CHAOS BOUND

CHAOS BOUND

Book One of the Mist Warden Series

By Adriaan & Rebecca Brae

Edition 1.0

Edited by Penelope Jackson, www.penelopejacksoneditor.com
Cover art by Derek Murphy, Creativindie Covers

Published by BraeVitae Inc.

PO Box 1897
Cochrane, Alberta T4C 1B7
Canada
contact@braevitae.com

This is a work of fiction. Names, characters, businesses, places, events, and incidents are either the products of the author's imagination or used in a fictitious manner. Any resemblance to actual persons, living or dead, or actual events is purely coincidental.

ISBN: 978-0-9918836-7-7

For J.K., my brother from another mother. You were always looking out for everyone else, but somewhere along the way you lost yourself. May you find your way back.

Rebecca Brae

For D.S. my home room teacher for grades 3-5. Your understanding and patience with this odd kid made this book, and many other successes in my life possible. Thanks.

Adriaan Brae

Chapter 1

Environment rebalancing. ALERT: Detecting Class 3 H-K
Shadow Drone remnant. Priority 1 removal. Establishing
contact with compatible Channel. 57-72% probability
event chain can be averted.

* * *

In a vast darkness, a murky halo of light surrounded four teens
as their joined hands jerked erratically across a Ouija board. A
curvy brunette leaned closer to the scarred workbench,
studying the board. The candle nearest her flickered and
distorted shadows danced across equipment-laden shelves.

"What's it doing now?" Panic lent an edge to her voice.
"It's not even making words."

Chris tilted his head to the side, looking puzzled. "Not in
any language I know."

"I don't have time for this," snarled the guy next to him.
"Lunch is already half over. Why don't you stow this séance
shit for a couple weeks until Halloween?"

"Can-it, Bill." Kirsten surveyed the group with cold, gray-
blue eyes. "It's never done this before. I wonder who, or what,
we've contacted?" She aimed a malicious smile at the brunette.
"What do you think it'll do next, Danni?"

They watched in silent anticipation as the planchette rasped back and forth across the board.

"I—I don't know if I'm up for this, guys," Danni said. "Let's just stop, okay?"

"Oh, grow a pair." Kirsten pinned her with a glare. "Don't you dare chicken out on me."

Danni's cheeks paled but she firmed her lips and kept her hand on the planchette.

"Guys…" Chris drew the word out and ended in a high, alarmed tone. "I think I recognize some words."

Kirsten examined the board. "Like what?"

"Devour. Hate." His eyes followed the planchette's trail across the board. "…T…H. Okay. It just spelt 'death.' This is officially creepy."

Danni pulled her hand off and nearly fell as she scuttled away from the table. Her stool toppled and hit the concrete floor with a ringing clang. The rest of the group's hands lost contact as their concentration broke.

"You selfish bitch!" Kirsten shot to her feet. "You ruined it."

The four sentry candles at the corners of the table wavered and flared. Spears of flame shot up a foot above the rapidly melting wax columns.

"Fuck this," Danni said as she ran for the door. She heaved the solid metal barrier aside, creating just enough space to slide through.

Bill eased back from the workbench, his gaze darting from the board to the flames and then to his friends' faces. "You know…I'd better go…make sure she's okay." He jogged after Danni into the anemic shaft of light.

"You could at least close the damn door," Kirsten called after him, then said more quietly, "I sooo don't need to get busted this y—"

"Uh, Kirsten?" Chris said in a hoarse voice, pointing at the board. "Look!"

The planchette was spinning wildly.

A curious dread settled over Kirsten's features.

The spears of flame guttered as the candles burnt down to the table. Liquefied streams of wax flowed from the corners and merged as a swirling black mass at the center of the board.

"Cool," Kirsten whispered, edging forward and stretching a hand out.

Chris shouldered her out of the way before she touched it. He knocked the planchette off the table and his right hand skimmed the top of the tar-like extrusion. It humped up, sliding a thin pseudopod along his skin, and then erupted upward to engulf his hand. Darkness swarmed up his arm. He screamed.

* * *

Jessica sat bolt upright, shaking her right arm, screaming, "Get it off. It burns!"

Eric, who had been peacefully snoozing in the grass beside her, leapt to his feet. After taking stock of his surroundings, he crouched down and held her still to examine her arm from freckled shoulder to pale hand.

"Did something sting you?"

Jessica writhed in pain, "It's all over me…" She let out a terrified whimper.

Eric saw her closed eyes and shook her gently. "Jess, wake up."

Jessica's face contorted. "I can't think…I can't…" Her voice faded and her head slumped against her chest as her body went limp.

Eric supported her as she collapsed against him and cradled her head as he laid her down. He knelt beside her, fanning her ashen face.

"Jessie. Wake up, babe."

Without warning, her body convulsed and her hand whipped out, striking him in the throat.

He fell backward, gasping for air.

Jessica growled and clenched her fists. Frothy spittle formed at the edges of her mouth as she panted like a cornered animal.

Then her body relaxed, her breathing normalized, and her eyes fluttered open.

* * *

Silver birch branches swayed overhead in a perfect, clear blue sky. Jessica turned her head and peered through the tall prairie grass, groggily trying to recall where she was.

Eric sat a few feet away, watching her, mute and wary. His breath wheezed as he massaged a red welt on his throat.

"Eric?" Jessica struggled into a sitting position, surprised at the hoarseness of her voice. Her throat was raw, her brain felt like it was trying to bash its way out of her skull, and her right arm was numb. "What happened? Are you okay?"

A wet drop rolled from the side of her mouth to her chin. *Oh gods. Please tell me I'm not drooling.*

She swiped a hand across her mouth and then spat several times as she tasted dirt. Her fingernails were encrusted with it and there was a row of angry half-moon marks on her palm. Frowning, she examined the ground. There were two intersecting circles gouged in a patch of dirt. A pebble sat in the center of the oval shape created by the overlap.

"You must have had a bad dream," Eric croaked. "When I tried to wake you up, you turned into some kind of mini sleeper ninja and took me out."

Jessica stared at him in shock, forgetting the strange symbol in a rush of shame.

Eric's guarded expression faded and his trademark grin reappeared. "It was a damn good punch. With skills like that, your nap time is safe." He waved her off as she tried to get a better look at his neck. "I'm fine. Really."

"How can you joke about this? I hit you." Jessica's voice rose. "I'm so, so sorry. You plan this amazing picnic and all you get is a knuckle sandwich. I'm the worst girlfriend ever."

"I'll get a T-shirt made." He wiped a tear off her cheek. Grabbing a couple of Dr. Peppers from the cooler, he handed one to her and kissed her nose. "Seriously. I'm fine." He ran a hand over his neck and rolled his head around. "See? Still attached. No harm done."

Not knowing what else to do, she took a swig of her pop. The cool liquid slid down her aching throat and brought a measure of relief.

"You know…you can tell me if you have a secret identity." He grinned. "I'm a modern guy. A superhero girlfriend wouldn't threaten my macho-ness. I can totally see you in an underground lab stuffed with cool gadgets."

Jessica cast an exasperated look at him. "This isn't funny. There's nothing super about me."

He wrapped an arm around her shoulders and gave her a gentle squeeze. "You're always so serious." He looked into her eyes. "You'd think after hanging with me this long, you'd know that laughing about shit you can't change is the best thing to do." He leaned in and brushed her lips with his. "Some would say the only thing. It's a beautiful day and I'm not about to let a silly accident ruin it."

His last words, a hollow echo of her nightmare, brought

the images and feelings flooding back.

Ruined indeed.

Shivering, she recalled the rage that had consumed her, coursing through her body like a charge along a power line.

Rubbing her right arm where phantom pain still prickled, Jessica laid her head against Eric's chest. "It felt so real."

"The kayak again?" He tucked a wave of copper hair behind her ear as a gust of wind swept past.

Eric believed that her nightmare about the first, and last, time she was in a kayak cropped up whenever she was stressed. She figured it cropped up whenever it damn well pleased.

"Nope. But Kirsten was in it. That's almost as bad. Her and Chris and two others called Bill and Danni, no idea who they are, had this Ouija board..." She paused and stifled a groan as the images flashed in her mind. "Actually, I don't think I want to talk about it."

"Kirsten? Sheesh. Enough said." He shifted position and pulled her with him as he laid down. "You're probably just stressed about starting school tomorrow. And I know my moving to Calgary upset you, no matter how much you try to hide it. But you have nothing to fear. Not even the siren call of the big city can make me forget my little Babushka." He tweaked her nose.

Jessica laughed, remembering the fifth grade show when they'd played an old Russian couple. Shaking her head, she set her pop down and cuddled up to him. "How do you always make me laugh?"

Eric's grin deepened as Jessica kissed his dimple.

Blades of grass tickled her cheek. Her headache was finally ebbing to a dull and infrequent throb, and the sun's warm rays tingled pleasantly against her skin. A fish splashed playfully in the little cove beside them. This was their secret place, hidden on the other side of Ghost Lake, away from the town's prying eyes. It had always been an oasis from the chaos. She wanted it to stay that way.

Jamming her nightmare deep into a recess at the back of her mind, she vowed to make the most of the rest of the day.

Chapter 2

Jessica woke up the next morning tired and mentally bruised. She'd managed to put aside her nightmare while she was with Eric in the comforting embrace of day, but after, when she was alone in her bed and the shadows of night grew arms and reached out for her, the nightmare images and sounds all crawled back.

The fact that she had woken up suggested she must have fallen asleep at some point, but she had no clear recollection of any dreams, only a lingering sense of dread and the feeling she was being watched.

She sat up, moving slowly to prevent a rush of blood to her already throbbing head, and surveyed her room. Everything looked normal but she felt exposed, as if the walls had suddenly become a tissue-thin barrier between her and...something...

Jessica's gaze paused on the mirror that hung over her desk, an area her parents referred to as the "black hole." Photos of friends and notes from Eric ringed the oak frame, leaving only a small gap in the center to use.

There wouldn't be any fun messages from Eric waiting in her locker this year. School wasn't always the happiest place, thanks to a particular group of students, and some days those notes were all that sustained her. Sometimes they were just jokes and other times they were much more. Her favorite was the semi-melted fruit-roll-up "I love you" heart from Valentine's Day. Silliness and sweetness wrapped up in one edible, butt-shaped valentine.

She caught herself twisting her comforter into a knot and smoothed it out.

Why do things have to change?

Jessica ran a hand through her hair and humphed as it snagged in a jumble of knots. Shifting position, she grimaced at the horror staring back at her from the mirror.

Her harried sleep had not been kind to her new haircut and she had to admit getting bangs and layers wasn't her most inspired idea.

I wanted more volume, but this is crazy. Jessica plucked at several orange clumps sticking at right angles from her head.

With a tired sigh, she slid out of bed to examine the outfit she had spent an hour picking out last night. She did this every year: new haircut, new clothes, new resolve to be more outgoing, more confident, more anything.

And now, the cheery red T-shirt and bright blue jeans held little appeal, not to mention the intense colors did nothing to assuage the bowling ball of a headache clanging around in her head.

Maybe being more outgoing wasn't such a good plan on the first day at a new school. Most of the class would be the same old crowd from last year, but she'd heard there were also quite a few new students. Some were transferring in from Calgary and others were imports from Coldwater's booming housing developments.

Blending until I'm settled sounds better.

Her stomach fluttered at the thought of meeting new people. The whole meet-and-greet thing never came naturally. Thanks to living in a small town where everyone knew everyone, she'd mostly avoided these situations except for brief, uncomfortable encounters at her parents' work functions or summer camps.

On the bright side, I might not be the only redhead anymore. That would be nice.

After downing a painkiller, she eventually settled on a faded purple shirt with Eeyore looking over his shoulder saying, "Oh well," and an old pair of jeans. With the clothes situation sorted, she hopped into the shower and easily fell back into her morning routine. The disturbing events of yesterday drifted further from her mind and by the time she made coffee and tucked into a bowl of cereal, her headache and dark mood had lifted.

High heels thudded down the stairs like automatic gunfire and her mom whipped through the kitchen in a coffee-gathering whirlwind. Jessica called out a greeting and received a mute wave of a briefcase as her mother disappeared into the garage.

It was nothing new. Her mother was always running late. She wouldn't see her dad, either. He always left before the birds even realized dawn was imminent.

She struck up a conversation with her cereal bowl. "So, how are you? Fine? Well, isn't that nice. It's a fine day to be fine. Me? How nice of you to ask. I start grade ten today and I'm super nervous. I think I'll take a raincoat. There's clouds coming in. Well, can't chat all day. Important things to do and all that. You just chill out in the sink until I get home and I'll tell you all about my day."

Wow. I should have skipped that third cup of coffee.

Jittery from the combination of caffeine and nerves, Jessica collected her carefully pre-stocked backpack and resolved to stop talking to inanimate objects. She briefly considered how that would impact talks with her parents and decided it wouldn't.

It's not like we have two-sided conversations.

She had long ago stopped expecting them to respond to her in any normal or immediate fashion, even though, in-line with the illogical nature of the universe, the reverse never seemed to apply. She sometimes managed to squeeze in a few words between meetings, client sessions, conferences, and research projects, but she had stopped trying lately. It wasn't worth the effort.

On occasion, she was proud of her busy parents. Her dad was a top physicist with a mind buried in equations and theory. Her mother was a psychologist who helped high-needs clients. Both taught at the university. Both were in demand worldwide. Both were 110% dedicated to their careers.

Not long after her thirteenth birthday, they had sat her down and told her she was old enough to take responsibility for herself, that it was time for them to concentrate on work. She supposed they were right. Most kids would jump at a chance to get rid of their parents. And she had, at first, but there were only so many weeknights her friends could come over. After she had faced an empty house and dinner alone for a while, the feeling of privilege wore off.

Most of the time it was fine—she certainly had more freedom than most of her friends. But sometimes, she would have liked one of them to be around, wish her luck on her first day, give her a hug, tell her she would do great.

The silence of the house bore down on her. Jessica took one last look around the vacant hall, opened the front door, and listened to the sounds of a garbage truck picking up bins, the muffled roar of traffic, the warbling songs of birds. She relished those traces of life, letting them wash over her.

A gust of wind blew her bangs into her eyes. Jessica blinked and irritably brushed them away. Rifling through her backpack, she found a hairclip, gathered her rebellious bangs to one side, shoved the clip into place, and headed out, thinking, *Change is definitely not a friend of mine.*

* * *

Jessica stopped at her best friend's house and watched as Beth's mother hugged and kissed her goodbye. Beth escaped the mauling and dashed out to join Jessica, her ruffled miniskirt showing off her long, tanned legs. An RCMP car pulled up as they reached the sidewalk and Beth's dad emerged to give her a quick hug. He waved hello to Jessica and she waved back as Beth anxiously pulled her away.

"Sheesh. You'd think I was leaving for a tour in the Middle East." Beth stopped and stared at Jessica. "I thought you were going to wear your new red shirt? I mean, this looks…comfortable, but…" A delicate crease appeared on her forehead. She shrugged and continued walking. "You're probably right, though. That red with your hair was a bit much."

Jessica stalled for a second, staring after Beth, and then caught up to her. *But she was with me when I bought it. Why didn't she say something then?* She worried her lower lip. *Probably being polite, but I would have appreciated the truth more. Now I'll have to return it and I've got no idea where the receipt is. Did I even keep it? Damn.*

"Yeah…well, you know me…thought I might step out of my box and try some brighter colors this year, but I guess not. I like my box. It's a comfy box." Jessica glanced down at Eeyore. Maybe he wasn't the height of fashion, but he was an old friend.

She inhaled a strand of hair and spluttered. "Damn it. I'm never leaving my box again. This crap happens every time."

Beth flipped open a compact to check her lipstick and then dropped it back into her purse. "Right...your new do. I think it'll work for you. The whole choppy, messy look is totally easy to style."

Easy to style...not exactly a resounding compliment.

Jessica wedged her hair behind her ears. "I told the hairdresser to leave it long enough to put in a ponytail, but did she listen? Noooo. Of course not. And she cut my bangs at the perfect length to stab me in the eye. Do I have a big 'ignore me' sign strapped to my ass?"

Beth raised a dainty eyebrow and leaned back to look at Jessica's posterior.

After a calming breath, Jessica changed topics. "Check out my new backpack. There's tons of pockets *and* a special anti-static padded sleeve for my laptop."

"Geek." Beth grinned. "Only you would get excited about that...and maybe Kathy. Now, if it was a Louis Vuitton purse..." Her expression became dreamy.

Jessica snorted. "You think anyone who pays attention in class is a geek. Which reminds me, if Dave's in your math class again, don't you dare sit near him or I'll end up tutoring you. And that is painful...for everyone." Deepening her voice to imitate their old principal, Jessica added, "Your grades are the foundation of your future, young lady."

"Stop being such a worrywart. Dave is so...last year. This is high school. I'm onto bigger and better things."

"Oh, terrific. Judging from the size of Dave, in a few years you'll graduate to elephants and whales. That'll make for an awkward intro to the parents. 'Don't mind the spray, Lenny had a barnacle stuck in his blowhole.' "

Beth playfully shoved her and Jessica stumbled sideways, watching her friend laugh. Her blonde hair gleamed like spun gold as it billowed in the wind—cold comparison to Jessica's own carroty locks, which flapped around her like a flock of angry birds. She spat out another strand and jammed it into her hair clip.

If this keeps up, I'll look like Pebbles Flintstone by the time we make it to school.

* * *

The bell rang just as the girls reached the parking lot. They were relieved to find they weren't the only last-minute arrivals and followed a throng of students inside, hoping someone knew the way to the gym for the welcome assembly.

The crowd carried them through broad hallways with towering ceilings and row upon row of dull green lockers.

And this is just the first floor, Jessica thought as she passed a steep stairwell, identical to one they had passed a ways back.

She was surprised at the number of unfamiliar faces and looked with interest when she spotted a group of First Nations teens heading into the administration office. She nudged Beth and nodded in their direction.

Beth extricated herself from the press of students after they made it into the gym and peevishly smoothed her skirt. "They're from Ozade. The reserve school got torched this summer so they're coming here now. Lots of people aren't happy about it. Dad thinks there'll be trouble. Told me to stay out of it."

"Trouble?"

"You know…fights and stuff. Like I'd get anywhere near a scrap." Beth mumbled as she scanned the students scrambling for spots near friends in the stands. She waved and grabbed Jessica's arm. "Kathy's here. Looks like she's saving seats. Come on."

Beth dragged Jessica through the crowd, bypassing a cluster of harried faculty at center court trying to connect a laptop to a projector. They reached Kathy at the same time as a group of guys. One of them shoved Kathy's jacket and bag aside and started to sit.

Beaming a plastic smile at him, Beth planted her bottom on the jacket before it slid off and tugged Jessica down beside her. Kathy's bag, already half-off the bench and in Jessica's way, landed on the feet of a girl sitting in the next row up. Jessica's face reddened as she apologized and tried to free the bag, which was now wedged between the rows.

The guy they had cut off poked Jessica's shoulder. "Hey. You jacked our spot."

Jessica glanced at Beth and Kathy. "Let's just move."

"Don't be stupid," Beth said with a flip of her hair. She turned to Kathy, who looked as though she wanted to melt into the floor, and whispered something in her ear.

"Yeah, well, we were here first." A broad-shouldered jock pushed his way between Jessica and Beth and squeezed Beth's knee. "But you can sit on my lap anytime."

He turned to face Beth, shoving Jessica off the seat. She would have fallen, but a steadying hand grabbed her elbow. Flustered, she spun and almost lost her footing again when she saw Chris standing beside her. Staring fearfully at his hand on her arm, she reflexively jerked away and then cringed inside.

I've got to get that damn nightmare out of my head.

She stuttered a pathetic "thank you" as he leaned forward and jabbed the arm of the guy who had forced her out of her seat.

"You're new here." Chris held his gaze as the jock scornfully smoothed out his sleeve. "And I'm guessing you'll be trying out for the football team?"

"What's it to you?" His tone was arrogant and challenging.

"Just thought you should know…" Chris nodded at Beth. "Her dad's a cop who's a bit overprotective and a good friend of our coach." The jock retracted his hand from Beth's leg. Then Chris patted Jessica on the head. "And she's just nice, so stop pushing people around, all right?"

Chris returned a wave to a group at the other end of the stands. "Why don't you and your buddies come with me and I'll introduce you to the rest of the guys who'll be trying out. You can size up the competition." He grinned good-naturedly.

The jock frowned, stood to see who had waved at Chris, and then shrugged. "I'll make you a deal; introduce me to that hot chick with the killer legs and I promise to only half-crucify you on the field."

"You don't waste any time." Chris chuckled. "That's Kirsten, and she should be wearing a neon 'handle with care' sign, so don't say I didn't warn you. I'm Chris, by the way."

They wandered off, exchanging names and discussing what positions they wanted on the team.

Jessica breathed a sigh of relief and sat down heavily. The girl behind her loudly cleared her throat. Remembering Kathy's bag, she resumed her efforts to pry it loose.

Beth sighed for an entirely different reason, inclining her head as she watched Chris walk away. "Did you have to get seats at the very front, Kathy? I feel like a total loser."

Kathy regained motor function and gestured to the benches extending upward behind them. "These stands aren't safe. All it takes is one loose screw and the whole thing comes down. I read an article. Some kids died watching a basketball game last year and their parents are trying to raise awareness about how dangerous it is. The stands...not basketball. Actually, basketball is pretty risky too..." Kathy re-focused at Beth's warning growl. "Anyway, the expert said collapsible stands should be banned."

Jessica paused in her tug-of-war. "There's collapsible stand experts? Really?"

Kathy belatedly noticed Jessica's battle and grabbed one of the straps to help. "I don't think the article said what type of expert. Probably some kind of engineer."

Jessica, now crouched on the bench for added leverage, felt the pack suddenly give and toppled backward. She swung her arms to regain her balance and stumbled across the floor, narrowly managing not to fall.

Kathy's backpack sailed overhead and slammed into the back of a man whose bald head gleamed like polished marble under the stark fluorescent lights. He fell against the projector, sending the wheeled table careening across the gym. Several teachers chased after the errant cart and the man turned to glare at the bag.

Everyone sitting near enough to see what had happened started laughing. Kathy froze, half hidden behind Beth. Beth edged lower in her seat, blushing delicately. For an irrational moment, Jessica raged against a universe which chose to make Beth look good, even when embarrassed.

People should look sweaty and blotchy. Not cute.

Coming back to herself, Jessica blurted, "Shit...your laptop wasn't in there, was it?"

Kathy stared at her backpack and shook her head.

Kissing her plan to blend in goodbye, Jessica took pity on Kathy's paralyzed state and went to collect the bag.

The man transferred his glower from it to her as she approached and Jessica whispered, "I'm so sorry. It was an accident. It got stuck and…"

He held up a hand. "I'm not interested in excuses. What's your name?" His voice boomed off the distant walls and ceiling, growing in force, swelling until it drowned out the laughter behind her.

"Jessica Clarke," she stuttered as a reinvigorated flush spread across her face. She didn't need a mirror to know it wasn't a pretty shade of red.

"Miss Clarke, I trust this little stunt isn't indicative of how you plan to spend your time at my school." When Jessica meekly shook her head, he continued. "Sit down and don't move for the rest of the assembly. And if I ever hear such foul language come out of your mouth again, you'll be in detention for the remainder of the year."

Shoulders drooping, Jessica grabbed the bag and retreated to her seat, hoping her face would stop burning and that she'd eventually remember how to breathe. Kathy took her backpack and secured it under her feet.

The rest of the assembly passed uneventfully. Once the teachers figured out their presentation, they launched into the standard barrage of welcome speeches. As Jessica had suspected, the bald man she had assaulted turned out to be Mr. Johnson, the principal. He looked directly at her during his speech outlining acceptable student behavior and school policies.

She was relieved to escape his glare when teachers began collecting their students for what was left of first period.

Chapter 3

Jessica decided to hunt for her locker during the lunch break. Her morning classes were sciences and, although interesting enough to keep her awake and engaged, they also landed her with monster textbooks, and her shoulder was starting to hurt.

After wandering the halls for long enough that she began to mutter, "You are in a maze of twisty hallways, all alike," she finally broke down and stopped a teacher to ask for directions.

"Locker seven?" A pensive wrinkle creased the young woman's forehead. "Well, I'm new here too, but I think it might be in the basement."

Jessica thanked her. "I don't suppose you know how to get to the basement? All the stairs I've seen go up."

Smiling sympathetically, the teacher held out a hand and introduced herself. "I'm Mrs. Anderson. Let's figure this out together and then it'll be one less thing I have to do later. I knew I should have stocked up on breadcrumbs."

The basement's convoluted layout surprised both of them, but they eventually found Jessica's locker tucked away in a dingy hall lit with flickering fluorescent lights. A few grimy half windows dotted the outer wall, doing little to alleviate the gloom hanging in the stale air.

As soon as Jessica successfully opened the combo lock, Mrs. Anderson rushed off to prepare for her next class. The stench of old sweat laced with mold wafted out as Jessica dumped her books into the locker. Pinching her nose, she made a mental note to bring an air freshener tomorrow.

She texted Beth to find out where she was, and then met up with her and Kathy in the cafeteria. Jessica barely had time to recount the locker saga before the bell rang. She bought the least flattened sandwich of the few remaining and a can of pop, wolfing them down as she walked to computer science.

Jessica spent most of the class cursing her choice of beverage and trying not to burp too loudly. She had held high hopes for the class, computers being one of her favorite things, but between the obsolete desktop units and the textbook that might as well have been titled *Archaic Adding Machines for Cavemen*, it wasn't looking good.

Her otherwise bleak afternoon improved slightly thanks to her last period math class. When she walked in, Mrs. Anderson's friendly voice greeted her.

"I see you made it out of the crypt."

Jessica let out an amused snort. "The crypt. I like it. I might have to steal that."

The teacher fidgeted with a piece of chalk, twirling the white stick in her hand until her fingers were thoroughly coated. "Do me a favor and don't say where you got it."

"No problem." Jessica slid into an empty seat in front, unsure whether to be relieved or not that adults weren't immune to first-day nerves. "Your secret's safe with me."

* * *

Jessica found her locker again after school with only a few false starts and gathered her stack of books before meeting up with Beth and Kathy.

Their homes were all close, so they were able to walk together for a ways. Jessica's was the farthest, on the edge of an older development overlooking the barren, grassy slope of Coldwater Hill.

After a few blocks, she looked over at Kathy, who was also flagging under the weight of her backpack. Jessica grimaced as she re-adjusted the strap cutting into her shoulder.

Beth skipped ahead, humming and occasionally twirling with the grace of someone who had taken ballet classes since she was able to walk. As usual, she had opted to leave her books at school and Jessica suspected they would not see the light of day except for their outings to class, and even then it would be for show.

Kathy stopped to rest her pack on the ground and Beth rolled her eyes. "Did you guys have to bring *everything* home?" Kathy opened her mouth to respond and Beth held up a hand. "Never mind. Forgot who I was talking to."

Relieved for the break, Jessica dropped her own bag and stretched out her back. "Why even bother giving us such out-of-date texts? I'm surprised they aren't carved on stone tablets."

"Feels like they are," Kathy agreed.

Beth pulled moisturizer out of her purse and started to apply it to her hands, tuning out the discussion.

Jessica continued moaning. "My physics book was published ten years ago. And I can't believe they even assigned one for computer science. What a joke. I mean if any class should have course material online, it's that one."

"I know." Kathy sneered at her bulging bag. "My biology

text is even older. Also, it looks like someone threw up on it. All the pages are warped and stained."

Beth scrunched her face up. "Yuck! That's why they stay in my locker. The school should disinfect them before handing them out. You need to ask for a new one."

Kathy shrugged and hefted her bag. "I can still read it. I guess it's okay."

Beth shook her head and shared an exasperated look with Jessica. Kathy's timidity annoyed Jessica on occasion too. As much as Jessica liked to fade into the background, she knew there were times you had to make some noise and get noticed.

* * *

Jessica sat cross-legged on her bed with textbooks laid out around her. Thankfully, there were no pukey ones. She flipped through their pages, reading indexes and skimming chapters that caught her eye.

Despite her tirade, she had always loved the look and feel of books, and was willing to overlook publication dates because they held an interest beyond factual content. Each dog-eared page, scribbled notation, scrawled name, and margin doodle gave a book history…a unique life of its own.

She picked up her chemistry text. *I wonder who used you? What was going on in their life? Where are they now?* She let the book fall open to where the binding betrayed its heaviest use and a ripped condom wrapper fell out. *Okay. Maybe I don't want to know.*

Jessica rubbed her stomach as it gave a ferocious growl and glanced out her window. Darkness had settled. The clock on her bedside table read quarter past eight. No wonder her stomach was complaining. She had yet to eat supper and it was almost time to call Eric.

She heated some leftovers and ran back to her room, gingerly holding the scorching plate by the edges. Shoveling down a few forkfuls of chicken stew to pacify her stomach, she checked to see if Eric was online. A quick IM later and they were video chatting.

Eric jumped into how his day had been. "It's really weird not knowing anyone and the school is seriously huge. I think there's more students than people in the whole of Coldwater. I got lost and almost missed signing up for tryouts because I went to the wrong locker room. I wish I was with you guys."

"Me too. At least we could get lost together," Jessica sighed. "I swear our school is larger inside than outside. There's a Timelord somewhere wondering where he left his Tardis. Hold up, since when do you worry about meeting people? That's my neuroses. Everyone always loves you."

"Yeah, right. People in Coldwater might have liked me, but here...I don't know. Most of them already know each other, so they aren't exactly scrambling to introduce themselves to the new kid from Hicksville."

"Hicksville! So that's what you think of us now."

Eric paused. "Of course not...it's just what people here think of anyone not from the city. I didn't mean—"

"I'm just bugging you. And hey, if you get lonely, I'm only forty-five minutes away." Jessica didn't know which one of them she was trying to reassure.

"True. But until I save enough to get the old Crown Vic roadworthy, I'm subject to the vagaries of the mom-mobile. She doesn't mind me borrowing it, but there's no guarantee it'll be free when I need my Ginger fix."

"Not the Green Machine," groaned Jessica. "I thought you agreed to let it shuffle off this mortal coil after the engine fell out on the way to the drive-in." They hadn't even made it down the block. "My back still hurts from pushing it. Which reminds me, I owe Beth a kick for sitting on the hood 'directing.' Valet shoes, my ass."

Eric choked with laughter. "I don't know how she didn't break her neck in those heels. Ah...good times. And, for the record, the engine didn't fall out. It was just part of the transmission. That car is a classic. It used to be an old cop car—"

"Yes...I know," Jessica interjected. "You've told me a million times. But that thing is so big you'll need a docking permit to park in the city."

"Oh, now you're just being cruel." Eric said in a phony hurt tone. "The Green Machine won't like you anymore if you keep insulting her."

With Eric's mood now lighter, Jessica diverted the conversation away from cars. They talked for an hour, until he was called away to help his brother move boxes. Promising he'd visit that weekend, they reluctantly hung up.

Jessica felt a pang of loneliness as she sat in the oppressive quiet. The same feeling she'd had that morning, of being watched from around a corner that wasn't there, started to creep in. She resolutely plugged herself into her mp3 player and turned to the web, losing herself in her favorite comics and news sites.

When her eyes grew heavy, she put herself to bed, sleepily rehashing the day. It hadn't been all that bad, barring the unfortunate mishap with the principal. She'd found her locker, made it to her classes mostly on time, and was even looking forward to some of them.

All in all, not too shabby. Now, as long as I stay out of Johnson's way, this could be a great year.

Chapter 4

Channel ineffective. H-K Shadow acquired host. Locality rich in core Shadow sustenance. Estimate 17 days to replication. 82-100% probability of Shadow infestation. Imperative to activate Channel. Risk of permanent damage acceptable. Initiate direct feed when threshold receptive state detected.

* * *

Six weeks later, Jessica had long-since downgraded her outlook on the year from great to acceptable, with a chance of dismal.

She waved from the front of math class as Beth slid into her customary back-row seat. Beth half-waved back and continued a whispered conversation with Matt, the handsome behemoth sitting beside her.

Jessica felt a pang of jealousy as she watched the intimate exchange and firmed her resolve to talk to Beth tonight at the mall. If she'd pissed her off somehow, she wanted to know. She had seen less and less of her over the last few weeks. Every lunch hour Beth came up with an excuse to join another table, but even that pretext had trailed off lately. It was bad enough that Kathy, renowned for her astounding level of social obliviousness, was starting to notice.

The bell rang and a hush settled. When no teacher arrived, everyone launched back into their boisterous discussions. Frustrated, Jessica paged through her textbook to last night's homework. There were several questions she needed to resolve before the mid-term next week. If Mrs. Anderson was late and had to spend five minutes getting the class into order, she wouldn't have time for questions at the end of the period.

A wadded-up ball of paper smacked into Jessica's head and she whipped around, scanning the class. There were several potential culprits snickering, but each of them looked as guilty as the next. Shaking her head, she noticed a huddle of students around Beth. Her peaches and cream complexion flushed with excitement as she regaled her spellbound audience.

Jessica wondered if they were talking about Kirsten. The popular blonde had stormed out of the principal's office in a blind rage a couple of days ago. Luckily, Kirsten had been distracted enough to miss Jessica's presence. She shuddered at the thought of running into her nemesis in that mood.

Curiosity overcame shyness and Jessica slipped back to listen in. With Beth making herself scarce, her prime source of gossip was gone and she felt seriously under-informed.

"…but they don't know for sure. Dad said they found him washed up…"

She lost track of what Beth said next. The classroom door opened and the principal lumbered in, followed by Mrs. Anderson and a middle-aged woman dressed in a fitted charcoal gray pantsuit.

Mrs. Anderson looked drawn as she made her way to the front. She didn't smile, which was odd for her. Something was wrong.

Jessica reluctantly slunk back to her desk while the rest of the class carried on, oblivious to the newcomers. She watched the principal and other woman with a growing sense of foreboding. Mr. Johnson was as twitchy as a dog with a flea in an unreachable spot.

The principal frowned and repeatedly cleared his throat with increasing vexation. When no one took notice, he barked, "That's enough. Everyone sit down and zip it."

Startled students trailed back to their desks as the suited woman whispered something to him. Mr. Johnson nodded and cleared his throat again.

"Students…please direct your attention to Ms. Oreiller."

He waved a hand at the woman standing patiently beside him. She inclined her head with a quick nod of thanks and stepped forward, smiling reassuringly.

"I'm afraid I haven't had a chance to meet all of you yet. I'm your school counselor." She paused to make sure she had everyone's attention. "I wish I were introducing myself under better circumstances, but unfortunately I have some very sad news."

Continuing in a low, soothing voice, she said, "One of your classmates, Christopher Fowler, passed away yesterday. His passing is a great loss to our school and to the community, and is deeply felt by all."

A litany of shocked denial ran through Jessica's mind.

Chris, dead? It's not possible.

An icy wave crashed over her, leaching in until she felt like a flash-frozen bird, teetering on a wire, waiting for a stray breath of wind to send her plummeting.

Is this shock?

She laid her head on the desk. Her throat tightened and she stretched her neck to open her windpipe.

I need to focus on something else…anything else.

She latched onto the calm logic of today's math lesson.

Her textbook was open, pencil lined up to one side, waiting. Its solid, hexagonal reality felt reassuring against her fingers.

A few sobs broke over the soft buzz of conversation as the counselor carried on. "A memorial assembly will be held after lunch tomorrow. I encourage all of you to come, so we can say goodbye to Chris and remember what a special person he was."

No matter how hard Jessica stared at the equations and geometric diagrams in her book, they would not come into focus. The lines and symbols roamed across the page, joining in unexpected patterns that almost made sense. A buzzing in her ears and a creeping numbness in her hands and feet distracted her. She gripped the pencil harder, barely able to feel it.

The page, desk, and classroom receded as if she were on a speeding train, leaving her suspended in a cold, dark void. Light and warmth were far below.

The counselor's faint voice reached her. "When someone passes away, it's normal for…"

* * *

Words faded to nothing. What Jessica thought were classroom lights below formed into an array of car headlights and small fires. They were clustered on a boat launch at the foot of a bridge, the railing of which she was dangling from, head-down over inky black water.

I should be afraid, she thought, but an icy presence filled her mind, leaving no room for fear.

Her body felt wrong. Looking up, she realized it wasn't hers. The chest was broad and flat, decidedly male. Her gaze traveled higher, past her muscular legs, and she saw Chris's face distorted in a rictus of hunger, stark against a backdrop of stars. His eyes, the gentle gray eyes that rescued his square-jawed face from jock-ish indifference, were swirling black voids. She knew with absolute certainty that he was going to kill her, and he was going to enjoy it.

As she watched, the mask slipped. Some of the darkness in his eyes retreated. A glimmer of the real Chris pushed back, usurping the maniac.

"Bill," he rasped. "What's happening?"

Bill. Jessica recognized the name—one of the strangers in her Ouija nightmare had been called Bill. She must be seeing through his eyes.

Chris's grip tightened around her ankles. He pulled back and her body jackknifed up. Her hand grasped the edge of the rail and dragged the rest of her over. She landed painfully, jamming her knees into the rough bridge deck.

"What the fuck is wrong with you?" she heard herself say in deep, gravelly tones. "This bi-polar psycho shit has got to stop. Is this about Kirsten?" Her—his—body tensed for a fight. The mix of adrenalin and anger was exhilarating.

Chris rocked back and forth with his head buried in his hands, tugging at tufts of his curly brown hair. Every tendon in his arms and neck stood out. His harsh panting mingled with the music straggling up from the boat launch. He peered from between shaking forearms, watching her, as the oily shadow pulsed sluggishly across his eyes, reclaiming the pieces it had lost.

Terror seized Jessica's heart. She wanted to bolt, but Bill's body just edged back a few feet.

Can't you see it? she screamed inside him. *Run!*

Chris threw his head back and a howl tore from his throat, spilling rage and revulsion into the night. He took a halting step forward, screamed again, and then launched himself at the bridge rail.

Bill yelled as his—their—body sprinted forward in an effort to intercept him.

They were too late. Chris dove headfirst over the rail in a final and oddly beautiful display of athletic skill.

Despite Bill's amazing reflexes, they only grazed Chris's ankle with an outstretched finger. That brief touch became an endless, searing pain as snaking black tendrils latched onto their hand. It burrowed in and their body collapsed, curling up on itself in a spasm of mindless agony.

* * *

Jessica couldn't move. Something was pinning her to the ground. She flailed her one unrestricted arm and whacked an elbow on something hard and angular. More pain. More darkness. Amoeboid red spots undulated around her, swimming in a fathomless ocean of black.

Abandoning the idea of movement, she focused on examining the sensations prodding at the edges of her awareness. Jessica narrowed the list of immediate concerns to whatever was digging into her side and a sharp pain in her left hand.

She opened her eyes when she remembered she could and saw that she was laying on the floor, tangled in an overturned desk. Jessica looked around in a daze at the startled faces of her classmates.

She tried to sit up, but her limbs were heavy and out of sync with the instructions firing from her brain. Frustration and panic grew as each ungainly action piled upon the next, until she was sure she resembled an upside down turtle. She stopped moving, forcing her eyes closed again as the room spun sickeningly.

Jessica felt rather than saw Mrs. Anderson hovering over her. It was as if her skin recognized the teacher's unique radiance. Contemplating the oddity of this, she realized she knew where everyone was in relation to herself. Then she felt herself pulled into a sitting position as Mrs. Anderson gently checked her head for injuries.

The strange sense of presence emanating from people gradually abated and Jessica hesitantly cracked an eye open. The world was no longer spinning.

She watched Mrs. Anderson's lips move but her words were lost in a resonant low buzz, as if someone had stuffed bumblebees in her ears. She rubbed them, trying to quell the horrid tickling.

Sound exploded. Jessica recoiled from the onslaught of yells and laughter, pressing herself against Mrs. Anderson as she tried to figure out what the teacher was saying. The confused jumble of noise steadily thinned until she connected one voice to Mrs. Anderson's lips.

"...all right? Do you know where you are?"

"Math?" Jessica croaked.

Mr. Johnson's voice roared over the din, demanding the class settle down.

The counselor pressed a tissue into Jessica's hand and asked if she could stand.

Jessica belatedly saw the trail of blood dripping off her finger. Its source was a small but ugly gash in her left palm. She closed her hand around the tissue and nodded.

Wrenching her gaze away from the blood, Jessica extricated her legs from the desk and struggled to her feet with Mrs. Anderson's help. Heat shot up her neck and spread across her face when she became aware of all the eyes focused on her.

Desperately needing a friendly face, Jessica sought out Beth. Their gazes met and Beth broke contact, laughing tensely at something Matt said. Jessica stared down at her feet as the counselor had a hushed conversation with the principal.

Someone near the front of the class stage-whispered, "It's always the quiet ones. She must have had a serious obsession going on."

The guy beside him snorted. "Bet she just wants out of class. Shit. Why didn't I think of that?" He laid his hands over his heart and flung himself to the floor crooning, "Oh Chris! How could you leave me like this?"

The class erupted in hysterical laughter and indignant yelling. Mr. Johnson's head snapped to attention and he stalked over to the prone joker, looking like a boiler ready to blow.

Shaking a stubby finger in the boy's face, he snarled, "You. Get up, get your things, and follow me." He turned to the unlucky neighbor. "And you. Do the same, and not a word from either of you. Ms. Oreiller, let me know as soon as you're done with Miss Clarke. I want to talk to her too."

Great. Jessica groaned. *Guess he remembers me.*

He addressed the class, "I will not...I repeat, NOT...tolerate outbursts like this. I can't think of a more inappropriate time for such a shockingly disrespectful and tasteless display. You are all new here, and so far, the impression isn't good. Strive to do better or you won't be here long." As he completed the last sentence, his gaze fell on Jessica and she flinched.

The counselor took her arm and waved at Mrs. Anderson, who was still hovering nervously. "She'll be fine, Emily. I'll take her to the nurse's office. If anyone else is having trouble, please send them down to me right away. Good luck."

Chapter 5

The nurse pried her hand open and removed the blood-soaked tissue. Jessica stared at her smeared palm, feeling detached from reality as the counselor relayed what had happened. She tentatively poked her numb hand as the nurse whipped around the room collecting supplies.

"It's just a sliver. I'll have it out in a jiffy," she promised over the clanging of instruments. "Nothing to worry about. One of those things that looks worse than it is."

She came back and before Jessica could react, she plucked a thick splinter of yellow wood from her hand and squirted on a clear liquid Jessica was sure should hurt, but didn't. After vigorously wiping her hand clean with gauze and slathering on antibiotic cream, she slapped on a bandage and declared the emergency over.

"There you go. Looks like part of a pencil. No stitches needed. Should be good as new in a week or two. If it gives you any trouble, make an appointment with your doctor. You've had your tetanus shot, right?"

Jessica paused to assimilate the barrage of information and then nodded. She stopped when the room began to tilt and slip sideways.

"Now, dear," the nurse continued. "About your fainting spell, has that happened before?"

"Never." Jessica kept her head steady.

"Been feeling extra tired lately? Distracted?" She droned on as if reading from a script, but the questions seemed random. "Have you been daydreaming more than usual?"

"Um, not really. Same as always, I guess. Not that I daydream a lot." *Oh great,* she thought. *I'm starting to babble. Gotta lock it down or I'll talk myself in to a psych eval.* She muted the little voice inside suggesting that might not be such a bad idea.

"Any chance you're pregnant?"

Jessica's eyes widened. "Uh. No."

"Righty-ho, then. Fill out this form and you can be off." She shoved some papers into Jessica's lap. "Talk with your family doctor about ruling out low blood pressure, diabetes, epilepsy, that kind of thing."

Wow. Those would suck. Jessica's gut lurched as she stared blankly at the pages.

The sharp scent of bleach flooded the small room as the nurse wiped down the steel counters.

When Jessica grimaced, Ms. Oreiller moved to her side and took the form. "You're left-handed, aren't you?" The counselor smiled as Jessica nodded carefully. "Right, then you'll need a bit of help filling these out. Let's go to my office."

Jessica followed her out, thankful to at least escape the nauseating tang of disinfectant.

* * *

The counselor's eclectic office was a welcome antidote to the nurse's sterile workspace. A giant computer monitor, more suited as a museum piece, and a keyboard, so well used the letters were half worn off, consumed the top of a pockmarked wooden desk. A lumpy, high-backed chair and plaid couch occupied most of the floor space. The eye-watering pattern was reminiscent of pants she'd seen in classic Dr. Who episodes, and she wondered how old it was. Bookcases covered every available wall, their shelves bowed under the weight of stacked books.

If I ever have an office, this is how I want it to look, minus the antique technology of course.

Ms. Oreiller gestured at the couch and they sat down to complete the medical form. Once done, the counselor patted the cushion beside Jessica and told her to lie down.

"You might as well rest up while I take this back to the nurse. I'm planning to have a quick word with the principal as well." Noting Jessica's cringe, she hastened to reassure her, "Please don't worry. You aren't in trouble. You had a shock and were understandably upset. Were you close to Chris?"

Jessica sank deeper into the couch wishing it could swallow her. "Umm, no, well, kind of." She wracked her brain trying to figure out something reasonable to say. "I know him...uh...knew him. Everyone did. He's lived here for...uh, a long time."

Oh my god, stop babbling, you moron.

"What I'm trying to say is that I...actually, I don't know what I'm trying to say." Jessica glared at the ceiling, widening her eyes in hopes that the moisture pooling at the corners would evaporate. "I've never known anyone who died before."

"Loss is hard to process, especially when it happens suddenly like this. You aren't alone." She patted Jessica on the shoulder and stood. "Just relax for a bit and, if you feel up to it, we can talk when I get back."

Ms. Oreiller turned the lights off as she left. Jessica

stretched out on the surprisingly comfortable couch and tried to make sense of her muddled thoughts and emotions.

What the hell happened? Did I faint? Did I hallucinate? Am I totally losing it? Gods…I'm so selfish. Chris is dead and I'm thinking about myself.

Her stomach clenched as the image of Chris diving over the railing into nothingness flashed in her mind. Unable to stay still, she leapt off the couch. Her right arm twinged at the sudden movement and she had a vivid recollection of the last time she'd felt that particular pain. It was at the cove with Eric.

Why do I keep hallucinating about Chris and some kind of black goop? Is it possible to keep an obsession secret from yourself?

As she paced the room hoping to find something else to fixate on, a fleet of sticky notes bordering the counselor's computer screen caught her eye. Flowing handwriting relayed dates and times of staff meetings, phone numbers, and miscellaneous reminders.

Jessica re-read one of the notes. *She didn't. No. She wouldn't have…would she?*

Casting a guilty look at the door, she tapped a key to wake the computer up and tried to log into Windows, which didn't work. Jessica stared at the sticky-note. *Damn. What else could "pass = Baddy1115" mean?* Then she saw the photo of a young black lab peeking out from behind a mass of papers. She grinned and typed in "Buddy1115."

The password prompt was replaced by the counselor's desktop. Shaking her head in disbelief, she scanned the cluster of files and shortcuts. Drawn more by a sense of curiosity than any urge to violate privacy, she clicked on the link labeled "student records."

An archaic green-on-black text console took over the screen. Clumsily navigating with the cursor, she picked a year and a student name at random. She found herself in Malcolm Davis's student record. She had no idea who he was, but she knew his age, class schedule, grades, contact information...

Holy crap...what am I doing?

Jessica nervously glanced at the door. The hall outside was quiet and there was no hint of movement behind the frosted glass panel. Unwilling to push her luck any further, Jessica logged out.

She paced the length of the room, flexing her stiffening left hand until a fish screensaver appeared. Letting out a relieved sigh, she dropped back onto the couch and wedged her good hand under her back for safekeeping.

I can't believe I did that. What if she checks her last login time? I can't believe she stuck her password on the monitor. I thought that only happened in movies. Should I warn her? No. She'll know I was snooping. Crap!

The mellow hum of the computer fan eventually lulled her into a post-adrenalin stupor. Tension drained from her muscles and she closed her eyes.

* * *

Ms. Oreiller gently tapped Jessica's leg to wake her up and set her backpack on the floor beside her.

"I picked up your things from class. You'd better double-check that everything's there. They were a bit scattered."

Jessica rubbed her eyes and smiled gratefully as the counselor settled into the chair across from her. "Thanks. Wow. How long was I out?"

Ms. Oreiller checked her watch. "About forty minutes. Looks like you had a good nap."

Jessica rummaged through her backpack. "I think it's all here. Only forty? I feel light-years better. Wish I could sleep that well all the time." As soon as she'd said it, Jessica knew it was a mistake.

Ms. Oreiller leaned forward. "Do you usually have trouble sleeping?"

Oh boy. Here we go. Jessica stared at the counselor in dismay. *This had better not turn into a repeat of the life-coach debacle.*

Halfway through grade eight, her parents decided she needed to be more "at home with taking risks." They hired a life coach, who signed her up for a lesson at an indoor climbing wall. She'd struggled her way up, to the capricious enjoyment of a horde of gawking onlookers, only to discover her paralyzing fear of heights near the top. In the end, an instructor had to climb up the wall and pry her off. It had not been a good day.

The experience taught her two things: Number one, ground = good; number two, avoid anyone in or related to the counseling field, including her mother.

With that in mind, Jessica took a deep breath and considered how to dig herself out of this conversation. She settled on the old deny and deflect strategy.

"I just meant I don't normally feel so rested after a nap. This couch must have some kind of relaxation field around it. Seriously. You could market this thing."

Her jaw tensed as she watched Ms. Oreiller, waiting for a sign she had found something in the statement to delve into.

The counselor smiled. "I spoke to the principal and he won't need to see you. Mrs. Anderson let your class go early, so you didn't miss anything. I think everyone was having a hard time concentrating." She paused. "Is there anything you'd like to talk about? Anything I can help you with, or even just listen to?"

Jessica looked into her warm hazel eyes and felt herself relax.

Wow. She's good. How does she do that?

Jessica busied herself zipping up her backpack. "I'll be okay. Thanks for talking to Mr. Johnson. We didn't have the best introduction and things aren't getting much better." She bit her lip. "Is he going to call my parents about this?"

"No, but I'll be touching base with anyone's parents who shared classes with Chris, which includes yours. I need to make sure everyone's notified. And just so you know, my meetings with students are confidential, so please talk to me if you're having a hard time. The nurse will also be calling your parents about your injury. I suggest you get to them first. She tends to be...abrupt. I'm sure you'll do a better job of explaining what happened. And she was right about seeing your doctor. Make an appointment."

Jessica considered how a truthful conversation with her family doctor would play out. She'd end up on a two-week vacation in a padded room with a jacket that did up from behind. Not good. She looked terrible in white.

Jessica sucked her lower lip into her mouth to stifle a hysterical giggle.

Ms. Oreiller patted Jessica's uninjured hand. "You look much better. I've never seen anyone as pale as you were earlier. Would you like me to call a taxi to take you home?"

"Thanks, but I'm meeting a friend. She's probably pissed that I'm cutting into her mall time."

"Okay. But please, pop in sometime to say hello." An impish grin spread across Ms. Oreiller's face. "People seem to avoid my office and I need reassurance every so often that I haven't sprouted horns or cloven hooves." She held a finger up on either side of her head and waggled them.

Jessica left the office smiling and double-timed it down to her locker to meet Beth.

Chapter 6

The hallway was deserted when Jessica arrived at her locker. After checking the closest bathroom and finding it equally vacant, she concluded that Beth had taken off. It wasn't much of a surprise. Beth was easily bored.

She called her friend and was taken aback when Beth answered with a breathless laugh. Her "hello" was barely audible over a mélange of background chatter.

"Beth? Where are you?"

"What?"

Louder, Jessica repeated, "Where are you? We were supposed to meet at my locker."

There was a long pause filled with raucous cheering before Beth responded, "Jess? Hey. How are you?"

"Still kinda freaked. Where can we hook up?"

Another pause. "Ah, thing is…" Beth's words became muffled as if she were holding the phone some distance from her mouth. "Piss off, Adam. I'm trying to talk. No, it's not."

Jessica jerked the phone away from her ear as Beth's voice blared, "Sorry. Anyways, I figured you wouldn't be up to going out…after everything…so I made other plans. We'll get together some other night, okay? I should go. Feel better."

Jessica found herself listening to dead air and glared at the phone. Her grip tightened as she raised it above her head, preparing to hurl it down the hall, picturing it smashing into a million pieces. She stopped herself. It wasn't the phone she was mad at.

How could she not know how much I need to do something, anything, right now?

She wanted to call Beth back, tell her what an insensitive jerk she was, but a lone rational holdout in her brain reminded her of why she had made tonight's plans. An argument would only drive a deeper wedge between them and she had no idea what had put it there to begin with.

Maybe Eric's free? She checked the time. *Nope. He's got at least another hour of football practice. Kathy. That's it. She won't let me down.*

Jessica called Kathy, already feeling her angry panic subsiding. Kathy was always looking for a study-buddy. Not the most exciting night, but then neither was the mall, and at least this way she'd get some work done.

After reaching Kathy's voicemail for the third time, she gave up and texted.

<< call me

Jessica watched particles of dust float through a weak beam of sunlight. They sparkled like miniature shooting stars. It wasn't entertaining for long.

She decided to head home. Snatching up her coat and bag, she threaded her way through the crypt and upstairs.

Lively voices issued from the auxiliary gym as she approached. Peering in, she saw a girl leap gracefully and spike a volleyball at an opening on the opposing court.

Another new student, Jessica mused as she took in her petite frame and soft Asian features. *And, judging from all the back thumping and high-fiving, a popular one, too. Must be nice.*

The team resumed practice and Jessica watched, amazed as the mini dynamo dove around the court. She was all lean muscle.

Spectators were gathered in clumps at the corners of the gym. Jessica ruefully pegged them to be ninety percent prospecting male jocks and ten percent annoyed girlfriends who looked as though they'd rather be wrestling alligators.

One exuberant onlooker hollered, "Yeah! Go Mac!" He slapped a guy standing beside him on the back. "We might actually have a shot at the championship this year."

Jessica watched the players for a moment longer, trying to figure out what the draw of competitive sports was. She admitted defeat and carried on down the hall. There were far better things to think about, such as how to explain Chris's death and her fainting spell to her parents without freaking them out. Not an easy task given her own gut-seizing fear and confusion about the situation.

Trying to convince someone else not to panic while I'm panicking will be a new trick.

She judged success unlikely.

As she drew near a group of students, she caught the edge of their conversation.

"Killed himself? Bullshit!"

Jessica slowed her pace and listened more intently.

"No joke. Jumped off the fucking bridge. Steve heard it from some chick whose dad is a cop."

"No way! Chris would never, just, like, no!"

Their voices lowered as Jessica passed.

She kept walking robotically until she rounded a corner and then stood in shocked silence.

So that's what Beth was talking about. The hushed words she'd overheard in class clicked into place. *Suicide? Why didn't she tell me?*

Everything suddenly felt heavy; even the air pressed in on her. She saw Chris falling toward black water and jammed the heels of her hands to her eyes, trying to banish the image. She leaned back against the wall and slid down, drawing her legs up to her chest. Wrapping her arms around them, she rested her chin on her knees.

It was bad enough to lose someone like Chris, but to have freaky hallucinations about it? With real details? She stopped herself from traveling too far down that path. Her brain was overloaded, her emotions too raw.

A piece of paper taped to the opposite wall fluttered as someone walked by. She absently read the scrawled text: Grade 10 Science Club Orientation. Oct 19 @ 4:15.

That's today. She checked the time: 4:06.

This was the first she'd heard of a science club here. The prospect was intriguing and potentially distracting enough to force her mind back on track.

She'd been in one last year with Kathy. They had designed and built a robot that could navigate through a maze using the "always turn left" algorithm, remembering dead ends as it went. They'd had a blast laying out huge, complex mazes in Jessica's garage until her mother had accidentally crushed the robot with the car.

Jessica stood and brushed her jeans off. *Why not? Anything's better than going home to an empty house right now.*

* * *

The meeting turned out to be in the same lab as her chemistry class—a lucky break since she felt as mentally aware as a stale cheese sandwich. When she arrived, there were five occupied stools.

Yikes…guess I wasn't the only one who didn't know about this.

Jessica recognized most of the occupants from her junior high club, but did a double take when she saw Kathy sitting on the far side of the room.

Kathy's eyes widened and a guilty flush spread up her neck when she noticed who had come in.

"Fancy meeting you here." Jessica gave Kathy a quizzical look as she sat down beside her.

Kathy fidgeted with her pen, dropped it on the floor, picked it up, dropped it again, and then gingerly placed it on the counter, looking as if she expected it to throw itself off at any moment. Several seconds passed in silence as they both watched the pen. It didn't move.

With her gaze still fixed on the writing implement, Kathy eventually replied, "Hi. I, uh, I didn't know you wanted to join."

"That's probably because I had no idea it existed."

"I meant, I didn't think you'd want to join. Not after our project tanked last year."

"It didn't tank. We just couldn't rebuild it in time for the fair. At least we had a blast doing it…" Jessica trailed off as a walking stack of library books pushing a roller backpack ricocheted off the doorframe and clattered into the room.

Kathy perked up and waved. "Over here, Kelly."

Jessica stared at her in disbelief. "Please tell me you didn't just call Machiavelli Kelly over here."

Kathy shushed her. "She's…nice, in her own way." She paused. "Well, maybe not nice, but she is super smart. Her science project got first place last year."

"She also plied the judges with lemonade and cupcakes."

Jessica grimaced. "She wrote her name on the icing. And I wouldn't put it past her to have laced the drinks."

Kelly arrived after rearranging her load several times and reluctantly leaving her roller bag at the end of the row.

"Whew...wasn't sure I'd make it in time. You should see all the project outlines in the library. I went through the recent ones and copied anything good. We should play it safe and expand on a project someone else did—preferably one that won a science fair. That way, we don't waste time thinking up an idea."

"And yea it came to be that Creativity died a quiet and gasping death..." Jessica mumbled as she leaned to the side, avoiding Kelly's teetering stack of books and papers. She had spoken flippantly, but the correlation to recent events belatedly registered and she felt sick inside, feeling she had somehow belittled Chris.

Kelly nodded at Jessica. "Heard you passed out today. Claire said someone saw you down a mickey at lunch, but they must be full of crap. You'd still be drunk and you look all right to me. Anyway, do you mind moving? I need to talk to Katherine about our project and I don't want anyone scooping my ideas."

A mickey? Our project? No wonder Kathy didn't mention science club.

She glanced at her friend, eyebrow raised.

Kathy slunk lower on her stool.

Jessica stood and walked away, back ramrod-straight, eyes staring directly ahead at nothing, feeling not just abandoned, but thrown away. Twice.

She made it to the door before giving herself a mental slap.

What am I doing? So what if Kathy doesn't want me here. She doesn't dictate what I do. In fact, I should stay. Screw her.

Jessica surveyed the room again. Most of the others were already paired up, talking, but there was one guy sitting on his own at the back of the class. She recognized him from computer science, though the familiarity was faint. He never said anything in class.

Lush, raven-black hair styled in an uneven shag fell to his shoulders and hid his eyes. His long, thin nose was the only visible feature on his face, lending him the shrewd, aloof air of a hawk. His watchful stillness suggested he was on edge.

Her surprise that one of the First Nations students was joining science club caught her off guard. The underlying prejudice crept forward and flashed its ugly, naked truth in her mind. A disgusted blush heated her cheeks as she conspicuously dithered at the door.

Looks like he feels as out of place as I do. Probably more, she decided. Coldwater's relationship with the neighboring reserve was strained, to say the least. It had been ever since she could remember. And her classmates weren't exactly the most unbiased bunch. *Myself included, apparently.*

She took a step toward him and stopped.

What if he just likes being on his own and is going to blow me off? Everyone else has today.

Irritated by her hesitation, she strode over and asked in the most confident tone she could muster, "Mind if I sit here?"

He leaned back on his stool, stretching out his long legs, offering no indication he'd heard.

Jessica's mind stalled. She'd been prepared for acceptance or rejection. She didn't know what to do with indifference.

After enduring her blank stare for a while, he shrugged.

Based on the quickness of the movement, his beat-up leather biker jacket camouflaged a wiry frame. The garment looked like it had been run over by a semi and thrown into a herd of stampeding cows. She guessed he either had a rough lifestyle, or was seriously committed to the grunge look.

Jessica climbed onto the stool next to him. "I'm just here to see what it's like. Don't know if I'll join." She pointed to a couple of guys sitting in front of them. "Gordy and Boxer were in our club last year and they did this experiment with fire-crackers that set their table on fire at the science fair and…" As Jessica helplessly tried to put the brakes on her verbal diarrhea, she saw the corner of his mouth twitch up.

He turned to face her. "You must have missed the memo. Townies aren't supposed to talk to us. Apparently we're rest-less."

His voice was so surprisingly deep that she stopped mid-word. Jessica snapped her mouth shut and tried to think of an intelligent retort. She failed. Assuming her muteness was the desired outcome anyway, she busied herself retrieving a note-book and pen from her backpack.

The uncomfortable silence stretched out until Jessica couldn't stand it anymore. "Yeah, well maybe I was busy pass-ing out when that note got sent around. You don't have to be so rude. You're not the only one having a shitty day." Jessica fiddled with her binder, a chorus of *Lame, Lame, Lame* running through her mind.

The arrival of her chemistry teacher, Mr. Bakshi, merci-fully saved her from his response. He waddled to the front of the class, carefully transferring a stack of paper from his brief-case to his desk. Groaning, she watched as he meticulously re-arranged the beakers lining the front of the table according to height. She heard chuckling beside her and glared at her neigh-bor.

He was nodding and grinning. "You're the one who—"

"Yeah," snapped Jessica. "I'm the one…is that all right with you?" she continued, grumbling to herself. "Might as well write 'freak' on my forehead."

"Or 'Chris.' With some little pink hearts."

Jessica slid off her stool. Her hand had just closed around the strap of her bag when he grabbed her wrist.

"Ignore me. I'm an asshole sometimes. It's kinda my thing." He let her go. "I'm Drew, by the way, and believe me, I know what it's like to be tossed in the freak pile."

Jessica climbed back onto her stool, glaring at him. "I don't know what you've heard, but for the record, Chris is the guy who died. He was a friend."

"Sorry," Drew muttered.

They sat in silence, sizing each other up, until Mr. Bakshi called the group to attention.

"Ladies and gentlemen, welcome to science club. Is there anyone here who has not been in one before?"

Drew was the only one to raise a hand and various snickers erupted. James, alias Boxer of the flaming table incident, twisted around on his stool and mimicked a war cry.

"You got a problem, buddy?" Drew ground his words out slowly.

Boxer stopped laughing. "Nope, but you do. You're in the wrong room. The AA meeting's down the hall."

Jessica stared at Boxer, stunned. Drew was half off his stool when Bakshi brought a yardstick down with a resounding crack in front of Boxer.

"Enough! There is no room for that kind of narrow-minded idiocy in science. You will accompany me to the principal's office after we are done for what I imagine will be a long and uncomfortable conversation."

Drew slid back onto his seat like a wildcat reluctantly

withdrawing from combat.

Bakshi straightened his lab coat. "It doesn't matter whether you've been in a science club before. I'll just explain how this works in a bit more detail."

Groans and lolling heads greeted this news, but the teacher continued undaunted. "Science club meets here at 4:15 p.m. sharp every Monday and Thursday for one hour. All of you will…"

Jessica listened as he outlined what membership entailed. Not only did he want them to prepare individual or paired projects for the provincial science fair in December, he planned to continue the club through their second semester and enter a combined group project in the national fair in May. Her mind was spinning by the time he asked if anyone had questions.

Bakshi gazed around the silent room, making a clicking noise with his tongue. "I don't suppose anyone is prepared to discuss project ideas?"

Kelly's hand shot up before he finished the sentence. He nodded to her and she launched into speech.

"I really think it's best if we discuss these things privately. I wouldn't want to influence anyone else's ideas, even though you would obviously know it was my idea first, since I talked about it first…"

He held up a hand. "Miss…?"

"Uh…Kelly Macintosh. It's just that these things are so sensitive, and—"

"Yes, all right Miss Macintosh. Calm down. This isn't the CERN research center." He wearily turned back to the rest of the class. "Please use the remainder of the meeting to choose partners and outline project ideas. If you need inspiration, talk to me or visit the school library." He pointed at Boxer. "Except you. You are to keep your mouth shut and stay put until I collect you."

Bakshi settled into his chair and waved Kelly up. She practically vibrated with excitement as she grabbed Kathy and started toward him.

Before they descended, Bakshi stood and aligned a sheet of paper perfectly with the corner of his desk.

"This is the member list. If you wish to join, please legibly print your name and phone number on here. Anyone whose name is not on this list by the end of next Monday's meeting, will not be participating."

The group began talking amongst themselves.

Drew crossed his arms. "I didn't think science club would be so…strict. Feels like a military recruitment center."

"That's just Bakshi. I have him for chemistry and he's the same in class." Jessica shook her head at his neat row of beakers. "He's driving me batty with those stupid things. He has to make sure they're arranged before he starts. And if any of them move out of alignment, he stops to fix them all over again."

"Sounds like a nutbar," said Drew, his disappointment evident. "And here I thought they sent all the crazies to our schools. Maybe this club isn't worth bothering with."

Jessica nodded, wondering the same thing herself. "Bakshi's definitely a bit cracked, but he's also genuinely brilliant. I saw him working through an equation so long that he used up all three blackboards. And his writing is *small*. Sadly, he's not much good at teaching. Doesn't get why we don't always understand things the first time around."

She was distracted as Boxer whacked his partner on the arm and jabbed a finger at a diagram they were drawing.

"I'm sorry about what he said. I don't know what's wrong with people sometimes."

Drew followed her gaze. "Same shit. Different day." He

muttered a quick "Later" and made for the door.

Jessica eyed Bakshi's list but couldn't decide whether to sign up. She had until Monday. Presumably her brain would start functioning and arrive at a decision before then.

She shouldered her bag and left, too hurt to say goodbye to Kathy.

Chapter 7

By the time Jessica arrived home, there were already voicemail messages for her parents from the nurse and counselor. She resisted the urge to delete them and stared at the fridge's uninspiring contents until she caught a chill. Deciding her stomach wasn't ready for anything heavy, she grabbed an apple and trudged upstairs.

She opened her laptop and sprawled out on her bed before taking a bite. The apple's satisfying crunch and juicy tartness boosted her flagging spirit, and she hungrily consumed the rest as she scanned news sites. Chris was only mentioned on the local paper's webpage:

BODY FOUND

The quiet serenity of Coldwater was shattered late Thursday evening when the body of a teenager was discovered near a public boat launch on Ghost Lake. Cause of death is unknown. The RCMP are conducting an investigation into the circumstances and ask that anyone with information about the deceased's activities on Wednesday, October 18, come forward. No further details are being released at this time.

Jessica read and re-read the article. The blunt, detached language grated on her nerves. It was empty, both of feeling and detail. She'd read similar news stories before, but this was different.

Tears welled as she remembered how vibrant and full of joy and...life...Chris had been. And now he was reduced to "the deceased." As if the single act of dying erased everything.

She looked around her room, at the bookcases and tchochkes, soaking in the familiar surroundings, trying to force back her growing depression. She paused on a photo taken this past summer: Kathy, Beth, Eric, and her, hands linked as they jumped off a dock into the lake. The same lake that had swallowed Chris.

Both moments were frozen in time. One in her mind, staring from within, and one in front of her, staring from without.

She focused on the photograph—a joyful memory now tainted with doubt and betrayal. Beth pursed her lips into a kiss for the camera, Kathy's eyes were squeezed shut, Eric grinned as he looked at her, and herself, her eyes were shining as she stuck out her tongue, carefree, content. Of course, she was a squat dwarf compared to the rest, but she looked happy. They all looked happy. She missed that.

Jessica leapt up and rooted through her overflowing desk drawer, eventually pulling out a silver necklace with half a heart pendent reading "st end." She hadn't worn it since elementary school and wondered if Beth still had the other side.

Not likely, she answered herself. *She's far too image conscious to keep anything so cheap.*

She sighed and carefully replaced it in the drawer.

Nostalgia coaxed her to phone Beth, but she pushed away the temptation.

Jessica lay down on her bed and rifled through her homework assignments. Her hand ached, but she ignored it. She pulled her math book out of her bag and then nervously dropped it, remembering the strange symbols moving across its pages. She flipped it open with a pen and discovered that several of them were stuck together.

After hesitating for a second, she peeled the pages apart and gaped in disbelief.

Crudely drawn in thick, brown-red smears was the same double intersecting circle design she'd seen gouged in the dirt at the cove. Her mind tardily connected the dried blood to the bandage on her hand. When she looked back at the book, the symbol flared like a reflector hit by passing headlights.

Her eyes snapped shut but the image did not dim or change—it stayed, blazing in the dark behind her eyelids. She opened them again but the symbol remained, interposed over the mundane landscape of her bedroom.

Paralyzed, she sat with her heart pounding until the figure faded from her vision. She glanced down at the textbook, half believing she had imagined everything, but saw that the symbol was still there.

She kicked the book off her bed.

Crawling up to her headboard, she pressed her back against the solid wood frame and drew her knees up to her chest. She stared at the inert math text, listening to her teeth chatter.

What the hell is going on?

Chapter 8

Jessica barely registered the cafeteria's hectic lunchtime activity as she picked at the dissected remains of her ham sandwich. She had bought it hoping to stimulate her appetite, but her stubborn haze of hunger-sapping depression remained intact—unlike her lunch. Mostly inedible before, the sandwich now resembled something a mama bird had regurgitated for her chicks.

She pushed the plate away and glanced across the table to Kathy, who was devouring a soggy burger. They hadn't said much to each other since yesterday and Jessica figured she should make some kind of effort.

As she contemplated what safe topic to start with, a group of guys swaggered by their table. One of them veered closer and crossed his hands over his heart, sighing, "Oh, Chris!" His crooked leer magnified the ugliness of his laughter as he backed away, performing a series of dramatic bows.

"Jerk!" Jessica flipped him the finger.

Kathy gave her a blank look as she shoved a mammoth hunk of burger into her mouth and squeezed out a muffled "Huh?" between chews.

"That jackass made a crack about my fainting and now he's over there laughing it up with his buddies. It must be all over school. He's not even in our grade."

"So? He's an idiot. Most people are." Kathy shrugged and resumed eating.

Jessica watched in disgust as a limp pickle slithered out of the bun and flopped onto Kathy's plate.

She could at least pretend to be interested, she thought gloomily as they fell back into uneasy silence. Jessica read the ingredients on her juice box, trying not to give in to the temptation to lay her head on the table.

Last night had been all kinds of bad. Her parents came home late, but her mother had insisted on discussing what had happened. Once that was over and exhaustion set in, she had closed her eyes and begged for sleep, but all her brain would do was replay images of Chris leaping to his death or that stupid glowing symbol. She spent the rest of her night reading *The Last Herald Mage*, hoping her favorite comfort series would lull her into slumberland. No such luck.

Jessica's eyelids dropped like weighted drawbridges and she forced them open again. She scanned the cafeteria for something more interesting than ascorbic acid and blue #2. Spotting Beth at a table, she waved hopefully.

Beth turned away, wrapping an arm around Matt's shoulders as she leaned close to whisper in his ear. He grinned and ran a finger along her jaw.

Jessica self-consciously lowered her hand.

Nice. Guess I'm not even worth a wave now.

She poked Kathy's hand and discreetly pointed at Beth. "She's with Matt again. She must really be into him."

Kathy licked a glob of ketchup off her fingers. "Yeah. I bet they're going out. Probably why we haven't seen much of her. You know how she is with new guys. He's from Calgary."

Jessica quirked an eyebrow and Kathy explained, "I accidently witnessed this morning's kiss-a-thon when he got off the bus."

Kathy haphazardly shoved her lunch detritus onto a tray and stood. "Anyway. I gotta run. I'm late meeting Kelly. She's totally psyched about our project. Are you joining up? You didn't sign the sheet."

"I'm thinking about it," she grumbled as Kathy bent to pick up her bag and dumped everything off her tray. Jessica helped her gather the garbage and then relieved her of the tray before she dropped it all again.

"Thanks, Jess. Catch ya later."

As Kathy hurried off, Jessica had a sudden thought and called after her. "Are you going to the memorial?"

She turned and shrugged. "I guess. I think everyone has to go."

Jessica waved at Kathy's retreating back, relieved she wouldn't be on her own. "I'll…" Her voice trailed off as she realized Kathy's mind was already elsewhere.

She dumped the garbage and sat down with a huff.

Why do I bother? My cereal bowl shows more interest. She contemplated her plastic tray and shook her head. *Nope. Not here. People already think I'm strange enough.*

* * *

A riptide of students swept Jessica into the gym. They funneled through the doors and spilled in all directions, noisy, boisterous, and pushy. She was elbowed, stepped on, and dragged for a short distance when her hair snagged on someone's backpack. By the time she found Kathy in the stands, predictably sitting on the first tier, Jessica felt like she'd survived a street fight.

She stopped in front of Kathy, staggering as those still searching for seats knocked into her. Jessica narrowly resisted hugging her when she saw the spaces Kathy had reserved with her bag and coat. If she hadn't known how cringe-worthy Kathy considered PDA, there would have been a love-fest.

Jessica glanced back as a loud chorus of "ouches" and "hey, watch its" approached. It was Kelly, using her formidable roller bag to clear a path through the crowd. Jessica groaned and carefully relocated Kathy's backpack, hoping to clear the decks before Kelly landed.

She was too late.

Kelly bustled up, giving Jessica an odd look when she stifled a cry of pain as a wheel rammed into her foot.

Jessica gritted her teeth and stepped back, flexing her toes to ensure they were intact.

Kelly loudly congratulated Kathy on securing seats, in the same way someone would praise a puppy the first time they shit outside. She brusquely shoved Kathy's jacket off the bench and plopped down with a grunt.

"This is a gong show," Kelly grumbled. "What idiot decided it was a good idea to stuff everyone in here at once?"

Kathy glanced nervously behind them. "These stands are going down for sure this time!"

Jessica limped back to the bench and turned to sit. She was halfway down when a boney knee jabbed her in the ass. Whipping around in surprise, she saw that Kirsten had slipped in behind her.

"That hurt." Jessica glared at Kirsten. "And I'm sitting there."

Kirsten raised her backside a few inches and looked at the bench. "Funny. I don't see your name on it," she said in a syrupy drawl, as if addressing a half-wit.

This can't be happening again! Jessica steamed as Kirsten stuck her nose in the air and began chatting with a friend sitting one tier up. She experienced a moment of mental vertigo, thinking back to the disastrous welcome assembly.

Only this time, Chris isn't here. And he never will be again.

Her heart hurt.

Kathy gave Jessica a nervous shrug as their eyes met. Kelly busily rifled through her bag, having either missed or ignored the exchange. There would be zero backup from them.

Jessica weighed her options. Causing a scene was out. She had little empathy for Kirsten, but she had been Chris's friend and maybe that warranted some extra slack, today, of all days.

Or not. Jessica scowled as Kirsten laughed at something her friend said. *She's remarkably chipper for someone attending a friend's memorial.*

Kathy's eyes pleaded with Jessica to leave it be and she gave in with a disgusted growl.

Sending Kirsten one last scathing glare, Jessica walked away, scanning the crammed stands for a free seat. It was a futile effort. People were now sitting on the floor, while others stood to either side of the stands, vying for wall space.

Jessica swore as she threaded her way to a space near the door.

After the last stragglers filtered in, she ended up stuck behind the tallest guy she'd ever seen. Whenever she shifted position to peer around him, someone else would move and block her view. She briefly considered asking if she could sit on his shoulders, but dismissed it as a hysterical whim. With her luck, he'd be game, and she'd end up looking like an overeager parade spectator. Besides, it would no doubt attract the principal's attention, and that was the last thing she needed.

Jessica caught glimpses of Mr. Johnson, various teachers, and a pastor during the tributes. The last speaker was the volleyball star she'd seen practicing yesterday.

The girl stepped up to the microphone and spoke in a strong, clear voice with a hint of an accent Jessica couldn't place.

"My name is Michiru, or Mac, if you like. I started here a few weeks ago. New town. New school. New people. I felt kind of lost. Three days in, I met Chris. He stuck up for me when someone was rude, and since then, he went out of his way to talk to me. He'd see me sitting on my own in the caf and join me. He introduced me to his friends and cheered me on in practice. Because of him, I don't feel like an outsider anymore. I only knew him for a short time, but he made a big difference.

"He made everyone feel like they mattered." Her voice cracked and she took a moment to steady herself. "Chris didn't just care about people, he took the time to listen and helped where he could. All his friends said the same thing; Chris lived life with his heart and arms wide open."

Michiru lowered her head. Flipping her ponytail out of her face, she straightened and continued in a level tone. "Chris is gone, but that doesn't dim the light he brought into our lives. Let's honor his memory by carrying his compassion with us as we meet each new day and each new person. Let's make a difference he would be proud of. Thank you."

There was a brief silence as she stepped back from the podium and then the gym exploded in cheers, whistles, and thunderous clapping.

Jessica stood rooted to the spot, tears pricking at the corners of her eyes. Michiru's speech brought back memories of a day she'd spent with Chris. Kirsten had said something mean on a fieldtrip, she didn't even remember what now, but Chris had noticed she wasn't enjoying herself. When it came time to partner up for a lame assignment, he'd grabbed her and they'd spent a goofy couple of hours talking about everything from anime to world politics.

It was so wrong that someone like that could be snuffed out, with so many gifts of kindness left un-given, a hole torn in the fabric of intersecting lives.

Jessica backed slowly out of the gym, not wanting anyone to see that she was crying, and then ran to the nearest bathroom.

Shit. She stared at her reflection in the mirror, cursing her splotchy skin and puffy eyes. *The middle of school and I do this. I'll look like a half-boiled lobster for hours now.*

Jessica could already hear the acerbic jokes, feel the burning assumptions in her classmates pitying looks and sneers. She'd long ago given up on using cover-up. All it ever did was draw attention to the fact that she was trying to hide something. And that was like dropping raw meat into a piranha tank.

Her anger turned inward and she berated herself for being too sensitive, too weak, too uncontrolled to hold her emotions in check until after school.

Why the hell is his death hitting me so hard? Chris was a nice guy, one of the nicest, but we weren't really all that close. It's not like he was my best friend. We had classes together, chatted occasionally, but...

Maybe that's it. He was a nice guy, but did I ever tell him?

I don't think so.

I hope someone did.

A tear splashed into the white porcelain sink and slid down the drain.

Chapter 9

H-K Shadow consolidating control of new host. Shadow ex-
hibiting difficulty adjusting to changes in local population. Priority task: Bring Channel to receptive state.

* * *

Jessica splashed her face with cold water, trying to counteract
the spreading lobster effect and headache that invariably
accompanied her tears.

A stampede of footsteps and voices approached from the
hall. Groaning, she soaked a paper towel, grabbed her backpack,
and dove into a stall. Locking the door, she crouched on the
toilet seat, hoping they'd pass by.

The bathroom door squeaked open and she belatedly
snatched her bag off the floor. Jessica set it down on the toilet
tank behind her, praying for balance as the seat wobbled. She
pressed the cool towel against her swollen eyes and listened as
the girls rushed in.

"You should have seen her face. I thought she was going
to cry." Kirsten continued in a high-pitched, whiny voice, "'But
I was going to sit there. Wah.' "

*Crap and double crap! Of all the people…*Jessica froze, a reflex that for once served her well as the toilet seat finally settled.

All she could see was a sliver of activity through the gap between the door and frame. There were four or five girls milling around the sinks, checking makeup, brushing hair, spraying perfume, and adjusting outfits. She stifled a sneeze as a waft of flowery scent drifted into her stall, goading her headache into full swing.

Kirsten called everyone to attention. "Anyone who's chicken better take off. Once we start, no one leaves. I heard about some girls who ran out in the middle and a janitor found them a week later in the furnace room…with no faces. Something tore them off."

There was shuffling, but no one headed for the door.

"Are you sure this is safe?" one of the girls hesitantly spoke up.

Jessica recognized the voice as Natalie, one of Kirsten's regular followers. That she even dared to question Kirsten was telling.

After a brief pause, Natalie added, "I mean, with, you know, Chris and all. I heard you'd done some kind of ritual that went weird? You don't think maybe that's why he…"

Cold fear traced down Jessica's spine as she recalled her Ouija board nightmare. She shoved the images from her mind and thought about nice things—kittens, minty ice cream, smartphones with better specs than her laptop.

"Don't blame me for Chris's mental issues." Kirsten's voice snapped like a whip. "Anybody who's feeling psycho, please, please, use the door." Her tone seamlessly shifted from angry to hurt. "I can't handle a repeat of the whole Chris thing, so if you're feeling suicidal, just stay the fuck away from me, all right?"

The group was silent.

Jessica had witnessed enough similar altercations to guess that Natalie was looking cowed.

Assured there would be no further defiance in the ranks, Kirsten continued, "Okay. Jenny, you light the candle and I'll make sure the door is wedged shut so nobody interrupts us."

Kirsten breezed past the stall and Jessica instinctively shrank back, setting the toilet seat wobbling again. The lights clicked off and the soft glow of a candle struggled against the gloom, casting distorted shadows on the walls and ceiling.

What the hell is she planning? wondered Jessica as moving darkness eclipsed the light trickling through the gap. Guessing it was Kirsten rejoining the others, Jessica gave into her curiosity and gingerly stepped off her perch. She pressed her pounding head against the cool metal door and peeked out.

Faces torn off? Is it wrong of me to hope that Kirsten makes a run for it?

Kirsten ordered everyone to gather at the candle. "I'll explain this once more so nobody screws up. We all stand nice and still, with our eyes closed, and say 'Bloody Mary' thirteen times. Then we can look. If everything goes right, Bloody Mary will appear in the mirror and tell us something about the future."

That old stinker?

Jessica breathed a sigh of relief. She remembered trying it in grade six with Beth and Kathy. Kathy had freaked out and bolted, and was thankfully still in possession of her face. Beth and Jessica had stuck it out, only to find their own expectant mugs staring back from the mirror. At which point, Beth had said in a deep voice, "Jess will grow boobs when she's forty-two."

She grinned at the memory.

The girls began chanting in a serious, steady tone.

Against her will, Jessica counted. At the third "Bloody Mary," she considered sneaking out while the group was occupied, but by the time they reached six, she decided it was safer to wait it out.

When they reached eleven, the warm yellow candlelight edged into blue.

At twelve, a hush thickened the air. Noise from the busy school no longer penetrated the room. She heard only the low, constant chanting.

Jessica yawned, trying to clear the cotton-ball feeling in her ears. A prickling sensation crawled over her exposed skin, making her shiver.

"Bloody Mary."

A pure white light flared and then faded into a diffuse silver radiance, drowning out the candle's glow. Jessica started in surprise, unable to see where this new light came from.

There were several screams and Kirsten blew past the stall. Jessica jumped back onto the toilet as the group charged after their retreating leader, stumbling and pushing each other. Jessica kept as still as possible in the awkward position she'd landed in, listening as they frantically banged on the bathroom door, which was stuck.

Kirsten yelled, "The doorstop!" and after a second, the door crashed open.

I'm not going to panic. Jessica closed her eyes. *Whatever happened, it can't have been set up by Kirsten, or she wouldn't have scrambled out of here faster than a cheerleader in a slasher flick. Someone must have played a trick on her. That's got to be it.*

As she shifted her weight to climb off the toilet, her shoe slipped on the rim and splashed into the bowl. Grabbing the toilet-paper dispenser narrowly saved her from a nasty fall, but didn't save her foot. Disgusted, she pulled it out and squelched to the stall door, skidding as the grip of her soaked running shoe refused to live up to its name.

Jessica cautiously peered through the gap, but the silvery light source remained maddeningly out of sight. She knew she should run for the door. That would be the smart thing to do.

Who am I kidding? I can't leave without seeing what scared them.

She sidled out of the stall and moved nearer to where the girls had stood. A thick black pillar candle sat in a sink, its flame lost in the intense white light streaming from the mirror behind it. Looking into the light didn't affect her eyes the way it should have. She had no urge to squint; just the opposite—her eyes opened wider, ushering in more of the brilliance.

Jessica's breath caught when she saw the figure floating within the mirror. It was impossible to see where the light ended and the hazy, vaguely feminine form began. They were one. Her wild, flowing hair and robes shimmered. The face was oddly smooth, as if a loose shroud concealed its features.

She took a halting step toward the figure. Its radiance sought her out, seeping into her body, drawing her closer.

Jessica tore her gaze away and pushed out her left hand—a feeble barrier. Her bones stood out in dark relief against glowing red flesh rendered transparent by the light. Even in the depths of her fear, Jessica felt awe for the sheer impossibility of the phenomenon before her.

Against every notion of sanity, she inched closer, stepping fully into the light.

It was like plunging into a stream of glacier runoff. Her thin T-shirt and jeans offered no protection. In the back of her mind, she wondered what sort of light radiated cold instead of heat.

Jessica watched in horror as her hand reached for the mirror. She forced it back to her side with agonizing slowness, feeling as though she was fighting against a rushing current.

The figure reached out to her, its arms draped in sleeves of dripping light. Fear lent Jessica enough strength to take a small step back as the spectral hands groped inches from her face.

She retreated a few more steps, past the edge of the icy white illumination, until she stood in shadow once more. The ghostly face tilted to the side and stretched down. A thin crease appeared on its forehead and the arms withdrew, blending seamlessly back into the light.

Warmth trickled over Jessica's frigid skin and the numbness in her body subsided. The wavering light surrounding the figure began to flash and roil. Its hair and robes whipped violently in an unseen storm.

The door was only a few meters away. Too afraid to turn her back, she kept her eyes fixed on the mirror and edged toward the exit.

The figure let out a grating screech like a dull blade sliding across ceramic.

Jessica covered her ears and sprinted for freedom.

There was a blinding flash behind her as she tore the door open and threw herself out.

* * *

Jessica slid across the floor and lay in the middle of the hallway staring at the bathroom door, afraid the dancing spots clouding her vision were the creature's minions. She scrabbled back until she whacked her head against a locker on the opposite side of the hall.

The door clicked closed and she rubbed her eyes. A blurry ring of silhouettes appeared. They were vaguely human-shaped gray blobs surrounded by green auras, and they were visible whether her eyes were open or closed.

A loud cry sounded and she blinked at the milling forms, wondering who was yelling. Her skin still tingled from the cold and was so sensitive that even her breath felt harsh against her forearm.

Jessica realized who was screaming when she ran out of air. She clamped her mouth and eyes shut, willing everything to go back to normal. Pressing her hands against the floor, she focused on the solid, polished surface.

No more ghosts. No more hallucinations. No more dead friends. She repeated it in her mind like a mantra until she sensed movement near her.

This is a bad dream. I'm going to wake up in my bed. Cracking one eye open, Jessica saw the school hallway. *Okay…not a dream.*

The humanish blobs slowly resolved into recognizable people. Kirsten was one of them, standing off to one side, pale and shaken. A teacher was bent double beside Jessica, peering worriedly at her.

"You!" Kirsten said, sounding surprised and angry. "What the fuck were *you* doing in there?"

The teacher straightened and frowned at Kirsten. "Language!" He pointed at the bathroom. "That's ground zero, is it?"

She nodded vigorously. "It's in there, Mr. Darien. I swear." He walked toward the door and Kirsten clutched at his arm. "Are you stupid? You can't go in."

"Young lady. I don't know what you are playing at, but I don't appreciate being called stupid. You stay put until I've had a look. Then we'll have a chat with the principal about your language, lack of respect, and why you felt the need to participate in such an attention-seeking sham. *Comprende?*"

Kirsten glared defiantly as he beckoned over a nearby

student.

"Make sure she doesn't move." He said, indicating Kirsten. Then he jerked a thumb at Jessica. "And make sure she sticks around too, or you'll be joining our little get-together with Mr. Johnson."

Mr. Darien wrenched the bathroom door open and felt around for the light switch. When he disappeared inside, Jessica scanned the hall, noting that none of the other girls from the bathroom were among the crowd.

She glanced over at Kirsten and almost smiled.

Good to know I'm not the only one with fair-weather friends.

Jessica peeled herself off the floor. Wishing there was a convenient patch of sand she could stick her head in, she made her way to where Kirsten stood, her wet shoe squelching loudly with each step.

Ignoring the muffled giggling, she leaned against a locker and flinched as someone grabbed her arm. Although the grip wasn't tight, the touch felt uncomfortable against her skin, like scratchy wool on a sunburn.

The guy who had been charged with watching Kirsten was now stationed between them, with one hand on each of their arms. He obviously did not intend to spend his afternoon with the principal.

Kirsten leaned around him and gave Jessica a puzzled look that still managed to be menacing. Jessica ignored her and waited anxiously for the teacher to return.

Time stretched out. Jessica was just starting to worry when he emerged—intact and relatively calm.

Mr. Darien held up a hand and addressed everyone in an exaggeratedly soothing tone. "Ladies and gentlemen. I'm happy to report there's no need to panic. The situation has been re-solved." He directed a sharp look at Kirsten and Jessica. "Girls, next time this happens, I suggest flushing instead of creating a general panic. Granted, it was frightening, but in the end, it was easily dealt with."

Kirsten's cheeks flushed.

He turned back to the laughing crowd and continued. "Now, get to class."

They didn't move, and Mr. Darien irritably waved at them. "Shoo."

With the teacher distracted, Kirsten leaned forward and glared at Jessica again. "This is your fault. You hid in there and did this. I don't know how you pulled it off, but I'll make you pay."

Jessica fixed her gaze at a point straight ahead, pretending she wasn't listening. Not for the first time, she wondered how she managed to get into these situations.

When only a few students straggled away, Mr. Darien threw his arms in the air. "All right. Let's try this: Anyone here in five seconds is going to the principal's office with us."

It was like magic. In the blink of an eye, the corridor was empty except for Mr. Darien, Kirsten, Jessica, and the guy doggedly holding onto them. The teacher waved at his deputy, and he vanished as quickly as the rest.

Now, why couldn't I have that for a power? Jessica thought giddily. *A wave of my hand and, poof, people disappear. Handy.*

She surreptitiously waved at Kirsten and then humphed in disappointment.

Mr. Darien looked between Kirsten and Jessica. "I don't know what went on in there, and I imagine all I'll get from you two is more nonsense." Kirsten opened her mouth to speak and he held up a hand. "Don't even try. I'm not interested. Tell it to Mr. Johnson." He ushered the girls ahead of him down the hall.

Jessica cringed. The principal wouldn't be happy to see her again. She stopped a few squelches into the forced march. Kirsten and the teacher bumped into her.

She pointed back to the bathroom. "Uh…my bag's in there."

Mr. Darien adjusted his neck, cracking his vertebrae in a way that made Jessica feel sick. He jerked his head toward the bathroom and growled, "Fine, but be quick about it."

She licked her lips and stared at the door.

The teacher glowered at her impatiently.

Jessica croaked, "Um, I don't suppose you would…"

Kirsten took a step back, pre-emptively distancing herself, as a warning flush crept up Mr. Darien's neck.

Jessica shook her head. "Never mind. Sorry. I'll get it."

She slowly approached the bathroom and peered in, ready to bolt at the slightest provocation. When nothing untoward happened, she scurried over to the stall she had hidden in.

As she grabbed her backpack, which was mercifully still perched on the toilet tank, she noticed Kirsten's bag sitting on the floor under the bank of sinks. Keeping her eyes averted from the mirror, Jessica scuttled over and retrieved it.

Then she remembered the candle. Mr. Darien couldn't have seen it when he came in, or they'd be in trouble for that too. Standing as far away from the mirror as possible, Jessica blindly felt around the unnaturally chilled porcelain until she had hold of the candle. She stared at the garbage can for a moment and then shoved the candle into Kirsten's bag.

It's hers. She can deal with it.

When she reached the door, curiosity overcame anxiety and she snuck a quick peek at the mirror. Jessica nearly dropped the bags in shock.

The same symbol she had seen in the dirt and on her

math text was drawn in the condensation on the mirror, though this version was no quick smear. It was laid out with consistent lines in smooth, geometrically precise curves. And it was big, covering the entire surface. Where the two circles intersected, she could clearly see the shape of an eye, staring blindly out at the room.

Her gaze followed the curves, around this way and that. She marveled at the perfect symmetry and felt herself drawn into the design. Her vision narrowed and cold pricked along her skin. The sensation knocked her out of her stupor and she stumbled into the hall.

Jessica heard Ms. Oreiller a short distance away, talking earnestly. "I quite agree with you. This is inexcusable. Kirsten, you owe Mr. Darien an apology. You know better than to call people names."

Kirsten's mouth opened and closed several times. Eventually, she peevishly mumbled, "Sorry. I was just scared." Then she sneered and jabbed a finger at Jessica as she arrived. "It's all her fault. She did something to make us think there was a ghost in the mirror."

Jessica spitefully dropped Kirsten's backpack on her foot. As Kirsten massaged her toes, Jessica said, "I found your bag. No need to thank me."

Ms. Oreiller frowned at Jessica, taking in her red eyes and disheveled clothes. The counselor's eyebrows shot up when she reached her soaked pant leg.

"Girls, I think we should talk. I'll take it from here, Mr. Darien."

Mr. Darien spluttered that they were on their way to the principal's office, but the counselor cut him off.

"I understand. Unfortunately, Mr. Johnson has a lot on his plate at the moment. He's meeting with the RCMP, and I don't think it's going to be a short discussion. Best not to disturb him with something I can handle."

Grudgingly nodding his assent, Mr. Darien stalked off, muttering under his breath about women and teenagers.

* * *

Ms. Oreiller listened to an hour of heated accusations, at least on Kirsten's part. Jessica couldn't bring herself to look the counselor in the eye as Kirsten skewered her in every possible way. Ms. Oreiller did her best to coax Jessica into the discussion and curb Kirsten's jibes, but Jessica wasn't tuned in. She was busy going over what had happened in the bathroom, occasionally listening as Kirsten described what she had witnessed.

Unless someone had secretly graduated from film school with mad FX skills, Jessica didn't think it could have been a prank. Kirsten's description of the specter was identical to her own, so she was left with two possibilities: Either they had been subject to a group hallucination, or their bathroom was haunted. Neither seemed likely, and the first didn't account for the symbol.

The hairs on the back of her neck prickled. Had she drawn the symbol and somehow blocked it from her memory, or had the specter left it? Three times she'd seen it, and all after nightmares or disturbing hallucinations. The whole point of symbols was that they stood for something, but this one meant nothing to her.

Over the haze of thoughts running through her head, she registered the counselor dismissing Kirsten with a warning to think seriously about how her words affected others.

When she was gone, Ms. Oreiller turned her full attention to Jessica. She tried again to draw her out, but Jessica's only response was a desultory, "Sorry."

Frustrated, the counselor leaned forward. "Jessica?"

Jessica was locked deep within her own mind, rehashing and analyzing every detail from her Ouija board and bridge dreams. Was there more to the nightmare images than subconscious fears? Some guy called Bill had been in both, but she didn't know him. Did he exist?

A hand shook her knee and she snapped back to the present.

"Please look at me when I'm talking to you, Jessica."

She raised her eyes to meet the counselor's.

"I'm worried about you. I reviewed your school records and, apart from a few minor incidents, you have no reprimands or suspensions. Your marks are consistently high and you've pretty much been a model student. Something has changed this year. I think you should talk about what's happening. If not to me, then to your parents, or friends."

Jessica snorted as she imagined telling her parents. "Sure. Just as soon as I figure out how to explain the un-explainable."

The counselor sighed. "Don't put up roadblocks. You are a bright, determined young woman, but being independent is only good to a point. If you can't work through this yourself, do the smart thing and ask for help. Talk it out. Sometimes that's all it takes to put things in perspective. I don't know why Chris didn't reach out, but I am begging you to, before things get worse. You know my door is always open."

Ms. Oreiller stood, indicating their conversation was over.

As Jessica reached the door, the counselor asked in a quiet voice, "Why is your leg wet?"

Jessica looked down at her damp shoe and simply responded, "Toilet."

Ms. Oreiller sucked in her lower lip, coughed, and then nodded. "Hmmm. I see. Well. Carry on. I believe you can still make the last few minutes of class."

Chapter 10

Direct link with Channel failed. Channel untrained. Possible breakdown of pre-interregnum culture. Generating new decision trees.

* * *

Jessica sat on her bed that night, stroking her pet sock, trying to make sense of what was happening—two nightmares and a ghost in a bathroom. It sounded like the beginning of a twisted Christmas carol.

Am I crazy? Would I be questioning my sanity if I were?

She gazed down at the floppy green microfiber in her hand. It was nothing special, except there was something incredibly reassuring about the soft material rhythmically sliding through her fingers. It never failed to calm her mind when she needed to work through a thorny problem. This time however, she was fast coming to the conclusion that she wasn't going to come to a conclusion.

The sock caught on the bunched-up bandage stuck to her palm and she yanked the loose covering off in frustration. She tossed it at her garbage basket and missed.

Groaning, she gently rubbed her itching palm and looked

down in surprise when her fingers met with smooth skin. Her left palm was red, but the puckered skin and open puncture were gone.

Even though it felt like a week, not even two days had passed since they'd announced Chris's death. There was no way her wound should be this healed. Then she remembered the ghost in the mirror, and how she'd held up her hand.

The hairs on her neck prickled. The sensation ran across her shoulders and down the backs of her arms.

She shivered, recalling the eerie cold of the light, and glanced at her mirror. Never before had its reflective surface felt ominous. And the photographs of her smiling friends clustered around the edge just seemed mocking now.

Friends indeed. Where are you?

She didn't have to think too hard for that answer. Beth would be on a date, probably with Matt, and she knew from an earlier call to Kathy that she was happily holed up in the school library with Kelly.

Jessica leapt off her bed in a fit of irritation and threw the yellow baby blanket her grandmother had knit over the mirror, effectively blocking both it and the photos from sight.

She plucked her laptop off the desk, unwilling to sit near the mirror, and returned to the bed. Jessica opened her computer and confirmed Eric was online. She paused to savor the comforting normality of her actions before calling.

He answered on the first ring. A video window popped open and his handsome face took over her screen. His hair was getting long, falling over his eyes, and Jessica longed to brush it aside.

"Howdy, stranger," Eric drawled in a mock western accent and then switched to his normal voice. "What happened to you last night? You were online, but you didn't answer when

I called."

Jessica heard the counselor's voice in her head, urging her to talk. She bit her lip, angry at the tears threatening to spill. She couldn't tell him. He'd think she was crazy, just as sure as her parents would, and Ms. Oreiller, and any other sane person.

After an extended pause, worry edged into his voice. "Jess? What's up?"

She needed to talk, she knew it, and so she told him about the only semi-normal thing she could—that Chris had died and that he might have committed suicide.

Eric was shocked. He had known Chris better than Jessica and never pegged him as unhappy, let alone depressed enough to do something so drastic.

Hearing the distress and sympathy in his voice, Jessica broke down and told him about passing out when she first heard. Then she started telling him about the bathroom specter, but midway through heard how crazy it sounded and chickened out, re-framing it as an elaborate prank.

After explaining, she added, "And...FYI, if I wind up dead in a ditch somewhere...Kirsten did it. She's convinced I orchestrated the whole thing. Then, just to top today off, I find out Ms. Oreiller called mom at work. She phoned me while I was walking home, wanting to know why the school counselor was concerned. I'm totally screwed."

When Eric asked how Kathy and Beth were handling everything, Jessica couldn't keep her tears at bay. All her pent-up confusion, anxiety, and fear poured out like a dam tearing open.

She apologized, embarrassed, swiping her sweater sleeve across her eyes. "These last few days have been awful, and Beth and Kathy are being total jerks. Beth has this new boyfriend and Kathy's hanging around Kelly, if you can believe it.

They've paired up for science club. She never even told me she was joining."

"Do they know what happened with Kirsten today? And why do I get the feeling this has been going on for a while?"

"Because it has." Jessica sighed miserably. "I didn't want to bother you. I thought things would blow over. And you know what the rumor mill is like. Half the town probably knows what happened, but Beth and Kathy are too wrapped up in their own lives to give a crap." Jessica ended by excusing herself to blow her nose.

When she came back, Eric said, "You're right. They suck. I don't know what their damage is. I mean, Beth's always been a bit fickle, but not Kathy." Eric continued slowly, as if planning while he talked. "Sounds like you need some sexy fun time with your boyfriend. Between my practices and your crazy workload, we haven't seen much of each other lately."

Jessica flinched at the word crazy.

"Tell you what. I'm gonna get down with my rebel self, skip Saturday practice, and hijack mom's car. A little food…a day at the cove…you'll be good as new. I won't even complain if you bring a book. It'll be chilly, but I'll bring blankets and we can cuddle…while you read, of course. What do you say?"

Jessica couldn't help smiling as Eric's eyes twinkled mischievously. "Sounds perfect. Just don't let me nod off this time. I don't want to be responsible for any more injuries."

"Agreed. I'll pick you up around eleven. I need my beauty sleep."

Jessica snorted and shook her head. "You're such an ass. Don't ever change."

"No worries, sweetness. This firm, yet oh-so-squeezable ass plans to remain young and perky forever."

Jessica grinned and related how Mr. Darien had accused

her and Kirsten of leaving a load in a toilet. She finished amidst Eric's easy laughter. "You know…the look on Kirsten's face almost made the whole ordeal worthwhile. Not quite, but almost."

Chapter 11

A jagged white hump interrupted the smooth row of lockers ahead. Jessica's Monday morning zombie shuffle ground to a halt as she squinted in the crypt's dim light, trying to bring the mass into focus. Confirming it was in the vicinity of her locker, she approached cautiously.

With my luck, it's got rabies.

Eric had done his best over the weekend to keep her occupied and happy, but the dread of facing school was never far from her mind. The first few days would suck, she just wasn't sure what inventive torments her classmates would employ. She suspected she was about to find out.

As she drew nearer, the locker deformity resolved into a fleet of miniature tissue ghosts. Muffled snickering drifted down the hall as a pair of heads poked around the far corner. She ignored them and opened her locker as if nothing was wrong.

Well, at least I'm set up to treat nosebleeds for the next century.

She retrieved what was needed for morning classes and pulled the grinning ghosts off the door, piling them in the bottom of her locker.

Despite her newfound dread of school bathrooms, she scouted out an empty one near the theatre and locked herself in a stall to wait for the bell. This morning, encountering a ghost ranked lower on her fear scale than a run-in with Kirsten, and she knew her nemesis would never frequent the drama nerds' bathroom.

Jessica read the graffiti etched on the cubicle's metal walls, hoping Rachel's herpes cleared up and Dizzi learned the difference between "your" and "you're." She had to give props to whoever drew the giant penis with a monocle and top hat. There was some real artistic talent there.

When the bell rang, she waited a few seconds and then dashed to class, mostly tuning out the whispers that rose in her wake. She slipped behind her desk and pulled her chemistry text from her backpack.

After saying a tense "hey" to Kathy and receiving a noncommittal grunt, she noticed a handwritten note taped to her desk's laminated top. It read, "Open Me."

The room was unusually quiet. Her classmates twirled pens and flipped pages in notebooks. Several shuffled in their seats.

She glanced over at Kathy, who was chewing her pencil. Her friend's gaze kept sliding toward her, but she looked away as soon as she realized Jessica was watching.

Jessica studied the note. The thick, boxy lettering wasn't familiar.

Biting her lip, she pulled out her binder and dropped it on her desk with a resounding bang that echoed through the room. Then she primly crossed her ankles and leaned back in her chair, waiting for Mr. Bakshi to arrive and commence the daily dance of the beakers.

He arrived shortly before the bell rang and set about organizing his desk. His beakers were in disarray again. Jessica felt a flash of annoyance on his behalf. Every day he stood up there, arranging his beakers in the proper order, and never once did he complain or accuse anyone. He simply fixed them and carried on. She wished she could do that with her life.

Jessica's gaze gravitated back to the note. The words goaded her, teased her, dared her to give in.

Is ignoring it really going to make a difference? They'll just find some other way to bug me and I'll end up wondering what this was all day.

With a resigned sigh, Jessica moved her books to the floor. She never could leave a mystery alone.

Something shifted inside as she eased the desk lid open a crack, but it was impossible to see far into the shadowed interior. Cursing herself for not replacing the battery in her keychain flashlight, Jessica raised the lid another inch and leant down to get a closer look. There were no scrabbling noises, so she was relatively certain it wasn't alive…either that, or it had no legs.

Her eyes narrowed. *If they think I'm scared of snakes, they're going to be disappointed.*

Now certain it was a prank involving someone's hapless pet, she began to worry about how long it had been in the desk and whether it was warm enough.

The asshats probably didn't bother to put a heat mat in.

Out of the corner of her eye, she saw Mr. Bakshi aligning the last beaker. Class was about to begin.

Figuring it was better to get it over with quickly, she steeled herself and pulled the desk fully open. There was a loud pop and a distorted white face flew at her head.

She let out a high-pitched scream and several students jumped and giggled. Mr. Bakshi dropped his beaker.

Recovering in record time, Jessica yanked the ghost mask off the underside of the lid and searched for the source of the noise. Taped to the side and top of the desk were several thin strips of cardboard, no doubt the pillaged innards of Christmas crackers. She had to give the pranksters credit. It was simple but effective, and at least they didn't endanger something alive. Except possibly herself. She put a hand over her pounding heart.

Jessica felt a presence and grimaced when she saw the pressed and starched lab coat sleeve. Mr. Bakshi hovered beside her like a ripe storm cresting a valley ridge. She handed him the mask. He blinked at it and then pointed to the pile of glistening shards in front of his desk.

"I'm sorry. I didn't think…" Her words trailed off as the teacher's lips thinned and a muscle twitched in his jaw. "I should clean that up?"

He nodded.

"And I guess I'll see you after class?"

He nodded again and resumed his post at the front, casting a pained look at his foreshortened row of beakers.

* * *

Jessica was relieved when the last bell of the day rang. She had stoically endured the snickering, inexpertly dodged the wet tissue ghosts launched at her in the halls, and ignored the sidelong glances from faculty members. Pretending to not care was exhausting.

She shoved the new math text she'd borrowed from the library into her backpack and called after Beth, who was about to reach escape velocity.

Beth turned back at the door and hissed, "For God's sake, don't yell my name like that. The whole school probably heard you."

"Sorry. Can you lend me the notes from last class? I

was…uh, indisposed, as I'm sure you've heard."

Beth fidgeted with her shirt. "Yeah. I heard. What the hell were you thinking, pissing Kirsten off? She doesn't need any more reasons to hate you. You're soooo dead."

Matt sauntered up and slid an arm around Beth's waist. "Hiya, sweetcheeks. Gettin' your daily dose of freak?" He leaned in until his nose was an inch from Jessica's and yelled, "Boo!"

She stepped back, her expression wooden and fists clenched tight enough to hurt.

"Oh, hi, you." Beth chirped sweetly. "I'll just be a sec."

Matt frowned. "Well you'd better step on it if you're coming."

"Of course. I'll meet you at Tyler's truck."

Jessica fought down revulsion as Matt planted a sloppy kiss on Beth's lips and smacked her on the ass. The guy was a world-class jerk, with a hefty side of chauvinistic prick. She had no idea what Beth saw in him.

As soon as he was out of earshot, Beth leveled a pitying look at Jessica. "Listen. I didn't want to have this conversation. I figured you'd get it, but you obviously don't. We've been friends a long time, but things are different now, we're different. We might have had a great time playing dress-up and sticking worms down Jamie's pants in elementary, but this is high school. We aren't interested in the same things anymore. We don't hang around the same people. We don't even hang out at the same places."

When Jessica remained silent, she continued. "I think it's best if we go our separate ways. I don't know what's been going on with you lately, but I hope things get better."

By the time Jessica found her voice, Beth was already walking away. "I just wanted to borrow your notes." Her tongue felt dry and ungainly and the words came out in a slurred mumble.

Beth stopped and looked back. "What?"

Jessica felt the distance between them open like a crevasse under rotten snow. Anger forced her voice louder.

"All I wanted was your fucking notes. Things haven't changed at all. It's always about you. Kathy and I do whatever you want, and then you hook up with some guy and ditch us like used toilet paper. Don't bother calling me when Matt and his cronies decide to move onto the next hot ass that walks by. I'm done."

* * *

Jessica shoved her way through the crowded hallway with no specific destination in mind, just an overwhelming need to get away. When she reached the main school doors, she remembered the science club, and stopped. She'd forgotten to think about it over the weekend.

She glanced down the hall toward the lab and then back to the doors. They beckoned, and for once she longed to escape to the quiet solitude of her room.

Jessica stumbled as someone bumped into her. Grumbling, she made her way to the library.

She slumped into a chair at the nearest table and laid her head on her arms, weighing the pros and cons of joining. The positives were compelling: It would look good on her school record, which needed a boost at the moment; she'd get to go to the science fairs; she'd maybe learn a thing or two. Of course, she'd also have to deal with new best buds Kathy and Kelly, work on a lame group project, and listen to everyone bicker about whose project was the best. Those were substantial negatives. But then there was always the possibility Gordy and Boxer might incinerate something again. It would be a shame to miss that.

The library doors banged opened in the middle of her deliberation and Drew skulked in, accompanied by two other guys. They all looked annoyed.

The tall, gangly one poked Drew in the back. "You must be shitting me."

"I said I was thinking about it. I don't know if I want to or not yet." Drew batted at Gangly's finger.

The other one, a stocky guy with his hair in two long braids and legs as broad as tree trunks grumbled, "Man, why are we still here? School's out." His gaze roamed over the bookshelves. "Fuck, there's a lot of books."

After a short, astonished pause, Stocky shook his head. "Time to blow this rat hole. You promised to help me get my dirt bike running." He grabbed Drew's arm and started walking toward the door.

Drew struggled to pull away, but his efforts were futile until he caught the door handle and jerked them both to a stop.

"You can both piss off. And Bobby, even if we had a time machine, we couldn't salvage that pile of rust."

Bobby let him go and held up his hands. "Fine. What DO you wanna do?"

"Check out some books for my social studies assignment." Drew waved an arm around in a vaguely theatrical gesture. "Hence, the library."

Gangly snorted. "Hence? What kind of word is that? If you're trying to suck up to those science club nerds, it won't work. Teach probably won't even let you in. You skipped half of last year's classes and your skin isn't the right color, in case you've forgotten."

"Fuck you, Sam. Nobody tells me what to do. If I want

to join, I will. And if you guys want to waste your time here, when we've got half-decent teachers and computers that aren't rejects from the '90s, then that's your problem." Drew attempted to shove Bobby, who proved immovable, and staggered back a few steps.

Bobby's expression darkened. "I get it. You're too good for us now. You think you're gonna fit in with these rich white hicks? Think you're Mr. Independent?" He jabbed a finger at Drew's chest and knocked him back another step. "Well, go ahead and pretend you're one of them. See how far that gets you. Just don't come crying when you find yourself cornered by your new 'friends' with no one to back you up."

Drew clenched his fists and took a step toward Bobby. Bobby held his ground, meeting Drew's glare.

The librarian hustled through the door and cast a warning look at the tense group before disappearing behind a stack of books on her desk. She peered out occasionally, no doubt checking to make sure there were no shenanigans disturbing her ordered domain.

Bobby spun on his heel and stalked out, followed by Sam. Drew stood for a minute, glaring after them, clenching and unclenching his fists. He threw his bag to the floor and there was a crash as it skidded into the leg of Jessica's table.

The librarian half stood and pointed a stern finger at them.

Drew sagged down in front of a computer beside Jessica and she instinctively edged away. She could hear his teeth grinding as he stared at the blank screen.

The sound set her own teeth on edge and she pressed the ear closest to him tighter against her arm, trying to block it out. After squirming for several minutes, she reached critical mass.

"Need help looking something up?" She asked curtly,

motioning to the idle computer.

His lips thinned.

"I'll just move then, shall I?" Jessica shoved her chair back and bent down to grab her bag.

"Awww. Aren't you sweet, offering to help the poor dumb Indian figure out the mysterious high-tech computer? That your good deed for the day, princess?"

Jessica stopped moving. In her mind, she saw Bakshi stoically rearranging his beakers. She took a deep breath and raised her gaze to his.

"Listen. Obviously, you've had a crappy day...again. So have I...again. I'd love nothing better than to take someone's head off right now too, and that's exactly why I'm going to walk away." She stood and then hastily added, "And calling these lumbering beasts high-tech is ridiculous."

Jessica turned to leave and heard him laugh. Her last scrap of Bakshi Zen went up in smoke and she dropped her bag. "What the hell is so funny?"

"You," he wheezed, grinning broadly. "Well, actually more the idea of you taking someone's head off wearing that fuzzy pink sweater." He dissolved into laughter again. "I bet you've never even seen a real fight. Plus, someone's stuck a note on your bag. 'I see dead people.' What's up with that?"

Jessica ripped the note off her backpack and shoved it in her pocket. "Yeah, well, I punched my boyfriend and nearly collapsed his windpipe a while ago. Plus, I'm a five-time survivor of Boxing Day at the mall, so I've seen my fair share of fights. Last year there was even a stabbing in the parking lot. And my sweater isn't pink. It's coral. I don't wear pink." She paused, wondering why she had told him all that.

"Well, as long as we're sharing such vital information, I'd like to point out that these computers aren't that bad. Cheap-ass, generic pieces of crap, but technically modern. I could hack them in my sleep, but they're still way better than the shit my old school had."

Jessica was impressed and decided to test his tech savvy. She wrinkled her nose, feigning disdain. "I don't think I care to associate with someone who considers a desktop I could re-place with a single Raspberry Pi 'modern.'"

"A temping thought," he agreed with a grin that signifi-cantly bumped up his cuteness factor. "And the Linux OS would be a definite improvement."

She grinned back, relieved to be in good geek company. "Can you imagine the looks on the faces of the school board IT crew?"

A surprisingly genuine laugh burst out of him. "You're a strange duck. But, seriously, what's with the note? You some kind of mystic trying to drum up business?"

Jessica rolled her eyes and sat back down.

"No." She breathed out the word and let her head fall back until she was staring up at the drop ceiling. One of the fiberboards had a footprint on it, which suddenly struck her as hilarious.

She quelled her giggling when she noticed him staring and asked, "Did you hear about the ghost in the bathroom on Friday?"

When he nodded, she continued, "I got blamed for it, at least by Kirsten. Don't know if you've met her. She considers herself queen bee of…everything."

Drew nodded. "I know a few people like that."

They sat in silence, each wrapped in their own thoughts.

After a while, he asked, "So, did you do it?"

"No." Jessica snorted. "I can't even figure out how it was done."

A haunted look crossed her face and Drew leaned closer. "What did you see?"

"I don't want to talk about it." She blinked as a lock of hair poked her in the eye. "Weren't you here to find some books?"

Drew shrugged and hit a key to wake the computer up. He deftly navigated through the library site, searching the online catalog with easy competence.

Curious, Jessica leaned in to read the titles he was browsing. "I thought you needed books for a social studies assignment."

"You're kinda nosy." Drew's mouth quirked. "Why do you care what I'm looking up?"

"Just curious. Ultra-low-frequency noise?" Jessica sounded puzzled. "Are you sure you understood the assignment?"

"You're really not into subtlety, are you?"

"Waste of time. Gave up on it long ago." She scrolled down his screen to see the other books his search had brought up. "Oooo, this one looks interesting."

Drew shooed her hand off the keyboard. "If you must know, I'm trying to think of a project for science club. I don't want to join if I haven't got something interesting to work on." After copying a final ISBN from the list, he kicked off a new search on human pattern recognition.

"Oh no," Jessica groaned. "Tell me you're not looking up explanations for ghost sightings."

"Good guess, Bossy Pants," he said, scanning the titles. "Our talk got me thinking about creating a ghost booth. Cool, right?"

"Not." Jessica said flatly. "If I do a project this year, and that's a big 'if,' I was thinking of something more internet related." An idea she'd had a few weeks ago popped into her head as she spoke. Budding enthusiasm displaced her glum mood. "There's some cool work going on with collective intelligence, getting large, anonymous groups to help solve difficult problems by making decisions that are hard for computers, but easy for humans—like tagging images or the mood of a comment."

Drew's face brightened as he caught her excitement. "I've been curious to play around with that stuff too. It's amazing how you can siphon knowledge from the crowd, but I have to admit I haven't managed to wrap my mind around the math yet."

"Oh, the math shouldn't be too bad. It's mostly probability and genetic algorithms, though I guess knowing some calculus helps." She felt heat rising to her cheeks. "I'm a bit of a math geek. Where I run into trouble is thinking up a good hook. People need to be motivated to spend time, even if it's just a couple of minutes, and I'm not that creative."

"Hey," Drew swiveled in his chair to face her. "What you need is a way to gamify the experience. Give people virtual rewards, let them level-up and compete. They'll eat it up."

"I like it!" Jessica was fully geeked-out now. They volleyed ideas back and forth in rapid sequence, most of them utterly impractical but entirely awesome. Drew's face transformed as his interest grew. Once pinched and withdrawn, his eyes were now shining.

"We could do it if we teamed up," blurted Jessica.

"Sure." Drew answered quickly and then looked as if he wished he'd played it cooler. He pulled out his phone to check the time. "We'd better hustle. I bet Bakshi will lock the door at precisely 4:15 and count us AWOL. I wonder if he shoots deserters?"

Jessica grabbed her bag. She wasn't sure this was a good idea, but it might work out.

Plus, it's worth it just to see the look on Kathy's face when I show up with a partner and kick-ass project.

Chapter 12

```
Reverting to preliminary Channel Preparation Process.
Priority 1: Gain trust. Initiate basic demonstration of
predictive ability.
```

* * *

Mr. Bakshi's eyes narrowed into thin slits as Jessica and Drew slunk into the lab and took seats at the back. Drew elbowed her in the side as Bakshi pointedly glanced at his watch and then resumed scribbling on the blackboard.

Jessica deciphered his scrawl. He was writing out suggestions for the group science project. From the number already crossed out, the endeavor didn't appear to be going well.

Boxer yelled out, "What about a machine that demonstrates the harmful effect of smoking? People care about that crap, right? I saw this show where scientists taught monkeys to smoke and then dissected their lungs. It was wicked gross."

Mr. Bakshi's shoulders sagged. "I'm quite certain the school won't be funding any monkeys, present company excluded. And I don't feel like explaining to the board of education why I bought ten cartons of cigarettes for my science club. Anyone have an idea that doesn't involve getting me fired or arrested?"

Drew put up his hand and Jessica's eyes widened in horror. His mouth was curved up at one corner and she had a sneaking suspicion the teacher wouldn't find his suggestion as entertaining as he did.

Bakshi scanned the class and stopped when he came to Drew. After a suspicious pause, he nodded. "You have an idea...what's your name?"

"Drew...uh, Andrew...Gray."

The teacher glanced down at the list on his desk and Drew hurriedly continued, "Haven't had a chance to sign on yet, but I will. Anyway, I was thinking—what if we set up some basic social networking sites, each directed at specific populations. For instance, one to attract people in software sales, one for environmental activists, and so on. We can target whatever groups we want."

Mr. Bakshi frowned as he fiddled with his beakers.

Drew hopped off his stool and began to pace as he explained, "But the trick is, we use obviously bogus privacy agreements to see who pays attention. We can bury statements like, 'Thank you for supporting our identity-theft effort,' or, 'We claim all legal rights to your firstborn,' in with the normal text. Then we track how many discreet IP hits there were compared to completed registrations or partial registrations."

The furrow on Bakshi's brow deepened until his eyes nearly disappeared under his bushy eyebrows. Jessica wasn't sure whether Drew was uncaring or unaware of the impending doom, but she suddenly wished she hadn't sat next to him.

Drew carried on. "Best part is, we'll get demographic info on anyone who completes the registration. So we can see what ages, education levels, incomes, even geographic locations are most likely to skip reading privacy agreements. We could publish the results and warn at-risk groups, as a kind of public service. I bet lots of people would be interested to know who's most susceptible to these types of scams."

The piece of chalk Mr. Bakshi was holding snapped. "That's quite enough, Mr. Gray. Although there are undoubtedly people who'd be interested, I fail to see value in attracting the attention of criminal organizations or the police. It skirts far too close to fraud and we don't have the legal resources to deal with that."

"But—" Drew stopped as the teacher's cheeks puffed out with indignation.

Jessica dropped her head to hide her face and bit down on her pencil to stifle a giggle. It was a good thing Bakshi didn't get mad often; he looked like a crazed Cabbage Patch Doll.

"If you don't have a serious suggestion, keep your mouth shut or leave." Bakshi turned back to the blackboard, retrieved a new piece of chalk, and asked, "Now, anyone care to share a reasonable suggestion?"

Drew slid back onto his stool and crossed his arms.

Kelly raised her hand and, without waiting for a prompt from the teacher, launched into her idea of studying the effects of pesticides on amphibians, in detail.

"…simply everyone's up in arms about pesticides nowadays. I did extensive research over the weekend on the major players and I think…" Her voice droned on. After a few minutes, everyone, including Bakshi, shared the same bewildered look of someone who had just been mugged on a busy street in broad daylight.

Experiencing a rare moment of gratitude for Kelly's vociferous brown-nosing, Jessica leaned closer to Drew and whispered, "Are you nuts?"

He shrugged. "Seemed like a good idea to me. Not my

problem if Bakshi's too chicken to do something interesting."

"It did sound interesting," agreed Jessica, "but he's right. I've been to the national fair before and the judges are pretty traditional. A hacker-culture project wouldn't go over well."

She retrieved a bottle of water from her backpack and took a swig to relieve her throat, which had dried up under Bakshi's scathing attention. "This is not good. I'm already in hot water after chem class this morning. He's going to be doubly thrilled to talk to us about our project now."

"What happened?"

Jessica explained the desk prank and glared as Drew chuckled.

He pressed his lips together and whispered hoarsely, "You get into some weird shit. This partnership might be more fun than I thought."

As she opened her mouth to reply, a disturbingly familiar chill crept into the crevices of her brain. Her hands and feet tingled and an odd green glow began emanating from people. It became brighter, melding inanimate objects into indistinct shadows, until the room turned into an overexposed photograph.

Jessica grabbed the edge of the counter.

Crap. Am I having another seizure?

But the world did not rush away as it had in math class, and Jessica remained firmly rooted in her own body.

Confused, she looked around the lab and a figure in the next row caught her eye. A soft nimbus of green light surrounded Lindsey, a girl she knew from junior high. Bright plumes of white flame trailed from her moving hands.

Jessica blinked hard as the weird visual effects in the room faded. Only the fire enveloping Lindsey's hands remained.

The acrid scent of burning flesh and smoke was overpowering.

Jessica jumped off her stool, sending it flying back into the wall, and yelled "FIRE!" as she threw her water bottle. For once, her aim was true. It landed on the desk in front of Lindsey, bounced, and splashed water all over her, her notes, her bag, and her partner.

Mr. Bakshi ripped a fire extinguisher off the wall, ran over, and spun in a circle like a demented figure skater.

As Jessica raced around the counter, the cold presence in her mind evaporated, and her brain and body snapped back into sync. She realized halfway to Lindsey that she looked remarkably calm for someone whose hands were engulfed in flame.

Jessica skidded to a stop.

Lindsey spluttered as water dripped off her chin.

A grave apprehension settled in Jessica's mind. No one was reacting properly. Drew looked confused and amused, Lindsey's mouth was opening and closing in mute anger, and Bakshi was marching toward her with a thunderous expression.

She seized Lindsey's wrists and examined her hands. Her skin was perfect. No blisters. No sores. No charring. Not even a paper cut blemished her manicured pink fingers.

Lindsey yanked her hands back and screeched, "Get away from me!"

Trying to simultaneously apologize and comprehend what was happening, Jessica took a few steps back and ran into Mr. Bakshi's formidable stomach. He took her by the arm and dragged her out of the classroom.

"What the hell was that?" he roared once they were in the hall. His neatly combed salt-and-pepper hair was now a riot of frizzy curls that would have made Einstein jealous.

Stammering, Jessica tried to explain what she'd seen.

He cut her off. "Young lady, a lab fire with gas lines and chemicals present is a very, very serious situation. People die. Don't you EVER pull anything like that again. This is the second time today I've had to talk to you. Get your priorities straight, or you'll find yourself expelled." Bakshi's thick-rimmed glasses slowly descended his nose as he talked and he pushed them back into place. "Now, are you prepared to participate or are you here solely to make my life difficult?"

Jessica blinked saucer eyes. "No...I mean, yes, I want to participate and no, I don't mean to make anyone's life difficult. It just seems to happen. I really thought there was a fire. I've been seeing some weird things and I—"

"All right." Mr. Bakshi sighed long-sufferingly. "Collect your books, go home, and come up with a project that'll blow my mind. I want to see a thoroughly researched and professionally presented outline *before* Thursday's meeting. Impress me and you're in. But if you're not ready to do real work, save us both the time and don't bother."

On their way into the classroom, he added, "And while you're collecting your belongings, you can apologize to Miss Baker."

Nodding, Jessica headed for the back. Lindsey was standing by a sink, mopping her hair and shirt with paper towels. She cast an acerbic look at Jessica.

Drew grinned as Jessica arrived. "And you were worried about *me* pissing him off?"

"I'm not in the mood." She shoved her things into her bag. "I'll talk to you tomorrow about the project...assuming you still want to partner with me."

Drew nodded vigorously. "Wouldn't miss it for the world."

After a faltering apology to Lindsey, which was ignored,

Jessica wended her way through the deserted crypt to her locker. She dragged her feet as she walked, feeling useless and defeated.

Nobody else had seen the fire. As scared as she'd been after the ghost in the bathroom, at least there had been witnesses to prove she wasn't totally crazy. Now she was back to square one.

Not quite, she mused, as it occurred to her the two scenarios weren't mutually exclusive. *Is there a square zero? It's entirely possible I'm going nuts, and weird things are happening.*

Jessica stopped at her locker, wondering how much a one-way ticket to Abu Dhabi would set her back. She watched as chunky green slime oozed down the metal door and pooled at her feet. A handwritten note sticking out of the hinge-side gap read, "Who ya gonna call?"

She leaned closer and sniffed.

Lime. Yuck.

Carefully opening the door, she rifled through the contents to see how much of the slime had made it inside. Her Physics text had a splotch on its cover, but the tissue ghosts had selflessly taken the brunt of the attack.

Jessica pulled them out, saying a silent eulogy for the absorbent guardians, and went in search of paper towels—lots and lots of paper towels.

Chapter 13

Jessica wiped up the last of the goo and dumped a mountain of garbage in the nearest bin. When she returned to her locker, she noticed a movement down the hall.

A shadowed form was partially visible at the corner. She couldn't make out who it was, but they were wearing a school jacket. The school colors of puke yellow and robin egg blue were unmistakable.

Warning pricked at the back of her neck, but she shrugged it off.

Probably checking to see how well his plan came off. Asshole.

Jessica sorted through what books and notes she wanted to take home. As she transferred a text to her locker, she glanced back and was pleased to see that the spectator had left.

Trying not to think about what pranks tomorrow would hold after the fire incident made the rounds, she slammed her locker and headed out.

The fluorescent lights flickered as she walked. One moment the hallway was awash in a sallow glow, and the next, it was plunged into shifting shades of gray. No light trickled in from the windows. Night was starting to fall earlier and earlier with the approach of winter. Soon, she would be coming to school in the dark and leaving in the dark.

Her mind redrew the lockers as mummy caskets, their brittle inhabitants lined against the walls, waiting for eternity. She imagined one of them opening and a shriveled hand reaching out for her...

Jessica took a firmer grip on her imagination.

A sudden twinge of pain shot up her right arm. She rubbed it and quickened her pace as she rounded the corner.

Some part of her mind registered the obstacle before she saw it, and she staggered to the side, narrowly avoiding a collision.

She was in the middle of an apology, when she recognized Bill, the mysterious guy from her Ouija board and bridge dreams. Her words trailed off into silence.

Guess I don't need to wonder if he's real anymore, thought Jessica as her gaze traversed his substantial bulk.

She froze when she reached his face. His eyes were black holes.

Or I could be hallucinating again, she tried to reassure herself. Because being crazy was infinitely better than this.

Frothing spittle clung to the edges of his mouth which gaped open, exposing more black nothingness within. Menace radiated from him, prickling against her skin like a thousand needles.

The lights flickered and died, plunging the hall into darkness.

Jessica staggered back toward her locker and the stairwell on the other side of the basement, one hand trailing along the wall as a guide.

Her mind looped a single panicked thought: *Have to get out. Have to get out.*

A low, arrhythmic rumble approached from the direction she was running. She skidded to a stop and pressed herself against a locker, hoping whatever it was would pass her by in the dark.

The lights flickered and Bill was standing in front of her, spit dribbling off his chin and running down his jacket collar.

He stepped forward.

Hot breath wafted against her forehead.

"Delicious," he moaned.

The rumbling grew louder.

Jessica opened her mouth to scream, but only a mute exhalation of fear escaped.

Bill raised a beefy hand to her cheek, not quite touching, but close enough that she felt its heat.

A group of girls in gym clothes thundered around the corner and headed toward them.

The blackness in Bill's eye sockets thickened and bulged.

"So bright!" he gasped, pulling his hand away and balling it into a fist.

The girls came closer, breathlessly chattering and jostling for the lead.

Bill's pained expression blanked. He stiffly turned and walked away, as if strings and pulleys were maneuvering his limbs.

Jessica tried to find her voice as she watched the last girl pass. Her knees kept threatening to give out and she was shaking so badly, the locker behind her rattled.

A girl in the middle of the pack broke free. She jogged back and ran in place beside Jessica. It was Michiru.

"Hi. We're in physics together, right?" she asked cheerfully.

Jessica stared blankly at her bouncing face, still light-headed from unused adrenaline. She peered past Michiru in the direction Bill had gone. There was no sign of him, but she kept staring, certain he would reappear.

Michiru stopped jogging. "Are you all right? Was that guy bugging you?"

Jessica's knees buckled and she slid to the floor.

Okay, so he wasn't a hallucination. Damn.

Michiru glanced around. After a slight hesitation, she crouched down and laid a hand on Jessica's shoulder.

"You don't look so good." Leaning closer, she whispered, "Did you take something? Do you need a hospital?"

"Seriously?" Jessica groaned and put her head in her hands. "Now I look like a whacked-out junkie? This day just won't die." She tilted her head back and glared at the girl. Jessica wanted to be mad, but there was no judgment on Michiru's heart-shaped face, only concern.

She sighed. "I'm not on drugs, but I'm starting to think I should be." At Michiru's shocked look, she hastily asked, "Um…what did you want…I mean originally?"

Michiru frowned and flipped her ponytail over her shoulder. "I think you're in my physics class. Second period?"

Jessica nodded.

"I was going to ask if I could borrow your notes tomorrow, but don't worry about it. I can get them from someone else."

Jessica's brain slowly shifted back to the world of classes and homework.

"No, it's fine," she said, and then muttered, "Not like it's hard. Only takes a few seconds out of someone's day." Jessica refocused on Michiru. "Meet me in the library at lunch. There's a photocopier there."

"Perfect." Michiru stood in one fluid motion, holding out

a hand. "Are you sure you're okay?"

Jessica caught her hand, felt Michiru's grip tighten like a vice, and was pulled to her feet as if she weighed nothing.

Leaning against a locker to steady herself, Jessica admitted, "I'm not sure about much at the moment—except that I want to go home, go to bed, and pretend today didn't happen."

"Maybe I'd better walk you upstairs." Michiru grabbed hold of her arm as she took a step and teetered to the side.

Jessica glanced fearfully down the hall and then back to Michiru. She moved like a cat and radiated competence. Everything was precision and grace.

In essence, thought Jessica, *she's pretty much everything I'm not.* Smiling timidly, she said, "Thanks. I'd like that."

Chapter 14

Shadow evidencing interest in Channel. Acquiring local Channel protector. Direct interaction of Shadow and Channel limits infestation probability. Increased risk of Channel destruction acceptable. Alternate Channels available.

* * *

Jessica didn't sleep well that night. Whenever she lay down, the strange events from the past week clawed their way to the surface of her mind.

She sleepily greeted Tuesday morning with vague thoughts of academic redemption. Ghosts, weirdoes, and hallucinations were way out of her comfort zone, but she could do homework and extra-credit assignments with the best of them. If she could win Bakshi over it might help get the other teachers and the principal back on her side. At least that would be something.

Between classes, Jessica threw herself into planning the science project. She was pleasantly surprised when Drew proved equally willing, dispelling her suspicion that he had only joined for a laugh.

He wasn't as comfortable with the math as she was, but

he came to her house Tuesday night armed with a list of open-source implementations for her to review. He'd also coded up the core of the website in Python, which struck her as an odd choice, and they spent an engaging half-hour arguing the merits of strongly vs. weakly typed programming languages. It was almost 9:00 p.m. by the time he left.

Jessica made it to lunch on Wednesday Bill-encounter free, but she still expected to see him around every corner.

She had rearranged her life to accommodate the fear. Trips to her locker were painstakingly timed to coincide with groups of other students. Her walk to and from school took twice as long because she avoided secluded areas. Whenever she was in a crowd, she scanned the faces of anyone close to Bill's size—and the halls now seemed full of candidates. Add to that her classmates random pranks, trying to avoid Kirsten, and a general mistrust of her own eyes, and Jessica's nerves were stretched to the absolute limit.

She ate lunch on the move, sticking to main hallways on the way to the library, her new lunchtime haven. When she arrived, Sarah, a twelfth grader whose little sister Jessica used to babysit, barreled through the door, almost knocking her off her feet.

Sarah looked rough. Her sweater was inside out and her funky, purple-streaked bob looked like birds were not only nesting in it, but had thrown one hell of a party.

Jessica considered asking if she was okay, but the way Sarah looked at—through—her made her reconsider. Sarah had always been one of those "together" people, doing it all without seeming overwhelmed. Senior year was clearly not being kind to her. Jessica could relate. Her junior year wasn't exactly what she had expected, either.

She rubbed her arms in a sudden chill, feeling that there

was something off about Sarah. Something more than the obvious. She stopped at the re-shelving cart and stared after her.

Jessica blinked and then rubbed her eyes. There was a large gray wolf where Sarah had been, slinking down the middle of the populated hall. Her brain ceased to function.

"Sure, she's got a nice ass, but is she your type?"

Jessica stifled a scream as Drew materialized at her side. His grin brought heat to her cheeks and she stumbled over her words, "What? No, it's...it's nothing."

She looked back at the hall, but Sarah and the wolf were gone. There was only the normal chaos of bickering cliques and harried staff.

Okay. Pretend to be normal. Nothing weird here.

Jessica spun on her heel, turning her back on the hall.

The librarian frowned at them and Jessica absently wondered how the woman managed to draw her brow down with her hair so tightly bunched into a French braid.

There must be special classes in advanced disapproval techniques for librarians.

"We're getting the stink eye." Drew transformed her thoughts into words. "We'd better sit or she'll give us a severe finger wagging again."

They found a free table and Drew's tone became more serious. "We still on after school? I think we've got enough reference material to write up the proposal now." He leaned forward and whispered, "I brought my laptop, so we can both work on the report."

Jessica raised an eyebrow. "Is that a secret? I bring mine to school all the time."

"It's kinda expensive and I don't like to advertise, if you know what I mean."

"I guess." Jessica shrugged. The average person wouldn't

consider her laptop worth stealing, but that was because no one but Kathy knew her generic-brand case hid top-of-the-line components, thanks to one of her dad's contacts at the university.

"Ha...maybe you don't know what I mean." He scanned the handful of students browsing the library shelves. Several were staring at him and looked away when their gazes met. "Sometimes I get the feeling people are waiting for an excuse to take a chunk out of me. But then I remember that most of these assholes think my being here *is* an excuse. It's not paranoia if it's true."

"Yeah. That, I understand."

Drew gave her a skeptical look. "What do you have to worry about, Whitebread? This is home territory for you."

"Oh right. Because I find this prickly nest of vipers so relaxing." Jessica bristled. "Maybe I don't know what your life looks like, but you don't know jack shit about mine, either. Stop making assumptions."

Drew leaned back. "Whoa...you're wound a bit tight."

Jessica's glare intensified until he shook his head and held up his hands. "All right. Truce. I'll check the 'tude at the door if you do. Tonight?"

Growling faintly, Jessica nodded. "Meet me at the main doors after school." She checked her watch and noted there were fifteen minutes until the bell. Not wanting to strain their partnership any further, she grabbed her bag and left.

* * *

A wall of puke yellow and blue approached as Jessica made her way down the hall. She ducked into a nook between blocks of lockers, pretending to look for something in her bag. As the group drew near, she saw Bill wasn't among them and relaxed.

She recognized another of the boys as Tim, a footballer Eric used to hang out with. He trailed silently behind his buddies with a preoccupied look on his face.

Before she had time to chicken out, Jessica stepped forward and touched his arm.

He jumped. "Hey! What's your problem?"

"Complicated question," she mused. "Not really sure at the moment. You're Tim, right?"

He nodded slowly. "Didn't Eric used to hang with you...Bess?"

"Jessica. I'm Eric's girlfriend." She tried not to bristle. "I was just wondering if you know a guy called Bill? He's new. Tall, blond, into sports."

He frowned and stepped closer, as if worried someone would overhear. "Bill? Yeah, he's on the team. Why?"

Jessica sank back against the wall. She'd only heard Bill's name in her Ouija and bridge nightmares. She could understand if she'd seen him around town during the summer and her mind had unconsciously transplanted his image into her nightmares, but guessing his name correctly in a dream? *How is that possible?*

Struggling to refocus her scattered thoughts, she mumbled, "I think he...that is...I think I found his social studies book and wanted to give it back. It has 'Bill' scribbled inside with a football doodle. Is he around?" She cringed. None of that explained how she knew what he looked like.

Tim considered her for a moment. "Sounds like Billy boy all right, but he didn't come in today. He's been...uh, he's got the flu or something. Just give it to me and I'll make sure he gets it."

"Well, I...I don't have it with me right now. Think he'll be here tomorrow?"

"Dunno. Maybe." He shrugged.

Jessica forced a smile and eased around him. "Thanks. Do you know his last name? I'd like to write it into the book so next time he leaves it somewhere, it won't be so hard to return."

Tim looked amused. "What are you, Billy's fairy godmother?" Then his eyes widened in enlightenment. "I see. The long-distance thing with Eric isn't working out. Well, let me save you the heartache, shorty. You're not Bill's type." Waving at her chest, he added, "He likes a bigger rack and longer pegs."

Jessica's smile edged into a snarl.

Tim tsked. "You need thicker skin, babe. I'm just tellin' it like it is. His last name's 'Decker,' but don't say I didn't warn you. He won't be interested. And besides," he looked down at her, caution and honesty warring on his face. "Between you and me, he may not be the safest guy to be around right now. I think he's going through some personal shit."

Jessica nodded and slipped away, her mind busily digesting the new information.

Something must be up if Bill's friend is warning people to stay away, but at least I can track him down now that I have a last name. Wait, why would I do that? That's a bad idea. Very bad.

* * *

Jessica sat on the front steps after school, ignoring the open chemistry text on her lap. People-watching was far more entertaining. Everyone was laughing, hugging, and chatting. They playfully teased each other and waved at departing friends.

One girl shyly defected from a group of eleventh graders and joined a testosterone-laden pack of jocks. She was quickly engulfed in the hulking crowd and Jessica heard her tinkling laugh as they marched to the practice field.

Everything seemed normal—for everyone else.

She gazed miserably around the school grounds. The grass was still green. The sky was still blue. There was a series of thuds behind her, and Jessica turned to see Kelly easing her roller bag down the stairs.

Yup. Normal is king. So why the hell am I the only one seeing people on fire, wolves wandering the halls, and salivating boys at my locker…and not in a good way?

She gave her bag a disgruntled kick and swallowed a yelp as she was painfully reminded of how many books she had packed.

The school doors swung open and another swarm of students emerged. Drew stalked out after the bulk of the crowd, saw her, and came over. Bobby and Sam followed him down the steps, looking disgruntled.

Jessica shoved the textbook into her bag and rose to meet them.

Here we go again.

"What do you mean 'find another ride'? You're our ride." Bobby glared at Drew's back.

"Not today." Drew zipped up his leather jacket. "I've got stuff to do in town."

Sam peered around Drew and then looked back at him incredulously. "By stuff, do you mean the midget standing behind you? Didn't know you were into nerdy schoolgirls."

Bobby shuffled to the side, his gaze ranging over Jessica's body. "He's got a hot date with Kermit the Frog."

Jessica glanced down at her apple green overalls. *Kermit?* She sighed. *I guess the color is a bit similar.*

She blew her bangs out of her face and decided to play it cool. "Hey, cut the frog some slack. It's not easy being green."

Sam, who was watching Drew's face, snorted with laughter. "Guess that makes you Miss Piggy."

Drew grabbed his arm and led him a few steps away. "We're working on a project. That's it. If you want to come with us to the town library and spend a couple hours researching genetic algorithms, then be my guest. Otherwise, you'll have to get home on your own."

Bobby grumbled, "Can't. Tate's already gone and Jenna ditched."

"The bus is right there." Drew waved at a yellow school bus idling at the curb. "That's kinda what it's for. Listen, I don't mind if you guys hitch a ride when I'm going somewhere, but I'm not your personal taxi. I'm not taking you home and then coming all the way back. You know how much gas my truck burns."

Sam sneered at the bus. "You want us to take the fucking cheese wagon?"

A muscle in Drew's cheek twitched as he started for the parking lot. "And another thing," he hollered over his shoulder to Sam. "Call me Miss Piggy again and I'll karate-chop you into the middle of next week."

Jessica stared after him and then back at the appalled expressions on his friends' faces. Shrugging, she trotted after Drew before Bobby and Sam recovered.

"Why would we go to the library?" Jessica asked when she caught up.

He stopped beside a rusted sky-blue truck. "I just said that to get rid of them." He slid into the driver's seat and leaned across to unlock the passenger door from the inside.

She caught herself admiring the truck's classic, rounded lines and thought of Eric. He would have loved it. She missed being able to share everyday things like this with him.

They were doing their best to stay connected, but video

chats and weekend visits weren't the same as living down the street from each other. She missed being able to cuddle up to his warm chest after a hard day, missed the soothing rhythm of his heartbeat. Neither one of them was talking about it, but she knew he could feel the difference too.

Jessica shook herself out of her melancholy and pulled the door handle. Neither her melancholy nor the door budged.

Drew appeared in the window and motioned for her to try again.

Wrapping both hands around the handle, she heaved with all her strength. Drew disappeared, there was a thud as he gave the door a kick, and it reluctantly creaked open.

"Sorry. Needs grease." He motioned to the seat and said, "Hop in," with only a slight twitch at the corner of his mouth.

Jessica narrowed her eyes. Running a hand over her soft green overalls, she acknowledged they probably weren't worth defending. She wore them because they were comfortable, not to make a fashion statement.

"You know, it's a five-minute walk to my house. We don't need to drive."

"Oh yes we do," Drew said emphatically. "No way am I walking back here in the dark to get my truck. I couldn't shake the feeling someone was watching me when I left last night. You getting in or what?"

The truck shook as the engine growled to life.

Jessica shoved her bag into the passenger foot well and searched for a foothold or handhold within reach. The vehicle was so jacked up that the bench seat was level with her shoulder.

She made it in after several abortive attempts, by jumping up to get her torso onto the seat. From there, she swung her legs into the cab. There may have been some flailing, but she decided to purge that part from memory.

After shuffling around so her butt was on the seat instead of her face, she leaned over, dragged the door closed, and straightened her overalls, which had wedged themselves somewhere they weren't welcome.

When she finished buckling her seatbelt, she noticed Drew staring. His strained expression suggested he was wisely attempting to keep a straight face.

"Well, are we going or not?" she asked in her best nonchalant tone.

Drew reversed out of the parking space. "I've never seen anyone's face get that red," he said in an unnaturally flat voice.

"Just go." Jessica glared at him through hair that was now plastered to her face, thanks to the static charge she had worked up. She roughly gathered her bangs and rammed a massive Hello Kitty hair clip into place on top of her head.

Drew lost it when he saw her new hairstyle. Laughing, he jammed the truck into drive and peeled out of the parking lot.

They rode in silence for a while. Drew kept his eyes on the road even though they were crawling along at thirty kilometers per hour in the school zone.

"Sorry. But it was pretty funny."

"I guess." Jessica smiled despite herself. "Big trucks and short people don't get along."

"Next time, I'll pack mom's exercise trampoline." Drew offered.

She chuckled, imagining launching herself from a trampoline into the truck.

The heat inside the cab became stifling as the day's last rays of sunlight beamed through the windows. Jessica searched the dashboard for the air conditioning controls and found a hole. Dangling wires hung like colorful spaghetti where the knobs, glove box, and radio should have been.

She located a handle to roll down her window and gave it a few turns. Drew looked over as the window inched down. He opened his mouth to say something, but snapped it shut as the glass dropped with a loud thunk into the door frame.

Jessica stared at the gap and then transferred her gaze to Drew, asking timidly, "Did I break it?"

"Nah. It hasn't worked for a long time. I'll dig it out later." Drew sighed. "I should get a newer truck, but this one kinda grew on me and I can't bring myself to junk it."

There was movement on Jessica's side of the road.

A huge wolf darted onto the street and she screamed, "Stop!"

Drew slammed his foot on the brake and swerved. They skidded to a stop as the wolf loped into a park. It was headed for a cluster of trees, but its steady gait faltered before it reached the tree line and it collapsed in a disturbing blur of gray and pink.

Jessica leaned out of her window to get a better look and gasped.

She tried unsuccessfully to shove the passenger door open. Cursing, she swiveled in her seat, grabbed the strap above the door, and awkwardly pulled herself up to slide feet first out the window. She landed heavily on the pavement, but her busy mind never registered the jolt.

Drew stepped out, asking if she was okay, but she was already running for the park. Chasing after her, he yelled, "What are you doing? It's not safe to…" His voice trailed off when he saw the writhing figure she had stopped beside.

Blood drained from Jessica's face as she watched the creature thrash, its body grotesquely stretching and bloating, its skin alternating between smooth flesh and matted fur. The elongated muzzle gaped wide in a choked howl and its face twisted into that of a young woman. The howl became a piercing scream as her body forced itself into human form.

Chapter 15

Jessica stared down in shock at the naked girl. She stared up at Jessica, her eyes wide with horror and confusion.

Jessica squeaked, "Sarah?" as her mind screamed, *you saw this! You saw the wolf in her at the library!*

Giving in to her wobbly knees, she knelt down and touched Sarah's arm. She recoiled and Jessica moved back to give her more space, wanting to help but unsure of what to do or say.

Behind her, Drew cleared his throat and Jessica spun to see him holding out an old woolen blanket. His eyes were shut. Pleasantly surprised by the unexpected chivalry, she took the blanket and wrapped it around the trembling girl, who had curled herself into a tight ball.

Jessica decided to play to her strengths and started babbling in a soothing voice about classes and her latest date with Eric. After a while, a flicker of recognition appeared in Sarah's eyes and her shivering lessened. She uncoiled enough to flick away a branch which was poking into her cheek and the blanket slipped, exposing her chest. Sarah looked down and froze.

Slowly leaning forward so as not to alarm her, Jessica

pulled the blanket up and glanced back to see that Drew had thoughtfully returned to the truck.

"Sarah? Can you walk? Can you make it to our truck?"

When she didn't respond, Jessica waved a hand through her line of vision and repeated the question.

Sarah looked wildly between Jessica and the truck. "What did you do to me? Where are my clothes?"

Jessica rocked back on her heels. *I should have known*, she berated herself. *What haven't I been blamed for lately?*

"We found you like this. Well, sort of..." Jessica wasn't sure how to describe what she had witnessed. She tried to smile reassuringly, but guessed she failed when Sarah staggered to her feet and backed away, clutching the blanket.

"Stay away from me."

"It's okay. I'm not going to hurt you. I just want to help you get home."

Sarah kept backing away until several meters separated them, at which point she bolted for the trees. Jessica ran a few steps and then stopped, remembering that Sarah had taken a medal in track last year. Within seconds, she had disappeared into the woods at the top of the hill.

Drew jogged up. "Guess that blanket's gone, eh?"

Jessica raised an eyebrow. "Did you miss what just happened? How can you be worried about a freaking blanket?"

"I don't think I missed anything. Some chick shapeshifted and ran off with my blanket. It's a good blanket. Many happy memories." He noted Jessica's frown. "But I can get another one."

Tugging her arm gently, he motioned toward the truck. "Look, she's gone. Let's get a move on. Our project proposal won't write itself."

Jessica followed him back in a daze. Drew yanked open

the passenger door and boosted her into the cab, before lithely jumping into the driver's seat.

Accelerating away, he said, "I'm sure she'll be fine. If you're still worried later, give her a call. If she isn't home, we'll come back and look for her. Okay?"

"Drew?"

"Yeah?"

"Why aren't you freaked out?"

He shrugged. "Uncle's always talking about that stuff. I mean, I've never actually seen anything before, but I hear about it enough." Drew glanced over at her. "Hey, are you all right? You're a bit gray. Didn't figure a shape-shifter would faze a girl who has visions and sees spirits."

Jessica drifted in a haze of uncertainty and fear. She stared at her hands, adding shape-shifting Sarah to the long list of weirdness that had become her life.

"Listen," Drew said quietly. "You don't want to talk about it and that's fine. Your house is the one with the brown garage, right?"

When she nodded, he continued, "Now, onto the tricky business of science."

* * *

Jessica struggled to concentrate on their proposal. She'd finish a paragraph, rifle through her research notes, and then find herself thinking about Sarah. After an hour and a half, all she had completed was one thin page outlining the clustering algorithms they planned to use.

Drew peeked over his laptop as she groaned and dropped her head onto the kitchen table. The tuft of copper hair held vertical in her hairclip flopped dejectedly onto her book.

Feeling Drew's stare, she lifted her head and huffed in annoyance, "What?"

He pointed at the hairclip. "There's pink on it, you know. I thought you said you didn't wear pink."

She gave him a warning look. "I make an exception for Hello Kitty. What did you mean by 'visions'?"

"Huh?"

"Earlier, when you said I get visions. What did you mean?"

Drew lowered his laptop screen. "I meant you see things. You don't have to play dumb. When you instigated the wet T-shirt contest in science club, I guessed you were having one. Let's just say I plan to sit near the door and keep an extinguisher handy."

When Jessica stared at him blankly, he continued, "Uncle gets them too. My grandparents thought he was having fits when he was a kid, but an elder said it was visions. Sometimes what he sees comes true, sometimes not. Says it's because life is a mess of possibilities. Most people think he's full of shit, but he's been right often enough to make me think twice."

Jessica mulled that over and then blurted out, "I had a vision today that Sarah was a wolf."

Drew leaned forward, resting his elbows on the table. "Wow. That's quick. Sometimes Uncle's don't happen for years."

Afraid of what demented thing she might say next, she jumped up and rummaged in the fridge for a snack. Finding nothing interesting, she moved to the pantry and stood in the dark cupboard staring at the shelves.

With Drew's corroboration of today's freaky event, she was sure there was something beyond her subconscious driving her dreams and visions.

Now if only I could figure out why I'm getting them and what to do about it.

In her mind, she heard Spock repeating Holmes's adage, "If you eliminate the impossible, whatever remains, however improbable, must be the truth."

But what is impossible, you pointy-eared prick? Never explained how to figure that out, did you.

This morning, shape-shifting had been impossible.

Jessica wrestled with her resistance to talk. She wasn't just afraid people would think she was crazy, she couldn't shake the feeling that describing what was happening, actually using the words, could somehow conjure them into being. If they had solidity, she'd have to deal with them, and she had no idea how to do that.

She held up the hand she had injured in math class. There wasn't even a scar to show where the wound had been. And then there was Bill. A shiver ran down her spine. Things were already frighteningly solid, and if Drew had any insight, it might give her a starting point.

She slammed the pantry door shut and faced him.

"I was beginning to think you were going to stay in there. I know a few people who came out of the closet, but the pantry's something new." His amused expression changed when he registered her barely controlled fear. "You weren't playing dumb about visions, were you? You didn't know you were having them."

They both flinched as Jessica's overalls started playing "Pocketful of Sunshine." She stared down uncomprehendingly and then dug in her pockets. She pulled out her cell phone and held it up. "Heh…my phone."

The cheery pop-tune continued.

"You planning on answering that? If you start singing

along, I'm out of here." He looked pained.

"Oh, right." Jessica laughed nervously and answered the call. "Hello?"

She listened for a second and then snorted. "Eric, I know it's you. Your nose whistles when you breathe heavy." She laughed and then grimaced as she checked her watch. "I know, but can I call you back in a bit? The project proposal is due tomorrow."

Another pause. "Yeah, I know, but we're almost done."

Pause. "Didn't I tell you I partnered-up?"

Pause. "No...Kathy's still stuck on Kelly." She glanced at Drew, who was busily typing away on his computer, pretending not to listen. "I got talking to this guy, Drew. You don't know him. He's new. Anyway, the idea just clicked into place. Neither of us were sure we wanted to bother, but since we came up with such a cool idea, we figured we might as well team up."

Long pause. Jessica shuffled her feet. "Listen, I'm sorry, but there's still a lot to do and I don't know what time Drew has to be home. I'll call you later, hon." A sweet, slow smile spread across her face. She said "Love you too," and hung up.

She shoved the phone into her pocket and apologized to Drew.

He shrugged, resuming their conversation as if there had been no interruption. "You really didn't know you were having visions?"

Shaking her head, Jessica sat down and fidgeted with her pen. "Nope. The only exposure I've had to visions is in fantasy novels. To be honest, so many strange things have happened lately, I thought I was going nuts. Just to get things absolutely straight...you did see Sarah change, right?"

He nodded. "By the way, thanks for warning me to stop. Man, I'm glad I didn't hit her. She looked as confused as us. I wonder if it was her first time. I'll ask Uncle if we should do anything."

"You don't think she'll attack anyone, do you?"

"Unlikely. All she wanted to do was get to those trees— I'm guessing to hide. I can't be sure about her, but normal wolves are pretty timid. We don't see much of them because they go out of their way to avoid us. Can't blame them."

Jessica nodded with feeling. "Does your uncle have dreams that come true? I mean, similar to the visions, but while he's asleep?"

"I think so. Do you want me to ask him about that too? You seem kinda lost."

Jessica rolled her eyes. "Understatement of the year." Her computer beeped, letting her know new mail had arrived, and she stared at the screen, thinking. "Maybe we can find something useful online about lycanthropy, or visions, or dreams."

"Or ghosts." Drew added.

She scratched her palm. "Yeah. Those too."

Drew cracked his knuckles. "The problem is filtering out the junk posted by crackpots, but let's see what we can do."

His fingers rapidly clicked away on the keyboard. He treated it like a musical instrument, making the machine an extension of his body. Text and windows flashed up on the screen. He hadn't been joking when he said he could probably hack the library machines.

He was using some kind of non-Windows desktop, presumably a Linux distro, but the only visible branding read "Awesome."

Jessica smiled. *Pretty much what I'd expect from him.*

She felt some of the isolation of the past few weeks slough off.

Her stomach growled and Drew looked around in surprise.

Jessica blushed furiously. "That wasn't a dog. It's my tummy reminding me to eat. I was thinking about ordering a pizza. Are you getting hungry too?"

"I always work better on a full stomach."

She dug out her cell and auto-dialed International House of Pizza. "In that case, we'll get along just fine. Let's do some more research on this, eat, and then get back to the project."

Drew nodded absently, his attention already reclaimed by Wikipedia's extensive article on werewolves.

* * *

"I don't believe it." Jessica blinked to moisten her dry eyes. "The proposal's finally done." With a sharp click, she hit print and listened as her printer started churning out pages upstairs.

Drew scrounged in the pizza box for another slice. He grimaced as he caught sight of the time on the microwave.

"Eleven? We sure know how to kill an evening." He munched a piece of pepperoni. "Actually, it was fun. Help out a werewolf, do a little science, eat a little pizza, check out what the net has to say about prophetic dreams...most interesting day I've had in a while."

Jessica grinned as he folded the last bit of pizza and shoved it in his mouth.

"We certainly managed to cram a lot in," she said.

He grinned back at her, catching the pun. "Touché."

Drew licked his fingers clean and resumed typing. "Speaking of time...I noticed something interesting. Most of what I read online associates werewolves with full moons, but that doesn't fit with Sarah transforming today." He hit a key and sat back. "Yup. This says the moon is 'Waning gibbous at 51% full.' "

Jessica was skeptical. "A disappearing monkey moon? You playing Donkey Kong or something?"

"Gibbous, not gibbon. And just a general PSA, gibbons are apes, not monkeys. It means we're well past the full moon. Plus, she changed while the sun was up." He narrowed his eyes. "I'll ask Uncle about that. I don't remember our shape-shifter stories being tied to a time of month or day, but I could be wrong."

A memory tugged at Jessica's mind. "My grandma's always sending me books about weird things. I wonder if there's anything in them."

"Ooo, I like weird things." He said, rubbing his hands together. "Let's check it out."

Leading the way to her room, she pondered the time for an entirely different reason. Her dad was away and her mom wouldn't be home from therapy group until at least midnight, so she figured she had about forty-five minutes. There would be hell to pay if her mom found a guy in her bedroom in the middle of the night. Still, she was reluctant for Drew to leave.

The defensive, cynical mask he wore at school had fallen away, revealing a hidden calm and introspective nature. His relaxed approach inclined Jessica to the same, when normally she would have been freaking out. He methodically tackled the project proposal and their unusual online research, treating them as equally commonplace endeavors.

She watched as he strode over and studied her packed bookshelves. The utilitarian metal frames took up the entire far wall of her bedroom. She had everything from Dr. Seuss to hard science fiction, with a smattering of her favorite graphic novels and fantasy collections. Two entire shelves were stocked with programming and mathematical reference books.

Jessica joined him and knelt to examine the books on the

lowest shelf.

"These are the ones from Grandma."

Crouching beside her, he pulled out an ancient-looking, leather-bound volume entitled *The Book of Werewolves* by Sabine Baring-Gould. He carefully opened it and skimmed the table of contents. The musty scent of old paper drifted up from the foxed pages.

"Looks like a good place to start." He nodded approvingly. "Your grandma has interesting taste in literature."

Jessica hefted a thick hardback titled *Dreamer's Guide* and leafed through the first few pages.

"Tell me about it," she said without looking up. "Every year I get a new collection of oddities. I don't bother to check what they are anymore. I just shove it all down here."

She contemplated a pile of clothes lumped in a corner, and then shoved them out of the way, pulling out a plain brown box tied with twine. "I didn't even open the last package."

Sitting cross-legged on her bed, Jessica tore away the brown paper and pried open the box. She pulled out a modern paperback titled *Nature Magic*. The next thing she retrieved was a clear plastic bag filled with plant stems and leaves braided into small bundles. Her eyes widened and she shoved it behind her, hoping Drew hadn't seen.

He had.

Drew sat down beside her and examined the contents, chuckling at her exaggeratedly innocent expression. "It's not weed." He opened the bag and pulled out a bundle, breathing in deeply. "I think it's sweet grass and sage."

Relieved, Jessica sniffed the dried plant. It smelled like spring, when leaves and grass began to turn green. "What's it for?"

"There's probably something about it in that book." He gestured to *Nature Magic*. "There's a similar bundle pictured on the cover. Uncle burns something like it when he's sick or having too many bad dreams. Says it clears things out." He held up the book on werewolves. "Mind if I borrow this?"

"Go ahead." She glanced at the stack of books in the box and then over at the thirty odd books cramming the bottom shelf. "I won't be running out of reading material any time soon. Never thought I'd find these useful."

"Things change," said Drew, getting up and sauntering out to the hall. "I'd better head home."

Sitting alone in her room, she remembered their project proposal and checked the printer. Stapling the report together, she called after him, "Do you want to take the report or should I bring it tomorrow?"

Drew reappeared wearing his jacket and dropped his backpack on her bed.

"Can I take it? I'd like to do one more read through. Don't want Bakshi asking me a question about our algorithms that I can't answer."

She eagerly handed him the report. "It's all yours."

He opened his backpack and a crumpled piece of paper fell to the floor. Jessica smoothed it out and discovered a page of notes on *Romeo and Juliet*. Its edges were shredded and there were holes punctured throughout.

She held it out for him with a smirk. "Not fond of the bard?"

"That would be Nihna." He shoved the page into a battered binder. "I can't say *Romeo and Juliet* is his best work, but I would have preferred if she hadn't clawed up my notes."

"Please tell me Nihna isn't your girlfriend," said Jessica nervously. "I have enough to worry about."

Drew snorted. "You'd think so, the way she acts." Jessica choked in alarm and he laughed. "She's an eagle I found injured a few years ago. She stuck around and built a nest near my house. I usually bring a treat when I visit, but I didn't this morning and she took it out on my homework." He slid their report into a plastic folder.

"Cool. Does she let you get close?"

"Sometimes. Mostly she glares at me from her nest, but she likes to be sneaky. She stole my notes while I was going over them for a test. It wasn't the first time. I think she likes the way paper moves or sounds. Took me half an hour to coax her into dropping them and then I had to chase them down, thanks to the wind." He shook his head.

"Could I meet her sometime? I've never seen one up close. I mean, I've seen them flying, but you can't really see them, if you know what I mean."

Drew looked surprised. "I'm not sure how she'll do with a stranger. She might just take off."

"That's okay. Even a chance is worth it."

"Sure. Why not." He slung his backpack over his shoulder. "I'd better get going."

Jessica caught his arm. "Wait...we forgot to call Sarah." Drew bit back a laugh as she slapped her forehead. "Crap...I forgot to phone Eric back too. I suck."

"It's pretty late. She might be in bed."

"I'll hang up if her parents answer." She rifled through her desk and fished out an old day-timer. Flipping through the pages, she found the sheet listing her babysitting contacts and unlocked the screen on her phone.

Drew took it away when she started dialing and cut the connection.

Jessica frowned. "What's up?"

"Is your number blocked?" When she shook her head, he ran a hand through his hair. "You really aren't used to this kinda thing, are you? If you're going to hang up on someone, at least make sure they can't call back and find out who you are."

"Right." Jessica sheepishly stared at her phone. "We can do that?"

"It's just a setting on your phone, should be under caller ID." When she hesitated, he offered, "Want me to do it?"

"No," she grumbled, irritated at her incompetence. Jabbing at the screen, she scanned through menus, disabled her caller ID, and then dialed. She held the phone to her ear and waited. After a moment, she disconnected with a satisfied look.

"Sarah answered. She made it home."

"Glad to hear it, but why'd you hang up? I wanted to know how she's doing. And ask for my blanket back."

"I don't know her that well," Jessica said. "And if you're really that upset about your blanket, I'll get you a new one."

"Nah. Wouldn't be the same."

They walked downstairs together and Drew gave her a mocking salute as he said goodnight. "Let's meet up tomorrow morning and talk about how to approach Bakshi. Now that we've come this far, I'd hate to lose my partner."

Jessica agreed.

She watched him stroll to his truck and drive off in a cloud of diesel fumes. When he was gone, she stared out at the empty street. She didn't feel as lonely as she thought she would. It felt good just to have someone know—someone she didn't have to hide things from and who didn't think she was crazy.

Jessica felt lighter and tomorrow seemed less dire, except for Bill. She'd forgotten to tell Drew about him. In fact, she'd forgotten about Bill entirely for several hours. It was glorious and terrifying.

The street suddenly seemed more shrouded than empty. Anxiety knifed through her, and she quickly locked and bolted the door.

Chapter 16

Chris wavered, panting from the exertion of holding back the consuming evil. Oily darkness oozed across his eyes. His expression hardened as he lost the battle.

Jessica tried to force Bill's frozen muscles to reach out and grab him, to prevent what was coming, but she was locked in slow motion.

Chris launched himself over the railing.

In her mind, she followed his silent descent, leaving Bill on the bridge, writhing in agony as the darkness burrowed into its new, more congenial, host.

She imagined Chris's horror, the crushing finality of his failure, as he sank in the freezing black water.

* * *

"Chris." Jessica choked his name, throat tight with the helpless sorrow that accompanied each nocturnal re-run of his death.

As she shrugged off the last vestiges of nightmare sleep, her leg muscles relaxed and she felt herself falling. She locked her knees, threw her arms out, and grabbed the edge of something hard. One of her hands bounced off the surface, feeling heavy and unnaturally cramped. She looked down and saw that she was clutching a book.

Where the hell am I?

Jessica examined the wooden bookcase she was leaning against and then peered nervously into the darkness around her. The vague impression of a hulking box to her left with the dull sheen of leather behind it took shape. Her nose itched and she sniffed. A headache throbbed to life as the bitter chemical scent of Chanel No. 5 assaulted her senses.

She was in her mother's home office.

Jessica willed her numb fingers to let go of the book and they eventually responded, dropping it with a thud onto a shelf. Pins and needles prickled through her hand and wrist and she rubbed them vigorously, trying to get her circulation back.

Her gaze slid along the book's glossy spine, the white lettering alternately coming into focus and then dissolving into fog. She blinked to clear her eyes and managed to piece together a title—*Psychology of Possession*. She tilted the book up to see the cover and her breath caught in her throat.

The publisher's red logo hovered above the cover, winking at her through the gloom like a boat's emergency light flashing in a storm. It was the same haunting, intersecting circles she had now seen several times.

The symbol...this is where it's from?

She opened the book and held it an inch from her face to better see the text. She scanned a few pages and found the rest of the title: *Psychology of Possession: A treatise on the modern psychological etiology and treatment of spiritual possession.* Her mother's books always had ridiculously long titles.

As she wondered if the scientific community gave out awards for longest title, an image of the oozing blackness stretching between Chris and Bill rose unbidden in her mind.

She dropped the book.

The implication was heinous, but she felt the truth of it down to her marrow.

Possession.

Jessica backed away, staring at the upturned cover. The symbol was gone. The publisher's mark was now a stylized fountain pen and ink well. She looked away and then back again, but the pen logo was still there.

Shivering, she wrapped her arms around her body and groaned when she encountered bare skin. She was naked.

Jessica had stopped wearing nightgowns and pajamas years ago. As an active sleeper, her tangled blankets were enough of a mess to contend with in the morning. Though, she'd never been this active before.

Guess I can kiss sleeping in the buff goodbye.

She tiptoed to the door and cautiously scanned the hall. Her mother's office was on the main floor, so getting back to her room involved going up the stairs. She cringed, trying to remember which of the steps creaked.

How did I make it down here without killing myself? And since when do I sleepwalk?

Her life kept getting weirder and she fervently hoped it would stop. Doing things without being aware was deeply disturbing.

The grandfather clock standing solemnly at the foot of the stairs read close to seven. Dawn crept through the front window and inched down the hall.

Jessica swore under her breath. Psyching herself up, she clenched her fists and whispered, "I can do this. It's now or never. Go…"

Her feet remained firmly planted on the polished maple floor.

She heard the faint shrill of her mother's alarm and glared at the clock. Grandpa Time was running slow.

Jessica charged upstairs, not worrying about noise until she tripped over the last step and sprawled across the hall carpet. Wincing as it abraded tender bits, she heaved herself up and sprinted for her room. Slamming the door shut behind her, she dove into her disheveled bed and pulled the covers up to her chin.

A sharp knock came seconds after she landed.

Her mother's head poked in.

"Jessica? Did you just slam your door?"

Feigning sleep, Jessica mumbled something and rolled onto her side. She opened her eyes and peeled her tangled hair off her sweat-slicked face.

"Mom? What's up?"

Her mother frowned. "Jessica Belinda Clarke. Someone slammed a door. You and I are the only ones home and I know it wasn't me, so that leaves you."

"Uh...sorry. I went to the bathroom. I might have closed the door a bit quickly."

Coming fully into the room, her mother picked a sweater off the floor and laid it over the back of a chair.

"Honestly, Jessica. I'm sure the neighbors heard it. And please, make time to tidy up this room. I know your father and I have been busy, but that's no excuse for your room to fall into chaos. You've got clothes and books all over. It's a wonder you can even make it to your door to slam it."

"Sure." Jessica pulled her comforter higher to hide her rolling eyes. "I'll get right on that."

Because a messy room always takes priority over evil entities possessing people.

She shuddered.

Her mother tsked in annoyance as she stepped on the corner of a binder. "Remember, a disorderly environment signifies a disorderly mind. I'm sure that's not how you want your friends to see you."

She closed the door behind her and Jessica listened to her slippered feet pad away.

Glancing around, Jessica had to admit she might be onto something. Her room used to be tidy and organized, just like her life.

Chapter 17

Jessica drifted through morning classes and found herself in the cafeteria at lunch with no memory of how she got there. Her mind stubbornly refused to focus on anything but what had happened that morning.

Possession. It made a bizarre kind of sense. It was exactly how she'd describe the feeling of the Ouija and bridge nightmares.

She shivered, recalling the bitter pain of the entity consuming her arm, the frenzied rage as it insinuated itself, usurping her body and will.

She thought back to the first time—that lazy picnic at the cove when chaos slammed into her life. A beautiful day shattered by violence and guilt. At the time, she'd thought she could leave the horror behind if she didn't think about it. That's what you did with nightmares, put them out of your mind.

But too many ugly pieces were clicking into place. She'd been shown the truth, like a puzzle made of knife-edged glass, and she'd been too scared to examine the pieces.

When is a nightmare a blessing?

When it saves lives, she thought bitterly.

All she wanted to do was go home and cry, but that was just another way of running out on her responsibilities.

So what am I dealing with? What do I know?

She replayed the nightmares in her mind, watching with a more informed eye, recalling them in as much excruciating detail as possible.

Something ate its way through Chris and then took over Bill. Something full of rage and ruthless cruelty...

* * *

Drew ducked through the crowd in the cafeteria, searching for Jessica. She had ditched their meeting that morning and he was worried. She didn't seem the type to blow off something that would affect her marks. Bakshi was not the forgiving type and acing this presentation was probably their one chance to get off his shit list.

He found her standing at the fruit counter, staring at an apple as if she expected it to sprout legs and do a jig. Annoyed students shoved past, complaining loudly. She was so deep in thought that he had to shake her shoulder to get her attention.

"Apple, banana...I've experienced the heartrending pain of that choice too, Sophie." He leaned closer, pulling her out of the flow of hungry teens. "Trust me. Go with the apple. Less slime, more crunch."

She gave him a confused look.

Drew sighed. "Nobody gets my humor. So, what happened to you this morning?" Jessica's face stiffened and he prompted, "Bakshi. Science project. We were going to meet and talk...are you feeling all right?"

Jessica groaned. "I'm so sorry. I totally forgot. I..." Her voice trailed off. "I can't think straight today."

Drew took a step back and looked her over. The sparkling green eyes he had seen last night were now dull and red-rimmed. Even her freckles seemed washed out.

"No worries. We can chat now if you've got a moment," he offered.

Apparently giving up on the lackluster cafeteria food, Jessica clumped over to an empty table and sat down heavily.

Drew slid into the chair opposite. "Seriously, are you okay?"

"Not really," she said with a weak smile. "I was supposed to finish a physics assignment before school and I forgot about that too. Guess I'm getting a zero on that one. Anyway…operation Dazzle Bakshi, after school. I'll be there."

Jessica stared down at her hands which were clenched into fists.

"Excellent. And hey, good news—I shoved our docs into slides, added graphics, and *voila*…foolproof presentation." He kept his tone light, hoping to ease some of her tension. "Probably a good thing. You pull an all-nighter or something?"

"I had a nightmare. Do I really look that bad?" She yawned and gazed down at herself, trying unsuccessfully to smooth out the rumple in her misbuttoned shirt.

Drew pointed under the table at her socks; one had blue polka dots and the other was covered with cartoon robots.

She twisted in her chair to look, blushed, and pulled her jeans down to cover them.

He leaned forward, his interest piqued. "Your nightmare, was it about the chick in science club? Should I start wearing fire-retardant underwear?"

"No. It was something else." She pinched her lips together, slipped into the same thousand-yard stare she had at the fruit counter, and absentmindedly re-buttoned her shirt.

Drew hid his grin behind a hand. Luckily, she'd sat with her back to most of the room and the few people on his side weren't paying attention to the peep show. Not that Jessica was baring much—just little glimpses; a tiny purple bow here, a pale curve of flesh there.

Once she was fully buttoned, he deemed it safe to interject and carried on their earlier conversation, trying not to look too guilty. "One of those things you don't want to talk about?"

"Not yet, but I will. I need to sort some things out first." She shook her head. "Some of this, it's just...too much."

His uncle had said the same thing many times and Drew felt a sudden pang of sympathy for Jessica. The oddities his uncle dealt with mostly made people think he was crazy. He suspected the visions, especially the tragedies he saw coming and couldn't prevent, did drive him crazy for a time. Many people treated him like the village idiot, others reacted with fear, and a very few adopted a kind of isolating reverence. In the end, all it amounted to was loneliness.

"So, anyway," she said after a moment, her eyes becoming more focused, less haunted, as if she'd drawn a curtain on the horrors in her mind. "If you wanted to find a person's address, how would you do it?" When he opened his mouth to answer, Jessica added, "Oh, and pretend they're not in the phone book."

Drew closed his mouth and picked at a scratch on the table. He was still curious about her nightmare, but knew from experience with his uncle not to push her on it.

"Ask one of their friends?"

"Uh...pretend you don't run in the same circles. I did get his last name, though."

Drew chuckled. "Ah. So we aren't talking hypothetically. Someone you're crushing on? I expected better of you."

"It's not like that," she snapped, and then apologized. "But seriously, how would you find him?"

Drew ran a finger over his bottom lip and leaned back in his chair. "He goes to this school?"

When Jessica nodded, he suggested, "Follow him home?"

"He hasn't been at school lately."

Drew's eyebrow quirked. "Bad boy, eh? Guess asking him where he lives is out of the question?"

Jessica pursed her lips and nodded again.

"Bribe the school secretary to look up his address?" She gave him an incredulous look and he grinned. "All right, something a bit more minor league then. How about getting someone to distract the secretary while you sneak in?"

"How is that more minor league?" Jessica shook her head. "Anyway, it won't work. The file cabinets might be locked and for all we know student records are kept somewhere else, like in the principal's office. And I'm sure as hell not sneaking in there."

"Good point." Drew rested an elbow on the table and dropped his chin onto his hand. "If you had this guy's phone number, you could call and pretend to need his address as part of a contest."

He glanced hopefully at Jessica and saw her shake her head. "Okay...just hack into the school admin system, then. Based on the caliber of our computer teacher, their network security probably sucks, so it should be easy."

A slow smile spread across Jessica's face.

"Of course! The counselor!" She hopped out of her chair, rounded the table, and hugged him from behind. Her hair tickled his ear and he caught a whiff of strawberry.

"You're the best! I'll meet you outside science club after

last period. We'll catch Bakshi before he goes in."

By the time he'd turned to face her, Jessica was halfway across the cafeteria. She collided with another girl, waved a half-hearted apology, and disappeared through the door.

He had met some strange characters, but Jessica kept surprising him.

A little voice in the back of his mind whispered, *That girl's going to bring trouble.*

Perfect, he shot back. *Can't wait.*

* * *

Fifteen minutes before lunch break ended, Jessica's patience finally paid off. She was camped near the counselor's office hoping she would leave, when a group of students thundered down the hall to the nurse's office, hollering for help.

The nurse dashed out carrying a bulky first aid kit and bustled away with them.

Jessica weighed her options and then ducked into the nurse's office as soon as the troop was out of sight. It wasn't what she had planned, but if there was one thing she'd learnt from all the military sci-fi she'd read, it was that no plan survived contact with the enemy and improvisation was key.

There was no knowing how long the nurse would be gone. Thankfully, the computer was booted up, so all she had to do was switch users, plug in the counselor's password, and she was in.

The same text console popped up displaying the student database and she scrolled down until she located "Decker, William." Taking a pen and a random pamphlet from the counter, she scribbled down his address and phone number. She was about to close the program when an entry in his file under "Disciplinary Action" caught her eye.

Biting her lip, she glanced between the door and screen, and decided to risk it. She hit enter and read a terse note dated a few days ago. He'd been given a week's suspension for trying to bite the football coach. She had just reached the end of the text when the computer made a loud popping noise and the screen went dead.

Jessica hit keys and jiggled the mouse. The screen remained dark. She ducked under the counter to examine the box and reeled back when she inhaled acrid smoke.

"You've got to be shitting me!" she hissed.

Holding her breath, she yanked the power cord. The plug was hot to the touch and the computer continued puffing out thin blue tendrils of smoke.

Coughing, she decided a hasty exit was in order and headed for the door. She was almost there when it swung open, missing her nose by inches.

The nurse rushed in, supporting Lindsey.

"Scoot!" she boomed, steering her charge to the examination table.

Jessica staggered back. A knot tightened in her stomach.

Lindsey stared straight ahead, her face slack and unresponsive as the nurse ordered her to hold her hands away from her body.

Her hands.

Jessica caught a glimpse of them and turned away. If there was skin on her left hand, it was unrecognizable. Seared muscle, tendon, and tiny globules of fat barely covered the bones. Her right hand wasn't as bad. The skin was blistered and patchy, but at least it was there.

The nauseating smell of burnt flesh mingled with electrical smoke.

Jessica leaned against the wall, her head spinning. She

heard the nurse exclaim and looked over to see her staring at something on the floor. It took Jessica a second to realize it was one of Lindsey's fingernails.

"You're going to be okay, honey. The ambulance is coming." The nurse continued muttering encouragements until the principal charged through the door with two paramedics and a gurney.

The paramedics went to work on Lindsey. The nurse quickly relayed what witnesses had told her; that Lindsey had been studying in the library one minute and then was suddenly on fire. Nobody knew what had happened.

The principal's face tightened. "Damn it, Deirdre, you should have told me there was a fire right away."

"There wasn't any sign of one—except her hands. The daft girl probably did it to herself. Her textbook was bit singed, but that's it." The nurse puffed herself up and glared.

"Burns like that don't happen without extreme heat. Either way," Mr. Johnson dialed his cell phone, "there's procedures. We need to evacuate the school and get the damn fire department to look things over."

He spoke to Lindsey as the paramedics transferred her to their stretcher. "How did you burn your hands?"

Lindsey stared blankly at him. "It was just a model…" she whispered plaintively as she was rushed away.

A muffled voice issued from the principal's phone and he put it to his ear. Barking into the receiver, he informed the emergency dispatcher that there was a possible fire in the school and then slid his phone into his suit jacket.

He turned back to the nurse. "Set off the fire alarm and then show me where you found her."

The nurse stuck her nose in the air and left.

Mr. Johnson was about to follow when he noticed Jessica

huddled against the far wall.

"Were you with her?"

Jessica wrenched her gaze away from Lindsey's fingernail. The principal's face was beet red and his nose was turning purple.

She shook her head.

"Then what the hell are you doing here?" he snapped. "And what is that smell? It's not smoke is it?" Waving a hand under his nose, he glanced suspiciously around the room.

Jessica tentatively answered, "I had a headache?"

The principal's gaze fell to the pamphlet she was holding and she looked down. Her nervous smile stiffened as she read, "GENITAL WARTS AND HPV: WHAT YOU NEED TO KNOW."

She shoved it into her pocket.

A muscle in Mr. Johnson's cheek twitched. "Right. Make sure you get that headache looked into."

Mortified, Jessica fled as the fire alarm wailed. She joined the surge of students and faculty streaming toward the exit.

The crumpled pamphlet pressed against her hip.

Yet another person hurt because of her bungling. She sent a silent apology to Lindsey and resolved to do something about Bill, today, right now if she could.

Chapter 18

Initial prediction display complete. 94% probability of message comprehension. Channel remains inaccessible.

* * *

Students and staff milled in the schoolyard, waiting to find out what was happening. With the exception of a few distraught students and twitchy teachers, everyone looked happy to have an unexpected break.

Jessica found a cement pylon at the edge of the crowd and sat down, her mind miles away, busily plotting.

If I speak to Bill's family, maybe I can get a better read on how much he's changed.

Before buying into her new and inconceivable possession theory, she wanted to rule out medical or psychological causes. Nobody in town had known Bill long, so it was possible he'd had problems before. Maybe that was even why his family moved here.

Problem was, she couldn't think of a way to check things out, other than in person. She needed to get his family talking and guessed they would be more inclined to chat with a friend who dropped by than someone on the phone.

She breathed in a lungful of crisp fall air, trying to displace the burnt flesh smell clinging to her nose. It didn't work. She raised an arm to sniff her sleeve and grimaced. The stench was embedded in her clothes.

Enthusiastic applause erupted as the principal announced that afternoon classes were cancelled.

Jessica spotted Drew on the steps, scanning the crowd, and joined him to hunt for Bakshi.

They found the teacher clutching his briefcase, alternately gazing longingly at the school doors and checking his watch. Jessica suspected he'd be there, waiting patiently, until the fire department cleared the school.

Bakshi listened to their request to reschedule the project pitch. Although agitated by the disruption to his carefully planned day, he accepted the change calmly enough. He flipped open an immaculate day-timer and penned in an appointment with them over lunch the following day.

Thankful for the reprieve, Jessica mumbled a distracted goodbye to Drew and went home for a shower. Once she'd dried off and changed clothes, she sat on her bed, skimming the first few chapters of *The Psychology of Possession*.

It was hard to decipher the information, as it was written for an audience with post-graduate knowledge of clinical psychology and neuropsychology. The more she read, the more Jessica questioned its utility in the current situation.

She remembered Bill's eyes in the crypt. Black wasn't an adequate description. The dull nothingness in his sockets hadn't just made holes in the light, it had consumed it. Somehow, she didn't think telling him to talk to a professional about his feelings would help.

After struggling through technical terminology, statistics, and clinical studies for two hours, Jessica plugged Bill's address into the map on her phone and headed out. His house was part of a posh new development on the hill east of town, overlooking what must be the most expensive golf course in the province.

Rather than follow the winding road down Coldwater Hill, past the school, and walk all the way back up along the highway, Jessica cut cross-country, uphill to the radio tower. It was technically private land, but it was empty.

She paused among the clustered pines at the top to catch her breath, admiring the expanse of prairies and foothills sweeping toward the white-tipped mountains. All the random ugliness of mud, dry grass, and trees homogenized into a beautiful rolling carpet of browns and greens.

Jessica reluctantly pulled her eyes away and followed a gravel service road to the highway and Bill's neighborhood.

This was where high-powered executives, government officials, and loaded retirees lived and played. The view of Ghost River Valley, the Rocky Mountains, and the pristine golf course was breathtaking; and people paid dearly for it.

Jessica remembered when they had first started building. Interest was so great that the houses had to be sold by lottery. Each peach-stuccoed monstrosity came with a mandatory golf membership, raising the appeal for those who preferred to close deals while chasing little white balls around an over-manicured park.

She felt out of place amongst the hulking houses. Everything about the area felt artificial and forced. Every front yard had the same ultra-green strip of grass, the same anemic chokecherry tree, and the same massive three-car garage. The looming steel doors looked like gaping mouths lined up, hoping an unsuspecting victim would stray close enough to suck in and swallow.

Pulling out her phone, she checked her location and confirmed she was getting close. She wasn't sure what to do when she got there, but figured presenting herself as a concerned friend would at least get her in the door. If she could keep his family talking and watch them interact, she might get some clues as to what was happening.

She wasn't comfortable using the term "possession." The religiousness of it didn't sit well in her rational mind, not that much of what had happened lately sat well on any level. She fervently hoped she wasn't going to end up on a street corner, wearing an aluminum foil suit and preaching about evil body-snatchers.

Jessica stopped at the foot of Bill's driveway, fighting the urge to run. She gave herself the tenth woman-up talk of the day and approached the front door, briefly hesitating before ringing the doorbell.

After waiting a minute, she peered through a clear diamond pane in the frosted window beside the door.

The house was dark.

Unwilling to turn back after coming this far, she tried the bell again, listening as the cheery melody chimed its tinny notes.

Nothing.

Jessica looked up at the second-floor windows and couldn't tell if there were any lights on. She checked the time. It was still early. His parents probably weren't home from work yet.

Apprehension swamped her resolve as she eyed the sterile neighborhood.

No. I am NOT leaving until I get some answers.

She retreated to a clump of bushes at the end of the driveway and sat down, planning to wait until someone came home.

A dog yapped excitedly and Jessica swiveled her head, trying to pinpoint its location. It sounded like it was in Bill's backyard.

Glancing down the street, she saw a young woman walking with a baby stroller.

Jessica debated with herself and decided the risk was acceptable, now that someone was near enough to hear her scream if something catastrophic happened.

She rounded the house and approached a cedar gate. A sharp yelp quickened her pace.

The gate swung open to reveal a lawn that was trimmed to within an inch of its life and a central, oriental-style gazebo surrounded by gardens stuffed with late-season flowers.

She heard a faint splashing noise and called out a tentative "hello?"

No one answered.

Knowing better, but now committed, she entered the yard. The sounds of water sloshing intensified.

Jessica crept closer and peeked around the gazebo.

She'd pictured a puppy retrieving an errant toy from a water bowl, but what she saw was Bill forcing a young beagle's head into a garden pond. The terrified animal squirmed in his grasp, choking on dirty water as it scrabbled to find leverage in the loose gravel.

A strangled cry of rage burst from Jessica and Bill's head whipped around.

She stood rooted to the spot as he released the struggling puppy and straightened to his full, formidable height. There was something like glee on his face, tainted with need.

The dog heaved its head out of the pond, threw up a deluge of brown water, shook itself, and trotted over to snuffle Jessica's feet as if nothing had happened.

She stared from the puppy, to Bill, and back again.

Bill stepped toward her.

Acting on pure instinct, she grabbed the dog and ran.

Bill's pounding footsteps followed as she raced around the house and bolted down the street, which she noted with resigned annoyance was now deserted.

The beagle clambered onto her shoulder as she ran and let out a volley of high-pitched barks, enjoying the impromptu excursion.

At least the damn dog's okay. She glanced over her shoulder and saw Bill gaining on her. *Maybe not for long.*

Her mind was in overdrive, but her legs were not.

If I yell for help, someone will come, she reassured herself, *or at least dial 911.*

Then, she remembered the recent news report about a woman being beaten to death by her boyfriend on a busy street in Calgary. Nobody wanted to get involved.

With renewed panic, she forced her burning legs to keep moving, her breath coming in sharp gasps.

Grasping the corner of a fence to slingshot herself around, Jessica aimed downhill, toward the highway. It beckoned in the distance like a mirage.

There's always traffic there. I'll run right down the middle if I have to!

She picked up speed on the downward slope, her feet flying, but Bill's slapping footfalls were close behind.

Between the increased speed and the added weight of the puppy dragging at her arms, she was severely off balance. Her rubbery legs had no coordination left. Staying upright became more a matter of luck than skill.

Her heart leapt as someone jogged into view, down where the road met the highway.

"Heyyy…" she called out as loud as her laboring lungs would allow. "Hey…aaah!"

In her relief at seeing the jogger, she missed the sidewalk ending. Her knee buckled as she hit the hummocked prairie grass and sent her tumbling. She lost her grip on the dog mid-fall and he rolled off on his own trajectory.

When the world stopped spinning, she lay on her back in the grass, legs numb, arms and elbows aching. She fumbled around, trying to get all her limbs moving in the right direction at the same time.

The beagle yipped as something blocked out the sun.

Jessica wheezed as Bill crouched beside her and she re-doubled her efforts to move. Her right arm burned with phantom pain as he slammed a hand down on her sternum, his fingers digging into the top of her left breast.

He was in no hurry now. The bastard wasn't even breathing heavily.

Foam gathered at the corners of his mouth and a string of drool ran down his chin. The ravening shadow consumed his eyes.

Terror spiked through Jessica. She couldn't draw any strength into her limbs. She struggled for breath as he increased the pressure on her chest.

Her vision tunneled and filled with a red haze.

"Wasn't going to take you yet." The thing wearing Bill smiled. "But you're so…sweet." He moved his hand to her face, taking pleasure in the way she squirmed to keep him from touching her flesh. "Such terror! I haven't even tasted you yet."

She felt the darkness gathering in his hand, like the itchy pain of bleach on skin.

This is it, she thought. The utter futility of her life overwhelmed her. She couldn't even save a damn dog.

Bill suddenly grunted in pain and rolled to the side.

Jessica scrabbled in the opposite direction, catching a fleeting glimpse of black hair and a neon-pink hoodie.

She looked harder and was shocked to see Michiru standing between her and Bill. He was levering himself off the ground, snarling.

Mind reeling, Jessica barely had time to gasp out, "Don't let him touch you" before Bill howled in fury, dropped a shoulder, and charged.

Jessica pulled her arms and legs in toward her body, expecting to be trampled, but Bill never made it past Michiru.

She was a blur of motion. Rather than the expected thud of body meeting body, Bill's tackling leap became an uncontrolled spin. He landed heavily on his back on the concrete and lay motionless. Michiru flowed back into a resting stance and waited, watching him with diamond intensity.

Jessica crawled to where the beagle was crouched, tail wagging even as he shivered in frightened confusion. He whined and she gathered him into her arms.

Bill staggered to his feet and came at Michiru again, stalking around her. A predator isolating his prey. He was easily twice her weight. A fight between the two seemed laughable, and yet it was Bill who was visibly shaken.

Michiru's face remained expressionless as her lithe form adjusted to mirror Bill's movements.

"You won't win this one. Leave," she ordered in a cold, flat voice.

Jessica quietly stood, hoping the combatants attention remained on each other. She examined the soggy bundle in her arms and found no obvious injuries.

Bill circled Michiru, growling like a feral beast. He lunged and caught her hood as she spun away. Jerking her back toward him, he reached out with his other hand and wrapped his fingers around her throat.

Michiru drew in a deep breath before he cut off her air. She twisted her torso in a quick, fluid motion and landed a solid elbow to his diaphragm.

Air whooshed out of his lungs and his face contorted in pain. His grip on her loosened and his hand slid lower on her throat. He screeched and jerked back when he touched a jade pendent tied around her neck.

He backed away cradling his hand, which now sported an angry red welt.

His empty gaze flicked between the two girls.

He took a step toward Jessica, murder etched in the sharp contours of his face.

Michiru slipped between them and dropped into a stance, ready for another round.

Bill stood poised on the edge of action, a scant meter away.

Seconds stretched out.

He stepped back. When he was several meters away, still pinning Jessica with a glare, he snarled, "It can't protect you forever. I will take you."

He held her gaze for several beats of her heart, then jogged away.

Chapter 19

```
Channel fully engaged with Shadow. Protector subcon-
scious manipulation complete. Channel destruction proba-
bility reduced to 61%.
```

* * *

Michiru dusted herself off, watching as Bill disappeared behind a fence. "'It'? Really? What an asshole."

Jessica stared at her.

The diminutive girl, practically pocket-sized in comparison to Bill, casually pulled her hoodie back into place and stretched her neck. Long purple bruises marked where his fingers had squeezed her throat and her hoodie and shirt were torn down the front.

Despite Michiru having had physical contact with Bill, Jessica was relieved to see no moving shadows in her eyes. She went over the fight in her mind and confirmed that she hadn't witnessed any transfer of black goo. Either it hadn't wanted to take her over or had been stopped somehow.

She was shaken by how close they had come to total disaster.

"Holy crap. Are you okay?" Jessica asked shakily.

Her gaze caught on Michiru's necklace. The thick red leather cord held an intricate jade carving of three flowers nestled on five leaves. It would have been pretty but unremarkable if it weren't for the soft green glow emanating from the stone.

Michiru grinned sheepishly. "I'm fine. Just bruised. Serves me right for being so sloppy. I should have known better than to do *ushiro mawashi* with him so close."

She tugged at the ripped edges of her shirt. "My top's seen better days. Good thing there's not much to see down there." For the first time, she looked anxious. "I can't go home looking like this. Mom will freak."

Jessica realized her gaze had wandered lower on Michiru's chest and forced it back up. "Not much to see" wasn't entirely accurate.

"I'll lend you a shirt," Jessica offered, wincing at the darkening bruises on Michiru's neck. "Maybe a turtleneck. My place is close, about twenty minutes, back toward school."

"Great. So's mine. Sounds like we live near each other. Though, there's really nothing in this town that isn't close." She sounded vaguely disgusted.

Jessica took a few wobbly steps and groaned. "Okay, this might take a bit longer. Maybe you should just roll me down the hill."

Bending forward to massage her calf with her free hand, Jessica received a series of wet dog-kisses on her chin and lips. She jerked her head out of reach and wiped her mouth on her shoulder. The beagle's tail rhythmically thumped against her side.

Michiru laughed. "He's cute. What's his name?"

"Haven't the foggiest."

Michiru gave her a puzzled look. She took the puppy from Jessica and cradled him in her arms like a baby. He waved all four paws in the air as she scratched his round belly.

"Did you just get him?"

They started walking and Jessica nodded slowly, amused. "You could say that."

Michiru cast her a sidelong glance.

Jessica chewed her lip. "I guess I kinda stole him. But only to stop Bill from hurting him." She stared at the dog. "I have no idea what to do now. My parents aren't going to let me keep him and I can't give him back. Not with Bill the way he is."

"Bill being the big, pissed-off guy?"

Jessica nodded.

Michiru walked beside her, slowing her pace to match Jessica's hobble as they followed the winding highway into town. Jessica had expected some kind of negative reaction, but Michiru seemed unfazed.

Still tickling the puppy's belly, Michiru asked, "So he was chasing you because you nicked his dog?"

"Uh...no. Not exactly. At least, I don't think so." Not sure where to go from there, Jessica changed the subject. "So, where'd you learn to fight? You're amazing. I've only seen action like that in movies." She frowned and added, "It's a lot more terrifying in person."

"That was nothing. You should see me with Mum and Dad."

"You fight like that with your parents?" Jessica's voice went up several octaves.

"We don't beat each other up. Although, I do occasionally aim badly or misjudge distance..." Chuckling at Jessica's horrified expression, she explained, "We work out together, going through forms and sparring. Keeps me fit." She shrugged.

A faint blush dusted Michiru's cheeks as she fiddled with the dog's collar. Metal jangled against metal and she examined it closer. "Mystery solved. His name's Hamish."

The puppy barked and chewed her finger.

"Thanks." Jessica smiled weakly.

"No biggie. It's on his tag."

"For that too," Jessica's smile widened. "But I mostly meant for helping me back there. Saving me, really."

"Don't mention it." Michiru glanced behind them. "I'm just glad I decided to add some challenge to my jog today. Not my usual route."

Jessica watched Michiru out of the corner of her eye, considering whether to explain any further about Bill. She had to do something about him, and soon, but today's fiasco confirmed he was too dangerous to take on alone.

Michiru knew how to take care of herself, and then there was her pendant. It had burnt him. Maybe she already knew something about this sort of thing.

There was only one way to find out.

Jessica cleared her throat. "Did you notice anything strange about Bill's eyes?"

"Strange?" Michiru cocked her head to the side. "Not really. Except his right eye was a bit lazy. Good for me. A blind spot is always useful. Why?"

"You didn't see how black they were?"

"They were blue...oh, you mean the pupil." She leaned closer to Jessica. "Were they blown? You think he's on something?"

"I wish." Jessica sighed as she limped down the hill. "If you'll give me the benefit of the doubt, I'll fill you in on what little I know. I've been having these dreams..."

* * *

Michiru listened to Jessica, keeping an eye on their

surroundings as they travelled, worried Bill might double back. She remembered him now as the guy who'd been harassing Jessica at school. He didn't seem like the rational type, so her senses were on high alert.

By the time they reached Jessica's house, she had finished her account and Michiru was mulling things over.

She would have dismissed the crazy tale out of hand, but Jessica related everything with such an earnest and embarrassed humility that Michiru was certain she believed what she was saying. Which either meant her new acquaintance was deranged, or that she had in fact witnessed some truly odd things.

The latter would require significant changes in her world view—prophetic dreams, possession, strange floaty symbols…it all sounded ridiculous. Thugs, pimps, and addicts were more Michiru's style. She had no idea the switch from big cities to a small town would be so hard. Still, she couldn't bring herself to completely dismiss the unusual, just in case it came back to bite her on the ass. In light of that, she decided to provisionally accept Jessica's version of events.

From the way Jessica spoke and what she'd seen of her at school, Michiru pegged her as bookish—classically intelligent but timid and probably naive. Not the type she'd expect to buy into the paranormal or get involved in dog-napping. And definitely not the type to pick a fight with a big bugger like Bill.

Jessica was in way over her head, and from the look on her face after the fight, she knew it.

As they trooped up to her room, Michiru said, "Bill's going to hurt someone if something isn't done. Maybe you should tell the police."

She looked down at the beagle snuggled in her arms, knowing the pain people were willing to inflict on the helpless, but not understanding.

"What am I supposed to say?" Jessica collapsed onto her bed. "Hi. I think this guy is possessed. Please fix him. Oh...and I accidently stole his dog." She massaged her temples. "They'd stick me in a padded room. Believe me, I've thought about calling them. You have no idea how much I want to make this someone else's problem. It's really scary and I don't want to deal with it."

Michiru nodded. "Good point. The cops are probably as useless here as they are everywhere else."

Jessica pulled a floppy green sock out from under her pillow and started stroking it.

"How about you?" Jessica asked after a moment, the gleam of an idea in her eye. "I'm not the only one he attacked. You could report him for trying to strangle you."

"Not a good idea. Trust me." Memories of the Paris debacle came rushing back and Michiru felt her old anger rising. She paced the room, trying to work off the surge of adrenalin.

Her first encounter with law enforcement happened back when she was too naïve to know that interrupting a john raping a girl could get a person in trouble. When she called an ambulance for the barely conscious girl, the police had showed up, and the guy claimed he was the victim. Said they lured him into an alley to jack his wallet.

Granted, she had broken his arm to eliminate a knife and taken out his knee to keep him down, but she figured that was light considering what he did to the girl. The police hadn't shared her view. As usual, her parents overreacted and they'd moved to Amsterdam within a week.

Her jaw tensed. "Police don't take girls seriously unless they lose the fight, badly."

Michiru dragged her mind back to the present by concentrating on her surroundings. She was surprised by how normal

Jessica's room was. Apart from a book lying on the bedside table claiming to reveal the secret history of modern witchcraft, Jessica's taste, although eclectic and academically inclined, appeared fairly mainstream.

She set Hamish down and watched him roll in a pile of clothes, flinging shirts, bras, and pants in all directions. She'd always wanted a dog, but her parents were right—it wasn't practical given all the moving they did. Being practical sucked.

"He's adorable. I wish I could help, but there's no way I'd get him past Mum and Dad."

"I'm not sure I will either." Jessica sighed as the puppy ran into the wall with a thud. "I'll try hiding him in here. It's not like my parents are around much."

"Lucky. I have the opposite problem," Michiru grumbled. "Got any tips for me?"

Jessica snorted. "Offer them tenure and clients with around-the-clock mental health issues?" She delicately replaced the sock under her pillow. "If I wear Hamish out on walks before they get home, maybe he'll be calmer. I just have to remember to warn Lucy."

"Lucy?" Michiru asked, wondering if Jessica had a sister.

"She cleans the house on Tuesdays. Chocolate should buy her silence. We get along well."

Michiru glanced at the scattered clothes, hair clips, nail polish, mugs, and other odds and ends, including an open jar of peanut butter. Every surface in the room was covered. "Does she get paid by the hour?"

"What?" Jessica caught her drift. "Ah, you mean this mess. Not her problem. I'm responsible for my room, which I guess is pretty obvious."

Levering herself up, Jessica limped to her closet, handed Michiru a turtleneck, and then sank back down on her bed.

"Thanks for listening…and for not looking at me like I'm crazy. Sometimes I wonder myself."

Michiru pulled off her torn shirt and struggled into the turtleneck, digging her pendent out to sit on top of the heavy fabric. She tugged at the tight neckline. The pressure against her bruises made it feel like Bill's fingers were still wrapped around her throat.

Jessica was quiet for a while, then said, "I don't know what I'm going to do, but I think I need your help."

The plea was whispered so quickly that Michiru nearly missed it.

She sat down beside Jessica and awkwardly patted her hand, hoping Jessica wouldn't start crying. "I'll help if I can, but I don't know what to do either. That guy is seriously messed up."

Jessica nodded. "I need to do some research on possession." She gazed curiously at Michiru's pendant. "And maybe some on your necklace. It hurt Bill when he touched it. Plus, it glowed. You know anything about that?"

Michiru arched an eyebrow and held her pendant out to take a closer look. "Glowed? It's just jade." She turned it over in her hand, feeling the familiar ridges and crevices in the skin-warmed stone. "Maybe the sun hit it at an odd angle?"

"No…it's still glowing." Jessica reached out and gingerly touched the surface, as if afraid it might bite. "It's fainter now, but it was quite bright before."

Michiru closed one eye and then the other as she squinted at her pendant. No matter how she looked at it, there was no glow.

"Looks normal to me." Worry itched the back of her neck. It was disconcerting to have things happening around her, and on her, that she couldn't sense.

"You seriously don't see it glowing?"

Michiru shook her head. She slipped the necklace off and handed it to Jessica. "It was my mum's. She gave it to me when I turned seven. Her mum gave it to her. It's kind of a tradition."

Jessica examined the pendant, holding it up to the light and running her fingers over the surface. She handed it back and asked, "Does the design have a meaning?"

Michiru accepted the necklace with a shrug. "It's bamboo leaves with some kind of flower...gentilly, hmmm, no, maybe gentillan or gentian...something like that. Mum explained, but it was a while ago."

She retied the leather cord around her neck. "I've never thought much about it. It's supposed to bring good luck." Thinking further, she added, "Hey, I saw a documentary once that said Buddhist monks plant bamboo groves around temples because they think it wards off evil, but personally, I think it's because pandas are cute. That's about the extent of my knowledge."

Hamish ran by, dragging a sandal. He stepped on a strap and tripped, somersaulting into Michiru's feet in a roly-poly ball of cuteness.

She was distracted for a while, playing tug of war, and when she looked up again, Jessica was feverishly typing away on her laptop. Michiru peered at the screen and realized she was taking notes.

Jessica finished and hit save. "I'll see what I can find out. Your necklace did something to Bill. If I can figure out how and why, it might be useful." She sighed. "That sounded a lot more positive in my head."

Michiru laughed, deciding Jessica was the most interesting person she'd met lately, or possibly ever. If nothing else, investigating ghosts and possessed guys would be new. And, based on today, exciting.

"We'll figure something out." Michiru checked the time and grimaced. "I'd better make a move. Mum will be wondering what happened to me. If you give me your number, I'll call later to see how you're getting on."

They exchanged numbers and email addresses and said a hasty goodbye. Wind rippled through Jessica's hair, turning it into a wreath of flame as she stood in her doorway, waving.

Michiru waved back and set off for home at a quick jog, genuinely happy for the first time since moving to Coldwater.

She hadn't said much about it, but she'd been upset when her parents decided to relocate to small town Alberta. She enjoyed the bustling crowds and endless activity of large cities. There was always something new and interesting to do.

Michiru smiled to herself. Had she known this little town had a Jessica, she wouldn't have worried.

* * *

What a girl, Jessica mused. Tough and gorgeous, even after a brawl.

The image of Michiru's smooth skin and elegantly curved back popped into Jessica's mind, but she was too exhilarated to feel even a shred of jealousy.

She raced back to her room and pulled her grandmother's books out from under the bed. Jessica was sure the necklace was an important piece of the puzzle. She just needed to find the other three corners and start working her way in.

Sitting on her heels, Jessica spread the books out on the bed. Reviewing their cover blurbs and indexes, she kept anything with information on possession and charms, and dropped everything else on the floor.

There was a scratching noise from the corner of the room and she looked over to see Hamish tunneling through her laundry. He emerged chewing the bow off her favorite bra.

After rescuing her undergarment, she grabbed a pen and paper, opened the first book, and settled into research mode.

Chapter 20

After a sugar- and caffeine-fueled night of research, Jessica spent Thursday restless and twitchy.

The project presentation to Mr. Bakshi went surprisingly well, mostly thanks to Drew's slides, which eliminated the need for heavy thinking.

Bakshi was impressed with the math involved and seemed to feel there was enough interest in their topic to make it worthwhile. He allowed Jessica back into science club with a warning that any further outbursts would not only result in her removal, but a school suspension.

Jessica was overjoyed when the day ended. If she could have summoned the energy, she would have done a happy dance.

As she trudged through the crypt, an arm snaked out of the crowd and pulled her to the side. Too exhausted to even gasp, she was relieved when she found the slender copper fingers attached to Drew.

"Glad I caught you. Do you have any free time this weekend? I'd like to show Bakshi something next week so he knows we're serious."

Jessica shook her head. "There's…uh…something else I need to take care of." She had arranged to meet a local priest to talk about exorcisms, something she suddenly found herself embarrassed to reveal.

She'd barely scratched the surface with her research last night. Isolating the useful bits from the flotsam was proving more difficult than she thought. Each web search turned up millions of hits, and after a while, everything sounded crazy. Or perhaps that was just the sugar and caffeine.

Wondering if Drew could offer some insight, she asked, "I don't suppose you know anything about possession?"

His eyebrows shot up. "As in, 'I have no idea what that is, I'm just carrying it for a friend,' or, 'The devil made me do it'?"

Jessica stared at him, mystified. After a moment, her lips formed a silent O. "The last one. Something taking over a person's body and controlling it."

"I see," said Drew, his mind visibly switching gears. "Skinwalkers are probably the closest we have to Christian possessions. Funnily enough, I talked to Uncle last night about Sarah and he mentioned them."

"Sarah? Good crap. Are skinwalkers and shape-shifters the same?"

Drew pulled Jessica further into a corner. "Not even remotely. Shape-shifters transform into another creature. They are the same person, only their changed self exists as if they had spent their life as that creature. If Sarah is a shape-shifter, when she transforms, she's a wolf version of herself. Skinwalkers are…different."

His voice lowered and Jessica strained to hear. "They *steal* a person or animal's body. They can be anything from nuisances to homicidal predators and are pretty much immortal unless their host dies. Uncle thinks Sarah's a shape-shifter, based on what we saw. That's good news. Even talking about skinwalkers freaked him out." He paused. "You still with me?"

Jessica forced her mind back on track. "Just thinking. So, if someone isn't himself, there are two possibilities: another person has shape-shifted to look like them, or a skinwalker's running the show. I hadn't thought of the first. That would change everything."

"I've never heard of a person shape-shifting to look like another person. It's always human to animal or vice-versa. Why do I get the feeling we're not talking about Sarah anymore?"

"Because we're not. What else do you know about skinwalkers?"

"Who…?" Drew's eyes narrowed. "Why are you looking at me the same way Nihna looks at fleeing prey?"

"Just curious." Jessica tried to smile innocently.

"Yeah. I had a taste of that kind of curiosity when I tried to rescue a squirrel from Nihna last year." Drew rubbed his forearm, revealing a set of three thin, parallel scars. "There's a story Uncle told me about skinwalkers when I was little. It still gives me nightmares."

Jessica impatiently gestured for him to continue.

He lowered his voice until it was little more than a whisper. "A group of kids stayed out late one night, laughing and joking about how brave they were. One by one, they grew tired and went home, until there was one boy left. Proud that he was the bravest, he lay on his back staring at the stars until he heard whispered voices in the trees. He called out, thinking his friends were playing a trick, but nobody answered. His fear grew and he set off for home. Footsteps followed him down the path, but every time he looked back, there was nothing. He ran and the footsteps quickened to match his pace, but still, he saw nothing. Too scared to yell for help, the boy ran until he no longer heard the footsteps and stopped to rest. When he got home, he told his mother what had happened and she summoned a medicine man. He listened to the story and waved a candle in front of the boy's face. His eyes reflected the light like a cat's. The medicine man took the mother aside and explained that a skinwalker had been stalking the group. It stayed away until there was only one because they don't like noise. The boy stopped hearing footsteps, not because the skinwalker gave up, but because it jumped into his body. And there it would remain, hiding, until it gathered enough strength to take control."

"I understand your bad dreams," said Jessica, silently pledging not to walk alone at night again, ever. "So what happened?"

Drew shrugged. "The usual...the medicine man tricked the skinwalker. He convinced it that the boy was dying, and when it left his body, he trapped it in a mouse and killed it. Uncle always told me to whistle if I was out alone at night." He grimaced. "As it turns out, whistling isn't a skill that improves with practice."

He puckered his lips and let out a piercing note which warbled aggressively off pitch. Passing students leveled horrified glares at them and Jessica shoved her fingers in her ears.

"Well, that would certainly keep me at bay," she said, pulling her fingers out after checking to make sure he had stopped.

"I think Uncle was just trying to scare me into staying home."

"And everyone else. If I heard that racket at night, I'd run home too," said Jessica. "Not that I'm really into solo nighttime excursions."

"Do all your nocturnal wandering with partners, do

you?" he chuckled.

Jessica blushed, recalling her naked foray to her mother's study. "At least I don't generally leave the house."

She saw Drew's eyebrow rise and changed the topic. "So, if someone is taken over by a skinwalker, their eyes reflect light? That doesn't fit what I've seen."

"It's just what that story says. Uncle probably knows more. It'd be easier if you told me what's going on and then I could ask him more specific questions."

Jessica pondered how to best describe the situation. When her fatigued brain refused to cooperate, she decided to just wade in. Drew would catch up. He always did.

"There's this guy...I had a dream that something went into him and now he's acting weird. His friends think something's wrong with him too. Twice now, when I've seen him, this black film clouds his eyes, but nobody else sees it. And he bit a teacher. And tried to drown his dog." She frowned. "At least I think it's his dog."

"Okay." Drew's skepticism died when no punch line came. "Biting and drowning definitely qualify as weird. Is this connected to that guy's address you were trying to find? How did that go?"

"Better than I deserve." Jessica looked away, feigning interest in a lopsided, neon-orange sign taped to the wall.

It was a poster advertising the school Halloween dance next week. Black plastic spiders ringed the edges. The longer she stared at them, the more it looked like they were moving. She shuddered.

Jessica had been beyond relieved when Eric asked her to his dance. Although she was nervous to meet his new friends, the thought of getting out of Coldwater filled her with joy. Eric shared her love of Halloween, mostly due to the inevitable chocolate overload, and they'd spent hours last week picking out a cheesy couple's costume.

At least I'll have one evening where nothing insane happens.

"I'm surprised they let you go so quick yesterday. You should have said something." Drew's voice broke through her pleasant reverie. "You fall into more trouble?"

"Trouble?" Jessica sorted through the list of things she could be blamed for, paranoid she'd forgotten one that was about to pounce. She came up blank. Her heart raced and sweat prickled.

"The fire scare." Drew looked confused. "I heard you were running around the library yelling about a fire?" He gave her a serious look. "I've been avoiding the library today, just in case."

"I wasn't even in the library yesterday." Jessica snapped defensively. "It had nothing to do with me…" Her thoughts hiccupped as she realized that was not completely true.

Now it was Drew's turn to pierce her with his eyes. "You holding out on me, Red?"

"No!" She winced at the shrill edge to her voice. "It was probably Lindsey yelling, and for good reason." Her stomach churned with remembered nausea. "Her hands got completely fried."

Drew's face showed no hint of recognition.

"Lindsey…the girl I threw water at in science club?"

"Ah. The one with the big…glasses. Makes sense now. Guess I can stop worrying about the lab blowing up." He grew more serious. "I hope she's okay."

"I doubt it." Jessica swallowed hard, tasting bile.

Drew jumped as his phone buzzed. He checked the text message and swore as he slung a tattered army bag over his shoulder. "I won't have time to talk to Uncle tonight. Gotta wash dishes in hell."

"Huh?"

Drew headed for the exit with Jessica in tow.

"Mom's waitressing at Ehage. They're swamped Thursday nights and their dishwasher is AWOL…again."

Jessica's mind drifted back to the field trip her elementary class had taken to the reserve's museum/restaurant. Like many things in life, it had seemed full of promise from the outside. The building was beautiful, designed like a teepee with five huge cedar logs running from the main floor to a high domed ceiling. Exhibit rooms ringed an open central area, but most had been either locked or empty.

After thirty seconds of awe, it became clear the museum contained a sparse collection of poorly marked artifacts designed to distract tourists while they waited for their "authentic First Nations meal." And by that, they apparently meant hamburgers, fries, and pop. The day had left a lasting impression when Jake barfed his greasy lunch down Jessica's back on the bus.

She gagged at the memory and Drew raised an eyebrow. "Something wrong?"

"Just remembering the last time I was there. It was…" She searched for something to say that wasn't insulting.

"Don't worry. I hate the place too. It's a fucking embarrassment, but people go because it's the only restaurant on the Rez. And, get this, just to make it extra tacky, they're doing Bingo Thursdays in the lecture hall. I mean, come on. The only speaker it's seen is someone calling out 'B22.' That's just sad."

They emerged from the school into dying sunlight. The air held a sharp chill, heralding the passing of autumn into winter.

"It's weird," he said, rubbing the back of his neck.

"Neave's not usually like this."

"Neave?" Jessica tried to place the name.

"Sorry. Not used to talking to townies. She's Sam's girl-friend."

"Sam has a girlfriend?" She hadn't meant for her voice to sound so skeptical.

"He's not a bad guy, most of the time." Drew grinned. "Just a bit intense. The whole townie-school thing's got his panties in a bunch. Anyway, his girlfriend is the AWOL dish-washer. It's not like her to blow off shifts. Though, mom did say she seemed pretty upset about something lately."

He kicked a loose rock down the steps. "Sam doesn't know what's up with her either. I hope she shows up soon. I don't want to scrape slop off plates any longer than I have to." His shoulders sagged.

"Well, good luck," Jessica said distractedly, her attention absorbed by his bag. One of the punctures in the thick canvas looked suspiciously like a bullet hole.

"Thanks." He followed her gaze. "Don't look so shocked. We upgraded from bows and arrows years ago."

Jessica frowned and he ruffled her hair before she could duck away. "Lighten up. The bag was my grandpa's from his army days."

"Oh?" She stopped in the middle of fixing her hair. "He was in the army?"

"Yup. World War Two. People wondered if the stories about the war were true, but figured something halfway across the world wasn't their business. Grandpa was different. He wanted to see. So he did. Guess it runs in the family." He grinned. "I can't resist poking my nose where it doesn't belong either."

Jessica snorted. "Maybe we're related."

"Doubtful." He tweaked her button nose. "You don't have the Gray beak. For sure I can meet up with Uncle on Sunday, maybe tomorrow if Neave reappears. I'll give you a call." He started walking down the stairs and then turned back. "And try to get some sleep tonight. You look like shit."

Jessica groaned, remembering what was waiting for her at home. "That's up to Hamish. He pounces on my feet every time I roll over and he's got surprisingly sharp teeth."

Drew's head tilted to the side, both eyebrows vying for peak position.

Realizing she'd skipped some important context, she managed to gasp out "Dog" as she tried to stop laughing.

"But you don't have a dog."

Wiping away tears with her jacket sleeve, Jessica tamed her laugh into a wide grin.

"Long story. I'll tell you later. I need to get home before he chews an escape tunnel out of my room."

Jessica considered asking him for a ride, but decided against it. She didn't want to get lumped into the category of moocher. No need to burn that bridge before it was even fully built.

Drew gave her a last quizzical look, then shrugged and sauntered off through the parking lot.

Someone brushed past Jessica and she nervously scanned the flow of students. Readjusting her backpack as she rushed down the steps, she took the fastest route to the street. She needed to get home while it was light out and there were people around. The thought of encountering Bill alone filled her with dread, and she wasn't about to stake her life on the skinwalker whistling defense.

Chapter 21

The earthy scent of fallen leaves and bright sunshine almost made up for the cold gusts of wind nipping at Jessica's ears. She was not a morning person, especially on Saturdays. Instead of waiting until the last minute to get ready, she should have spent some time digging out her toque and mitts. But the sun had tricked her into thinking it was warmer outside. Rookie mistake.

At least the driving pace Michiru set was keeping most of her warm, and the travel mug full of caffeinated goodness was making a valiant effort at thawing the rest.

The cold didn't seem to faze Michiru. She was wearing her usual yoga pants and hoodie, bright yellow this time, with the hood pushed back. She didn't look rushed, but it was a challenge for Jessica to keep up.

And to think, this is after she jogged all the way to my place. Ugg.

"So we're not actually going shopping, right?" Michiru asked, sounding concerned.

"No, that was just for the parental units." Jessica didn't have time for the three-hour lecture on comparative religions her mother would have given if she found out they were visiting a Catholic priest. "Though I guess I do need some conditioner, and maybe deodorant..."

She tried to visualize the contents of her bathroom and another thought struck her. "I also totally owe you a new hoodie and shirt, to replace the ones Bill wrecked."

Michiru gave her a blank look. "Why? I chose to get involved."

"Sure, but it was my butt you were saving. I owe you."

"That's not how it works. You'll just have to save mine sometime."

Jessica snorted. "Like that'll happen."

"You never know. So, does this priest know what he's in for? Aren't exorcisms deep, dark, secret stuff?"

"I think so, and not necessarily." Jessica answered both questions and swallowed a mouthful of coffee. "According to what I read online, some exorcisms can get pretty freaky, but I doubt he'll talk to me about those."

Between the cold wind and the hot coffee, Jessica's brain lumbered to action. "I'm not even convinced an exorcism is what we need. I called with a couple questions and the priest, Father, um..." She pulled out a small reporter's notebook. "...Wojcikowski said it would be easier to talk if I stopped by." She sighed. "Early, unfortunately."

Michiru grinned, but didn't comment. "And who are we supposed to be? I assume you didn't tell him about Bill."

"Good grief, no. I've never met the guy, so I have no idea how he'd react. He could think I'm nuts or go all Van Helsing extremist. I said we wanted to interview him for a school project."

"On demonic possession?" Michiru looked doubtful.

"For our Religious History class. We go to St. Martin's Catholic school in Calgary and we're just a couple of students spending our weekend doing the Lord's work, or rather, poking our noses into the Lord's work." Jessica plastered an exaggeratedly vacant expression on her face and fluttered her eyelashes.

"You're a bit scary sometimes." Michiru couldn't help laughing, but her joviality faded. "I don't know anything about being Catholic. Won't we have to light candles or sing or something?"

Jessica downed the last of her coffee and stuffed the empty mug into her backpack. "Don't worry. The most you'll have to do is genuflect if we walk past a big cross." She demonstrated quickly. "And I don't think he'll expect us to do confession."

Michiru's brow furrowed. "Confession?"

"It's nothing. If we get stuck, just say you had sexy thoughts about a guy, or lied to a teacher about why your homework wasn't done, or coveted your best friend's new dress. Think Ten Commandments and break one."

"Great, the only one I can ever remember is 'Thou shalt not kill.' " She snickered. "I'd like to see the look on his face."

Jessica grimaced. "On second thought, I'll do the talking. Let's pretend you're an exchange student. You're Japanese, right?"

"My parents are. I'm British." Michiru's response was automatic, as if she was used to explaining. Nodding to herself, she admitted, "It might work. You be the good little Catholic and I'll be the foreign heathen you're trying to spread the word to." She grinned mischievously. "I think I'll like being the bad girl."

"You're from England?" asked Jessica, unable to contain her curiosity. "I mean, you have an accent, but it doesn't sound English to me."

"We've moved around a lot, but I was born in London."

She shrugged. "I suppose I have a mix of accents."

"Cool," Jessica huffed, as Michiru pulled ahead again, pushing up the walking pace.

Jessica's legs still felt abused from her terrified flight from Bill, not to mention the walk up and down Coldwater Hill to his house, so she was very glad when the outer gates of the churchyard come into view.

The little one-room chapel had been there since the area was first settled in the 1800s. Originally constructed outside of town, it was now firmly within the inner township, and despite the encroaching urban landscape, it maintained a gated park and cemetery.

Although she had walked by it many times, Jessica had never stopped to explore the grounds, feeling somehow she'd be trespassing. As she walked up the long drive, she studied the little white church. It looked sweet, peacefully nestled amongst the surrounding spruce and birch trees.

Thanks to Michiru's speedy pace, they arrived with time to spare and strolled through the grounds, examining the cracked and leaning headstones. Many of them were so abraded by the harsh prairie seasons that the etched names were no longer readable.

While exploring an overgrown section, Jessica heard a man say something sternly in another language. He sounded close.

She whipped around and tripped over a broken head-stone hidden in a thick tuft of grass.

Michiru fumbled in her pocket as the man repeated what sounded like an admonishment.

"W…who's there?" Jessica whispered, blood pounding in her ears.

Michiru chuckled and held up her phone. "It's my ringtone. Dad got tired of Mum freaking out when I missed her calls and recorded a message telling me to answer the phone."

She did. After a brief conversation in what Jessica presumed was Japanese, she shoved the phone into her pocket and rolled her eyes skyward.

"Problem?" asked Jessica. "You can take off if you need to."

"It's just Mum being Mum. She has to know everything I'm doing, who I'm with, and how long I'll be. Sometimes I feel like…I dunno." Michiru's face softened. "I get that she worries, but I wish once in a while she'd trust that I know what I'm doing."

"I don't hear much from my parents unless I've fucked something up," grumbled Jessica. "It'd be kinda nice if they called to ask how my day's going."

"Well, there's caring and there's smothering. Mum would wrap me in cotton balls and lock me in my room if she could get away with it. She's way overprotective. Dad probably would be too, except he knows Mum has the bases covered 24-7. I'm surprised they haven't lo-jacked me yet."

Jessica found the idea of Michiru needing protection vastly amusing. It was far more likely the rest of the world needed it.

It wasn't until Michiru moved to offer a supporting hand to him that Jessica noticed the old man in black priest's garb picking his way over the uneven ground.

"Is one of you the young lady I spoke with the other day?" His words were thickly accented, sounding vaguely German or Russian.

"That's me. Jessica." She extended a hand.

He smiled and gave her a firm handshake, despite his arthritically bowed fingers.

"Please, come inside. It is better to talk without fearing a loss of limb to frostbite, no?"

He shuffled back toward his chapel, motioning for them to follow.

Chapter 22

Once the old man reached the gravel path, Michiru left his side and fell back to walk with Jessica.

They entered the church through arched double doors and walked up the aisle to the first row of aged wooden pews. Jessica turned awkwardly to face the priest as she explained their assignment, her notepad held at the ready on her knee.

He nodded thoughtfully as she spoke, his bushy eyebrows lifting slightly when she mentioned the topic.

"Exorcism." He said the word slowly. "Yes. An interesting and thorny subject. There are those in our order who still adhere to the theory and practice, and those who believe it is an anachronism best left in the past."

"Which are you?" asked Jessica tentatively.

"Neither, and both." He smiled. "I have lived enough to not discount anything."

They progressed into a discussion of the rituals, tools, and recitations used, as well as the religious basis and physiological signs of possession. Although he had no personal experience, he knew several colleagues in Europe who did and outlined the testing they employed to rule out alternate causes such as disease or mental illness.

By the time Jessica paused to look over her notes, she realized forty minutes had gone by. She glanced at Michiru, who was sitting ramrod straight, hands folded in her lap, staring straight ahead. Her eyes were open but unblinking, and Jessica briefly wondered if she had learned to sleep like that.

The priest levered himself off the hard bench. Jessica heard Michiru cough as he suggested they retire to his cottage to look over some books and letters. She suspected the cough covered a groan, but she couldn't be sure, as Michiru's expression was carefully neutral.

After the priest made an obeisance toward the altar and cross, both she and Michiru followed suit, and they trooped back down the aisle.

Michiru peered beseechingly at Jessica behind his back.

Jessica mouthed, "Sorry," but blazing curiosity quickly swamped her pang of guilt. The priest was obviously a scholar and well connected to people still practicing exorcisms. What treasures would he have in his private collection?

As they passed a dark rosewood cabinet, Jessica did a double take and stumbled to a stop. Pointing to a dark, shriveled lump inside a glass display box, she asked, "What's that?" Her voice rose in excitement.

The old man turned to look and smiled broadly. "Ah. How appropriate you should ask. It is the glove of Saint Aloysius—a most wonderful relic. He is the patron saint of students." He fondly patted Jessica on the head. "You are a very perceptive young lady. It has been with me since my time as a deacon in Poland. So many years ago now."

He sighed and opened the lid. "I must look as ancient and shriveled to you as this relic. But old is not always weak." He grinned at them, picked up the relic, and knocked it against the cabinet top.

Both girls gasped, but closed their mouths upon hearing the solid thunk it made against the wood.

"I keep it in here so dust does not get into the folds. Glass is much easier to clean." He put it back in the case and closed the lid. "Old does not mean useless, as many young people are wont to think nowadays. But you two are different, are you not? You can see."

Missing Jessica's eyes widening, he continued, "This relic is a powerful connection to the past. It is our job, this relic and mine, to unite old and new. Understanding what has happened to us, our world, and our universe is vital when looking to the future. History is wisdom. It gives roots to young saplings, so that they may thrive. When old and new combine, humanity grows and each of us becomes something greater."

He gave them a rueful smile and resumed shuffling down the aisle. "Forgive me. I am lecturing. I should know better. Many times have I learnt more from listening to students than speaking to them, but still I fall into this trap. I am afraid my time teaching at the Vatican has made me prone to losing my mind in thought."

"I know how that feels." said Jessica, sharing a knowing look with the priest.

Michiru poked her in the side and discreetly gestured to a bulletin board near the door.

Jessica cringed when she saw the poster with a color photograph of Hamish reading, "Lost Beagle. $100 reward." It was tacked up with several other lost dog and cat notices.

She recognized Bill's home phone number, which at least answered the question about whether Hamish was his.

Jessica leaned close to Michiru and whispered, "Guess I'll be walking him at night from now on. Either that, or I'll have to find him a doggie disguise. Think I could make him look like a potbelly pig?"

Michiru waved at her to be quiet as the priest looked back at them. She moved quickly to take his arm and directed him out the door, smiling sweetly.

Jessica followed behind, trying to figure out what to do with Hamish.

* * *

They arrived at the priest's cottage after a slow but steady stroll through the graveyard. Jessica and the priest retired to his study, and Michiru settled onto a comfortably worn couch in the living room.

She was relieved to be alone. So far, she hadn't needed to say much, but the more time they spent with the priest, the guiltier she felt. He was a sweet old guy and what had started as a harmless charade now seemed more like a big fat lie. So much for being the bad girl.

Michiru eased into a meditative trance, clearing her mind with a chant. She evened out her breathing and slowed her heart until her body fully relaxed. She came out of it feeling calmer, but no less guilty or confused.

How Jessica was able to decipher the old man's convoluted explanations was a mystery. And she was equally impressed that he had kept up with Jessica's rapid-fire questions. His body may be frail, but his mind was razor-sharp.

She spent some time trying to develop a plan to dissuade Jessica from wandering the streets alone at night with Hamish. Hopefully she'd been joking, but Michiru had no baseline to determine her level of self-preservation. Bill had outright challenged her ability to defend Jessica, and she didn't intend to give him any easy opportunities.

After what felt like an eternity, the priest and Jessica returned, avidly discussing the influences of Latin on modern English. Jessica glowed with contentment as the priest saw them out.

He stood on his doorstep, giving both of them warm handshakes.

"I do hope you will stop by to see me again," he said to Jessica. "I do not often meet youngsters so interested in religious matters. I fear the younger generations slip further from God and the old ways with each passing day." His already stooped shoulders slouched lower as he gazed at his little chapel's silhouette.

A chill wind flattened the grass in the churchyard and the hushed rustling of leaves swelled into a spirited chorus. He shivered as amber birch leaves fluttered to the ground and playfully chased each other through the leaning gravestones. Casting a last melancholy look at his church, he nodded politely to the girls, and withdrew into the shelter of his rectory.

Jessica and Michiru walked down the winding drive in silence until the main gate appeared around the corner.

"So what now?" Michiru asked.

"I have a plan in mind, but it's not completely worked out, especially not after the boatload of info Nick gave me." She let out a long breath. "But there's one constant, no wiggle room: You need to be in control of the host's body during an exorcism. He said some seriously bad stuff can happen if they get free in the middle." Jessica threw her arms out to her sides, hands spread wide. "What if I'm wrong? What if Bill's just a psycho asshole and I'm imagining things? He's not going to volunteer to sit still for an exorcism, and I'm not about to bash him over the head and tie him up! Oh! That reminds me." She grabbed Michiru's arm.

Michiru tensed, narrowly preventing herself from evading.

"I almost forgot to tell you," Jessica continued, oblivious. "The relic in there glowed like your necklace, only brighter. And if your necklace makes Bill uncomfortable..." Her voice trailed off. "I wonder if he'd let me take it to school as part of the project?" She released Michiru's arm and patted it absently. "I need to think on that a bit more. It might be useful, but I'm not sure he'd part with it."

They walked for a ways in companionable silence.

"So..." Jessica began, staring at the ground. "You're sure you don't want to go to the police about Bill?"

"Absolutely not." Michiru replied instantly. She was just starting to get used to Coldwater. "You?"

"Nope." Jessica kicked a drift of leaves piled along the fence line.

"If it helps, I don't think it would do any good." Michiru offered. "Even if they arrested him, he'd be out on bail in no time, and we'd be back to square one. Plus, you did steal his dog. That's not going to win you any credibility."

Jessica's face reddened. "This is so fucked up."

Michiru sensed the walls slamming back into place around Jessica. Today, with the priest, she had come out of her self-imposed shell and her whole personality changed—she held herself straighter, her eyes sparked with energy, and her voice was confident. Michiru had been shocked to realize Jessica was an inch taller than her. All of that was gone now.

"Thanks for coming with me." Jessica's voice sounded husky. Her face was half-hidden by her hair—just one deep green eye was visible behind the shimmering copper veil. "I didn't mean to get you involved in all this."

Michiru considered her words carefully.

"Listening to you and the priest talk brought some things

home for me. I've never seriously considered there might be…what did he call them…'malevolent spirits.' I've seen evil acts, heard evil words, probably even met some truly evil people, but they were all real…" She struggled to find the right word. "Tangible. I can deal with tangible. Spirits…not so much. And the fact that I can't even see some things…let's just say, I'm willing to run with you for a while to see if things get any clearer."

Michiru watched a leaf float across the sidewalk and land in a puddle of ditch water. She crouched and plucked the golden scrap out of the mud, offering it up to the wind once more. Watching as it merrily whirled away to find another resting spot, she pushed herself back upright.

"And there's another reason," she added. "I didn't know Chris as long as you, but it was long enough to know that he was a good person. If there's a chance to kick the ass of whatever's responsible for his death, you'd better believe I'm in."

Jessica's lips curved into a small, shy smile.

Michiru slid an arm around her shoulders. "And it's not your fault I'm involved. I'm the one who barged in on your great escape."

* * *

Later that night, Jessica's phone buzzed. She hit the spacebar on her laptop, freezing the movie she was watching, and hunted through the pile of papers and books on her bed. She found her phone holding a place in the *Wheel of the Wiccan Year* book and read Drew's text:

>> stuck in hell again. what u up 2?

Jessica smirked and responded:

<< chillin w zombies

>> cold keeps the smell down?

<< lol just a movie. night of living dead

>> ooo remake or orig?

<< the old bw 1

>> sounds fun. sigh

<< :(

>> meant 2 call earlier. saw uncle today. was more scattered than usual but maybe something useful

Jessica hesitated with her fingers hovering over the keypad, waiting for a follow-up text. When nothing appeared after a few seconds, she sent a quick query:

<< and?

No reply.

She stared at the phone for half a minute, humphed, and then bounced off her bed. She searched out Hamish and found him sleeping amongst her shoes at the bottom of her closet, legs in the air. Even so, she was extra careful as she crept out of her room. The little bugger could move fast when he wanted.

With the door safely closed behind her, she went downstairs to make herself tea. Her dad was in the office on the computer, door half-closed. The living room was dark.

Mom must have gone to bed already. Good.

Thankfully, Hamish wasn't big on barking. *Probably because he puts all his energy into chewing,* she thought grimly. So far, her parents had passed off the few barks he'd let loose as coming from outside, but that wouldn't last forever.

If she managed to keep a lid on things until next Friday when her parents headed to Zurich for a week, she was golden. Surely, she could work something out before they came back.

She grabbed a mug and teabag and put the kettle on. It was on its way to boiling when her phone buzzed. She yanked it out of her pocket to read:

>> sorry. minor grease fire. what's hell without flames

right?

Jessica snorted.

<< hope everyones ok. so...back 2 ur uncle?

The kettle clicked. She filled her cup and stared at her phone. Eventually he replied.

>> yes. took all afternoon. he walks when worried. didn't get much about possession. just looked annoyed. said the warden knew what 2 do? no idea

Jessica swallowed her disappointment and keyed in a reply:

<< thanx anyway. hope ur night gets more interesting...or maybe less!

She'd been holding out hope that Drew's uncle would know something to make the problem go away. But easy outs never seemed to present themselves. Not to her, anyway.

She was pulling the milk out of the fridge when another text came in.

>> he said some other stuff. don't know what's important. said reality was thin. a new beginning. something about other worlds? again, no idea

It twigged something in her memory. Something she'd just read in a book. She stood in front of the open fridge, cold air raising goose bumps on her arms. Something about a new year...she typed out an excited response to Drew.

<< no. that's perfect. gave me idea. maybe we don't have 2 directly deal w bill after all. yay

A loud "Jessica!" from behind made her jump. She squeaked as she smacked her elbow on the fridge door and sent it crashing into the counter. Turning, she saw her dad.

"How many times have I told you not to stand there with the refrigerator door open? You may not pay the bills around here, but I assume you have some concern for the environment?"

Jessica flushed. "Sorry." She closed the fridge, rubbing a finger over the slight dent in the counter's wooden edging. "Got distracted."

He sighed when he saw her phone. "Texting again. I should have known. How on earth do you find so much to talk about?" He retreated to his office without waiting for an answer. "Don't be up too late."

"I won't," she replied, putting as much false cheer into her voice as she could.

Not like I could possibly have anything important going on.

Jessica finished up her tea, liberated a stack of shortbread cookies from the tin, and headed back to her room. She checked her phone on the way and saw there was a new message.

>> ? do I still get 2 meet uma thurman?

Jessica pondered the baffling text and then giggled, realizing she hadn't used Bill's name when she talked to Drew before.

<< sorry bill=possessed guy. no sword fights i really hope

>> ok. 2 bad

<< :P can u come over tomorrow aft? going 2 need ur help with plan

>> sure thing. c u about 2

Jessica practically skipped upstairs. There were still facts to check, but she felt some of the roiling anxiety in the pit of her stomach shrink. She had a PLAN!

Chapter 23

By Sunday afternoon, Jessica felt reasonably confident she had a workable plan to deal with Bill. She just couldn't bring herself to say it out loud. It had seemed logical in her head, but that morning, when she had practiced describing it, the words came out all wrong.

And now, Jessica sat across from Michiru and Drew in her living room, trying to work up the nerve to speak.

Drew stretched an arm across the back of the couch and gave Michiru an appraising look. "So…you're Mac. From what Jess said, I thought you'd be ten feet tall and have lightning flying from your eyes."

Michiru raised an eyebrow at Jessica and scooped up a handful of nuts from a bowl on the coffee table.

"I never said anything like that." Jessica glared at Drew. "I told him about our encounter with Bill. That's all."

"I see." Michiru tossed an almond into her mouth and gave Drew a quick once over. "She described you as an outdoorsy techie, but you seem a little light on the outdoorsy part. I suppose you do kinda remind me of a grasshopper—long legs, loud chirp."

"Thanks for noticing my legs. I can see how someone challenged in the height department might be envious." He turned back to Jessica. "So, are you going to fill us in, or what?"

Jessica forced her voice into action. "I know. I know. I'm trying to figure out how to explain things without sounding like a total wingnut."

"I wouldn't worry about that if I were you," said Drew. "Some of us seem pretty fond of nuts."

Michiru ignored him and expertly caught a hazelnut in her mouth. "Come on, Jess. Your plan can't be any crazier than the other things we've talked about."

"Um…" Jessica paused, repeating what Michiru had said in her mind. "Was that supposed to be reassuring? Because it really wasn't."

"I call it like I see it. I'm here, and I assume he is too," she jerked a thumb at Drew, "because we want to know what's up with Bill and if we can help you out. So talk."

Jessica took a deep breath. "Okay. Bear with me. Rabies was the closest physical illness matching Bill's symptoms, but given that he was drooling at me on Monday, he really should be dead or paralyzed by now, so I've ruled that out. Honestly, there's a host of mental illnesses that fit his weird behaviors, but they don't explain why his eyes are funky or why Michiru's pendant burnt his hand. Based on what Father Nick said and my own research, possession, however implausible, is the only explanation that fits all his symptoms and behaviors. I think Chris was originally possessed while using the Ouija board and when he…made himself unavailable, whatever was in him jumped into the nearest warm body, Bill. It makes sense, except that it sounds totally crazy. I—"

"Hold up." Drew waved to get Jessica's attention. "Could he have some kind of parasite in his eye that looks like a shadow when it moves?"

Jessica shook her head. "If that's the case, Mac would have seen it. And she didn't."

Drew looked at Michiru and she nodded. "Yeah. His eyes looked normal to me."

"Maybe you missed it?"

Michiru popped another nut into her mouth. "Unlikely. I got several really close looks. And like Jessica said, there's my necklace. He reacted when he touched it, pulled away like it burnt him. That's not normal."

"Allergy?" Drew asked, sounding somewhat unconvinced himself.

Michiru gave him an incredulous look. "To jade?"

"Actually, I wondered about that too, so I looked it up." Jessica straightened in her chair. "I couldn't find any cases of allergic reactions to jade. Lots of articles about mineral allergies, but nothing for pure natural stones, which I'm assuming your necklace is, because of its age."

Michiru nodded.

"Okay," said Drew. "That all sounds reasonable, relatively speaking. Just wanted to make sure the basics were covered. Carry on."

"Right. Possession." Jessica backtracked to where she had left off. "There's lots of stories about possessions…and when I say lots, think millions." She rubbed her temples, remembering the hundreds of likely hits she'd scanned over the last few days. "People from all over the world and all through history have described similar events. You know the saying, 'A person's eyes are windows to their soul'? Well, turns out you can take that literally. There are tons of reports about possessed people having something wrong with their eyes. And it's also typical for objects with religious or cultural significance to be harmful to possessing spirits.

"Which brings me to Mac's necklace." Jessica pulled a folded wad of notes from her pocket and consulted them. "I looked up the design and found out it's a family crest for the Minamoto clan. It's also associated with a city in Japan called Kamakura, which is associated with the same clan. Are your parents from that area?"

"I don't know. They don't talk about Japan much." Michiru ran a finger along the central bamboo leaf in her pendant.

"You should read up on the clan. It's fascinating. This Emperor had forty-nine kids and couldn't support all of them, so he demoted some from royalty to nobility and gave them the clan name Minamoto. Forty-nine kids. Can you imagine?"

Drew grinned. "I'm trying."

Jessica tossed a pillow at him and continued, "Anyway...sorry for the digression. Japanese history is way too interesting. Where was I..." She looked up at the ceiling. "Right. The necklace. So it's not a religious symbol, but it's definitely culturally important. If we have any more run-ins with Bill, keep it front and center. I'm worried the ghost or skinwalker or whatever it is might try to possess someone else if it thinks Bill is in trouble, like it did when Chris died, so we should avoid physical contact."

After stopping to take a swig of water, Jessica plowed on. "Okay. So that's what I think is going on. Now. What to do about it. Halloween is on Tuesday. A lot of what I've read says working with spirits is easier on Halloween—something to do with the barrier between the living and dead worlds being thin. I've looked through a bunch of rituals and I think I've come up with a way to send the spirit back to wherever it came from. And the best part is, we don't need to do a full exorcism, so we don't have to kidnap Bill."

She glanced at Drew. "I know Halloween isn't a First Nations thing, but what your uncle said about different worlds made me think of it."

"Great." Drew grabbed some nuts from the dwindling supply. "At least it made sense to someone."

"Well, 'sense' might be a bit optimistic." Jessica grinned at him. "There's not a whole lot of that going around lately." She grew more serious. "Now, the hard part. We have two problems. Number one: I need a personal item from Bill and I don't know how to get it. Number two: I need to find the Ouija board and I don't know where it is or if it's even still around. For all I know, someone threw it away. I hope you guys have some suggestions, because I'm dry."

She finished abruptly and nervously sipped her water. The room was silent. Even Michiru paused, mid-crunch. Her expression was blank, though Jessica thought she detected a pensive tilt to her head.

"Bet you wish we'd done the ghost booth for our science project." Drew stroked his chin. "Just think of all the lost opportunities for project material we're going to rack up."

Michiru emerged from her thoughts and resumed chewing. "I don't know about the Ouija board, but getting something of Bill's shouldn't be hard." She petted Hamish who had curled up on the couch between her and Drew. "I mean, you could even use Hamish since he's Bill's dog."

Hamish opened an eye, gazed adoringly at Michiru, and wiggled onto his side so she could rub his tummy.

Jessica grimaced. "Umm…well, the ritual involves burning the item, so no."

"Yikes. Okay…what about his collar, then?" Michiru suggested.

"It's not that simple." Pink crept across Jessica's cheeks. "We need something with…um…well something that has been very close to Bill."

Michiru leaned forward in interest. "Like what?"

Jessica focused on the puppy. "Hair, skin, fingernail…" The pinkness deepened to crimson. "Underwear." She muttered the last word and both Michiru and Drew strained to hear.

"What was that last bit?" asked Drew.

Jessica sighed. "Underwear. We either need part of his body or an item that has something from his body on it. So anything with saliva, blood, sweat…um…other fluids will do. Underwear was mentioned as the best."

Drew sat back on the couch with a disgusted look. "Well. I vote you two handle the ginch collection. He won't be tossing any in my direction." Both girls leveled identical exasperated looks at him. "Or…we can follow him around with swabs and hope he'll gnaw on another teacher. When does his suspension end?"

"Tuesday," Michiru said matter-of-factly. "I checked. In any case, I've got it covered."

Jessica's embarrassment turned to concern and Michiru reassured her, "Seriously. Don't worry. I've got an idea. I should be able to get the goods by Monday afternoon."

"But you just said he won't be back until Tuesday. How…" Drew fell silent as Michiru glared at him.

"She didn't say it had to be fresh." Michiru looked back at Jessica. "It doesn't, does it?"

"I don't think so." Jessica frowned as she set her glass on the coffee table. "Listen. I don't want any of us in direct contact with him. If you're planning on paying a visit to his house, forget it."

Michiru shook her head. "I think there's something at

school. And as we've established he won't be there on Monday," she narrowed her eyes at Drew, "it should be even easier."

After a slight pause, Jessica nodded. "All right. So that leaves the Ouija board." She pursed her lips.

Drew snatched the last nut from the bowl. Casting a triumphant look at Michiru, he popped it into his mouth and addressed Jessica. "You've only seen the board in a dream, right?" When Jessica nodded, he continued, "And you said they were talking about lunch being almost over, which means it happened at school. So describe the area."

Jessica closed her eyes and rested her head against the chair back. "It was dark, but I think it was a large space. Their voices sounded echoey. Unless that was just the dream." She frowned in concentration. "There were large, weirdly shaped objects, cords on the ground, maybe a wrench. And I think the floor was concrete." Her eyes shot open. "Some kind of maintenance room?"

Drew stood up and paced. "I've seen most of them and they're small, more like closets, really. We could check out the ones I haven't seen, to make sure. I was more thinking the machine shop. It's big and has lots of random equipment."

"Could be." Jessica shrugged. "I've never been."

"Bobby takes shop class. I'll see if he can let us in tomorrow, sometime when it isn't busy. From what you said, it sounds like the Ouija group ran off in a hurry. Probably didn't stop to clean up. Maybe the board's still where they left it, or…there's also a big dumpster outside the shop bay. It could be in there. Gives us a couple places to start looking anyway."

He settled back on the couch, catching one of Hamish's flailing paws as the puppy rolled toward him and started gnawing on his jacket cuff. "You need some toys to sharpen your teeth on, don't you, little fella?" Drew extracted his sleeve and tickled the dog's pink tummy.

"His teeth are plenty sharp." Jessica harrumphed, mentally listing all the furniture, books, and clothes in her room that could testify to that fact, not to mention her toes.

"Too bad I already have a task." Michiru grinned. "I'll have to miss the dumpster diving."

"Let's hope it doesn't come to that." Jessica watched the beagle flop back and forth between Michiru and Drew. With them competing for his attention, at least the house was safe. Hamish had two modes: sleep and destroy.

"Wait," Jessica groaned. "Slight issue. Won't the maintenance rooms be locked?"

"You'd think." Drew caught the smug look Michiru gave him as she shifted into a cross-legged position. Hamish immediately deserted him and curled up in her lap.

Drew turned his attention back to Jessica. "The janitors aren't that careful. Gerard, this guy I met in social studies, came across an open one last week and found a pack of smokes and turkey sandwich." He shook his head. "Anyway, if the machine shop doesn't pan out, we can check the maintenance rooms…and the dumpster. In that order."

"And if the recent burglary has convinced them to start locking up?" asked Michiru.

"Nah." Drew chuckled. "Gerard heard one of the cleaners accusing the other of eating his supper. Said it was funny as hell. The guy got so mad he threw a bucket of mop water."

"Nice." Michiru didn't sound impressed. "So, back to the plan. You mentioned something about Halloween and a ritual?"

"Right." Jessica fleshed out her idea as she spoke. "Actually, I'm glad Drew mentioned finding ground zero. If we can locate where the spirit initially came though, I think that's where we should do the ritual. It might make things easier…or make things work…" She scratched the back of her neck. "Honestly, I'm not sure. I'm working with a lot of unknowns."

"How involved is the ritual?" Michiru pulled her attention away from Hamish, who was now snoring contentedly.

"I'll do a run-through tonight, but I think it'll take about half an hour, set-up to finish."

Michiru chewed her thumbnail and then said, "That's a long time to go without being interrupted. And you said something about burning Bill's…contribution? A fire isn't going to go over well after what happened to that girl last week."

"Listen, I know there's problems." Jessica fussed with the hem of her T-shirt. "But this is our best chance. There's a dance Tuesday night. Everyone will be in the gym, so as long as we can sneak off to wherever this happened, we should be pretty safe."

Drew let out a snort. "And really…a trained monkey could disable a smoke detector."

"I don't like it," Michiru said, aiming a glare at Drew. "There's too many variables we can't control."

"Welcome to my world," snapped Jessica. "I've never done anything like this. Never even considered something like this could be done. You're talking about the mundane details, but all I can think about is the weird shit behind this ritual. I mean…banishing a spirit that's possessed someone? I still can't wrap my mind around that one." She stopped pulling at her shirt and looked at Michiru, whose face was set like granite.

Jessica sighed. "Listen. We don't even know if we'll be able to find where my dream happened, or if the board is still around, or maybe you won't be able to get something of Bill's. Let's just cross each bridge as we come to it, okay?"

"Agreed." Michiru narrowed her eyes. "But doing this at school is a bad idea. I don't mind taking risks; I just don't see the point in taking unnecessary ones. And I'll get what you need from Bill. Don't worry about that."

"I know." She reminded Jessica of a bullet; once aimed and fired, Michiru would relentlessly plow through anything to find her way to the target.

"Ah, shit." Drew slapped his forehead.

Jessica and Michiru stared at him.

"I have to cancel on Mom. I'm supposed to help her at the restaurant Tuesday. They've pretty much given up on Neave at this point. She's really buggered off. Nobody's heard a peep from her."

"I'm in a similar boat. I need to find a way to gracefully back out of a date." Jessica bit her lip as she thought about how disappointed Eric would be, how disappointed she was. At least his part of their matching costume was more-or-less normal.

Drew clapped his hands, making the girls jump and eliciting a groan from Hamish.

"What are dates and dishes compared to fighting evil?" He rubbed his hands together. "This is going to be fun."

Jessica wished she shared even a shred of his exuberance. It was all she could do to keep struggling forward.

Chapter 24

Jessica checked her watch for the third time and then resumed staring at the huge bay door. "You sure Bobby's coming?"

Drew leaned against the brick wall. "Relax. Have a smoke." He offered a cigarette and she backed away, waving a hand to clear the air.

"You're not supposed to smoke on school grounds." She coughed as a waft blew past her. "Plus it's gross."

"You're also not supposed to skip class and break into the machine shop, and yet, here you are."

"Don't remind me." Jessica scanned the parking lot, expecting to see a teacher pop out from behind every car, tree, and corner. "I don't like this sneaking around."

Drew raised his face to the sky and closed his eyes contentedly. "The gravel will give us fair warning if someone comes by. You worry too much."

"Really?" Her voice rose with incredulity. "We've got a human torch, possessed people, and a wolf-girl running around town…and you think I worry too much? Maybe I'm not worried enough."

Drew took a long draw on his cigarette and contemplated

Jessica. She flinched as if she'd been shot when a fat magpie landed in the grass beside them.

"Fair enough," he agreed. "Worry about all that, but don't lose any sleep over skipping class. Besides, the sun is shining and we're not stuck in computer class listening to idiots complain about how hard it is to sort spreadsheet data. It's not all doom and gloom."

"True. You're sure we'd hear someone coming?"

"Yup. Here, if you want something to do, why don't you check the dumpster?" He waved at the massive orange container stationed between the machine shop's two overhead doors. "If this is where your dream happened, the board might have ended up in there."

Jessica walked around the dumpster, stood on her tiptoes, and stretched an arm up. She couldn't reach the top edge. Looking around for something to stand on, she spotted an empty paint can and kicked the dirty cylinder to the side of the bin.

Drew watched, amused, as she tried several times to balance on the lopsided can, and then took pity on her.

Catching Jessica as the can scooted out from under her, he said, "As funny as this is, I don't feel like a trip to Emerg." He linked his fingers and bent forward, ready to give her a leg up.

Jessica glanced between him and the dumpster. "Wait a minute. You're taller. Why don't you do it?"

"Yeah, here's the thing." He looked up without changing position. "Don't let this svelte figure fool you. That bin is taller than me, I'm not particularly athletically inclined, and I can't see you being able to help me up. It's better this way. Trust me."

After a moment, Jessica placed a foot in his cupped

hands. "Fine. I'll give it a try."

She stepped up and hooked an arm over the metal rim. Drew swayed under her weight as she wiggled, trying to lift herself up to see over the edge.

Jessica's knee connected with something solid as she struggled and all support from below vanished. Feeling her arms slipping, she scrabbled her feet against the rusted bin, failed to find purchase, and fell. She landed heavily and tripped over Drew's outstretched leg.

Gravel dug into her elbow as she hit the ground. She rolled onto her back and saw Drew sitting propped against the dumpster rubbing his forehead.

"That went about as well as I expected," she said, easing into a sitting position and brushing herself off.

Drew spat out the remains of his broken cigarette and winced as he tentatively felt his forehead. "I think it's safe to say neither of us is athletically inclined. Let's—"

Hinges squealed and Bobby poked his head out of the shop's man door. He stared at the strange dumpster tableau, clearly baffled.

"I miss a fight or something?"

"Just enjoying the sun." Drew picked himself up and held a hand out to Jessica. "I'm demoting the dumpster to plan C, preferably after we've liberated a ladder from one of the maintenance rooms."

Nodding vigorously, she waved him away and levered herself up.

* * *

Drew sauntered over to Bobby, massaging his head to dull the ache. "Any complications?"

"Not yet. I'm the only one here. Miller let me in to work

on my project and then buggered off to the caf. He'll be gone for a while." Bobby held the spring-loaded door open, moving slightly to let them by his bulky frame.

Drew squinted in the darkness. The smell of burnt oil and hot metal hung heavy in the air.

Jessica limped past Bobby, each of them warily eyeing the other.

Once they were inside, Bobby let the door swing closed. The ear-piercing screech of rusted hinges terminated with a heavy thunk. He moved to Drew's side and they watched Jessica turn in a slow circle, surveying the cavernous machine shop.

"Were you two—?" Bobby began, but Drew cut him off.

"For the last time…no." He elbowed Bobby to wipe the smirk off his face. "It's not like that. She's a friend."

Drew shook his head and joined Jessica. "Anything look familiar?"

Jessica nodded and began picking her way through the labyrinth of wood and metal. He followed, interested.

"I remember seeing two walls, so they must have been in a corner." She looked around. "Not this one. There was more space between the machines." She squinted at the distant corners.

"You lose something?"

Jessica and Drew jumped as Bobby's voice cut across their thoughts.

She sent Drew a pleading look and he nodded, getting that she didn't want an audience.

He offered Bobby a cigarette and ushered him away. "So…what's this project you're working on? Anything interesting?"

Bobby glanced over his shoulder as he popped the cigarette into his mouth and patted his pockets for a lighter. Drew held his out, leading him further away.

He lit his cigarette and pocketed the lighter. "Just something I'm doing for the welding unit. It's not going well." He scowled and kicked a glob of metal fused to the floor.

The fact that Bobby was actually concerned about a school assignment tweaked Drew's curiosity. "Can I see?"

"Sure. But no wisecracks. I know it's crap." He led Drew to a long table, bowing under the weight of mostly unidentifiable metal objects. Bobby pointed to a welded raven mask.

Drew gazed in admiration at the intricately crafted seams and edges, brilliantly fashioned into a detailed replica of a dancing mask. If it wasn't for the distinct metallic patina, he'd expect it to caw and fly off.

"You did this?"

When Bobby grumbled his acknowledgement, Drew leaned across the table to examine it more closely. "So, what's the problem? It looks great."

"It's too fucking heavy." Bobby scowled. "I was making it for Cal to use at the powwow, but it'd snap his neck. I can barely lift it and I haven't even finished adding the neck and crest feathers yet. It's garbage."

Drew stared at the mask. He'd known Bobby all his life and never guessed he carried this in him. Bobby. The guy who had phoned bomb threats into their school every day for a week because he couldn't be bothered to put air in his bike tires.

"You moron." Drew turned to face his friend. "It doesn't matter if it's wearable. It's an awesome piece of art."

"Seriously?" Bobby looked like he was trying to figure out what the punch line was.

"Damn straight. This should be in a gallery. Nice going, buddy." Drew clapped him on the back. "I didn't even know you could weld."

"Me either." He shrugged self-consciously. "You were right." Drew raised an eyebrow and he continued. "When you said we had a good thing here. Our old school didn't have any of this, but I'm going to ask the council for it when they rebuild."

A loud clang drew their attention. Jessica had knocked a wheel rim off a pile of parts beside a car lift.

Bobby inhaled, long and slow, on his cigarette. The end glowed bright orange in the darkness. "That chick is weird. What's she looking for?"

"Who knows. Anyway…" Drew ran a finger over the eye and beak. "Why's this a different color? You use another metal or something?"

Bobby was soon oblivious to all else as he poured out information. Drew listened, amazed. Never in a million years would he have imagined Bobby discussing the melting points of different alloys and the merits of welding vs. braising.

* * *

Everything about the place felt right to Jessica. She just needed to find the spot. She checked the time and groaned.

Fifteen minutes down. How much longer will our luck hold?

Jessica quickly worked her way through the machinery. When she drew near the next corner, a wave of heat washed over her right hand and up her arm. She lurched to a stop and retreated several steps. The burning sensation eased.

She examined her arm, half afraid it was some kind of karmic blowback from her failure with Lindsey, but it was fine. Definitely not on fire.

Her gaze traveled over the shadowed corner and her scalp tingled.

This section of the bay contained an array of wheeled

tool cases and pitted workbenches. Carts with saws, drill press-
es, and other equipment in various states of disassembly lined
one of the walls. Thick bundles of colorful cords spilled from a
box to one side, and shattered bits of plastic and warped metal
trailed across the floor to another crate labeled "RIP."

Jessica dragged her gaze away from the morbidly accurate
label.

This is it. Dread and relief warred inside. *This is where it
started. Where Chris really died.*

Taking a deep breath, Jessica moved forward. She ignored the heat prickling her arm and the little voice inside
screaming at her to run. In her head, she screamed back, *No!*
She had to keep going.

She walked toward the machine carts and the burning in
her arm lessened. Jessica glared at the appendage.

Figures. Guess the old "no pain, no gain" cliché finally makes sense.

Grinding her teeth, Jessica followed the pain to a large,
upright toolbox. Several drawers stood open on the rusted case,
displaying a range of hammers and chisels.

A rectangular beam of light shot across the bay as the
door to the hall opened. A middle-aged man wearing dark blue
overalls shuffled in, pushing a projector.

Drew ducked under the table he had been standing behind and Bobby spat his cigarette out, making a beeline for the
teacher who was headed in Jessica's direction.

Jessica winced, hoping there was nothing flammable or
explosive where the cigarette landed.

*On the other hand, a minor explosion would make a great distrac-
tion.*

She crouched behind the toolbox, wondering when she
had become so mercenary.

Her arm throbbed as she frantically searched for an escape route. The corner of a flat piece of wood under a neighboring toolbox drew her attention. It was non-descript except for a faint green aura above the lacquered surface. Jessica dropped onto all fours to get a better look and gasped as she recognized the stylized moon.

There were also two sets of shoes, approaching fast.

Jessica glared at the Ouija board.

Great. Now what?

The projector cart's squeaky wheels stopped a few feet away and she listened as Bobby spoke to the man. "…just take a look. I'm sure you can tell me what to use."

"Listen. I've got another damn projector to take apart. It's the fourth one down and we've only got six. I don't have time to fix your project. Figure it out yourself."

"But you're the teacher, aren't you supposed to…you know…teach?"

She heard a loud clang as a heavy object dropped onto the table. "Yeah, well, right now I'm a projector repairman. And I can tell you were smoking. If I can't smoke in here, neither can you. Now, shoo…I got work to do."

Jessica could tell from his tone that he wasn't going to budge. She glanced back at the board. Even the thought of touching it stoked the pain in her arm to excruciating levels. She ground her teeth. Stalemate.

A table saw on the other side of the bay whirred and a shower of sparks erupted from the blade. There was a series of clinks and clashes as pieces of metal hit the floor, and the sparks stopped.

"What the hell?" The teacher took off at a run to investigate.

Jessica seized her chance. She reached into an open drawer, grabbed a hammer, and used it to nudge the Ouija board further under the toolbox.

Nobody's found it yet. It'll keep until tomorrow.

She backed away, still crouched, and ran into the work-bench. The abrupt halt knocked her off balance and she reached out to grab the table leg for support. Her hand encountered something lumpy and smooth on the wood.

She peered back and her heart stopped.

A black, amorphous mass dripped down the leg.

Jessica barely stifled a scream and let go, feeling as though her limbs were moving in slow motion. She was about to run, not caring if she was caught, when the solidity of the mass finally registered.

Its shape gave the impression of movement, but no inky tentacles reached for her. She poked it with the hammer and started breathing again.

It was wax. Leftovers from the candles she had seen burning in her vision.

The metallic whine of the saw stopped and she took off in a scuttling run for the back door, hoping Bobby was still in distraction mode. She rounded a rack of sheet metal and bar stock and collided with Drew.

"Holy shit." She gasped. "We are so dead!"

"Not yet." He headed toward the door, keeping low and moving swiftly between shadow and cover. Jessica saw him grab something from a shelving unit as he passed.

She followed his route as best she could, not daring to look over her shoulder. When they reached the door, he motioned for her to stay down and squirted the contents of an oil canister along the hinge side of the door. Jessica watched as the glistening liquid slid down the doorframe and onto the floor, thinking she didn't need a prophetic dream to tell her someone would be landing on their ass. She hoped it wouldn't be her.

"We need to move quick once the door is open." Drew said, setting the can aside. "The light is going to be a fucking beacon if he looks this way. You go first. I'll be right behind, so don't stop until I say. Got it?"

Jessica nodded and he turned the knob, easing the door open. The hinges squeaked slightly and then became silent. As soon as there was a wide enough gap, she shot through into the sunlight.

Congratulating herself on successfully navigating the pool of oil, she belatedly realized Drew hadn't said where to go. Jessica spun in a frantic circle, half-blinded by the bright light. She had just decided to head for the cars, when Drew blew past and grabbed her arm, uttering a string of swear words.

They charged through rows of vehicles until he pulled her down behind an SUV. They were both panting like overheated dogs.

"You suck at following directions." Drew peered around the vehicle. "So far, so good."

"I didn't know which way to go. I told you I wasn't good at this stuff."

Drew rolled his eyes. "No shit." He looked her over and sighed. "No luck, eh? Guess it's the dumpster for us after school."

"No. I found the board. It...I don't think it's a good idea to move it. We have to come back anyways to do the ritual."

"I'm not sure if you have the worst luck of anyone I know, or the best. Mac's not going to like this." His teeth flashed in a wide grin. "Can't wait to see her face when you tell her."

Jessica groaned. "One crisis at a time, please." She worked up the nerve to look and was relieved to see that the shop door was still closed. "Can Bobby let us back in tomorrow night?"

"No need." Drew grinned and held up a roll of duct tape. "That door won't be latching anytime soon."

"Well. I guess we're set then." Her gut did a somersault. "As long as Mac pulls off her part."

"She will." Jessica wiped a sheen of sweat from her upper lip. Drew hadn't seen Michiru in action, so he didn't know. "I'm pretty sure I don't want to know how, but she'll do it."

Chapter 25

The synthesized beat vibrated through the floor and up Jessica's legs as a robotic-voiced singer proclaimed the virtues of being pretty. She rolled her eyes at the shitty music.

Except for a few overplayed Halloween classics, the DJ wasn't making any effort to stay in theme. Unless the theme was crappy pop, then he was doing a stellar job.

Most of her classmates were in costume and had dressed to impress, revealing as much skin as possible, but their choices showed as little imagination as the latest movie releases.

Jessica watched a busty zombie in a bloodied and torn naughty-nurse costume shamble by.

Sexy zombies...really? Ick.

She would have told her to get a life, but doubted the pun would register.

Jessica gave herself a mental slap. Most of the resources she'd read held dire warnings about emotional states affecting the outcome of rituals. *Which means I need to shake this pissy mood before things get started.*

She closed her eyes and counted to ten, concentrating on taking deep, even breaths. It was something her mother told her to do. When she opened her eyes again, she felt well oxygenated, but no less stressed or annoyed.

Yup. Just as useless as it was in kindergarten. Thanks, Mom.

She surveyed the writhing gym, but there was still no sign of Michiru or Drew. Then again, she was half an hour early.

The whirling spotlights and flashing strobes made her dizzy, and the heat of so many bodies pressed together was doing nothing to elevate her mood. She wiped an arm across her damp forehead and sneezed as a feather tickled her nose.

A scandalously dressed angel brushed past, caught her wing on Jessica's costume, and spun her around without so much as a "sorry" or "excuse me."

Angel indeed, she mused, backing up against the wall to smooth her ruffled feathers. She watched a stray indigo feather drift to the floor.

Jessica patted the stuffed belly of her parrot costume. Her phone was somewhere in there and she wanted to make sure the others hadn't texted her. There was no way she'd feel the vibration or hear it ring through all the padding. She eventually located it and confirmed there were no new messages.

Swearing under her breath, Jessica edged along the wall to the refreshment table as unobtrusively as her big orange feet would allow. Although an original slant on the popular pirate theme, her outfit wasn't the easiest to blend into a crowd with. Plus, she was lacking her seaweed-encrusted, shipwrecked pirate, which made the whole thing fall a bit flat. There hadn't been time to put together a different costume, so she was dealing as best she could. Apparently, that involved wanting to eviscerate anyone near her.

I should have come as a pterodactyl.

A group of students by the games tables erupted with laughter as Jessica waddled by. She lowered her head and carried on. The costume had seemed like a good idea at the rental shop. She'd done the bird dance for Eric and he'd ended up with hiccups from laughing so hard. She smiled, remembering how he had wrapped his arms around her, giggling into her feathers. She'd felt warm, and glowy, and safe.

Boxer squawked and asked if she wanted a cracker as she passed. Jessica ignored him. Unlike Eric's, the laughter tonight felt abrasive.

Could be worse, she tried to mollify herself. *If we'd gone with a Greek theme, I could have ended up as the wrong end of Pegasus.*

Her loneliness swelled as she sidled around a kissing couple. The urge to call Eric, to hear his voice, was unbearable, and before she realized it, she had fished out her cell phone.

She was supposed to be at home with the flu.

Jessica stuffed her phone back into the pillowcase she had pinned inside the costume's torso. With so much of her normal life slipping away, she couldn't bear the thought of losing Eric too.

She hoped he was having fun. One of them ought to be. This was her favorite holiday, but she was far too anxious to enjoy any part of it. She'd even forgotten to stock up on cheap chocolate. And she'd miss trick-or-treating, not that it held much appeal this year. It wouldn't be the same without Beth and Eric as her sidekicks, cracking jokes and daring her to switch neighbor's pumpkins.

If change were a real, tangible thing with a face, she'd punch it.

Like a vision of the Holy Grail, a clear plastic bowl filled with red liquid and pieces of fruit materialized in the pulsing light.

Jessica slugged back a cup of the gloriously cool punch, stretched her back, and adjusted her heavy bird belly. The only convenience the outfit afforded was a well-concealed spot to carry her ritual supplies. Unfortunately, that also added to its weight.

Another angel shoved past and tripped over Jessica's protruding toes.

"Watch it, birdbrain," the angel threatened.

The sharp tone of self-righteous indignation was instantly recognizable. Kirsten was the last person who should be wearing a halo. She was also the last person Jessica wanted to deal with right now.

She grated out a clipped "Sorry" and turned to walk away.

Behind her, Kirsten started to laugh. "Jessica? I should have known. Hey, guys. Check out Big Bird's loser cousin, Sweaty Bird."

Kirsten's entourage obediently gathered, blocking Jessica's exit.

She backed into a table, staring at the faces around her, trying to fend off the trapped feeling weighing down her limbs. Colors began to swirl and bob.

Please. Not a panic attack. Not here. Not now.

She dropped her gaze to the floor, trying to slow her breathing. "My...my costume made more sense when I had a pirate."

"I see...and where is the rest of your flock?" Kirsten made a big show of looking around, lifting the black plastic tablecloth to peer underneath. "Hmmm. Not seeing anyone." She glanced meaningfully at Beth and Matt as they arrived.

Beth was dressed in the same Tinker Bell costume Jessica had helped her make last year. She looked gorgeous.

Jessica self-consciously petted her feathery tummy, trying to focus on anything other than the sea of laughing faces.

"Looks like your flock has flown the coop." Kirsten

aimed a sidelong glance at Beth. "What did you see in her?" Kirsten's cold, appraising eyes swiveled back to Jessica. "I suppose there's a certain amusement factor."

Beth just shrugged, and Jessica wished she could sink into the floor.

"Dave got stuck manning the Skull Toss," said Beth. "He promised to give us free tries if we keep him company."

Jessica edged away as Kirsten cast a bored look at the game tables.

"Go if you want. I think this is more fun." Kirsten resumed her icy glare and Jessica's limbs seized up.

Beth walked off, having never even looked at Jessica. Some of the group left with her, thinning the crowd.

"So where is your pirate, anyway? Didn't bother to show? It was only a matter of time. Eric is way out of your league." Kirsten looked her up and down with a toothy grin. Jessica pegged it as an exact duplicate of one she'd seen on a starving hyena in a nature documentary.

With fewer spectators, Jessica found it easier to breathe and her panic morphed into anger. She briefly considered dumping the punch bowl over Kirsten's smug face, picturing the red liquid running down her lily-white costume. Her lips quirked.

Kirsten blinked as Jessica raised flashing eyes to meet hers.

"Find some other way to make yourself feel important Kirsten. I'm tired of listening to your bullshit." Mustering as much dignity as she could, Jessica turned her bulky self around and waddled away.

Only when she had made it to the other side of the gym did she dare to look back. She had to stand on her tiptoes to see the refreshment table over the crowd. Kirsten was gone.

She glanced at her watch.

"So…how many times have you checked that?" Drew's deep voice issued from an amorphous tan colored blob beside her. "I'm not late, you know." His eyes glinted behind two holes cut in the flowing fabric.

Once she got over her surprise, she shoved her belly to the side and hugged him. "You have no idea how glad I am to see you."

"Whoa. Remind me to be on time more often. A guy could get used to this kind of reception." He held her at arm's length as he took in her costume. "Does this mean I won't get slapped if I call you a chick tonight?"

She smacked his arm lightly. "I'm half of a duo that didn't happen." She frowned and pulled up a corner of his sheet to examine it. "Why are you beige?"

"That's a bit racist isn't it?" He harrumphed in mock offence.

Jessica rolled her eyes.

Drew fluffed out his sheet. "Last-minute costume. Figured I couldn't go wrong with the classic Casper. Well, almost classic. This was the closest we had to a white sheet. Mom's going to be pissed when she sees the holes." He chuckled. "I wish you'd told me about yours. I would have dressed up as John Cleese and we could have enacted the Dead Parrot sketch. But, hey, at least I'm totally incognito this way. I couldn't convince any of my buddies to come, so I'm here on my own."

Jessica narrowed her eyes and he backpedaled. "Uh…well, you know…I mean my buddies from the Rez. I didn't…"

She grinned and interrupted, "You aren't the only one who can feign offence. And I think Kirsten already got a start on the Dead Parrot skit. I'm feeling a bit tenderized. Hey, why do we associate white with ghosts, anyway?" Jessica asked. "Why aren't they orange, or purple, or beige?"

"Probably a Christian thing. Most of our spirits look like normal animals or people."

"Interesting." Jessica squinted as a girl in a grass skirt, coconut bra, and colorful lei emerged from the jerking herd on the dance floor. Her eyes widened when she recognized Michiru's lithe stride.

"Hey, guys. Sorry I'm a bit late. Took me a while to work my way over here. You okay?" Michiru waved a hand in front of Jessica's eyes and glanced at the ghost hovering beside her. "Yoo-hoo. Anyone home?"

"Uh. Yeah." Jessica snapped her mouth closed. "It's just that…wow…that's quite the costume."

Michiru grumbled. "Tell me about it. I had it all planned—a pair of shorts, one of Dad's Hawaiian shirts, white socks, sandals, a bit of zinc sunscreen on the nose, and an old camera. Voila! Instant tourist. But no. Mum took over, as usual. Said I needed something more feminine."

She gestured to the coconuts strategically positioned on her chest with lengths of twine wrapped in plastic ivy. "And this is what she did. I mean, she actually went to the supermarket, bought a coconut, and had Dad saw it in half. Can you believe it?"

The parrot and ghost shook their heads in unison.

Michiru adjusted the coconuts. "I'm wearing nuts on my boobs. How is that feminine? Because as far as I can tell, it's just bloody uncomfortable."

Drew cleared his throat. "Technically, it'd be more authentic if you weren't wearing anything up there. Also, more feminine."

"If I have to be here long, that'll be a distinct possibility."

She frowned as Drew coughed. "I still don't like this plan, Jess. There's too many people about."

"This isn't my idea of a good time either. If I thought it would work somewhere else, anywhere else, believe me, I'd be there in a heartbeat." Jessica lost a few feathers as she flapped her arms in frustration.

Michiru stifled a laugh and put a hand on Jessica's shoulder. "Okay. Okay. Calm down. I'm not going to ditch you. And I guess it's not all bad. With this racket going on, we could set off a crate of fireworks and not be heard."

Jessica glanced nervously at the churning crowd. "Any sign of Bill?"

Michiru shook her head. "I talked to some of his friends on the way over. He's supposed to come, but nobody's seen him yet. To be honest, they didn't sound that eager. I think they're hoping he won't show."

"Yeah. I kinda feel the same," said Jessica, "but unfortunately I won't know if the ritual worked until I see him."

"Does that mean we can start without him?" A spark of hope flickered in her eyes.

Jessica chewed her lip, thinking. "We have the Ouija board and you have Bill's...um...item." Michiru nodded and she continued. "So we should be good to go."

Michiru motioned to the gym door. "Then let's do this. The sooner we get it done, the sooner we can all go home, and I can get rid of this torture device."

After Michiru retrieved her jacket from the coat check, the trio made their way to the school's main doors.

Jessica watched the grass skirt sway and part, showing off Michiru's trim legs. "You look really nice." She dropped her head to hide the flush spreading across her face and pretended to smooth out her tummy feathers. She was becoming fond of the soft, round protuberance. It was somehow comforting.

Drew pointed at a volleyball hung over Michiru's shoulder on a length of twine. There was a creepy red jack-o'-lantern face painted on it. "I especially like Wilson. Nice touch."

Michiru snorted as she held the door open for them. "A good volleyball was sacrificed for this. Thanks to Mum, there's nowhere to carry my stuff in this costume." Drew raised a hand and she leveled a warning glare at him. "If you say one thing about available coconut storage, I'll shove them somewhere very uncomfortable."

Drew's hand abruptly returned to his side and Jessica hiccupped as she swallowed a giggle. "I dunno, Drew. Might be worth it."

He shrugged noncommittally under his sheet, but the crinkles visible at the corner of his eyes indicated he was grinning. "Easy for you to say, Chiquita. You wouldn't be the one explaining to a doctor how it happened."

Jessica shuffled past him into the chill night air and tried to clear her racing mind. She was thankful for the distraction Drew and Michiru were providing, but their banter couldn't entirely stave off the fear nipping at her heels.

This is going to work. It has to work. It's a simple seven-step process. Close circle. Call gatekeeper. Summon ghost. Open portal to hell or wherever it came from. Send ghost home. Close portal. Open circle.

As she repeated the steps in her head, her heart pounded against her ribcage like a moth beating itself to death on a lighted window.

Chapter 26

Faint moonlight lit the way as the trio approached the machine shop.

Jessica watched as clouds consumed the stars, feeling as though the gray smudge was spreading across her soul. She wanted to believe this would work, that she could make it work, and then everything would go back to normal. But every time she thought about what she had to do and why, the utter absurdity of the situation came crashing down.

She bit her lip to stifle a burst of hysterical laughter.

Doubt and confusion wriggled through her like maggots in a rotting corpse, eating away at her certainty, leaving nothing but the barren, pale bones of self-confidence.

Am I seriously contemplating summoning a ghost, or demon, or whatever it is? Do I even believe in them?

Yes. Primal instincts honed over hundreds of millions of years screamed the answer in her head. *You do now.*

She had looked into Bill's eyes and seen only infinite pits of rage. No trace of humanity had looked back at her; that terrible shifting shadow was all there was.

Jessica's gut twisted and she wished she hadn't downed a

whole glass of punch. The sickeningly sweet liquid rose in her throat and she swallowed hard.

I will not throw up. I will not throw up…

"I'll go in and make sure nobody's about. You guys stay out of sight," Michiru said in a matter-of-fact voice when they reached the door. She popped a mini chocolate bar into her mouth, smiling in ecstasy as she savored the treat, and slipped inside.

Jessica gazed after her, wondering how she could eat at a time like this.

Drew pulled his sheet off, bunched it into a ball, and shoved it under his arm. Jessica gave him a strained smile, which morphed into a grimace when there was a muffled thud from the other side of the door.

"Guess nobody cleaned up our oil slick." Drew whispered, making no effort to conceal his amusement.

Jessica swore under her breath and stared at the door, wondering what to do. She took a step toward it and Drew grabbed her arm. He shook his head and pulled her behind the dumpster.

Jessica fidgeted with her wing feathers. "You think she's all right?"

"If we haven't heard from her in a few minutes, we'll go in. Okay?"

She nodded and then twitched as an owl hooted.

"Nervous?" Drew searched the nearby trees, hoping to catch a glimpse of it.

"I'm trying not to toss my cookies."

"Damn." He took a few hasty steps back. "There were cookies?"

She snorted and then froze. Her mouth opened and closed several times.

Drew backed away, motioning to the wall. "Um. Aim over there, please."

Jessica tried to form words, but only managed a pained wheeze and some vigorous pointing.

He looked up, flinched, and then laughed. He yanked a skeletal arm out of the dumpster and the lid shut with a reverberating clang.

Jessica watched in horror as he approached, holding out the dead limb like a macabre offering.

She stumbled back. Her bird feet tangled and she fell, landing on her ass. Cursing her bulbous belly as she rolled onto her side, Jessica worked her way into a kneeling position.

Her eyes remained fixed on the grisly remains. Bloody gauze clung to the jaundiced bones and flapped grotesquely in the wind.

Drew stopped and bent forward, resting his hands on his knees as he tried to quiet his laughter.

With her hands on the ground and her feathered butt in the air, Jessica shuffled her feet apart to untangle her toes.

"You look like a bird pecking for juicy worms," wheezed Drew between fits of laughter. He bent the plastic bones back and forth.

Jessica straightened, her expression changing from fear to annoyance.

Gravel crunched behind her.

Michiru caught Jessica as she spun and lost her balance. "It's all clear inside. You guys all right?" She glanced between them.

Drew held the skeletal forearm out to Michiru. "Need a hand?"

She rolled her eyes. "Lame. If you two are done playing silly buggers, can we get this show on the road?"

He clicked his heels together and pulled off a sharp salute with the arm. "Aye, Aye, Captain. Not that I know what the hell you just said, but I assume it means you're a party pooper."

"I'll file that gem under 'Don't give a crap.' " Michiru glided back to the door and held it open, motioning them through.

Drew poked Jessica in the side with his spare limb to get her moving. She batted it away and glared at him. "How did you know?"

He shrugged. "Bobby said someone left shit around to freak out the shop class. He suspects the teacher."

"Well you could have warned me. I almost pissed myself."

"Ditto. It was fucking hilarious when you…" Drew checked his grin as her face tightened. He held up his hands. "I didn't know they'd still be here."

Jessica's gaze lingered on the bones. "Get rid of it. I won't be able to concentrate with you waving that around."

"I'll try to restrain myself." Drew bristled at the order, but tucked it under his arm with the sheet. "Think I'll keep it. Never know when it might come in handy."

Both girls groaned.

Jessica stopped when Michiru touched her shoulder and pointed to the floor. "Careful. There's something slippery here."

She nodded and moved into the darkened shop, purposefully avoiding eye contact with Drew as he choked down a laugh.

After catching her toes twice on a pile of scrap metal, she stopped and pried off the shoe covers. She scrunched the orange feet up, shoved them into her ever-expanding belly, and continued on, reveling in her renewed agility. She'd never be as graceful as Michiru, but at least she felt a little less like a tipsy Donald Duck.

The ache in her arm started halfway across the machine shop. She had never been so relieved to feel pain. When she arrived at the corner, she eagerly shone her light on the toolbox and saw the Ouija board tucked safely underneath.

Jessica closed her eyes and let out a long breath. *One hurdle down. Onto the next.*

She grabbed a long metal pipe from a nearby box and inched the Ouija board out.

The trio contemplated the unassuming object.

"That's it?" Drew looked skeptical. When she nodded, he crouched to take a closer look. "Doesn't look very scary."

"Don't get so close." Jessica pulled him back, flinching as pain shot up her arm. "It doesn't look like much, but believe me, it feels like a whole lotta bad."

Rubbing her arm, she scanned the area with her flashlight. "I could use a hand finding the planchette. If the board's here, it might be too."

"And to think, you wanted me to ditch this." Drew brandished the boney appendage and danced away as Jessica growled and made a grab for it.

His laugh ended in a choke as the arm was suddenly plucked from his grasp. Michiru waved it at him from a few paces away. "It's mine now. Try to take it if you want, but I don't recommend it."

He deliberated and then said, "Whatever. Keep it."

"Good." Michiru hurled the arm onto a raised car lift platform. "Problem solved. Now, let's find this thing."

Jessica was already crawling around, peering under various bits of machinery. "If you find anything that looks like it, don't touch it. Just call me over."

She straightened as Drew passed, muttering under his breath, "…no sense of humor…no—"

"Drew." Jessica heard the strain in her voice and scowled. He stopped and looked down at her.

"This is serious." She stood, facing him. "Deadly serious. Fooling around is fine, just not right now. Chris died because of this…ghost or entity…whatever it is…and I'm pretty sure more will die if we don't do something. I need to know you'll listen to me, do what I say, because I don't want to die tonight, and I sure as hell don't want to watch either of *you* die."

He was silent for a moment. "Fine, but just for tonight, and you tell no one. Being ordered around doesn't sit well with me." He held up a hand when she frowned. "I'm not casting stones, just letting you know how it is. And, for the record, I really didn't know the Halloween shit would still be here, or that it'd freak you out so much. So, I'm sorry."

"I'm sorry too. I'm way high strung right now."

He gave her a crooked grin. "We'd better get a move on, or Michiru's gonna crack some coconuts. Mine probably."

Jessica returned his grin weakly and bent down to continue the search.

* * *

Finding the planchette amid a pile of disassembled instrument panels was relatively quick, thanks to Michiru's hawk eyes. With that task complete, they set about preparing the area and organizing supplies.

Drew laid a piece of sheet metal on the floor, dropped a wooden crate in the center, and started the overhead ventilation fan. The blades hummed quietly.

Jessica sorted through her various freezer bags, watching nervously as Drew used a pair of long-handled blacksmithing tongs to transfer the planchette and Ouija board into the crate.

The knot in her stomach tightened. Her heartbeat quickened to match the distant, steady thump of music. It sounded like war drums.

Jessica reviewed her notes, trying to hold the pages steady with numb hands. It was odd. Her whole body was numb. Even the pain in her arm felt muted. Maybe that was what happened when fear reached a certain level. Everything just stopped.

Her stomach lurched. Everything except the fear.

"Looks like we're all set up." Michiru put a hand on Jessica's shoulder. "You gonna to make it?"

Jessica nodded stiffly.

"Right." Michiru rubbed her hands together. "I'll set up camp in the hall. If we're going to be interrupted, it'll happen there, and I can at least claim to be getting something I left in the weight room. Drew, you keep one eye on the outside door and one on Jessica in case she needs help." She pulled out her phone. "I need your number. We can text updates to each other every few minutes, but make sure your phone's on silent."

"I'm not an idiot." Drew scowled as he retrieved his cell. "Between the two of you, I feel like I've been drafted."

Michiru hid a grin as he flipped through screens, checking his settings.

Jessica felt Michiru's arms rest lightly across her shoulders. For a second she thought Michiru was trying to hug her, but realized what she was doing as soon as the warm jade touched her skin.

When she finished tying the cord around Jessica's neck, she said, "You need this more than me tonight."

"Thank you." Jessica wanted to say more, but couldn't find the words.

"I know you'll take care of it and it'll take good care of you too." Michiru lovingly ran a finger down the central leaf and headed for the door.

After a brief pause, Jessica gasped, "Wait. I still need Bill's—"

"Crap." Michiru hustled back. "I'm really off my game. I totally forgot." She rummaged in Wilson and pulled out a bulging freezer bag. "I would have gotten it to you earlier, but coach had us training over lunch and after school. I barely squeezed in a shower tonight."

Jessica and Drew leaned forward to examine the bag. The contents were oddly shaped.

She poked it. "What is it?"

"Jockstrap." Michiru looked between the two of them as Jessica quickly withdrew her finger. "Don't tell me you guys have never seen one."

They shook their heads.

"How the hell did you get that?" asked Drew incredulously.

She shrugged. "I ducked into the change room when it wasn't busy and took it. Nobody bothers to use padlocks."

Jessica stared at her, wide-eyed. "You were in the boys' change room?"

"Yup."

"And nobody said anything to you?" Drew looked baffled.

"There were a couple of confused guys, well, more embarrassed really, but I told them it was a dare." She wrinkled her nose. "You know...I always thought the girls' locker room was rank, but it's nothing compared to the boys'. Seriously. If you ever go in, wear nose plugs, or at the very least, bring air freshener."

"You're sure it's his?" Jessica gingerly took the bag from Michiru and held it at arm's length.

"His name's on the band. And guys don't share straps, so it's definitely his...uh...remains. Good luck." Michiru walked away.

"Yuk." Jessica dropped the bag next to the Ouija board.

Horny zombies and dirty jockstraps. Happy Halloween to me.

Chapter 27

Michiru melded into the shadows. Not even her grass skirt made a sound as she left.

"She's, ummm…" Drew stared after Michiru, his voice trailing off.

Jessica nodded. "I know."

Drew sorted through an array of bottles on a shelf and retrieved a white plastic jug. "I must be doing something right to be in such interesting company." He grinned as he set the container down. "When you're ready to start the fire, dump this on, stand way back, and toss a match."

Jessica examined the section of floor they had cleared for the ritual. "How far back?" She had to create a circle and she couldn't cross the boundary until the ritual was complete.

He shrugged.

She decided to make it as large as possible.

Drew unhooked a fire extinguisher from the wall and plunked it down beside her. "Maybe don't use the whole bottle, just a bit, okay?" Jessica's eyes widened and he added, "I'm sure it'll be fine."

She stared at the Ouija board and took a deep breath.

"Riiiiight. What could possibly go wrong?" Her eyes shifted back to her notes—bits and pieces of information and instructions she'd stitched together like Frankenstein's monster, only without any experience or training.

What am I doing?

Frustrated by her hesitation, Jessica threw down the papers and grabbed her direction markers. She had already determined where north was, so she placed a stone there, a smoking incense stick to the east, a lit candle to the south, and a bowl of water to the west.

Her heart raced as she snatched up her notes and walked to the outermost edge of the cleared space. She flipped to the circle ceremony, glancing at Drew. He was wandering back and forth, looking for an observation post.

"I'm going to make a circle that covers this whole area." She suppressed the rational part of her brain in preparation for what she was about to say. "It's a magic circle, so I have no idea if you'll be able to see anything. Don't know if I will either, but there'll be a line of salt marking the edge. I'm inside, and you're outside. You can't cross it and neither can I. Not for any reason. Understood?"

"I hear you." He watched curiously as she began pouring a trail of salt in the shape of a rough circle.

Jessica eyed him. The scamp had conveniently sidestepped agreeing, but she decided it wasn't worth pursuing. After their talk earlier, she was fairly certain he understood the gravity of the situation. She just hoped he wouldn't have to make that choice. Especially since it would mean something had gone terribly wrong.

She forced her doubts down and read from her notes. "I create this circle to contain all forces that would do harm." Her voice sounded faint and hesitant even to her own ears. She tried for more volume. "None whose will is set on destruction or injury shall cross the barrier. I ask for assistance from those energies in harmony with my intentions. This circle is a place beyond time and space, between the worlds, where my intentions manifest."

Jessica stopped short of joining the trail of salt to complete the circle, leaving a foot-wide gap by which she placed the bowl of sea salt.

Thin wisps of smoke rose from the incense stick. She inhaled the spicy scent, watching the wraithlike eddies spin in her wake. Their shifting patterns were hypnotic and the smell reminded Jessica of her grandma's house. All that was missing was a whiff of brewing tea and lavender shortbread.

Jessica retrieved a barbecue lighter from her pile and held the flame to a charcoal briquette. When miniature shooting stars sparked from its surface, she set it into a bowl and blew on it until a rich orange glow consumed the coal.

She dug out a handful of prepared herbs, dropped them on, and a gray cloud puffed up.

Jessica didn't pull back quick enough and sneezed three times.

There was a snort of amusement from the darkness.

She panned her flashlight over and saw Drew sitting on the runner of a partially raised car lift. He was swinging his legs like a little kid, looking entirely innocent in that practiced way he had.

Jessica shushed him, and he mimed zipping his lips and throwing away the key.

She sighed, wondering how Michiru was doing. The image of her banging the coconuts together and trotting around the hall Monty Python style rose unbidden in her mind.

Nah. She's all business tonight. Probably wishing she'd added them to my bonfire pile, though.

Jessica gripped Michiru's pendant, felt the solid warmth of the jade in her palm, saw the ghostly green glow of it envelop her fingers. She expected to see its light twinkling against the salt in the bowl, but it didn't. The glow stopped a few millimeters above her skin.

She forced her mind back to the task at hand and read out the rite to call a gatekeeper: "I invoke the gatekeeper, guardian of the path. I call upon you to open a gateway between this realm and the one connected to the spirit board before me. An entity trespasses in our world, preys on people, sows pain and death. I ask for your assistance. Open a gate, so that the spirit can return to its home. Open a gate, so balance between our realms can be restored. OPEN!"

Jessica shouted the last word, tossed another handful of herbs onto the charcoal, and watched the smoke billow up. Her voice bounced off the high ceiling and echoed back. She waited for a sign of the gatekeeper's arrival or of a gate opening.

Nothing.

Her chest tightened as the dread of impending failure overtook the bone-gnawing terror of the unknown.

What if I can't even open a gate?

Smoke from the herbs began to drift and coalesce, creating improbably clean lines and angles. A seated woman with long flowing hair formed in the cloud and a geometric structure appeared superimposed over her. With a start, she recognized the intersecting circles and eye of the symbol from her visions.

Interesting.

A quick glance at Drew confirmed he saw something. He'd stopped fidgeting and was watching with a deep, focused stillness.

As much as the figure appeared insubstantial, it brought

with it a solid presence she felt in a way that went beyond physical senses. Jessica had visited the base of Hoover Dam on a family trip, years ago. She remembered pressing her back against the concrete wall, thinking of the millions of tons of water on the other side, invisible but undeniably present. It was exactly like that.

That must be the gate.

Funny, she'd expected the gatekeeper to be invisible and the gate to appear as an old-fashioned door, or high-tech energy portal, not the reverse. Not this looming presence that seemed a hair's breadth away in every direction. She could feel its cool tingle against her skin and hear...just the faintest hint of a melody. There was something familiar in it...

Her stomach lurched. She was stalling.

Tendrils of smoke coiled expectantly in the air.

This was the moment she had been dreading. The thing she most didn't want to do, but had to. She didn't want to come face-to-face with that darkness again, gaze into its bitter emptiness and have it gaze back into her.

And now I'm going to call it to me.

She looked at the ethereal figure of the gatekeeper.

It sat. Waiting.

There was nothing to do but carry on and hope it amounted to something—much like her approach to the annual sports day at school. *Just keep your head down and go through the motions.*

Picking up the bag containing Bill's jockstrap, she held her breath and dumped the contents onto the ground just inside the opening she'd left in the circle. Holding the bowl of salt in one hand and her notes in the other with the flashlight, Jessica faced the gap. It looked wider than she remembered. Maybe too wide to close quickly.

Her hands shook as she squinted at the blurred words, trying to make them out. Crouching down beside the jockstrap, she cleared her throat and focused on the dingy white fabric.

"Unknown spirit, be bound to my words and attend. I command you to leave the vessel you invaded. From this moment, you have no refuge in this realm. No haven exists in man or beast. The skies, oceans, and earth are closed to you. This circle alone is your sanctuary. Attend and be bound by my words."

A sudden rush of weakness and bone-deep pain caught her by surprise. Her flashlight clattered to the ground, followed by her notes, as her right arm cramped and spasmed.

Behind?

She had been focused on the gap, expecting— something?—to pass.

What she saw when she spun around turned her limbs to lead. The beam from her flashlight spilled across the cement floor and terminated at the crate, as abruptly as if severed by a knife. An undulating pool of nothingness seeped through the cracks in the wooden box. Thin black feelers consumed the light as they flailed in the air, searching, probing, testing.

Fixing her eyes on the questing tentacles, she dumped the rest of the salt in the general area of the gap. The salt ring was a bit ragged, but she held the idea of a perfect sphere in her mind, willing it to impose itself on reality.

"The circle is closed." She forced the words out.

Her flashlight beam flared and died. A ripple of energy coursed through the air as darkness settled. Jessica's knees buckled with sudden weakness and she staggered sideways as a dizzy spell hit.

She dropped the bowl and grabbed her notes.

In the brief flash of light, she had seen inky-black tentacles extending toward her. The cloudy form of the gatekeeper was visible, sitting in serene isolation on the other side of the circle. If it was doing anything, it wasn't obvious.

With the area now solely lit by the southern marker's weak flame, the tentacles were nearly invisible, but she felt their caustic energy all around her. She started to hyperventilate and forcefully slowed her breathing, countering her panic with logic, knowing she was getting enough oxygen despite the feeling of suffocation.

Come on. Get it done.

She looked down at her notes and realized there wasn't enough light to read.

"Crap," she muttered, then, her voice louder but still shaky, she began reciting the ritual from memory as best she could.

"Gatekeeper? Uh, the gate is open now. So…guide the spirit demon thing back to whatever hell it came from."

She didn't feel any lessening of the entity's miasma.

Is there something else? Right.

"Uh, evil entity thing, I command you to get back to where you came from. You are bound by my words. I COMMAND you to leave this place and, uh, get banished!" She winced. "Let the balance be restored." That sounded better, but it still didn't seem to have an effect.

A metallic crash and low curse from Drew reminded her that time was passing. She quashed the sudden terror that he might blunder into the circle, releasing the entity.

"Fine, gatekeeper, since you're having issues, we'll do this the hard way." She rummaged in her bird belly until she found her backup bag of salt and tore it open. Pouring out a handful, she flung it in an arc at the darkness in front of her, willing the loathsome tentacles to back the hell off.

The bone-chilling presence receded.

Jessica tossed another fistful of salt. "That's right," she growled. "You are Not. Wanted. Here." She punctuated each word with another spray of salt, ignoring the stabbing pain in her arm.

Michiru's amulet was glowing brightly now and the entity's tentacles were starting to pick up a faint, matching, green aura of their own. Now that she could see them more clearly, her panic subsided slightly. In her imagination, in the dark, the entity had filled the entire space, but in reality, it had simply cornered her against the edge of the circle with a few thin tentacles. Her advance had caused it to shrink in on itself, and it was now hardly larger than a basketball.

Jessica sensed the gate again, stronger than before. An infinite depth she could lose herself in. Its icy presence saturated the air, creating a faint blue mist. It felt soft against her skin; chill, but in a good way that soothed her singed nerves. The tantalizing thread of melody drifted back. She could almost distinguish a pattern—

The entity struck out with a tentacle in a quick jab.

Jessica threw her hands up to block. Warm green and cool blue energy swirled over her skin, and pooled at her hands, absorbing the strike. She had expected to feel the shattering pain from her dreams, but instead felt a light slap on her palms.

The entity's tentacles wriggled obscenely around the barrier, trying and failing to reach her.

Jessica was giddy with relief.

"How do you like that?" she snarled. "Eat my friend. Try to eat me?" A deep rage consumed her. She wasn't going to share her world with this abomination for one more second.

Jessica grabbed a tentacle. It squished between her fingers like rotten fruit. She gathered the entity up, working it like soft putty, compressing it down to the size of a softball. When she was done, she picked a direction that felt right and shoved the entity through the edge of reality, into the gate.

The mist and the great blue wall behind it convulsed and evaporated, taking all trace of the entity with it. The image of the gatekeeper blew apart, dissolving into random eddies of smoke.

In a gravelly voice, Jessica ordered, "Gatekeeper, guardian of the path between this world and the next. I call upon you to close the gate and depart." It was probably redundant, but this was the one part of the ritual she remembered clearly.

A brilliant light suddenly bathed the area. Her heart skipped a beat before she realized it wasn't some new magical manifestation, but the glare of a 100-Watt bulb.

Jessica shaded her eyes and saw Drew holding a portable lamp over his head. He looked frazzled.

"How's things?" he asked, missing nonchalant by a few octaves.

"Spiffy." She glared at him. "Point that somewhere else. Crap on a stick, you nearly gave me a heart attack!"

She tossed the jockstrap into the crate with the Ouija board. Its human effluent seemed almost homey after the revolting squishiness of the entity.

"Just figured you could use some light."

Jessica waved him back and sloshed the crate with a good quarter of the sharp-smelling liquid from the jug. She was happy to note that she didn't get so much as a twinge from the board.

She picked up the incense bowl and dropped its smoldering contents into the crate.

Fortunately for her eyebrows, Jessica's hind-brain responded a split second ahead of the audible pop as the air ignited. She ended up crouched at the edge of the circle as fire engulfed the crate. The heat was bearable, but the smoke spread and thickened. She pulled her face into the neck of her costume and tried to breathe as shallowly as possible, her eyes burning and watering.

"Jess!" Drew yelled. "The smoke's not clearing, like it's stuck in a bubble or something."

Of course! Jessica fought down her panic. *The circle is meant to keep things IN. Dolt!*

There was an entire ritual for opening the circle. She skipped it and rolled across the salt line, hoping the consequences for breaking the barrier were better than dying of smoke inhalation.

A jolt zapped through her body as she crossed the barrier. Trapped energy dispersed along a series of meandering cracks in the fabric of reality, like the flaring steamers of a lightning strike following lines of electrical potential.

Smoke burst in all directions and funneled up toward the fan. Jessica barely had time to fill her lungs with fresh air before there was a loud hiss, and a frigid blast hit her belly.

The world turned white. She closed her mouth as a salty tang coated her tongue and stung her eyes. Coughing weakly, she rolled away wiping at the powdery residue clinging to her face.

She ran into something solid and struggled to her knees, squinting through the fog in the direction of the assault.

A dark form bore down on her and she scrabbled to the side.

"For fuck's sake, stay still." Drew growled, as another arctic jet slammed into her side.

Jessica turned her face away and held her breath. Her oxygen-deprived lungs ached with the effort. Incipient dizziness descended as the expanding white cloud roiled around her. Her stomach heaved and she swallowed a lump of smoky bile.

There was a metallic plunk as Drew set down the extinguisher. "I think you're mostly out."

Jessica sucked air into every recess of her starved lungs. For a few merciful seconds, the world retreated, and that sweet, clean air was everything.

Her vision cleared as she stared down at her costume. Under a blanket of talc, jagged lumps of melted and charred feathers trailed down one side. She fingered the snow-kissed bumps.

That was a closer call than I thought.

She sensed Drew hovering and gazed up at him. He looked uncharacteristically worried.

"Thanks," she croaked, forcing a weak smile.

"No problem. I'm sure you'd do the same if I was on fire." He held out a hand. "Did it work?"

"I think so. Can't say for sure until I see Bill."

Jessica stared at his hand for a second, weighing the relative benefits of curling up into a ball and taking a nap versus moving. Sighing, she grasped his hand and stiffly stood up. It was quite a process. Her limbs felt as reliable as a box of frogs.

She shook her costume and dislodged most of the powder, but the coating on the severely charred feathers refused to budge—they had become fused together.

"Guess I can kiss my deposit goodbye."

Drew grinned. "Better than having your goose fully cooked."

She shot him an unimpressed look and then blinked as a dazzling light flashed in her eyes. When the field of red afterimages cleared, she saw him examining his phone with a bemused expression.

"That's a keeper." He slipped it into his pocket and backed away as she took a wobbly step toward him. "Trust me. It'll be funny later." She took another step. "Seriously. I'd hate for you to miss out. Wouldn't be fair." His hip hit the corner of a workbench and he limped to the other side, keeping the table between them. "Okay. It's too soon. No more jokes. I promise."

Jessica's growl morphed into a groan as her legs reached the end of their endurance. She let herself sink to the ground. It felt like a hoard of giant mosquitoes had sucked the life out of her. It wasn't a natural exhaustion.

"What the hell are you two doing? You can see that bloody light halfway down the hall." Michiru emerged from behind a pillar.

Rubbing his hip, Drew pointed innocently at Jessica's dead flashlight. "It went out."

Michiru strode over to the work lamp and turned it to face a stack of boxes. With the light radius restricted, she returned and crouched down beside Jessica. "Are you done?"

"A bit overdone, really." Jessica grimaced as she slid a leg out from under her bum.

Michiru's gaze traveled over Jessica's singed costume long enough to determine the damage was superficial. She nodded once. "Okay. What next?"

"Well…" Jessica couldn't believe she'd made it this far, and her mind hiccupped on the concept of "next." "When the fire burns out, we should collect the ashes and dump them in the bin outside. That's about it." Her voice was flat. With nothing left to focus on, her doubts resurfaced. Was it over? Not knowing was the worst part.

Drew patted her on the head. "Leave the cleanup to us. The sooner we get this done, the sooner we can get the flock out of here." He slapped a hand over his mouth, looking genuinely surprised. "It slipped out. Sorry."

He retreated and went to work, sweeping the area with a broom he found propped against a shelf.

Despite her exhaustion, Jessica couldn't sit and watch them deal with her mess. She crawled around, collecting her supplies and stuffing them back into her costume pouch.

Michiru and Drew moved the boxes and equipment back into place. When the fire guttered, they swept the dead embers and salt into a pail, and hauled them out to the dumpster.

Jessica touched the ashes before they tossed them, and her painless arm confirmed that there was nothing left of the entity.

Drew wiped down the soot-covered sheet metal and dragged it back to the scrap pile. He glanced at Jessica as he propped the metal against the wall.

"How are you doing?"

"Better." She had stayed upright long enough to find a chair and squeeze her padded butt between the armrests. "Still beat, but my head feels clearer."

Michiru materialized beside Drew and he let out a startled yelp. A smug smile flickered across Michiru's face before she counseled her expression back to neutrality.

He glared at her. "Someone should put a bell on you."

"Someone could try, but they may not like where it ends up." She surveyed the area and nodded approvingly. "Looks good. I think we're done."

Drew switched the light off and the trio silently trailed outside and back around to the front of the school. Michiru diverted them to the parking lot as they neared the entrance.

Jessica leaned against a car and peered through the windows at the school doors. A group of students emerged and bundled into an old VW van for a smoke break.

"I can't believe we did it. We were lucky. The..." Jessica hunted for words, "darkness I saw attack Chris and Bill, it was there, in the circle with me." She shuddered. "It attacked me, and would have got me, too..." Her hand spontaneously rose to her throat. "Definitely lucky." She undid the cord and handed Michiru's necklace back to her. "Thanks for this. I think it saved my life."

"Anytime." Michiru smiled, caressing the pendant "It's funny how you don't really notice something until it's not there."

"I know what you mean." Jessica's throat tightened and she steadied herself on the vehicle. Her dizziness wasn't diminishing. It felt like she was on a boat in stormy seas. Not a bad metaphor, actually. Her cozy life from last year with Beth, Kathy, and Eric seemed like another country. One that she was rapidly sailing away from into uncharted territory.

Drew pressed a set of keys into her hand. "My truck's over there." He pointed to a section of the lot near the football field. "Go lie down for a bit. You look ready to drop."

Though her weariness bore down on her, she shook her head. "I need to find Bill."

"Sure. But it looks like you've had a cage match with the Stay-Puft marshmallow man. Kinda hard to explain. Mac and I can do the legwork. We'll text you when we spot him."

Jessica picked at the white crust on her belly. Based on her earlier reception at the dance, people were bound to notice her re-appearance. Especially Kirsten. And she couldn't think of any benign reason to explain a half-melted costume.

"Okay," Jessica agreed. "But don't go near him."

"Not to worry, my feathered friend." Drew gently clapped her on the back. "I saw some weird shit go down tonight, and I'm no hero."

Michiru rolled her eyes. "Come on. I think I saw a wizard inside. Maybe he has a bowl of courage for you."

She started off without him. Drew shook out his sheet with the air of a matador challenging a bull, tossed the fabric over his head, and jogged after her. The side of his sheet bulged as he caught up. Michiru smoothly stepped out of the way, and Drew stumbled sideways when his poke met no resistance. She waved coyly at him and skipped ahead.

Straightening his sheet, Drew sullenly glided into step behind her, narrowly dodging the door she pretended and then neglected to hold open as they entered the school.

Jessica shook her head and made her way to the truck. Sooner or later, Drew would realize he wasn't going to get the better of Michiru. For his sake, she hoped it would be sooner. For the sake of general amusement, she hoped it would be much, much later.

She crawled into the truck with great difficulty, locked the door, and then gratefully stretched out on the bench seat. Being short had some benefits: She fit nicely, with her head and toes just touching the doors on either side.

Eyes half-closed, she belatedly remembered to dig out her phone. She had to re-start it twice before the screen would display anything other than random squiggles. With that taken care of, she tried to snuggle in again, but was jolted by a sharp pain in the back of her neck, near the base of her skull.

She ran her fingers over the area and found something stiff. Thinking a feather from her costume had become tangled in her hair, she felt up the length of the narrow shaft. It went all the way to her scalp. The end was embedded in her skin.

She struggled upright and adjusted the rear-view mirror, so she could see. It was a natural brown-and-black-striped turkey feather. Odd, since the feathers in her costume were all dyed bright colors.

Damn thing must have stabbed me while I was rolling around.

Jessica set her jaw, locked her fingers around the feather, and yanked.

Cursing loudly, she jammed a finger over the bleeding hole and laid back down. After a few minutes, the pain subsided and her exhaustion kicked in, dragging her down into sleep.

Chapter 28

Channel link interrupted. Unexpected evocation of Shadow
remnant. Normalize communication via dispersion of gate
energy to Channel. ALERT: Gate Integrity Breach—Class 2.
Divert all resources to gate stabilization.

* * *

Michiru moved through the crowded gym like a stream around
a rock fall. She stopped someone she knew from the football
team and, after a quick dance, confirmed that he hadn't seen
Bill. Several unsuccessful orbits of the party later, Michiru
relocated Drew and ushered him into a corner.

"Anything?" She made no effort to keep the frustration
out of her voice.

The beige ghost shook its head. "It'd be easier without
the costumes. Any idea what he's supposed to be wearing?"

"Nope. Let's widen our search. I'll find some more of his
friends and ask if anyone's heard from him, and you can go
haunt the halls to see if he's wandering. The teachers aren't
paying much attention, so they shouldn't be hard to avoid."

"And if we come up empty?" he asked.

Michiru surveyed the confusing mash of masks, painted

faces, wigs, and props heaving on the dance floor. "I'll tell the DJ to announce that someone's here to meet him at the main door."

She nodded to herself, liking the idea. "Should work. If he's here. But let's try to find him in a less obvious way first."

"Right. Hasta la vista. And not a moment too soon. This music's gonna melt my brain." His sheet billowed dramatically as he spun and headed out.

"Drama queen," she called after him. "Text your location to Jess and me if you find him."

The ghost grumbled noncommittally.

Michiru cracked her knuckles, adjusted her coconuts, and threaded her way through the crowd with renewed vigor.

* * *

Drew attached himself to a random group wandering down the main hallway. One of the pack, a disreputable-looking pirate, brandished an empty rum jug at a bored teacher manning the coat check by the main doors. Drew took advantage of the distraction and ducked into an intersecting hall.

Having no set destination, he skulked through the darkened school, staving off boredom by contemplating what mischief he could get into. The halls were mostly empty, except for one amorous couple hiding under a stairwell. Luckily, their extreme inattention to anything but each other made them easy to bypass.

He risked a peek as he tiptoed past, just long enough to confirm both figures were too small to be Bill. Their costumes were realistic, and he marveled at how they managed such an involved kiss without getting their antlers tangled. He shook his head, deciding they must be practiced.

The classrooms, labs, storage closets, offices, and cafeteria were disappointingly locked. He had just given up all hope for fun when he remembered what Michiru had said about the unprotected gym lockers.

Visions of jockstraps flapping in the morning breeze on the flagpole brought an evil grin to his face.

The change rooms were back near the dance and he'd only done a cursory check before.

No one would blame him for being extra thorough.

He started down the hall and his phone buzzed. He stopped at a break between two banks of lockers to check the text from "Hardass."

>> Nothing. You?

Drew smirked at his recently added contact name for Michiru. Before he could reply, he heard footsteps and raised voices approaching. He pressed the screen against his chest to hide the light and slid further into the nook.

There was a loud thud, followed by a shock wave that rattled down the row of lockers. Then, an animalistic panting started, punctuated occasionally by a weak gasp as the lockers clanged and vibrated.

"That's right, bitch. Squirm." The panting grew quicker, more excited. "Your fear is sweet."

Drew knew angry, but the guy's voice held a sharper edge of cruelty than anything he'd heard. Pulling off his sheet to get it out of the way, he looked down the hall and groaned.

The ritual hadn't worked. It couldn't have.

A shiver of revulsion rippled through him as Bill's spongy tongue snaked out and licked tears off the girl's cheek. His thick hand squeezed her neck, pinning her against the lockers. Even in the low light, Drew could see her face darkening, her mouth gaping as she desperately tried to pull air down her constricted throat.

"Shit. Shit, shit, shit." Drew swore under his breath.

Bill knocked the girl's head against the locker, and she let out a rasping cough.

There wasn't time to call Michiru. Whatever had its talons in Bill was a nasty sonofabitch. As he watched the hulking footballer lift the girl one-handed, he didn't believe for a second someone Michiru's size had a chance. At least not while he was in this state.

"So much for my policy of avoiding heroics." Drew muttered.

He switched his brain off, stepped out, and hurled his phone at Bill. It sailed straight and hit him on the side of his head.

Bill howled and cradled his ear. Temporarily forgetting the girl, he turned to face Drew, huffing like an enraged bull. "Your turn to scream, grub."

Drew's surge of adrenalin fizzled, leaving behind a hollow, gnawing fear.

They were only five meters apart; a short distance for the footballer to cover. Drew backed away, trying to recall which way to turn at the end of the hall, and how far it was to the gym.

Behind Bill, the girl held her throat as she choked down air. "You sick fuck." She swung her purse and whacked him on the back, before staggering away. "Find someone else to be your punching bag. We're through."

Bill half turned to watch her go and then took a step toward Drew.

The air between them rippled, like heat waves rising from sunbaked pavement.

Drew blinked hard, trying to clear his vision. He couldn't afford to take his eyes off Bill. The supercharged athlete would be on him without the few precious seconds of warning afforded by those five meters.

The walls wavered between opaque solidity and a distorted, semi-transparent film. A distant crimson skyline flickered in
and out of view beyond the confused barrier.

Bill narrowed his eyes. "What did you do?"

Drew continued backing down the hall. "Listen. I don't
want any trouble. Let's just go our separate ways." He blinked
again as the haze on the floor resolved into something like
smooth, white sand.

There was a movement to his right. A tall, bronze-
skinned man strode out of the wall and crouched to stare at the
ground. The hallway was visible through his body. He ran a
scarred hand over the sand, became very still, and then looked
up at Bill, as if registering his presence before seeing him.

The ghostly stranger stood slowly, as one would when
trying not to alarm a wild animal. His long white robe fluttered
in a phantom wind.

He frowned, examining his surroundings. When he came
to Drew, he nodded politely.

"Strange. I was tracking a wagistu, not a skinwalker."

His voice sounded muffled and tinny, like a bad phone
connection, but there was also something odd about what he
said, or how he said it. Drew understood most of it, but his
brain had to switch gears, as if the words were familiar and at
the same time foreign. He repeated them in his head and
sucked in a breath.

The stranger was using a language similar to the dialect
his uncle spoke. The inflection and pronunciation was off, but
it was close.

He gave Drew an appraising look. "You are me-en-
hawi?"

Drew shrugged, not understanding. He glanced at Bill,

who was backing away with animal caution.

The man followed Drew's gaze and scowled. He raised a robed arm to point at the footballer and barked, "You don't belong here."

"Neither do you, dog." Bill retreated another few steps.

After a second, Drew realized Bill had spoken in the same dialect as the stranger.

All three turned as a shrill screech emanated from the bleached sand dunes and massive slabs of cracked stone visible beyond the row of lockers. The sound made Drew's skin crawl. A spiny, beetle-like creature burst out of the sand and dove into another dune before the lockers shifted back into solidity.

The stranger nodded to himself. "Rocky ground is good for me, bad for wagistu. I must go." He studied Drew with a keen interest. "Take care, brother."

He strode toward the wall and walked through without hesitation.

Drew reached out and his hand struck the cool, unyielding metal of the lockers, even as they alternated between opacity and translucence.

"Fools." Bill snapped. "You've disturbed the barriers." He looked around, visibly shaken as the hazy image of sand faded into the floor.

The creature's piercing call sounded again. Bill spun on his heel and ran, disappearing into the shadows at the far end of the hall.

Drew cautiously touched the lockers again, half afraid to move in case he ended up somewhere else. They felt solid. He stared down at his hand. It looked solid too. But then, who knew anymore?

He retrieved his sheet, puckered his lips, and whistled as loud as he could as he crept to where his phone had landed.

Maybe it had just been some old tale Uncle told to keep them at home, but sometimes a lie was better company than the truth; especially when you weren't alone in the dark.

His phone's screen was cracked and it didn't respond when he tried to wake it. He shoved it into his pocket, tossed the sheet over his head, and took off at a jog for the gym, still whistling, wondering how much weirder this night was going to get.

Chapter 29

Something woke Jessica up and she groggily stared at her phone.

Nope.

She glanced around the truck's dark interior and a sudden horror occurred to her. Cursing all eight-legged fiends, she swept her hands over her face, body, and legs. No black lumps fell off or skittered away. She resisted the urge to tear her costume off, telling herself the crawly, tickly sensation on her skin was a figment of her imagination.

When she stopped moving, she heard a muffled chattering outside. Jessica grabbed the steering wheel and pulled herself upright.

The noise stopped.

She peered out into thin moonlight, checking for movement amongst the cars. Nothing. She scanned wider, across the football field, and saw a strange lump in the southern corner. One second she swore there was a thin trail of smoke rising from the mound, and the next, she wasn't even sure there was a mound.

Groaning, she flopped back down and curled up, pulling

a dusty blanket off the seat back. She sneezed and rubbed her nose as she huddled under the cover.

Must have fried a few brain cells tonight. I can't even see straight anymore.

After re-checking her phone, she laid it beside her head and closed her eyes.

A steady rustling, like a forest of leaves fluttering in a strong wind, circled the truck.

Jessica's eyes popped open. There weren't any trees that close.

She slowly sat up.

A howling creature covered in luminescent scales dropped through the windshield, passing inches from her face, and disappeared through the floor. The interested, logical part of her brain categorized it as a cross between a sloth and a radioactive iguana, the rest of her screamed as she threw herself out of the vehicle.

She staggered away from the truck, into a swaying mass of translucent purple vines that suddenly clogged the area.

What the hell is this? Another vision?

The creature was still howling, though the sound came from far below.

Jessica looked down. Her heart gave a heavy thump as the ground shifted between dull concrete and a maze of thin, knobby branches stretching down for some ten meters into a swamp. Her head reeled and she grabbed the open truck door.

After a moment of clinging to the metal frame, she acknowledged that she was not, in fact, falling. She could feel hard ground beneath her, hear the crunch of gravel under her rubber soles, though her stomach still lurched when she glanced down into the muddy swamp.

Right. I just won't look down anymore.

She let go of the door and turned in a circle until she saw the angular bulk of the school through the jumble of foliage.

Something hissed behind her. Covering her face with her arms, she bolted through the vines toward the school. She had no idea what was going on, but she knew whatever it was wouldn't seem so scary with Michiru and Drew nearby.

* * *

Crossing the parking lot to the school was a harrowing experience. Jessica flung the doors open and plowed past the startled teacher at the coat check. He was just starting to stand, pointing an indignant finger at her back, when a rumpled beige blob barreled into her. They careened into the coat racks, scattering jackets, hangers, and pink tickets across the hall.

Drew surfaced in a pile of coats, found Jessica flapping under a velvet cloak, grabbed her wrist, and hauled her upright.

The teacher stared in horror at the overturned racks, groaning as a ticket fluttered past his nose.

A crude, stone-tipped spear sailed through the closed school doors, passed through Jessica's shoulder and Drew's chest, and then disappeared into the floor further down the hall.

Drew ran a hand over his chest and started breathing again.

Jessica grabbed his arms, trying to catch her breath.

Drew's eyes widened and he yanked her to the side, narrowly avoiding a stampede of students charging for the door. A few brave teachers waded in and tried to direct the crowd. Several people screamed as they passed a side hall and shoved past the slower runners. The horde reacted to the screams, becoming a churning mass of confusion, before once again surging toward the exit.

Trying unsuccessfully to stop people as they sprinted by,

Jessica yelled, "No! Don't go out—" She snapped her mouth shut as the doors clanged open and the frenzied mob poured into the night.

Shaking her head, she flattened herself against the wall and looked at Drew. "There's…a jungle…and cavemen or something out there. They were chasing me."

"That would explain the spear." Drew coughed, covering a chuckle as Jessica pulled in her stuffed stomach to avoid being shoved by the exodus. "You must have looked like an extraordinarily lucky break to a hungry caveman."

An undulating blue ball the size of a large watermelon emerged from the opposite wall, floated across the corridor, and melded into the wall they were pressed against. It sparkled as if filled with fireflies.

Several runners skidded to a halt to avoid the sphere and the group coming up behind collided with them.

Drew swore as a zombie in a lab coat fell. He grabbed the guy's leg and pulled him out of the way as the crowd pressed onward, either uncaring or unaware of those in danger of being trampled.

Jessica helped Drew lift the zombie. As soon as he was standing, he shook them off and, without so much as a glance at his rescuers, lurched back into the stream.

She poked Drew in the side and pointed to the thinning pack rushing out of the gym. Michiru sidled through the doorway carrying a pirate wench across her shoulders, fireman style. A grim reaper knocked into her, shoving her into one of the metal door jams, and she ruthlessly rammed the buccaneer's protruding backside into him. The black-robed specter bounced off, then wisely retreated.

Jessica saw the look on Drew's face and smacked him on the shoulder. "If you say one word about booty…"

He shook his head. "Don't worry. No joke's worth losing a limb." He took Jessica's hand and motioned toward Michiru. "Come on. We should help her."

They had just started moving when the air shimmered. People, floor, walls, and ceiling shattered, as if a glass image of the scene had broken into hundreds of geometrical shards and then been tossed into the air to hang randomly. Faces split into several panes. Pieces of floor intersected ceiling. Soft shadows splintered into angular, disconnected bits.

Jessica felt Drew's hand gripping hers, but when she looked, part of someone's leg was where their hands should have been. Drew's distinctive nose was above her and to the right.

"Drew?"

He squeezed her hand. "I hear you."

"Let's not move."

The nose moved up and down slightly. "Agreed. I think things might clear up if we wait. I ran into a desert earlier, but it only lasted a few minutes."

"Fuck." Jessica huffed. "This is like being trapped in a kaleidoscope. I was already dizzy."

"And to think, some people pay good money for a trip like this."

She groaned. "It just makes me feel ill."

"Ummm...since we seem to have a minute...I should tell you that Bill's still not right. Any chance the ritual has a delayed effect?"

"What? You saw him?"

The nose nodded. "He was strangling someone. She got away. I nearly didn't."

Jessica's last reserve of energy blew out as if she'd crossed into the vacuum of space. All the hours of research, all the work, the risk, the terror…all for nothing. Useless.

Drew cleared his throat. "Question. If the skinwalker's still in Bill, then what was in the circle with you?"

"Don't know." Her voice was cold, detached. "It looked the same to me, but I obviously don't know shit."

"Well, you're not alone." He squeezed her hand again.

Around them, people called out to each other and occasionally screamed as something brushed past. Someone was sobbing. The indifferent bass beat from the gym thumped in the background as slivered pieces of bodies randomly shifted.

Jessica kept a firm grip on Drew's hand and closed her eyes until he announced that things were back to normal, more or less.

Michiru appeared beside them and frowned at Drew. "Where the hell have you been? I texted you, but—"

"Yeah. Not the best timing." He interrupted, running a hand through his hair. "Long story short: I ran into Bill and my phone didn't make it."

"Is he…?" Michiru's voice trailed off as Jessica dropped her gaze to stare dismally at the floor.

Drew shook his head and extended his hands several times trying to figure out how best to help with the pirate. "He's still fucked. Need a hand? I think she's coming around."

The pirate's head bobbed up as someone ran past.

Michiru shrugged forward and caught the girl as she slid off. "Nope. We're fine."

"Wha…what happened?" The pirate groaned.

"You fainted." Michiru patted her on the shoulder. "Don't worry, Dee. Jerry fainted too, so no one's going to give you a hard time."

She blinked uncomprehendingly. "Oh. Okay. I'd better go home now."

"Whoa. Hold on a sec and I'll come with you." Michiru grabbed her arm and stubbornly held on.

Dee flipped her eye patch onto her forehead. "Uh…what happened again?"

There was a scream, back toward the gym. Jessica realized that the music had died.

They turned and saw the hallway morph into a cavern of pitted red rock. Mrs. Anderson was lying on the ground, or rather in it, her prone body only partially visible through a semi-transparent boulder jutting from the rough cave wall. A giant, pink-skinned, rat-like creature sniffed her leg, swiped a paw through her, and then trundled away.

Michiru slid an arm around Dee's waist as she slumped and carefully lowered her to the floor. "You guys stay with Dee." She nodded toward the teacher. "I'll get her."

She darted down the hall as the last of the dance crowd ran, crawled, and, in at least one case, rolled out of the school. Most, although bruised and scraped, looked healthy enough to travel under their own power. From the sounds filtering through the main doors, there was a fair amount of commotion outside, but the school was now clear and quiet, except for the receding scratching of the rat's claws against the cave floor.

Mrs. Anderson was already trying to sit up when Michiru knelt down beside her. After a brief exchange, Michiru pulled the teacher's arm across her shoulders and helped her back to the group. She gave Drew a gentle kick on the shin to get his attention. "Think you can handle Dee?"

He rubbed his leg, looking offended.

After several abortive attempts to lift the unconscious girl, he awkwardly heaved her upright. "She's…oof…worse than a bloody sack of potatoes." He grunted, staggering as she drooped bonelessly to the side.

Jessica grabbed the girl's arms and helped pull her over Drew's shoulder. She caught hold of his leather jacket as he tottered sideways.

"Right." Michiru's mouth twitched. "Let's go."

Drew followed her down the hall, with Jessica leaning into his side to straighten his course.

Mrs. Anderson shifted her arm on Michiru's shoulder and glanced back at them. "Jessica?" Her eyes were unfocused. "What's going on?"

"You're asking the wrong person. I don't understand anything anymore." Jessica immediately regretted snapping at her. "Sorry. I just really don't know. I'm sure everything will be fine." She lied.

Poor Mrs. Anderson. I bet this isn't what she figured teaching in a small town would be like.

The teacher gazed past them, to where the cave shimmered in and out of view. She blinked. "Was there a big rat?"

Jessica nodded and pushed Drew to the left as he almost ran her into the overturned coat check table.

Mrs. Anderson frowned, looked at Michiru, who smiled reassuringly, and then turned to stare straight ahead at the doors.

"Wait, Mac!" Jessica called out. "There's some kind of jungle and spear-chucking cavemen outside."

"I don't think we need to worry." Drew pressed Dee against the wall to take some of the weight off his shoulder. "None of this is solid. Your cavemen threw a spear right through me." He waved his free hand over his chest. "See? No holes."

Jessica nodded slowly, thinking aloud. "Okay. Yeah. The rat's paw went through her." She stared at Mrs. Anderson, who looked down at herself in alarm. "But just because some things are insubstantial, doesn't mean everything is."

Michiru cracked the door open and peered outside. Her body stiffened, she sucked in a sharp breath, and then relaxed. "Well. A slimy centipede thing just landed on Tom, but it went right through him, and Lucy ran across a pit without falling in. I think we're okay."

A massive golden lion head poked out of a wall beside the door and then swam through the air, swishing its long snake body through Michiru and Mrs. Anderson. The beast's burnished scales flashed as it swung around and shot straight up through the ceiling.

Michiru cleared her throat. "Yup. Time to go." She kicked the door open and guided Mrs. Anderson out. The teacher was shaking her head and obsessively patting her stomach where the creature's tail had passed.

There were still a few people running around outside, though the parking lot was emptying fast. A white pick-up truck stopped to let a group pile into the box before veering around a cliff wall that now occluded nearly half of the lot.

"Now, there's a good idea," said Drew, struggling down the steps.

Michiru glared at him.

"Based on what I saw earlier," he glared back, "things will sort themselves out in a bit. If we stick around, we'll just be in the way and probably get hurt. Better to bounce. If that's all right with Your Highness?"

A muscle in Michiru's cheek twitched as she ground her teeth. Her retort was interrupted as Mr. Darien raced up and took charge of Mrs. Anderson.

"Emily. Thank God. Dave's called the police and fire department. They should be here any minute."

He surveyed the rest of them and did a double take when

he saw Jessica. His lips thinned as his gaze traversed her ruined costume. "I'd better not find out you had anything to do with this, missy. You're already on shaky ground after the bathroom stunt."

"I had nothing to do with that...or this." Jessica paused and swallowed.

At least, I hope I didn't. Oh gods. Did I fuck up this bad?

She looked back at the school, realizing too late that the teacher had not missed her guilty expression.

"Am I glad we ran into you!" Drew cut in, smiling broadly as he shoved Dee at Mr. Darien. She was starting to wake up again.

The teacher staggered, trying keep hold of the wiggling girl.

"She fainted. I'm sure you know what to do." Drew backed away, collecting Jessica and Michiru as he went.

Dee bucked and screamed in remembered horror, snapping Mrs. Anderson out of her stupor. She held on to the girl's arms, reassuring her there was no giant rat, and that everything was going to be fine.

While the teachers struggled with Dee, the trio sprinted for Drew's truck. They dove in the open driver's door and quickly sorted themselves out.

Drew patted his pockets, stared at the dash, and then whipped around to Jessica.

"The key."

Jessica ducked down to check the floor. She found her phone, but no keys, and started searching the crevice between the seat and the seat back. Her hands shook with exhaustion. Every move felt as if she was fighting against a progressively stronger current.

"Shit." Drew saw his blanket lying on the ground. He

jumped out and shook it. The truck key clinked onto the pavement. He grabbed it, chucked the blanket at the girls, and scrabbled back into the driver's seat.

A large mechanized creature, resembling a six-legged stegosaurus with a double row of diamond-shaped radiator panels running down its back, thundered into view. Jets of white steam, brilliant in the truck's headlights, jetted from a multitude of gleaming brass tubes poking up at random intervals through the black-iron plates that covered its body.

The beast slowed and turned towards them.

Drew took off in reverse at top speed. He turned the wheel as he slammed his foot on the brake, neatly spinning the truck around. Dropping it into drive, he peeled away from the advancing creature.

Michiru extricated herself from the blanket and looked back at the machine. "Awesome! Whatever that is, I want one."

Jessica whimpered. The thing was massive, but she had no energy left to care. Even forcing her eyelids open after blinking was becoming a chore.

Drew frowned into his rearview mirror. "Uh-huh. It'd be even cooler if it wasn't chasing us." He turned right, heading for the highway, and accelerated hard.

The mechanical dino steadily gained on them with its clanking and hissing gait, passing unhindered through the translucent trees and vines. It slid into nothingness as it crossed the line where the cliff and jungle cut off and reality reasserted itself.

* * *

Drew ducked as a police car raced past, lights flashing and siren blaring. Worried his plan to flee the town might look suspicious, he turned down the first crossroad he came to. After snaking through a maze of residential streets, he veered to the curb, parked, and switched off the headlights.

The trio sat, mutely staring into the night. It was late enough that even the trick-or-treaters had packed it in.

A violent snort broke the silence. It came from inside the truck and Drew pressed back against his door, searching for the source. He looked over at Michiru, who was doing the same. Her expression would have been funny if he hadn't been trying not to piss his pants.

Between them, Jessica's head lolled back. Her mouth gaped open as she let out another snore.

Heat rose to his cheeks.

"Fuck me." Drew placed a finger under Jessica's chin and levered her mouth closed. "I thought one of you had turned into a goddamn grizzly."

Jessica grumbled in her sleep, wrenched her head away, and overbalanced. She slumped sideways, face planted into Michiru's arm, snorted once, and nuzzled in, trying unsuccessfully to curl her legs onto the seat around her belly.

Michiru winced and shifted Jessica's position so that she was mostly lying in her lap instead of grinding her head into her coconuts.

The sirens gradually petered out and normal nocturnal sounds once more ruled the dark.

Drew restarted the engine, thankful that it was feeling cooperative tonight. "Looks like things have calmed down. I'd better get you guys home." He glanced up and down the quiet street, unsure which direction to go. "Assuming I can find my way back to a road I recognize."

"I can get you to Jess's house." Michiru offered. "I'll walk from there."

"You sure?" He glanced sideways at her, wondering if

she was putting on a false bravado.

"I don't say things I don't mean." She stared forward, her expression unfathomable. "Let's just say I'd rather deal with a horde of giant rats on my way home than try to explain to my mother why I'm being dropped off by guy she hasn't met."

Her lips pursed in a flash of annoyance, and then relaxed as she schooled her countenance. "I guarantee she'll be waiting up, and she's…overprotective."

He raised an eyebrow. "That must be interesting."

"Interesting?" Michiru's eyes narrowed. "What's that supposed to mean?"

"Just that 'overprotective' must be hard to do with someone like you."

The temperature in the truck plummeted.

"Someone like what?"

The prickle on the back of his neck suggested he had missed a good opportunity to keep his mouth shut.

"Um…I mean…you don't strike me as the type…" He paused, wondering how to wrap up the conversation in a way that wouldn't end with a bruise. "…to enjoy being overprotected?"

Michiru remained silent for a few long seconds and then huffed, "No. I'm not."

Drew kept his mouth firmly closed for the rest of the trip, wondering how he managed to push people's buttons even when he didn't intend to. Most of the time, he enjoyed the innate ability. He learned interesting things and it kept people off balance, gave him an edge. But sometimes it was more of a curse than a gift.

Hoping to avoid waking Jessica's parents, he parked half a block down from her house. He and Michiru assisted their semi-conscious feathered friend out of the truck. Jessica woke up enough to walk, with Drew prodding her every now and then when she stopped moving.

They eventually made it to her house. The door swung open while Jessica was still groggily digging inside her costume for the key.

Jessica's mother frowned out at them. She looked from Michiru to Drew, and then back to Jessica. "What on earth happened to your costume?"

Jessica mumbled something incomprehensible, went to step over the doorjamb, and tripped.

Michiru lunged and caught her elbow before she fell on her face.

"Young lady…" Jessica's mom pulled her away from Michiru and propelled her inside. "You have some explaining to do." She pried one of Jessica's eyes open and stared into her pupil. "When I got home from work, I found a bag of candy on the front steps. Eric left it for you. From the note, I gather he was under the impression you were home, sick. Which is odd, because you told us that you were going to a dance with him."

She pinned Jessica with a professional you-will-tell-me-everything-and-quickly glare. "I don't know what's going on between the two of you, and I don't much care, but you will explain why you lied to me about your whereabouts. And why you're so out of it that strangers have to help you to your door."

Drew stepped back, trying to attract Michiru's attention by jerking his head toward the truck.

Michiru straddled the threshold, glancing worriedly between Jessica and her mother.

Jessica leaned against the hall table and closed her eyes. "They're not strangers, Mom…" Her words were slurred and trailed off as her thoughts appeared to stall. After a moment, she cracked an eye open and listlessly waved an arm at the door. "Mom, meet Michiru and Drew."

Her mother gave them a withering look. "I see. Well. Thank you for bringing my daughter home." With a curt nod, she shut the door, narrowly missing Michiru, who pulled her foot out just in time.

The porch light conspicuously flicked off.

Drew grimaced as he heard Jessica's mother through the door asking if she'd been drinking.

"Well, that was the worst first impression I've ever made." Michiru rubbed a hand down her face. "I should have said something, but I couldn't think of anything that didn't sound stupid."

"Wouldn't have done any good. Her mom wasn't in a listening mood." He started down the driveway. "According to Jess, it's a chronic condition."

Michiru followed him in a daze. "I hope she's okay. She looked pretty rough."

"Probably needs to sleep for about a week. Uncle's always drained after ceremonies." Drew hopped into his truck and waved at the passenger seat. "My offer's still open. I'll even let you out early so we don't have to go through that shit again."

"Thanks, but I want to walk. It'll clear my head." She rubbed her neck, her eyes focused inward.

Drew grabbed the blanket, which had fallen into the foot well, and tossed it at her. "How you aren't a popsicle, I'll never know. It's fucking freezing out."

"I suppose." She wrapped the blanket around her shoulders with a nod of thanks. After a moment, she asked, "Why is it that I can deal with bullies, championship games, possessed maniacs, even 'roided-up rats, but throw one disgruntled parent at me, and I turn to mush?"

Drew shrugged. "Everyone's got an Achilles heel. Eventually some cunning adversary has to stumble upon the hero's kryptonite. Keeps them humble." He grinned as he closed the door and rolled down his window. "Guess I know yours now."

He drove away, laughing maniacally.

Chapter 30

"I thought that was you hiding behind the tree." Drew sat down on the grass beside Jessica and peered interestedly at the dog-eared book she was reading. "Only someone truly desperate would be out in this cold."

Wind swept across the schoolyard and Jessica pulled her hood up to cover her ears. She reluctantly lowered her book and snugged her hands into her jacket sleeves. Leaning back against the trunk, she groaned as Michiru jogged up. "I was hoping to avoid people. Guess I suck at that too."

"There you are!" Michiru sat down with a cheery smile and tossed a toonie at Drew. "You win. This time."

Drew shrugged at Jessica as he pocketed the money. "I bet her I could find you first." He leaned over and fingered a jagged hole in the side of Jessica's jacket. "Hamish?"

She looked down and nodded, tenderly tucking her book into a pocket.

"That reminds me." Drew dug around in his bag and flopped a thick, knotted rope in her lap.

Jessica stared at it blankly, wondering if it was code for something, like the infamous pirate black spot.

"For Hamish," Drew said, when she didn't respond.

She stuffed it into her backpack. "Thanks. I'll give it to him tonight."

They meant well, but Jessica really didn't want company right now. She didn't want to think about what had happened, what could happen next.

"Soooo…" Michiru stretched her legs out and leaned back on her arms. "What happened after we dropped you off? I phoned, but you weren't answering your cell and I didn't want to call the house in case your mum still wasn't happy with me. Did she stop flipping out at some point?"

"Eventually." Jessica sighed, knowing they wouldn't give up. "School being cancelled yesterday was bad. Very bad. She stayed home so we could talk. I had to smuggle Hamish into the basement while she ransacked my room looking for drugs. She found a crapload of chewed-up stuff, so now she's convinced I let my room get so messy that mice moved in and Dad's set traps everywhere." She held up a hand, showing them a thin purple bruise across two fingers. "I went to get a sweater this morning and wham."

Drew bit his lip.

"Oh, that's not even the worst of it." Jessica leaned her head against the tree trunk and closed her eyes. "Her idea of talking was giving an hour-long lecture on addiction. I yawned, once, because I was so fraking tired, and she decided I wasn't listening. So I got to spend the rest of the afternoon with a friend of hers who runs an addiction treatment center." She shuddered. "It was horrible. All those people hurting themselves until there's nothing left."

"Not just themselves." Drew's eyes darkened. "They take everyone around them down."

No one could think of anything to add to that, so they sat

and listened to the wind rustling through the grass. It could have been an awkward silence, but it wasn't. They were lost in their thoughts together.

"On the plus side," Jessica said after a while, "Eric had a great time at his dance."

"Did your mum spill the beans about you not being sick?" Michiru immediately looked unsure about whether she should have asked.

"No. She said that was my mess to clean up. I hate lying to him, but what can I do?" Jessica pulled her knees up to her chest, thinking out loud. "If I tell him what's been happening, he's going to be pissed I didn't tell him sooner. And that's if he even believes me. He's equally likely to think I belong in a funny farm. I've really dug myself a deep one this time."

She suddenly realized she hadn't asked how they were doing and felt selfish. "Did you guys get in any trouble?"

Drew shook his head. "Mom doesn't worry as long as I'm in one piece. Though she was a bit pissed when I told her about the sheet." He looked at Michiru. "You?"

"My parents freaked when the school called, but I told them it wasn't as bad as it sounded." She ran a hand over the grass, caressing it. "They'll feel better when someone explains what happened, but then so will a lot of people."

Three firefighters strode across the parking lot, flanking the principal.

Jessica hunched further into her jacket, pulling the hood down to cover her face. She had a terrible feeling that if Mr. Johnson saw her, he'd read the guilt in her eyes and haul her off.

Michiru tilted her chin toward the group. "Apparently, the new theory is a gas leak."

"Oh?" Jessica raised an eyebrow. "They've done away

272 *Adriaan & Rebecca Brae*

with the LSD-spiked punch theory, then?"

Drew snorted. "It's still a favorite with some. There's a couple guys trying to take credit, but then I also heard a certain undesirable might have done it. Something about 'fowl play.' " He winked at Jessica.

"I was a parrot, not a chicken, but yeah," Jessica groaned. "Someone anonymously informed mom about that little theory. She was already mad enough thinking I came home drunk, but she totally lost it after that." She shook her head. "I do fifty things right and they ignore me. Then the minute there's even a hint something's gone wrong, they're all over me."

"Parents are tricky." Michiru frowned as she gazed at the neat rows of parked cars. "Do we know what happened here?" She turned to Jessica, who immediately looked away.

"It might be my fault." After a long pause, Jessica said, "Who am I kidding? It's probably my fault. I must have said or done something wrong. The ritual didn't affect Bill, but there was something in the circle with me. I don't know what I did to cause…" Her shoulders slumped.

"Could Bill have done it?" asked Michiru.

"No way." Drew said with certainty. "He was as freaked as the rest of us, maybe more. Said something about us disturbing barriers." He glanced at Jessica as she sucked in a sharp breath and hastily added, "But lots of strange shit has happened lately. It could have just been more random weirdness."

Jessica squeezed her eyes shut. "No. That's what I was afraid of. The ritual was all about opening a gateway, or rather thinning the barrier between our world and the entity's. The original instructions involved knowing the name of the entity and the realm it came from, but I didn't know either, so I kinda skipped that part. Maybe I opened more than one gate." She put her head in her hands. "I'm so stupid. I never should have tried it."

Michiru gave her arm a squeeze. "So it didn't work. Nobody was seriously hurt, and I'm pretty sure that was the most successfully scary Halloween party ever. Plus, now you know what not to do next time."

"Next time." Jessica snorted. "That's a laugh."

Michiru crossed her arms. "Well, *I* don't intend to sit on my ass while Bill hurts or kills someone. Do you, Drew?"

"I see you're as diplomatic as ever." Drew scowled at her and grudgingly answered, "But I guess not." He pulled a lighter out of his jacket and repeatedly flicked it, watching the flame flare and die in the wind. "You should have seen him with that girl, Jess. He was enjoying it."

"What do you expect me to do?" Jessica's eyes snapped anger. "It's perfectly fucking clear I don't have a clue what I'm doing."

"I don't know what to do either," admitted Michiru. "But I can't live with myself if I don't try something. Can you?"

Jessica looked away. "No." Her voice cracked. "That's why I did the ritual in the first place."

"Right." Michiru rubbed her hands together. "So where do we start?"

"Well, that's kind of the problem." Jessica worried her lip. "Even if we figure out how to fix the ritual, we're screwed, because our only tie with the entity's home is gone. Burned. Destroyed. Completely ruined, thanks to my ingenious plan."

"The Ouija board." Drew pinched the bridge of his nose. "Shit. Guess it's back to the drawing board, then."

"Guys..." Jessica's gaze paused on each of their faces. "I don't know if there is another way. That ritual was the best I could find. I really thought it had worked."

"What about your grandma?" asked Drew. "She seems

interested in the weird. Any chance she might have some ideas?"

"I tried calling her last night, but she's on a yoga retreat until next week." Jessica sighed. "To be honest, I'm not even sure what I was going to tell her. I mean, she's like eighty. I don't really want to freak her out too much."

Drew's eyebrow raised. "If she's on a yoga retreat, chances are she's hardier than you and me put together. I've seen my mom doing that shit. It's not easy."

The school bell rang, signaling the end of lunch.

Drew stood and dusted off his jeans. "Well, whatever you did at the dance, it scared the shit out of Bill. Maybe he'll lay low for a bit. And we'll do what we can to help."

Jessica stared at them. They honestly expected her to come up with something. She didn't know what to do with that kind of faith. But they were right. None of them were the type to sit back and watch crappy things happen. Though Jessica wondered if that might not be the safer course for everyone, as far as she was concerned.

What are the chances I'll just make things worse?

She silenced the answer that popped into her head and grabbed her backpack. "I should have some time to look into things, as I'm grounded for the foreseeable future. My parents are heading out for a week-long conference. Mom threatened to cancel, but she won't. They'll probably just have someone look in on me. My parents: Masters of overreaction, but their follow-through sucks. Especially when it interferes with work."

Michiru hooked her arm through Jessica's as they walked back to the school. "So it'll be safe to come over?"

"Yeah. I think they leave sometime Friday morning, so anytime after school should be good."

Drew gave Jessica a sharp look. "Wait a sec. Your parents are going away for a week?"

"Yeah," she replied, confused by his tone. "Is that a problem?"

"I don't know if it's a good idea for you to be alone." He suddenly sounded much less sure of himself. "I mean…after seeing Bill…he was going to hurt that chick, or worse, and it's not like he doesn't know who you are."

"I recognize that," Jessica said. He meant well, but his concern grated on her nerves after her mother's recent onslaught. "I'm careful to not be too far from help and I don't go out at night."

Michiru chimed in, "Why don't you stay over with her, Drew? You've both got mad research skills."

He grimaced. "I can't cancel on Mom again. Definitely not on a Friday. She still hasn't forgiven me for sticking her with Sam on Tuesday. He broke more dishes than he washed. I can come by on Saturday for a while, if that helps?"

"Good enough," Michiru replied. "I think I can convince my parents to let me stay over Friday." She looked at Jessica. "But you'll have to meet them first, tonight maybe, and they absolutely can't find out your parents won't be there."

"Guys," Jessica protested, "I have spent time alone before. Lots, actually. And I'm just going to be researching, and maybe trying out some spells and rituals."

"That's great, Mac," Drew said overtop of Jessica. "Why don't you spend the weekend, do girly stuff." They reached the school doors and Drew cut left, heading toward the auto-shop wing. "Gotta run, see you Saturday."

"Girly stuff?" Michiru grimaced and aimed a stern look at Jessica. "You even think about putting my hair in curlers and we're through, got it?"

Jessica giggled, imagining Michiru with a head full of baby-pink foam curlers. She held her hands up in mock submission. "Never crossed my mind."

Chapter 31

The girls met after class and walked to Michiru's house. It was farther from the school than Jessica's, but at least it was downhill. Based on Michiru's fidgeting, Jessica guessed the journey was taking longer than expected.

She probably jogs back and forth for fun, Jessica thought disgustedly. She was growing uncomfortably warm trying to keep up.

Her house was a brown bungalow in an older area, closer to the center of town. It was perfectly nondescript, except for a battalion of garden gnomes poking bulbous red noses out of every shrub in the front yard. Jessica eeked when she saw their beady eyes gleaming in the foliage. She ran up the porch steps, trying to ignore the paranoia that insisted they were creeping up behind her with pitchforks, shovels, and picks poised for violence.

Unable to stand it, Jessica nervously glanced over her shoulder. It didn't look as though they had moved.

Her gaze wandered past the yard, out across the dreary landscape. Clouds hung low over the hills surrounding Coldwater and mist was gathering in the valley. They joined in places and spread, reducing everything within their grasp to muted grays.

She couldn't shake the feeling that she was being watched. Thinking back, she realized she had felt that way for weeks— ever since her vision in math class.

Michiru gently tugged her arm. "What's up?" She spoke quietly, surveying the yard and street, searching for the cause of Jessica's unease.

"Those bloody gnomes. It's like they're hiding."

"They are." She laughed at Jessica's puzzled look. "In a way. Dad got it into his head that Mum liked them and he keeps bringing them home. She doesn't have the heart to tell him she thinks they're creepy, so they get shoved into the bushes."

"That's not making them any less creepy." Taking a last look around, Jessica turned her back on the stubby army and followed Michiru to the door.

Entering her house was like stepping into a different world. A bizarre assortment of furniture, tools, knickknacks, electronics, and art, spanning all styles, decades, and colors immediately overwhelmed her eyes. Colors and shapes swam together and she wondered how Michiru was ever able to relax or concentrate.

"I'm home," Michiru called out at the top of her lungs. "There's someone I want you to meet."

A soft, musical voice called from the back of the house. "Okay, Mi-chan. No need to yell. I'm in the kitchen."

Michiru ushered her down a long hallway lined with photos, paintings, posters, and tapestries.

Jessica would never have guessed they had recently moved to town. It looked as though they had lived in this house their whole lives.

They stopped at a doorway hung with a sparkling blue beaded curtain.

Michiru sniffed the air and wrinkled her nose. "Oh no. Boot leather." Jessica gave her a confused look and she whispered, "Mum's roast beef. It's like trying to chew old leather."

Jessica stifled a giggle as Michiru forced her grimace into a smile and entered the kitchen.

The beads tickled Jessica's arms and tinkled pleasantly as she passed through. The kitchen was remarkably barren compared to the rest of the house. A fleet of appliances crammed one section of lemon yellow countertop. The other two were clear except for a cutting board, a large knife, and a tidy pile of vegetables in a metal strainer.

A compact woman with black hair shot with silver wiped her hands on a brightly colored tea towel and beamed at Jessica. "What a pleasure to meet one of Mi-chan's friends. I'm Hatsumi." She bowed slightly as she held out a hand.

Jessica, taken aback by the formality, belatedly shook her hand. "Uh. Hi. I'm Jessica. Nice to meet you."

Hatsumi kissed Michiru on the cheek. "I'll make some tea. And I must get Oda-san. He will want to meet your friend."

"Aw, Mum. She can't stay for long…she…her mum wants her home for…"

Jessica jumped in as Michiru stalled. "For an early supper…because we are…going to a movie."

Hatsumi bustled around the kitchen, putting the kettle on the stove and collecting tea supplies.

"There's always time for tea. We'll be quick." She swirled hot water in a duck-shaped teapot and set it down beside the stove. "Mi-chan. Please find your father while I make our guest comfortable."

Michiru looked torn, glancing between her mother and Jessica, but eventually relented and left.

Jessica couldn't blame her. Although soft-spoken, Hatsumi had an underlying band of steel in her voice, and she radiated the same calm, commanding presence as Michiru. It made Jessica nervous.

Hatsumi led her into the living room, another space crammed with intriguing items. Jessica pushed aside a pile of throw cushions and sank into an overstuffed velvet couch. She curiously examined a hot pink, sequined stiletto shoe on the side table. There was a number pad inside. She picked it up and listened for a dial tone.

"It doesn't work, but I will fix it." Hatsumi placed a plate of digestive cookies on top of a stack of magazines. There was a coffee table somewhere underneath. "I think there's a loose wire inside."

Jessica nodded and put the shoe phone down, wondering if she was weird for thinking it was bizarre enough to be cool.

Hatsumi perched on a chair opposite and amiably asked questions about how long Jessica had lived in Coldwater, whether she liked her teachers, and how she had met Michiru.

Jessica found herself talking easily, but stumbled on the last question. Telling Michiru's mom that her daughter had scared off a possessed thug in the crypt wasn't going to facilitate their weekend plans. "Um. Volleyball."

"Oh, do you play as well?"

"Me?" Jessica laughed and then coughed. "No. Uh. I just watch. I like to watch…sports. Sports are…" She breathed a sigh of relief as Michiru rushed in with her father.

Jessica wasn't sure what she had expected, but the tall, neatly dressed man with high, sharp cheekbones and long, steel-gray hair pulled into a tight ponytail wasn't it.

Hatsumi returned to the kitchen as her husband shook Jessica's hand.

"It is a great pleasure to meet you Jessica." He grinned, shattering the severity of his face, and leaned closer to stage whisper, "We aren't introduced to many friends. I was starting to worry Mi-chan hadn't made any."

"Daaaaad." Michiru groaned and flopped down on the couch. "Nobody hangs out at home. We go to games, or movies, or the lake. Home is boring."

Jessica peered around. "I dunno. Yours seems pretty interesting."

Michiru gave her a shushing look and turned back to her father as her mother arrived with a tea tray. "We've got a project due next week and I'd like to sleep over at Jessica's tomorrow night, if that's okay."

Hatsumi paused on her way to handing Jessica a cup and looked at Michiru. "Mi-chan. This is very short notice."

Jessica half stood to take her tea and Hatsumi smiled at her. She relinquished the cup, gestured to the cookies, and resumed pouring and handing out drinks.

Jessica declined the cookies, reveling in the delicate jasmine scent rising in the steam from her cup. It smelled almost as refreshing as her grandma's fresh mint and honey tea.

Michiru and her father snagged two cookies from the plate with snakelike quickness. A brief frown furrowed Hatsumi's forehead as she sipped her tea.

"I know," Michiru sounded contrite, something Jessica never thought she'd hear. "But the teacher sprung it on us today. It's a lot of work and it'd be way easier if we could just do it until it's done, if you know what I mean."

Oda nodded, lost in thought. "Yes. Some things must be done like that."

"But not all things." Hatsumi frowned at her husband. "There's something to be said for breaks. Working too hard, for too long, ends with mistakes." She turned back to the girls. "I'm sure your teacher would not assign something so late that requires this much work. Perhaps you misunderstood?"

Jessica put her drink down and attempted to shake off the tea-induced serenity. "I wish. I talked to Jenny, who had him last year, and he did the same thing to them. I can't afford a bad mark. If I don't do well, I can't take the next level this spring, which throws off next year's schedule, and then I'll have to make up classes in summer, and I won't have time because I'm already signed up for mini-university, and…"

Jessica stopped when she felt her heart racing and tears burning in her eyes. None of it was true, but the panic she felt was. She hadn't realized it was nipping so close at her heels. She reached out to pick up her tea, saw how badly her hand was shaking, and drew it back.

Hatsumi set her cup down. "It's very good that Mi-chan has a friend who cares so much about schoolwork. Sometimes I worry too much focus is put on physical conditioning and not enough on training agile brains. There should be balance."

"True." Michiru leapt onto the bandwagon. "I love sports, but I've been thinking I should start doing more for my classes. Put my best foot forward. This is the perfect opportunity to show my teacher what I can do."

Hatsumi fixed Michiru with an appraising gaze and then transferred a softened version to Jessica. "Can you do your project here? We would be happy to have you."

Jessica opened her mouth to respond, but closed it when she couldn't think of an appropriate counter. She looked at Michiru.

Michiru paused and then smiled at her mother. "Okay,

but she'll have to bring Hamish. She's puppy-sitting."

Jessica nodded vigorously. "I promised a friend I'd take care of him." And then she added for good measure, "He got into some butter Dad left out last night and it's not doing good things to his insides. I hope there isn't too much of a mess to clean up when I get home." She looked at her watch and genuinely grimaced.

Her mother would be calling home any minute to make sure she was there and she really didn't want to miss that.

Damn it. If I'd been thinking this morning, I could have forwarded the phone to my cell.

An unfathomable look passed between Michiru's parents. Hatsumi picked up her cup and took a slow sip of tea. "I hope Hamish recovers soon. It sounds…uncomfortable."

Oda glanced worriedly around the living room. "Puppies get into a lot of things. Perhaps it is better if Mi-chan goes to your house, Jessica. I'm afraid ours is not dog proof."

Considering all the yummy chewables at Hamish's gobbling height in this room alone, Jessica agreed. "I think so. Plus he's used to my place. It may not be good to move him, especially when he's not feeling well. He chews things when he's upset."

Oda's eyes widened and Hatsumi sighed. "Very well, Mi-chan. You may sleep over at Jessica's. But next time, please give us more notice. It would have been nice for Jessica and her parents to come for supper first. We must arrange a dinner soon. It will be nice to meet other families."

Michiru hauled Jessica up and shoved her to the door, calling over her shoulder, "Thanks, Mum. I'll just run Jess home and be right back."

After a muffled "oof" from the living room, her father offered, "I would be happy to give Jessica a ride home."

"That's okay, Dad. She's only ten minutes away..." She paused and revised. "Uh...maybe fifteen, but this way I can slip in a jog before supper."

Michiru handed Jessica's backpack to her and quickly escorted her out.

"You don't need to walk me home." Jessica tried not to sound peevish. "It's not like I'm going to get lost."

Michiru waved a hand at the darkening sky and closed the door. "I'd rather not take any chances. We don't know where Bill is."

Jessica was forced to agree, though she was trying hard not to think too deeply about it.

"Well," she said as they set off. "That didn't go too badly."

Michiru jogged in circles around her. "Are you kidding? It went great. Way better than my introduction to your Mum." She shook her head. "Now we just need to come up with some way to prevent our parents from meeting, ever."

Jessica snorted. "Shouldn't be much of a problem. I barely see mine and I live with them."

"You're soooo lucky."

"I guess," she said, not really feeling it after the warm and quirky atmosphere in Michiru's home. She was not looking forward to returning to her empty house, even for a few hours, and was more grateful than she cared to admit that Michiru was sleeping over tomorrow.

Chapter 32

Hamish met Jessica at the door to her room on Friday afternoon. His tail was super-powered, wagging his whole back end like a magnetized pendulum. He coughed up a feather and flopped onto his back, assuming his well-practiced "rub my tummy" position.

There were several smelly landmines waiting for her. In addition, her bathrobe, duvet, several books, the cord to her bedside lamp, and an old stuffed moose she had lost years ago now bore the marks of a bored puppy.

Jessica barely had time to clean up the mess before Michiru arrived, looking as energetic and fresh after volleyball practice as the bounding puppy. She shed her shoes and jacket at the door, playfully shoving Hamish with her feet.

Jessica retreated to the kitchen to take stock of her supplies and Michiru interestedly scanned the amassed books, papers, herbs, candles, and crystals.

"Wow, you get all this today?"

"I picked up some more salt and herbs on my way home, but I had the rest." Jessica shuffled the items into piles. "Something happened on Halloween that shocked me."

286 *Adriaan & Rebecca Brae*

"You mean other than the kaleidoscope effect, giant rat, and steam-powered dinosaur?"

Jessica laughed. "Before those. When I was dealing with what I thought was Bill's entity, I somehow managed to extend the power in your amulet to my hands." She held her hands out, remembering how the green and blue energies had swirled across them. "If I can replicate that, maybe I can figure out a way to keep us safe during an exorcism. Because, unless I can shield us, it's way too risky, and I haven't come up with any other ideas."

"Worth a try." Expressions of encouragement and skepticism warred on Michiru's face. "Sorry, it's just all so weird."

"I'm with you on that one." Jessica shook some seeds from a packet into a stone mortar and began to grind them into a sharp-smelling powder. "Feel free to raid the kitchen if you're hungry."

She grinned. "If?" Michiru started with a glass of water and then scouted around until she found the pantry. Hamish scampered after her.

"So, where did your parents go?" she asked, her eyes widening as she surveyed the pantry's bulging shelves.

"Some conference in Zurich. Mom's presenting a dissertation on neuro-chemical anomalies in people with PTSD. Dad went along to meet up with people he used to work with."

Jessica groaned as Hamish returned and shoved him away from her feet. He had developed a bit of a toe habit, and hers were tired of being licked and nipped. She pulled her legs up and sat crossed-legged on the chair.

"Cool. My parents never leave me on my own." Michiru moved further into the pantry and caressed a bag of bulk peanut M&M's. She turned back to Jessica holding a box of Kraft Dinner. "Can we have this for supper?"

"Sure. I was thinking of ordering a pizza, but that works."

A look of pure bliss settled over Michiru's face and she grabbed a second box of Kraft Dinner. "We can order pizza too." Her eyes turned dreamy as she murmured to herself, "Kraft Dinner and pizza."

She moved to the stove, skimming the cooking directions on the back of the package. "Is it difficult to make? Mum never lets me eat stuff like this. She has a thing about junk food. Those cookies the other night...they only come out for guests."

Jessica snorted. "She'd better not see our pantry, then. We're strictly sugar- and caffeine-powered." Taking pity on Michiru's novice Kraft Dinnering, she joined her at the stove, opened the box, and pulled out the cheese packet. "It's easy— all you need to do is boil the noodles, drain them, dump in some milk, and mix in the powdered cheese."

"Powdered cheese?" asked Michiru, glancing at the packet uncertainly.

"It tastes better than it sounds." After pointing out which pot to use, Jessica ordered a large pepperoni pizza and pulled a twenty out of the envelope her parents had left.

With dinner sorted, she gathered up her notes, bowl of herbs, and salt. At the door to the garage, she looked back at Michiru, who was putting the water on to boil. "I'm going to work out here—keeps Hamish away from me and me away from anything fragile." She glanced at the display cabinet housing her mother's collection of blown glass figurines. "I'll get things set up and come back in for a quick bite before I start."

* * *

After preparing her ritual space, Jessica emerged from the

garage and deduced that Michiru had spent more quality time with the pantry. She was cuddling a container of premade cream cheese icing and a chocolate cake mix. Her expression suggested she had found Nirvana.

"Can we have this for desert?" Michiru's voice bubbled with anticipation.

"Fine with me, as long as you bake it. Drew's going to be pissed he lost out on this feast. He—" She tensed as an angry sizzling heralded the unmistakable smell of burnt starch. Turning to look at the stove with great trepidation, she saw the pot lid floating on a cloud of bubbles. Milky liquid oozed down the sides and into the burner.

Jessica ran over and yanked the pot off. "Then again, maybe not. How long has this been boiling?"

"There's a time limit?"

Wincing, Jessica drained the water and attempted to break apart the gelatinous mass glued to the bottom. After hacking it into chunks, she mixed in the cheese and gazed at the soggy neon yellow lumps.

"Good thing we ordered pizza." Jessica felt bad for thinking it, but at the same time, she was relieved that not even uber-together Michiru was infallible.

Michiru happily polished off most of the Kraft Dinner while Jessica satisfied her cheese craving by picking out a few extra cheesy pieces.

Just as Jessica began to wonder if she should phone about their pizza, the owner's grandson arrived, apologizing profusely for the delay. He shrugged when she asked how things were going, which was odd, because he was usually quite chatty. He forced a quick smile and then trudged back to his car.

She handed the pizza box to Michiru and frowned,

watching him drive away. The Filipino family who had taken over the local parlor a few years ago was nice and their pizza was the best in town. Their service had never been this slow before. She hoped it meant business was good.

The pizza was perfect, as usual. Jessica contentedly munched thick slices of crisp pepperoni, savoring the smoky, spice of it.

Michiru inhaled half the pizza in the time it took Jessica to finish her second piece, and then gamely proclaimed that she was ready to bake the cake.

After the gooey mess that aspired to be Kraft Dinner, Jessica forced her to thoroughly read the cake instructions.

Jessica sat down beside her at the table and contemplated the homey scene. It was vital they keep a lid on their activities tonight, on more than just the parental front. If it ever got back to Drew that their sleepover involved baking, she'd never live it down.

Next he'll be thinking we're having pillow fights in skimpy nighties.

She glanced at Michiru and blushed.

"I can't put it off any longer," said Jessica with an edge of frustration. "Time to get to work."

Before leaving, Jessica collected the utensils and bowls Michiru needed for the cake. Hamish barked and ran back and forth between them, begging for more pepperoni and attention.

"Hey, you'll need this." Michiru headed Jessica off at the garage door, untying the leather cord from around her neck.

"Right." Jessica looked back at the kitchen table where Michiru had been, wondering how she had teleported herself between the two spaces. Grinning sheepishly, she took the necklace. "I would have felt pretty stupid stuck in my circle with this on the outside."

Michiru patted her shoulder. "Give a shout if you need

me."

"Thanks." Jessica shyly raised her eyes to meet Michiru's. "I mean it. I can't thank you enough for everything you're doing and for your trust."

Michiru smiled and looked away. "Yeah, well…" She cleared her throat, looking slightly embarrassed as she returned to the kitchen. "Good luck."

Jessica watched her friend organize the baking supplies, and pondered the divergent realities of this domestic task and what she was about to attempt. It made her brain hurt.

* * *

Three frustrating hours later, Jessica emerged from the garage tired, cold, depressed, and smelling like a chimney. The warmth of the kitchen slapped her in the face and made her eyes water. Her deflated spirits revived slightly when she detected the rich scent of chocolate.

Michiru was standing at the kitchen table, smearing a thick layer of icing over a lopsided brick.

"Looks yummy." Jessica leaned across and swiped a finger through the icing. She closed her eyes, savoring the sugary goodness. "Oh yeah. I need a whole lot more of that."

Michiru frowned at the trench and added another dollop of icing. "I *was* almost done."

Jessica went in for seconds and received a gentle tap from the spatula. She gave Michiru a half-hearted glare and dropped into a chair, licking her knuckle to rescue the speck of icing the spatula had left.

"Er…how'd it go?" Michiru asked hesitantly, moving the cake to the counter, out of arms reach.

"Pathetic. Not a single thing I tried worked. Nothing." She clenched her hands into fists. "I don't know what I'm doing wrong. I couldn't even get the gatekeeper to appear, and no combination of salt and herbs had any affect on your pendant." She dug Michiru's necklace out of her pocket and placed it on the table.

Jessica crossed her arms and dropped her head onto the table, going cross-eyed as she stared at the glowing green pendant inches from her nose. "What a complete waste of time."

Michiru finished the icing, took a second to admire her crooked masterpiece, and then cut two gigantic slices. She brought the laden plates to the table, moving a stack of books, and sat down opposite Jessica. Before she dug into her slice, she retrieved her pendant and tied it on.

"Have some cake. Sugar will perk you up."

"Not hungry anymore." Jessica mumbled dejectedly.

"More for me, then." Michiru tucked into her slice with glee.

Jessica groaned. "Sorry. I know I'm being an idiot." She said in a small voice.

"If you need to vent, vent."

Jessica raised her head. "I don't see how we can do this. If I can't duplicate the power in your pendant, I can't protect both of us, and I sure as hell can't take on Bill by myself."

"Agreed," said Michiru, thoughtfully licking her fork. "Didn't you say the relic at the church glowed like my necklace?"

"Uh-huh."

"Well, what if we borrow it?" Michiru looked hopeful.

"That won't fly. It's priceless. I've been reading about relics online and that glove is second-class." At Michiru's dubious look, she explained, "No. Second-class is good. The only thing above that is an actual piece of the saint, like a leg bone." Jessica thought for a moment. "Maybe I could leave my computer as collateral?"

"It doesn't look like much. You could probably swap it with a bit of trash and no one would notice." Michiru stuffed a large forkful of cake in her mouth.

Jessica glared at her.

Michiru laughed. "The relic, dummy, not your laptop."

Jessica grumbled to herself as she pulled her plate closer, inhaling the chocolaty scent. "You mean steal it?" She took a bite and something hard crunched. Cringing, she spit the mouthful onto her fork and examined the blue shards nestled amongst the soft brown sponge. It was not the expected stray eggshell. Transferring her examination to the slice on her plate, she pried out an oblong yellow chunk. It tinked onto her plate and she looked up at Michiru questioningly.

"Peanut M&M's. They go with everything." Michiru nabbed the yellow candy and popped it into her mouth with a grin. "I'm not necessarily suggesting we do it, but technically, I don't think it would be difficult."

"Interesting thought, but..." Jessica carefully dissected her cake, working her mind around the idea, then stopped with a puzzled look. "What the...?" She stuck her fork into the squishy end of something poking out of the icing. Her expression changed to horrified as a long jiggling orange-ish strand emerged.

"Ooooo, you got the worm." Michiru said jealously. "Lucky duck!"

She wordlessly handed it over and Michiru ate the gummy worm with obvious delight.

"So, say we were going to do some B&E." Jessica couldn't help hypothesizing. "How would we get glasscutters and electronic code breakers on short notice?"

Michiru chuckled. "You watch too many movies. I saw

the lock on the chapel and it's just an old-style tumbler. Shouldn't take more than a few minutes to pick. There were security signs on the building, but from the look of the wiring, I'm sure there isn't a system."

"You can pick locks?" Jessica asked in disbelief.

"Dad taught me in case I get locked out."

Jessica decided to save that discussion for later. She massaged her temples, attempting to drive out the dull ache behind her eyes.

"I don't know. I'll go back and talk to the priest tomorrow. Maybe we can work something out." She yawned widely. "I've got some ideas about how to do a kind of exorcism, but it involves immobilizing Bill, using the glove, and probably a lot of random unpleasantness." Jessica scrubbed at her face, trying to rub away her fatigue and tension. "And to top it all off, if I can't duplicate whatever trick I pulled on Halloween with your necklace, I'm not sure it or the relic will fully protect us from the entity."

"You did it once." Michiru exuded confidence. "You'll find a way to do it again."

Jessica gave her a level look. "I'll let that one pass, since you haven't known me for long." She sighed. "I'm not known for coming though in a pinch. Last sports day, I ran a relay race and managed to grab the wrong team's baton. I got everyone disqualified."

"Well, I guess we'll see," Michiru said with an air of finality. She read the time display on the oven. "Wow. It's past eleven. Time flies when you're baking!"

"Seriously? No wonder my brain feels like porridge. I've been dead tired lately and I can't seem to catch up on sleep."

Michiru clapped her hands excitedly and massaged Hamish's tummy with her feet to wake him up. "Definitely time for a run."

Hamish raised his head, looked at her through heavy-lidded eyes, and then flopped back down with a grunt.

Jessica stared as blankly as the dog had, waiting for her words to make sense.

Michiru jumped up and danced around the kitchen, gathering dishes and slotting them into the dishwasher. "I didn't get a proper run in today after school, so I've got energy to burn. Plus, the sugar…"

Jessica shook her head. "Knock yourself out. I'm going to bed. Feel free to join me when you're ready. It's plenty big enough for two." She waved an arm, indicating the cooking debris littered throughout the kitchen. "We can sort this out tomorrow."

Jessica hauled her exhausted self up the stairs, pulled on her newly designated sleeping tee, and collapsed into bed. As tired as she was, her mind refused to shut down. Details of tonight's failed experiments ran over and over in her brain. She'd messed up somewhere. If only she could figure out where.

She heard Michiru and Hamish preparing to leave, listened to the front door open and close, and then lay awake. Rain pattered softly against her window, eventually lulling her into an uneasy sleep.

Chapter 33

ALERT: 87% probability current conditions facilitate Shadow transfer to influential host. Notifying Channel.

* * *

The scream came from all directions at once and ended in a moist wheeze. Silence descended. Headlights cut through the night, illuminating a patch of grass and picket fence. Blue and red emergency lights flicked on, adding their pulsing glow to the shadows.

A radio crackled. "Regina 271, what's your 20?"

An RCMP officer slid out of the patrol car and surveyed the area. He tilted his head down to his shoulder mic. "Control. Regina 271, 10-23. Request backup. Just heard a scream. Checking area on foot." His tone was even, but he cleared his throat several times after the transmission.

"10-4, 271." The tinny voice replied. "Regina 263 en-route."

The officer stealthily advanced down the road. He was in an old section of Coldwater. Bungalows and two-storey residences lined the street, some set almost at the sidewalk with little front yards, and others set farther back on larger lots.

After carrying out a quick visual inspection, he spoke into his radio. "Control. 271 here. Who's my RP?"

"Adult female reported disturbance outside residence at 03h16. Unknown orig—" A flood of static interrupted the dispatcher and the officer returned to his vehicle.

Scowling at his shoulder mic, he repeatedly clicked the transmit button and checked the dials on his radio. "Control, you're breaking up. Say again."

"271 RP is online and confirms scream. She said it might have come from her backyard or somewhere beside the residence."

"Copy. Checking residence now. Inform RP officer on scene and to stay inside. Any word on 263?"

"ETA 2 minutes. She's stuck at the rail crossing."

"10-4 Control. Standby." The officer retrieved a flashlight from the dashboard clip. He swept the beam up and down the street before turning onto a stone path running alongside the bungalow. A lit plaque beside the door read '53.'

Wiping a hand on his shirt, he unclipped his holster and rested his palm on the gun. "Probably just another damn cat run afoul of a coyote. Stupid pet owners," he grumbled.

His boots scraped against the uneven paving stones as he approached the backyard. A rusty chain-link fence resolved out of the darkness and he unlatched the gate with a shaky hand, cringing as the hinges squealed.

Ahead, there was a whisper of movement and a curious grunting sound.

He drew his gun, holding it level with his flashlight as he scanned the backyard and exterior of the house.

It was a large yard. Three groups of bulky spruce trees, a rickety shed, and more shapes shrouded in darkness stretched out beyond the reach of his feeble light. He glanced at the sky and cursed the impotent sliver of moon.

More rustling came from the trees as the dispatcher's voice chirped, "271. Update status."

His breath quickened as he growled into the mic, "Control. 271. Movement in backyard. Possible animal. Attempting to confirm. Stand by with radio silence."

He flinched at the abrupt, "10-4." The dispatcher sounded miffed.

The dry crackling of fallen spruce needles grew louder as he moved forward. Something shifted behind the branches. It panted, low and raspy.

Keeping his light and gun trained on the trees, he edged around and stopped as his foot squelched in a sodden patch of earth. Frowning, he squinted at the shadowed ground.

Another rustle from the trees, closer now.

His gaze jerked back to the illuminated bottom branches and the void beyond. The air held the clean scent of forest mingled with feces, and something else. Something tangy. A hint of copper.

Silence.

The officer flashed the light at his feet and flicked the gun safety off. He was standing in a spreading pool of dark fluid, too viscous to be water and too copious to have come from a house cat.

A soggy tearing noise was followed by a thwap, like a wet rubber band being snapped.

Backing toward the gate, he steadied his gun and flashlight, and yelled, "Police. Put your hands on your head and walk slowly toward me."

No response.

He stopped and listened. The shuffling sound continued. He took a few steps toward the trees again, repeating his order.

No animal fled. No person emerged.

He cautiously rounded the trees and the scene was lit with sudden, brutal clarity. Bloody remains of what was possibly a woman lay battered and torn in the dripping grass. Entrails and other bits hung from branches. A hunched figure, slick with gore, excrement, and viscera, crouched over the body, hands buried deep in the gaping stomach cavity.

The figure looked up, halting its grisly search. The officer stared at the bloody face, so contorted with rage that it barely looked human. For a moment, they stayed, unmoving, staring. Then the officer barked, "On the ground. Hands behind your head."

Metal flashed near the body. The killer snarled and leapt.

The officer shot once and moved back, trying to put some distance between them.

He kept coming.

In the darkness, with the amount of blood already on him, the officer couldn't be sure he hit. He took aim and fired another two shots.

The killer dropped to the ground and slid to a stop a few feet from the officer's boots.

He waited for signs of movement as the smell of sulfur hung in the air. When there was none, he jammed the flashlight under his arm and clicked his radio, working at gathering the breath to speak. "10-38. 10-38. Where is my fucking backup?"

The dispatcher hissed, "271. Officer Riley is arriving. Say again?"

Tires screeched at the front of the house.

"Control...oh God. It's a kid. He was tearing someone apart. He...I shot him. I think he's dead."

"271. What's your 20?"

He shakily holstered his gun. "Backyard. Send an ambulance." After a slight pause, he added, "And get the sergeant out here ASAP."

He laid his flashlight on the ground, directing the light at the boy, and kicked away a nasty-looking hunting knife. After clearing the immediate area, he crouched down to check for a pulse.

A torn hunk of flesh slithered off the boy's hair as the officer nudged his shoulder to get at his neck.

Liquid darkness oozed toward his hand. It flowed over the boy's blood soaked face, across his ear, and down his neck. He jerked his hand away, but not quick enough.

It stretched between his finger and the teen's body like molten toffee, engulfing his hand and sliding up his arm in a matter of seconds.

Officer Riley ran into the backyard. She stared, bewildered, as her colleague flailed and shrieked, "It burns. Oh God. IT BURNS. HELP ME." His last words rose to such a fevered pitch of panic, they were barely audible.

Chapter 34

Jessica woke up on the floor, her heart racing and her right arm spasming with a pale echo of dream agony. The side of her face hurt and one breast was squished between her body and the carpet.

She rolled onto her back and massaged the remaining tremors from her arm. It was second nature at this point.

A dim red light hovered above her, illuminating the flow of Michiru's hair, which brushed the floor as she hung over the side of the bed.

"Hey," Michiru said cheerfully. "I didn't kick you, did I?"

"Um, I don't think so," she replied shakily. "I think I fell out all on my own."

Hamish pounced from his hiding place under the bed and tugged on Michiru's hair. She giggled, rolled over, and pulled the tantalizing strands out of reach. Ditching her flashlight, she turned on the bedside lamp.

The puppy lay on his back for a few seconds, waiting for a rematch, but when the hair didn't return, he wriggled to his feet and began enthusiastically scratching an ear.

Jessica eased into a sitting position, rubbing the side of

her breast through her shirt. As the dream horror percolated through her shock, she recognized the vivid, out-of-body feel from her previous visions.

She sucked in a sharp breath.

That's actually going to happen, if it hasn't already.

"Mac." Jessica didn't recognize her own voice, it was so thick with despair.

Michiru tensed, perched on the edge of the bed with her legs curled to one side. "What's wrong?"

Jessica opened her mouth intending to describe the dream, but it was too real.

Fresh blood mingled with the sharp scent of gunpowder.

Sweat slicked Jessica's forehead and upper lip. She couldn't form words; she could barely get enough air to speak.

Bloody globules, black in the moonlight, spattered across grass.

No, no, Jessica scolded herself. *I have to keep it together. Can't fall apart, not in front of her.*

She tried to stand with a vague plan to run to the bathroom, but there was no strength in her limbs.

Frustration overwhelmed her. *I'm no use to anyone, even myself.* She let out a strangled groan as a hot tear trailed down her cheek.

Michiru slid off the bed and wrapped her arms around her.

Jessica laid her head on Michiru's shoulder. All her good intentions, her useless, bumbling attempts to make things better, swelled together and burrowed through her chest like a pack of razors. Hiding her face, she cried, only vaguely aware of Michiru patting her back.

She wanted the earth to swallow her up and make it stop. To make everything stop.

Why can't I be smarter? Why can't I fix anything? Why me? Why? Just, why?

Jessica raged at the horrific images burned into her mind, raged at the entity, raged at the world for letting such a thing exist, and raged at herself for not being able to erase it.

Eventually her anger burnt itself to embers, and her body sagged, and a while after that, the need to blow her nose overwhelmed her reluctance to leave Michiru's embrace.

Jessica pulled away and retrieved a box of tissues from her bedside table, shielding her eyes from the too-bright lamp.

She spent a moment cleaning up and reassuring Hamish, who was whining and pawing at her legs. She welcomed the concerned puppy into her lap and fussed over him, grateful for the distraction before facing Michiru.

This is fantastic. She's really going to think I'm unstable now, not to mention a complete wimp.

Jessica forced herself to look at Michiru. Expecting pity and condescension, she instead found her friend sporting a grin.

"Ribbit!" Michiru's grin widened.

Jessica stared at her, worried her sanity had finally given up and taken a permanent vacation.

Michiru pointed at Jessica's lap and she realized her sleeping-tee was riding high enough to expose her froggy underwear. She flushed and shuffled her shirt down over her hips.

"They're cute." Michiru bunched her shirt up to show off a toned hip clad in plain, light pink cotton. "My mum only gets boring ones."

Laughter bubbled up in Jessica until she couldn't help herself. She giggled, and then giggled some more. It really wasn't that funny, but she couldn't stop. "Thanks." She said between breaths. "I needed that."

"Anytime." Michiru's expression turned serious. "So, you

ready to fill me in?"

"Right." Jessica turned her mind back to the tangled mass of problems and found them ever so slightly thinned. She hadn't wanted to take this path, but it was their only option. She met Michiru's eyes. "We need to steal the relic. Now."

Michiru raised an eyebrow.

"I had another vision." Her heart beat faster with remembered fear. "Bill's going to kill someone, a girl. No...not just kill, he's going to literally rip her apart." Bile rose in her throat and she looked down to see that she'd shredded her latest tissue. Scraps of white littered the carpet.

"Shit. When? Or has it already happened?" Michiru looked ready to spring in any direction.

"I don't...I don't think so. It sort of felt like it was going to happen." She chewed her bottom lip. "I can't really explain."

"Okay." Michiru watched her intently. "Any idea when?"

Normally being stared at would have shattered Jessica's confidence, but there was no challenge in Michiru's gaze.

"Soon. And when he's done, whatever's in him, this entity, it's going to jump into a cop." She held her friend's eyes. "And then we're all well and truly fucked."

"I trust you." Michiru said, her voice echoing her conviction. "Let's do this."

Jessica found the strength she needed to get up off the floor.

* * *

After pulling on black leggings and a dark green sweater, Jessica trooped downstairs with Michiru. She rubbed her bleary eyes, questioning how Michiru looked as calm and rested as if she'd just come back from a weeklong retreat.

She frowned at Michiru's chosen outfit—jeans and a

thick, aqua-blue argyle sweater.

"Shouldn't you wear something darker? I could lend you some pants and a shirt." Jessica paused as a thought occurred. "Hey. I think I have some black face makeup leftover from my Death costume last Halloween."

Michiru blinked. "And if we're stopped by someone, say a cop, how do you plan on explaining the black faces and burglar attire?"

"Belated Halloween party?" Even Jessica didn't sound convinced.

Chuckling, Michiru headed to the kitchen. "I'll take my chances dressed as a normal person, thanks."

Michiru upended her canvas messenger bag on the kitchen table. She stacked her binders and texts to one side and then rifled around inside. Jessica heard the distinctive sound of Velcro as she pulled up a flap at the bottom and began unloading an interesting array of items.

She laid a small black leather case on the table and rolled it open. It contained what appeared to be dental implements.

"This really shouldn't require torture," Jessica said, glancing apprehensively between the instruments and Michiru.

She laughed. "They're lock picks. I suppose they could double as torture devices, but I'd hate to wreck them, so, that's not going to happen."

Jessica stared at the canister Michiru placed beside the picks. "Dog repellant?" She leaned closer, squinting at the metal bar with four holes that emerged next. "What's that for?"

Michiru slipped her fingers neatly into the openings. "Brass knuckles. Gives punches more oomph."

"Where did you even get those? Aren't they illegal?"

"Yup. But it's amazing what Dad finds at garage sales. He can't pass up a good deal. Honestly, sometimes I think he brings things home because he feels bad nobody wants them. Our house is an orphanage for unwanted bits and bobs." She flexed her fingers in the brass knuckles and then slipped them off.

"Does he know you have them?"

"He should. He gave them to me."

"He gave them to you?" Jessica repeated incredulously. "Why?"

Michiru looked confused. "To defend myself." She answered slowly, in the tone of someone unsure whether the question was a trick. "Mum and Dad would rather I hurt someone else in defense than get hurt or killed myself. I always have some kind of weapon on me." After a pause, she asked, "Don't you carry something?"

Jessica shook her head, trying to imagine Michiru's sale-addicted dad and cute mom having that conversation.

Michiru gave her an appraising look. "You should. You've got the same short reach as me, you're crap at sprinting, and you'll be weaker than most opponents. Even a small knife might distract someone long enough for you to get away." She gestured at the bay window. "Bill's out there, Jess. He's strong and he doesn't like you. You need to start thinking about how to defend yourself."

Jessica peered into the bleak night, mesmerized by the silvered droplets of rain running down the window.

Michiru pressed a thin black folding knife into her hand. After a cursory examination, Jessica figured out how to work the blade lock and dropped the weapon into her pocket, not sure whether she could bring herself to use it.

"Is there a specific plan or are we pretty much winging it?" Jessica asked, shuffling her feet. "I'm not too good at the whole flying-by-the-seat-of-my-pants thing. I do better with a plan. A detailed plan. A plan involving a spreadsheet or maybe a slide presentation. Maybe we should—"

"Oh, no." Michiru clapped her hands together excitedly. "We're winging it. We're out of time, and anyways, over-thinking might work against us here. Kinda exciting, right?"

"Wait a minute." Jessica narrowed her eyes. "This is exciting? And yet you're the one who freaked out about the Halloween plan! At least there was a plan."

"And we just about broke reality," Michiru countered. "Let's try not planning this time. It might be safer."

Jessica paled. "I'm sorry about that. If I'd—"

"Stop apologizing. It cleared up." Michiru reloaded her bag. "You've whetted my appetite for adventure. Halloween was like the epicenter of weirdness. I had no idea what would happen next. It was..." She searched for the right word. "...exhilarating. Besides, there's no way Father Wochecki... what's his name?"

"Call him Nick." Jessica giggled.

"There's no way Nick will be out and about in the middle of a beastly night like this, and the church is nicely secluded from the street. We'll be fine."

* * *

Between the dense clouds looming over Coldwater valley and the pelting rain, no sliver of moonlight or streetlight breached the dark to guide their way to the church. The night swallowed buildings and obliterated whole sections of the landscape, turning what should have been a short trip down familiar streets into a strange and alien pilgrimage.

Jessica followed Michiru, keeping her head down to prevent rain from sneaking inside her hood. Each stretch of pavement and ditch looked the same as the next. The trees lining the sidewalk, the occasional crack, the heavy scent of wet tar; everything seemed familiar, yet when she tried to figure out where she was, she came up blank. And it felt like they had been walking for far too long.

Tapping Michiru on the shoulder, she moved closer and whispered, "Where are we?" She could barely hear herself over the drumming rain.

Michiru frowned and leaned closer. "What?" She made no attempt at quietness, and still the word was instantly swept away by the storm.

Jessica raised her voice and repeated the question.

"We're almost back at the church gate," answered Michiru.

"What do you mean, 'back'?"

"We did a circuit of the churchyard. I wanted to make sure no one was about."

Jessica wiped rain from her eyes. "Tell me again why we couldn't bring umbrellas."

The wind stole Michiru's exasperated sigh. "Because they're bulky and make too much noise in the rain. You might as well bang on a drum." She started forward again and Jessica trotted to keep up.

"But I'm getting soaked." Jessica winced, hearing the whine in her voice. Shivering as a stream of water slid inside her jacket and ran down her chest, she clamped her mouth shut and told herself to suck it up. At least the cold and wet were keeping her awake.

The churchyard's imposing iron gate materialized out of the haze.

Michiru leaned close and said, "From here on in, we go silent...or as near to it as possible. Did you bring your cell?"

When Jessica nodded, she continued, "Then turn it off.

Or better yet, pull the battery out. This storm is great cover, but let's not push our luck."

Jessica did as instructed and watched Michiru scale the ten-foot gate using the decorative ironwork as foot and hand-holds. She smoothly straddled the top and jumped down to land lightly on the gravel road beyond. Jessica was still attempting to fathom her path when she noticed Michiru's expectant stare.

The gate stood impassively between them. Jessica looked at the top. It seemed miles away. She bit her lip. This was the dreaded climbing wall all over again, except with no safety equipment.

Michiru grabbed her arm through the gate and hissed, "Snap out of it. We need to do this quick."

Jessica tried to stop her arm from shaking, but couldn't. Embarrassment heated her chilled face.

"If you can't make it, go home," Michiru said bluntly. "I'll meet up with you when I'm done."

Jessica shook her head, peering unblinking from the shadow of her hood at the gate.

There was a spark of realization in Michiru's eyes and she nodded once. "Right. This is kinda new to you. The gate has a repeated pattern, so it's easy. Just plant your feet firmly and make sure your grip is good. The metal's a bit slippery."

Jessica looked past the frame at Michiru. She was smiling encouragingly, the way a parent does at a child scared of monsters in their closet. Unable to bear that look any longer, Jessica grabbed a metal curlicue, placed her foot on an iron leaf, and started to climb.

Through sheer determination, she dragged herself to the top. She hooked a leg around the top bar and was just sliding over when she suddenly jerked to a stop.

Jessica teetered, straddling the gate, trying to find what part of her was snagged. After acquiring bruises in sensitive areas from the bar, she realized the bottom of her sweater was hooked over a spear-point.

She had a bad moment, looking longingly for solid ground, only to find it veiled in misting rain. Her climbing instructor's voice rang in her ears, "Focus on your holds, not the ground."

She swung back to the other side, hanging by her elbow and knee, fighting vertigo as she felt for a foothold. Cursing Michiru for not allowing them to use flashlights, she finally located a spot to stand and wrestled her sweater from the gate's steely grasp.

When she painfully eased over the top again, Jessica felt as though she had climbed Mt. Everest, twice. She half slid, half fell down the slippery metal on the other side and landed on her hip.

Michiru stared at her in disbelief and then offered a hand.

Jessica grudgingly took it and stood, brushing bits of gravel off. She glared at Michiru. "Easy, my ass!"

Michiru made a shushing gesture and headed up the road with Jessica limping behind. They reached the church and Michiru pulled her into the shadows as she rifled through her bag. Handing a pocket flashlight to Jessica, she directed her to focus its red beam on the keyhole while she worked.

"Now we get to use one." Jessica muttered to herself.

Michiru hissed at her to be quiet without taking her eyes off the lock.

Jessica watched her nimble fingers slide instruments in and out of the keyhole. The rhythmic movement was hypnotic and Jessica found herself unable to look away. There was something almost musical in the repeated patterns, as if Michiru was working in tempo with a mysterious tune that she alone could hear.

Eventually, she clicked her tongue in triumph and pushed the door open. After a quick look inside, she grabbed Jessica and they slipped into the dark chapel.

Michiru took the flashlight, hooded the beam with her hand, and led the way to the cabinet. Jessica trailed behind, overcome with fear that the glove wouldn't be there. Based on her recent spate of luck, she wouldn't be surprised if it was gone, safely tucked under the priest's pillow or in a secret vault.

When they arrived at the cabinet and the glass case was conspicuously absent, Jessica sank to the floor with a hopeless moan. "It's not here. I knew it!"

Puddles of water pooled under the girls as they stared at the empty surface.

Michiru began opening drawers until she found one that was locked. She smiled. "You give up too easily."

"And you jump to conclusions. You don't know it's in there. He probably noticed how interested I was and sent it back to the Vatican for safekeeping."

"Oh, come on. Now who's jumping? Father Nick couldn't move that case far. It looked heavy. I'll bet you a bag of candy it's in here."

Tucking the flashlight under her chin, Michiru pulled out her picks and went to work. The lock quickly gave in to her persuasions and she triumphantly extracted the case, set it on the cabinet, and lifted the glass lid to retrieve the relic.

Jessica touched the wrinkled leather and a soothing warmth enveloped her chilled fingers. She instinctively jerked her hand back as a drop of water rolled off her raincoat cuff.

"It'll be safe in here." Michiru tucked the relic into a side pocket of her bag. "It's waterproofed on the inside. Not that a little rain's likely to hurt this fossilized lump."

Michiru replaced the case, pulled one of Jessica's hand towels out of her bag, and mopped up the puddles around the cabinet. She directed Jessica to move back to the door and followed, wiping the trail of water as they went.

"Oh." Jessica exhaled in sudden comprehension. "The towel makes sense now."

"Just in case someone comes in tomorrow, or really, this morning. If we're lucky, we might be able to return it before anyone notices it's missing."

"That would be good." Jessica whispered without much optimism. She opened the church door a crack and peeked out as Michiru shoved the towel back into her bag. Pulling her hood up, she ducked into the rain and waited as Michiru locked the door.

The girls moved quickly down the path to the gate and Jessica watched in awe as Michiru scaled the metal skeleton as easily as a spider on a web.

Jessica inched her way up the slippery frame, painfully eased over the top, and managed not to fall on her ass as she descended the other side.

Once her feet were firmly planted on the ground, she looked back at the gate, barely able to believe she'd made it.

It wasn't pretty or graceful, and definitely not without a price, she thought, rubbing her bruised hip, *but I did it. At least my twenty minutes of terror on the climbing wall were good for something.* She shook out her arms and legs and flexed her fingers, trying to loosen up her over-stressed muscles. *I swore I'd never climb anything again. But then, I also swore I'd never tackle the entity again, and that's exactly where all this is headed.*

Michiru hooked her arm through Jessica's and propelled her down the street, humming cheerfully. The rain was slowing and by the time they made it back to the house, it was nothing more than a fine mist drifting on a gentle breeze. There were even a few stars winking between breaks in the clouds.

Jessica glared at the sky. "*Now* you clear up."

She shoved her door open, shrugged out of her water-logged jacket, dropped it in a heap by the door, and stood shivering. Her sweater, the bottom of which had started the evening slightly below her waist, now sagged well past her knees, heavy with rain and stretched from its tussle with the gate.

Michiru stayed on the porch to shake her jacket off and then carefully hung it and her bag in the hall closet. Jessica watched, amused, as she went back onto the porch to wring out her drenched clothes. Evidently deciding it was hopeless, she stripped down to her underwear and bra, came in, and laid her shirt and pants in front of a heating vent.

Rubbing her arms vigorously, Michiru pranced into the kitchen. "Want some hot chocolate?"

Jessica suddenly couldn't think of anything she wanted more. She needed a boost if she planned to make it up to her bedroom.

"Sounds perfect. I'll be right there."

She tried to pull her sweater over her head, but the sodden mass had other plans. Feeling like she was wrestling an inebriated octopus, Jessica eventually escaped and flung it away. It made a satisfying squelch when it landed. She peeled her leggings off, vehemently threw her socks at the sopping pile, and stood, soaking in the warm air until her shivering eased.

After retrieving the relic from Michiru's bag, Jessica joined her in the kitchen. She was dancing between cupboards, finding mugs and spoons, completely unaffected by her near-naked state. Jessica stopped in the doorway, looking down at her own generous curves, warring against a surge of self-consciousness. Michiru was the freest spirit she had ever met. She envied her.

Jessica sucked in her tummy and sat heavily in a chair, feeling like a bruised lump of fat. She set the relic on the table, still shocked they had pulled off the theft. As painful and grueling as the endeavor had been, they were still in possession of all their limbs and nobody was bunking in a cell with Big Bertha. It was a win, but she wasn't entirely sure how she felt about it.

I'm a thief. She gazed at the glove's glowing maze of folds and crinkles. *If there is a god looking out for you, I hope they take good intentions into consideration. It would be horribly depressing to be smited before I get the chance to do something worthwhile.*

Chapter 35

Jessica woke up later that morning cuddled against Michiru's side. She might as well have been hugging a boiler...a really noisy boiler in need of maintenance. Inching back to find some relief from the heat, her bum met air and she realized she was already perched on the edge of her bed. With a sigh, she shoved the covers off and stared at her snoring companion.

Her double bed had always afforded ample room for sleepovers, but Michiru consumed more space than her diminutive stature suggested possible. Jessica gently poked her bedmate, hoping to shift her over.

Michiru mumbled in her sleep and inched closer.

Jessica put a foot on the floor to stop herself from falling out of bed.

How does she do it? She watched her friend's mouth gape open and emit a noise akin to a bulldozer running out of fuel. *Even like this, she manages to be beautiful.*

Her hair was fanned artistically across the pillow, in sharp contrast to what Jessica imagined her own rat's nest looked like. It smelled of green apples. She involuntarily stroked a strand, wondering why Michiru always wore her hair in a ponytail. It was so thick, and luscious, and gorgeously straight.

The smooth curve of Michiru's face reminded Jessica of Beth's collection of porcelain geisha dolls. She'd inherited them from a relative and they had risked parental wrath every time they'd snuck them out of their special cabinet to play with.

Jessica smiled at the incongruity. She couldn't imagine Michiru serving tea, head lowered, with that coy smile geishas always had in movies. A more likely scenario would be Michiru swinging through the peaceful scene on a rope to steal the evil empress's teacup and save the empire.

She reached under her pillow to retrieve her pet sock and the deep indigo numbers on her alarm clock caught her eye. *Almost noon.* Running the supple fabric through her fingers, she drew its comforting softness into her soul and shed the last muzzy residues of sleep.

Coffee time.

Jessica gingerly sat up and eased her other foot to the floor. Most of her pain and stiffness was concentrated around her inner thigh and groin area, no doubt the result of time spent on the gate's unforgiving top bar. She leaned forward to examine her thighs and caught sight of an odd green glow near the top of her bed.

It came from her pet sock, which was sticking out from under her pillow. A faint, wavering aura surrounded it. She ran a fingertip over it, feeling a weak echo of the warmth she experienced when touching Michiru's necklace and the relic.

She shoved it back under her pillow. *Now my sock's magical? What next, magic underwear?* She glanced down and was relieved to note her frogs were not glowing.

Something moved under Jessica's foot as she stood. A rapid volley of barking and yipping ensued, and she hopped away, trying to extricate Hamish's teeth from her baby toe.

Michiru sprang up and landed on the other side of the bed in a crouch, wielding a knife. It was twin to the one she had given Jessica. Her eyes darted around the room, searching for danger.

Jessica waved a hand at her. "I just stepped on his tail. No need to skewer anything." Jumping onto the bed to escape the disgruntled puppy, she groaned and rubbed her toe. "Great...now my foot hurts too."

"Nothing's simple with you, is it? Most people get up and go to the bathroom in the morning, but not you. You instigate a dog fight." Chuckling, Michiru bounced back into bed and examined Jessica's toe. "You'll live. He didn't even break the skin."

Michiru hung over the side of the bed and found Hamish licking his tail. After running her fingers along the offended extremity, she waggled a finger at him. "You'll live too, you big whiner."

Hamish forgot about his trauma as soon as Michiru's hair dangled within reach. He pounced and there was a thud as he ran into the bed frame.

Michiru straightened her twisted pajama top and turned back to Jessica, her eyes widening when she saw her bruised thighs. "Yikes." She winced in sympathy. "How'd that happen?"

"The gate." Jessica tried not to glare. Michiru didn't have a scratch or mark anywhere on her.

"Seriously? You had a bit of a struggle, but I didn't think it was that bad."

Jessica harrumphed as she inspected her purple splotches. She could almost make out the shape of one of the gate's iron leaves. "I don't suppose you have something in your magic bag of many things to help bruises heal faster? I feel like I've still got that damn bar wedged between my legs."

Michiru covered her mouth, but a snort of laughter escaped.

Jessica scowled. *Definitely not geisha material.*

Michiru composed herself and apologized. Clearing her throat, she offered, "Apart from cover-up and tiger balm, time's the only cure I know of."

Jessica giggled despite herself. "Slim chance I'll need cover-up down there." Then she asked, "Tiger bum? Gross."

"Balm. It's for muscle aches, but it's good for bruises too." She patted Jessica on the shoulder. "I'll see if your parents have some." Michiru headed to the bathroom and Jessica flopped onto her back.

After a few minutes, Michiru returned empty-handed. "Okay. I've never seen such a well-stocked medicine cabinet, except it's all pills and plasters. Is there somewhere else...?" She stopped talking when Jessica's eyes flared and her mouth opened in a silent O.

"What?" she asked, cautiously examining the section of ceiling Jessica was staring at.

Jessica sat bolt upright on the bed. A smile spread across her face. She clapped her hands like an overexcited child on Christmas morning. "That's it! You're brilliant!"

Michiru gave her a puzzled look and Jessica continued, "I know how we can get Bill, but we need transport." She pursed her lips. "Drew!"

She swung her legs to the floor, snatched her phone from her bedside table, and sat on the edge of her bed waiting for him to pick up. Scowling when she received his voicemail, she ended the call and texted:

<< Need ride tonight. Life or death. Call me

Michiru's hair tickled Jessica's arm as she peered over her

shoulder. "You sure know how to hook someone, but is he even going to get that? I mean, his cell is trashed."

Jessica gave her a look. "It's Drew. There's no way he'd go without a phone for more than a day."

Michiru shrugged. "Hey, doesn't your boyfriend have a car? Maybe you should set things up with him, just in case? He looks built in your photos. Certainly more than Drew. We could use the extra muscle."

"Well, Eric can borrow his mom's car sometimes, but not on short notice." Jessica grimaced. "Also, I'd really like to keep him out of this. I still haven't found a way to tell him about what's happening. Drew already knows, so it'll be quicker and waaaaay less complicated with him."

A crease appeared on Michiru's brow. "I'm not always on the mark about what girls do, but don't they usually talk to their boyfriends about stuff? I mean, what's the point in having one if you don't?"

Jessica snorted and then quieted, realizing Michiru was serious. "Um, well, there's other reasons." She focused on her feet, brushing her toes against the carpet. "I can't think of a way to explain what's going on with Bill at this point that won't end with Eric calling the police. Think about it…violent guy stalking your girlfriend. What would you do?" She held up a hand. "Let me rephrase that. What would the average person do?"

Michiru nodded. "I see what you mean. And I guess it's all pretty unbelievable unless you've seen what's been happening. I still can't wrap my mind around Halloween, but I'd give anything for a ride on that mechanical dinosaur." A wistful look came over her and then she refocused on Jessica. "So, are you going to explain your plan, or should I stew for a bit longer?"

Jessica grinned. "No. I'll explain. But let's get some coffee on while we talk. I think this is going to be another very full day."

Chapter 36

After ironing out a plan over two pots of coffee, they spent the afternoon searching for Bill at popular hangouts. It was just past four. Everyone else was heading home, or preparing for Saturday night parties, and they still had no idea where the elusive footballer was.

The girls stopped for a sugar fix at the local ice cream parlor. They found an empty bench nestled among the trees lining Main Street and sat, people watching, as they dejectedly licked their treats.

Michiru had been in hyper-drive most of the day, jogging everywhere and fidgeting whenever she had to stand still, but now she looked like a deflated balloon.

"Is there a jackhammer on my head?" She asked, wincing as she rubbed her forehead.

Jessica peered around her triple scoop cone. "Probably too much caffeine."

"I guess." Michiru flinched as a car horn sounded. "Does coffee normally do this? You look fine."

"Don't tell me you haven't had it before?"

Michiru shrugged. "My parents drink tea."

"Life without the mighty java bean." Jessica contemplated the horrifying prospect as she licked a drop of caramel chocolate chunk ice cream off her hand. "I used to get a headache if I drank lots, but not so much anymore. I guess that also explains why you've been flying around like a monkey on speed all day. I thought you were just really excited about the plan."

Michiru grunted and sucked a large strawberry out of her strawberry shortcake ice cream. "Remind me not to drink coffee again. I need a nap." She hung her head in disgust.

Jessica started on her second scoop. Her eyes drifted closed in ecstasy as she relished the pistachio ice cream's salty sweetness. "I think you're one of those people who don't need uppers." She paused mid-lick as a thought occurred. "What if Bill's left town? We'll never find him."

"Don't think so. He's got no wheels. Charlie said his parents took his keys away when he got suspended." Michiru bit into her sugar cone and winced. Jessica watched in dismay as she tossed the remainder in the garbage.

"Was there something wrong with it?"

"Too loud."

It took a moment for Jessica to understand. "Oh. But I would have eaten it."

Michiru snorted and winced again. "You'll be lucky to finish yours before you end up wearing it." Michiru ducked back into the busy parlor and came out carrying a wad of napkins. She wiped Jessica's shirtfront. "Good thing you're wearing tie-die. Nobody's going to notice a spill on this."

"I need to do laundry." Jessica gave her a sheepish grin. "Maybe a friend drove him somewhere?"

"Could be." Michiru pulled her up and started walking. "We'd better get to the shop. Doesn't it close soon?"

Jessica happily crunched on her cone as she hurried to

keep up. "We've got lots of time. They're open 'til five." Pausing to contemplate her last bite, she added, "You know, it is kinda loud when you think about it."

They approached the quaint little pet shop, sandwiched between an old-school barbershop and a second-hand bookstore. Jessica looked longingly at the rows of tempting books, remembering many a glorious afternoon spent investigating the wall-to-wall, floor-to-ceiling shelves. She wished she was here to do that now.

As she licked the sticky remains off her fingers, an angsty guitar riff from a heavy metal tune issued from her pants. She nearly pulled them down in her haste to retrieve her phone.

Michiru turned the pet shop's paw-shaped door handle and pulled. There was a muted tinkling as the bell quivered inside, but the door remained closed.

The smile that had sprung to Jessica's face upon answering her phone gradually fell.

"I see. No. There's three of us…four with you. A motorbike won't cut it." She smiled stiffly at an old lady walking by and lowered her voice. "I can't explain right now. Can you meet us at my house? Oh…not until then? Okay…"

Michiru frowned at the door. The sounds of birds chirping, fish tanks bubbling, and various scratching noises drifted through the glass barrier, but most of the lights inside were off.

Jessica pointed at a piece of paper tacked to the shop's picture window: "Trixie's in labor. Open Monday, regular hours, with new puppies! Thanx, Bonnie."

"We're fucked." Jessica glared at the note. "Random store hours—welcome to small-town Alberta. We'll never be able to catch a live mouse."

A muffled voice came from her phone and she pressed it back to her ear. "Sorry…no. Just come to my house as soon as you can."

She shoved the phone into her pocket and stared blankly at the ground, not ready to contemplate another round of B&E. "My idea for transport is a no-go. Not that it really matters now."

"One problem at a time." Michiru was silent for a moment and then said, "I might have an idea." She glanced down the street to the newly built, chain grocery store. It stood out in cold contrast to the rest of the quirky, old-west-styled shop fronts. "Does it have to be a mouse?"

"I don't know." Jessica followed Michiru's gaze and shook her head. "But I'm pretty sure it has to be alive. We can't just slap down a pork chop and expect the entity to think it's the next hot vacation spot."

Michiru pushed Jessica toward the grocery store. "Come on. I'll show you what I mean."

She led Jessica through the aisles to the back, where the fish counter stood. Jessica saw the big tank and Michiru's line of thought became obvious.

Michiru tapped the glass and watched one of the lobsters crawl over his comrades. "Probably not four-star accommodation, but it's alive." She waved at the tank like a game show host. "Think it'll work?"

Jessica frowned. "I haven't the foggiest. I'm not even sure a mouse will work. It's just what was in Drew's skinwalker legend." She contemplated the shellfish and shrugged. "It's worth a try, though it's a bit of a moot point right now. Without Bill, the game's up."

Michiru fixed her with a look. "One problem at a time, remember."

Jessica rolled her eyes and set about picking the friskiest lobster. The butcher bagged the unfortunate crustacean and the girls made their way to the till. Jessica ducked down the pop aisle with thoughts of resupplying her depleted Dr. Pepper stockpile.

"Figures!" Jessica glared at the last two bottles at the back of the top shelf.

She stood on her tiptoes and knocked over a diet Coke next to the Dr. Peppers, hoping it might tip one of her targets and encourage some rolling. It didn't. Annoyed, she climbed onto the lowest shelf and tested the next one to see if it was sturdy enough to hold her weight.

A chattering group bustled down the aisle and Jessica dropped to the ground as she recognized some of her more popular schoolmates.

She made herself as small as possible, hoping they would pass by so she could continue her quest in peace. Instead, they stopped a little ways off to stock their cart. Casting a longing glance at the Dr. Pepper mocking her from its lofty perch, she tugged at Michiru's sleeve to go.

Michiru smiled at the group. A tall, trim guy with wavy brown hair smiled back, straightened his jacket, and swaggered over.

"Hey, you're that wicked volleyball player…"

From the pained expression on his face, Jessica guessed he was trying to remember Michiru's name.

"Mac," Michiru jumped in to help him before he hurt himself.

"Right." His smile broadened. "I'm Dean. Basketball's my game." He glanced back at his gang's overflowing shopping carts and punched one of his mates on the shoulder. "Hey. Get some diet shit or the girls won't drink anything." He turned back to Michiru and grinned. "And that would be a shame…so…you got any plans tonight, Mac?"

Michiru shrugged. "Looking for someone." When his chest puffed out, she hastily added, "Bill. He plays football. You know him?"

Dean's grin cracked. "Sure. He should be coming. I'm having a little house party." His teeth flashed white as his smile widened. "Why don't you stop by and I'll show you how much more fun I am? Bill's a little...checked out lately."

"Yes!" Michiru clapped in excitement and then winced at the sharp noise. "For sure he'll be there?"

"In living color. He'll be smashed by eleven and passed out in a pool of his own piss by midnight. I, on the other hand, plan to be pleasantly buzzed and fully functional all night." He leered at her and Michiru forced a half-hearted smile.

"Uh...sounds fun. Where do you live?"

He rattled off a dizzying array of directions involving an old gas station, a dead pine tree that was struck by lightning three years ago, and a rock on someone's front lawn that looked like a giant penis.

Michiru glanced at Jessica, who was hunched behind her pretending to read the ingredients on a pop bottle.

Jessica gave her a quick nod and Michiru waved to Dean. "Great. Thanks. See you tonight."

Dean noticed Jessica. "Nice lobster."

Holding the bag up like a shield, she let out a nervous laugh. "It's for my parents. It's their anniversary tonight. Been married a long time. Twenty years. Big celebration..." Michiru poked her in the ribs and she ended her spiel with an explosive exhalation vaguely reminiscent of a whoopee cushion.

She turned to make a run for the till but was brought up short as Michiru grabbed her arm.

Michiru looked Dean over appraisingly as a rising tide of crimson flooded Jessica's face. "Could you do me a quick favor?"

He grinned and spread his arms wide in an encouraging manner. "Ask and you shall receive."

Michiru pointed to the Dr. Pepper. "Can you reach those?"

Dean didn't even try to keep his disappointment from showing. He looked between Michiru and the pop, shrugged, and easily retrieved the bottles.

"Thanks." Michiru called over her shoulder as she ushered Jessica to the front of the store. She nudged her in the ribs again. "Yay us. Now we've got a line on Bill."

"Providing Dean wasn't just saying that to get you to go to his party." Jessica said rubbing her side.

Michiru's face fell. "I hadn't thought of that." She watched the group push their mountainous carts toward an unimpressed cashier several tills down from theirs.

Kirsten joined the group and dumped a veggie tray on the pile.

"Shit." Jessica dropped into a crouch.

Michiru waved at her and said, "Wait here. I'll double check things."

She rose high enough to watch Michiru approach the group and pull Kirsten aside. Jessica shrank down again, hoping she hadn't been spotted.

The cashier's puzzled face appeared over the counter.

"Leg cramp." Jessica rubbed her leg and tried to smile.

The cashier nodded, clearly unconvinced. "That'll be $31.43."

Choking at the price, Jessica riffled through her pockets and slapped the money on the counter without rising. Michiru returned and Jessica motioned from the floor for her to collect the bags.

Shrugging at the baffled cashier, Michiru grabbed them and followed Jessica as she squat-walked out of the store. Once outside, she asked, "What has you so wigged?"

Standing and stretching her back, Jessica grumbled, "Kirsten."

"Really? She seems all right to me."

"Yeah. Because she didn't see me. Trust me. You don't want her to know we're friends." She cast a worried glance back at the store. "She's hated me since elementary."

"Ah. Is it a fox 'n' hound thing?"

"What?" Jessica tried to remember the movie.

"You know, once best friends become bitter enemies as they grow up."

"We were never friends." Jessica's lip curled in disgust. "She tried to take credit for a project I did all the work on. She thinks I ratted her out, but she did it to herself. She couldn't even remember the subject, let alone describe any work she'd done when the teacher asked." Exasperation tinged her voice.

"That's a long time to hold a grudge." Michiru shook her head. "And over such a stupid thing. Anyway…Kirsten wasn't there when we talked to Dean, so I thought I'd check his info. As far as she knows, Bill is supposed to be there tonight, so I don't think he was lying."

"Right." Jessica took one of the bags from Michiru. "So now all we need to do is crash the party, kidnap Bill, and perform an exorcism." Her eyes widened as she spoke. "No problem."

Michiru laughed. "That's the spirit." She put an arm through Jessica's. "Actually, we've got a lot going for us. You're smart, I have an invite, and it sounds like everyone's going to be pretty out of it. If we show up late, nobody will even notice us."

"Yeah, but Kirsten will be there." The lobster squirmed in the bag and Jessica felt a sudden kinship with the doomed creature. "I'm getting a bad feeling about this." She paused. "Actually, I had a bad feeling about this before, now it's a worse bad feeling. Dire, even."

"Oooo! You forgot…we have to find a ride, too." Michiru scowled. "And I need to convince my parents to let me stay over another night. We'd better stop by and talk to them on our way back. It'll give me a chance to pick up some extra supplies too. Can you cry on demand?"

Jessica's lips thinned. "Very dire."

Chapter 37

Jessica stared at the silver sedan, felt the sharp, heavy presence of keys in her hand.

What am I doing?

She shifted uncomfortably as the bag of crushed sleeping pills tucked in her waistband dug into her skin. Dull cement stretched out between her and the car—a vast wasteland, goading her to turn back.

Michiru glanced at her, probably wondering why they were stalled on the steps.

Jessica opened her mouth to ask if this was a good idea. She closed it again. She had no right to push responsibility for her decisions onto her friend.

"What's up?" Michiru asked.

"Just pondering the usual…grand theft, driving without a license, drugging a guy who's possessed by some otherworldly, murderous creature, and performing a ritual I have no right to even contemplate. Yup…just another Saturday night in my wacky life." Jessica obsessively clicked her keys together. "Mom will kill me if she finds out I took her car."

Michiru chuckled and laid a hand over Jessica's to stop the jangling. "Right. 'Cause borrowing your mom's car without asking is the worst thing we're doing tonight?" She moved her hand to Jessica's shoulder and gave it a reassuring squeeze. "Listen. The situation sucks, but this is the best plan we could come up with. We tried to think of something else." Michiru rolled her eyes. "We tried so much my head feels like it's going to explode. There's no other way. Not tonight anyway. So, let's just get it done."

She slid past Jessica and descended the stairs. "We managed to convince my parents to let me stay over again, so I figure we're on a roll. We've got this."

"It was nice of them to have me for supper. I hate to say it, but I think I might actually be tired of pizza." Closing her eyes, Jessica willed her feet to move and followed Michiru.

They both reached out to open the passenger door and Michiru pointed to the driver's side. "I think this'll work better if one of us is driving. And yeah, if you liked mum's meatloaf, you must be desperate."

Jessica laughed nervously. "Right. Habit. And the meatloaf wasn't that bad. A bit dry, maybe." She shuffled to the other side of the vehicle, unused to the heels she was wearing. They were from last year's prom, and within ten minutes of slipping on the gorgeous platinum gray strappy sandals, she had figured out why Beth had called them "valet shoes" at the store. Nice to look at, but a bitch to move around in. Unfortunately, they were also the only fancy shoes she owned.

She had convinced Michiru to dress up in the interest of blending. Problem was, neither of them knew what the popular crowd wore to parties as Michiru's parents never allowed her to go and Jessica had never been invited. They settled for prying on Jessica's tightest clothes, most of which she had to dig out of the pile she had outgrown, but kept forgetting to donate.

Jessica thought she was clueless about the finer points of cosmetics, until she saw Michiru trying to put on eyeliner.

How amazing it must be to not have to try to fit in.

She watched Michiru shimmy her skintight jeans up before sitting. She never seemed to give a second thought about how others saw her and yet she managed to be popular.

Jessica adjusted the uncomfortably tight bodice on her purple tunic. *And here I am, always trying and never quite making it.* She wobbled on her heels. *If only the world was logical.*

Her heart skipped a beat as she slipped behind the wheel and slotted the keys into the ignition. It wasn't that she couldn't drive. She had a learner's permit. She'd even aced the exam. It was just that she always did better with theory than with the practical stuff. She had driven a few times, but only in Eric's old boat of a car, and an accident wouldn't have altered its rusty charm. Her mom's pristine car was another story.

There was a click as Michiru fastened her seatbelt. Jessica squeezed her eyes shut and turned the key. The engine purred and Jessica heaved a sigh of relief as she put the car in reverse. She'd half expected to hear police sirens.

"Here we go." Jessica eased her foot off the brake.

There was a metallic thud and squeal. Jessica slammed her foot on the brake and turned, slowly, to see the unopened garage door. She rammed the car into park and dropped her head onto the wheel.

Is there anything left that I haven't fucked up?

The vehicle shook slightly as Michiru got out.

"It's not as bad as it sounded," Michiru called out. "There's only a few scratches on the bumper and I think the door's just bent. Nothing looks broken."

From her lively tone, she guessed Michiru saw this latest

catastrophe as another interesting hurdle, not a bone-chilling prophecy of disaster.

She joined Michiru and stared in horror at the bumper. "I am so dead! How am I supposed to explain this?"

Michiru rubbed one of the scratches. "Some of it's just paint from the door. See?" She continued rubbing and the mark diminished slightly. "Maybe if we wash the car, it won't look so bad?"

A muffled, cheery pop tune cut through the night, fanning the flames of Jessica's annoyance. She yanked the phone out of her tunic pocket and jabbed the "end call" button.

"It was an accident, Jess. We have a week to fix this and only one night to fix Bill. So, come on."

* * *

As they examined the partially raised garage door, a low rumble advanced up the street. A sleek black motorcycle pulled onto Jessica's driveway and a tall figure in an unmistakably disreputable leather jacket unfolded from the bike.

Michiru stopped fiddling with the door. "Hey beanpole, you're coming dangerously close to cool in that gear."

Jessica groaned. "Great. Another witness to my stupidity."

Drew pulled off his helmet, shook out his hair, and strolled up to them, glancing at the warped door. "You girls start the party without me?"

"Very funny. Why don't..." Jessica stopped herself. "Sorry. I'm not mad at you. Just tired of screwing things up...and why is this door so fucking flimsy?" Forgetting about her specialized footwear, Jessica kicked the door, lost her balance, and would have fallen if Michiru and Drew hadn't been within arm's reach.

"Fucking shoes. Shitty fucking door." Jessica massaged her foot. Guessing it was obvious what had happened, she skipped the explanation and commandeered Drew's help.

They eventually coaxed the door into opening far enough for Jessica to squeeze the car out. The gears sounded like a coffee grinder chewing pebbles as it screeched along the overhead rails. Drew stood on the driveway signaling directions, like someone flagging an airplane into a terminal.

Michiru leapt into the passenger seat and hit the garage door button again as soon as they were clear.

Drew slid in the back and leaned forward to rest his arms on the headrests. He glanced curiously between the two girls. "So…nobody's actually explained what's going on tonight. Sorry about the truck, Jess, but my brother took off with it last night." He sounded downcast. "Hope he brings it back this time. Last time I had to buy it back from a rancher up in Waiprous."

Jessica turned to stare at him. "Your brother stole your truck?" She paused and glanced at the dashboard. "Appears to be going around."

"I don't mind if he uses it. It's more that he never lets me know." Drew shrugged. "I've got my bike, so it's not dire. Usually."

Michiru motioned to the waiting street. "Time to hit the road, Jack."

"Let's hope not literally," drawled Drew, making a show of putting on his seatbelt.

Jessica took a deep breath and eased the car off the driveway. She drove in silence, winding cautiously through Coldwater's deserted back roads.

* * *

Michiru judged from Jessica's hunched posture and intent expression that she was hyper-focused on driving, so she laid out the plan for Drew. When she was done, silence dominated the car.

She turned, trying to read Drew's inscrutable expression.

After a moment, one of his eyebrows quirked. "Let me get this straight. You've stolen a priceless relic from a church and Jess's mom's car so you can kidnap Bill and perform an exorcism?" Michiru nodded and he muttered, "Okay. Didn't see that coming." His dark eyes twinkled and a bewildered grin tugged at the corner of his mouth. "I spend a night washing dishes and look what I miss."

"Count yourself lucky," Jessica interjected. "You'd have ended up a gelding. I can still feel that bar on my thighs."

Both of his eyebrows shot up. "Girl's night with you two isn't like in the movies, is it? At least not the ones in the theaters."

Michiru fixed him with a glare and he clamped his mouth shut.

When they arrived at Dean's house, they found vehicles lining the street and clogging the driveway.

"Must be lots of people from out of town," said Jessica.

Michiru strained to see into the house as they passed and nodded. "Looks crowded. Good. The more confusion and bodies about, the better."

A muscle in Jessica's cheek twitched at the word "bodies," but she kept her eyes glued to the road and turned down the next street.

The quest for a parking space was prolonged by her insistence on finding one with a car length between them and any other vehicle. As she drove further away, their headlights illuminated a jagged line of picket fence. It tethered Jessica's gaze like a boat to an anchor.

The car lurched to a stop in the middle of the road. Michiru's muscles instinctively tensed and she braced herself with her legs, preventing the seatbelt from biting into her neck.

Jessica flung her door open and stepped out in a daze. All the blood drained from her face and she wobbled sideways, catching herself on the trunk of a parked car.

Michiru yelped as the car carried on without its driver. The open door passed within an inch of a parked car's side mirror. There was a thud from the backseat, a string of swears directed at seatbelts, and a flurry of activity beside her.

The tires scraped on loose gravel as the car slid to a stop again.

Michiru regained her composure and hopped out. She jogged up to Jessica, scanning her and the area. "What the hell, Jess?"

"This is the house," Jessica whispered hoarsely.

Michiru found nothing of note in the bungalow's stucco exterior. "Uh. Okay. The house of what?"

She pointed at a plaque by the front door, reading "53." "Where Bill…and the cop…" Her voice cracked. She looked up, searching the sky.

Michiru followed her line of sight and saw a faint arc of light behind a filmy cloud. It was the same moon Jessica had described from her dream.

"You girls coming back or what?" Drew flicked the hazard lights on and stuck an arm out to wave on a car that had stopped behind them.

Michiru took Jessica by the shoulders and looked directly into her eyes until they refocused on her. "Then we are exactly where we need to be. We can stop this, but we have to find Bill."

Jessica nodded once and they walked back to the car, arm-in-arm.

Michiru helped her in and then ran around to the passenger side. Jessica gripped the steering wheel, the white of her knucklebones showing through her pale skin. She shifted into drive and eased her foot off the brake. The car didn't move. She squinted at the dashboard and pressed harder on the gas pedal. The engine revved, but the car remained stationary.

"Let's hear it for backseat drivers." Drew leaned into the front seat and released the emergency brake.

The car leapt forward and Jessica jammed the brake pedal to the floor. Both girls glared as he extricated himself from the floor, laughing.

"That wasn't nice." Jessica growled.

"I owed you one for leaving us driverless. Though it was kinda funny. You made Michiru scream like a girl."

Michiru huffed and turned her back on him.

* * *

By the time Jessica located a suitably large parking space, they were five blocks from Dean's house and two from number 53. She rested her head against the steering wheel, relieved they had made in one piece, more or less.

Michiru leapt out and grabbed the bulging silver purse she had reluctantly agreed to use. She shoved the strap over her shoulder and grumbled as it slid off, dropping to the crook of her arm. "I don't see why I couldn't use my bag. It fits everything I need. Hell, even Wilson was better than this. At least he had girth."

"Wilson?" Jessica tried to counsel her expression as she

heard a choke from the backseat. She shakily levered herself out and leaned against the hood. "Oh right. Halloween." She snickered. "Well, just be thankful there's no coconuts to worry about tonight."

Michiru scowled and wedged the purse under her arm. "Ugh. Don't remind me. I think I still have marks from those."

"And Wilson would go with your outfit about as well as that ratty old canvas bag of yours." She looked over Michiru's jeans and sequined aqua crop top, wondering why they had never looked so good on her. "The point is to fit in. Or try to, as much as possible. Besides, I warned you not to put so much in. It doesn't hang right when it's full."

Jessica took a tentative step and dipped down as her right ankle gave out. "At least you're not wearing these bastards." She propped herself against the car and tentatively rotated her foot, testing whether her ankle was sprained.

Wondering why Drew was so quiet, Jessica glanced around and saw him casually standing under a tree. He swiped a finger across his phone screen and began typing.

Michiru frowned. "Can't you text and walk? We're on a schedule."

Drew did not look up. "You're kidding, right? No way am I going to a townie party…at least not without ten or twenty buddies. Don't feel like getting the shit kicked out of me."

Jessica blinked at him uncomprehendingly. "I don't normally go either, but we're with Mac and she's invited. And I think they'd just ask us to leave. There'll be no shit kicking. Unless Kirsten spots me." She grimaced. "Then all bets are off."

Drew sank down onto the grass at the base of the tree, still focused on his phone. From his regular finger movements, Jessica suspected he was playing a game.

"I'm sure you'll be fine," Drew said. "It's my skin that's

the wrong color."

Jessica looked between him and Michiru, baffled. "But it's pretty much the same as Mac's."

He snorted. "It's not the same. Trust me."

She turned to Michiru and received an uninformative shrug.

Drew sighed. "Listen. Text me if you get into trouble and I'll find a way in…hopefully in one piece. But make sure you're in deep shit because I guarantee we'll be in it once they see me. The last time I crashed a townie party, the odds were more even and let's just say the cops ruined everyone's night."

The bass beat of the party rumbled in the distance and Michiru pursed her lips. "We'd better talk about how we're going to get Bill back here. There's no way we'll be able to carry him this far, especially not with you wearing those stupid shoes."

Jessica mulled it over. "I've got it. When we're ready, I'll fire off a text to Drew and he can bring the car around." She held the car keys out, but he made no move to take them.

"Oh come on," she grumbled. "It doesn't involve coming in the house."

"No way. Think about it. Native guy. Stolen car. Some drugged-shitless dude. Sounds like a plan that ends with me finishing high school from a jail cell."

Michiru muttered some foreign words. "Then you'll have to duck out and get the car, Jess. I'll babysit Bill. Problem solved. Does that plan work for Chicken Little?"

"So long as I'm not driving." Drew continued playing on his phone. "No cop's going to give me the benefit of the doubt. At least Jess can say it's her mom's car."

Michiru set off and Jessica took a few wobbly steps. Her shoes showed no sign of cooperation and her feet no sign of adaptation. This night was going to be long and painful on many fronts.

Michiru came back to offer an arm. "We should stick together once we're inside. I don't want to lose time hunting for you as well as Bill."

Chapter 38

Jessica gazed at the stars, trying to think happy thoughts, but tonight the usually reassuring lights felt like eyes winking down from the infinite black, watching. She shivered.

"I suppose it's too much to hope that Kirsten won't show?"

"Probably." Michiru quickened her pace. The pounding music suggested they were closing in on Dean's house.

Jessica took her shoes off to keep up. "I hope the neighbors are deaf, or out, or seriously heavy sleepers." She grimaced. "Police showing up in the middle of things would be bad. Very bad."

Michiru nodded, stepping over a guy sprawled across the driveway spooning an empty bottle of cheap whiskey. "Must be some party."

Jessica reluctantly slipped her shoes back on and followed Michiru into the house. She was thankful to note that her teetering walk fit right in.

From front door to backyard, the house was littered with a mixture of semi-conscious, unconscious, and manic people, most of whom Jessica didn't know well. Many were from higher grades, but there were a handful of younger kids, probably partygoer's brothers and sisters, and a few who looked close to her parent's age or older.

Jessica shuddered at the sight of an old man passed out, face down, in the lap of a girl who was in her grade. She was sitting, propped up like a doll in the hallway. Another guy was slumped to the side, also unconscious, with "sex" scribbled on his forehead in red lipstick. A group of giggling girls stopped to take photos of the scene.

As she edged past the disturbing tableau, the nagging sensation that she had forgotten something returned. She had ignored it throughout the day in lieu of more immediate worries, but it kept creeping back.

Someone bumped her roughly from behind. She stumbled and fell onto a leather sofa. The current occupant laughed, overly heartily, and fixed his wandering gaze somewhere in the vicinity of her chest.

"All righ! Wanna dansh?"

A wave of beer fumes hit with his words. Jessica recoiled and struggled off the sofa.

Michiru grabbed her arm. "Hey…stay close."

"I'm trying." Jessica muttered as she scanned the crowd, hoping and dreading that she'd catch sight of their prey.

They moved through the main floor, avoiding groping hands, suspicious candy hearts, and unidentified puddles. When they couldn't find Bill, they moved to the backyard and then searched the upstairs rooms. After looking behind the first door, Michiru refused to open any more, so Jessica had to play peeping tom.

When they reached the end of the hall, Michiru said, "We must have missed him. Maybe he was in the bathroom or something. Let's take another look…downstairs."

Jessica followed her, wondering why drunk people's heads always bobbed around uncontrollably on their necks. Never having been drunk, she wasn't sure whether it was a side effect of alcohol or some kind of bizarre social convention.

It's not even in time to the music, so it can't be an attempt at dancing. Can it?

Keeping a finger hooked in Michiru's belt loop to avoid separation, she curiously watched people bump and grind their way around the living room, trying to stay vertical. Scenes from the zombie movie she'd just watched played in her mind. The jerky movements were eerily familiar.

"If anyone mentions fresh brains, I'm outta here."

Michiru stopped at the wet bar. "What?"

"Nothing." Jessica put her fingers in her ears to muffle the throbbing techno beat. "Just talking to myself."

Michiru hopped onto the bar top and surveyed the crowd. Several people whooped and clapped, expecting a show. Another girl attempted to climb up and slipped when the stool she was kneeling on toppled. She lay on the floor grinning stupidly.

Jessica glanced around nervously. She wanted to keep as low a profile as possible and Michiru was not helping.

A guy leaning against the bar made a drunken grab for Michiru's leg and received a knee to the head. He sank down beside the prone girl and put an arm around her as he took a swig of the beer he had miraculously kept hold of.

Jessica heard the unmistakable sound of retching and swallowed, pledging never again to feel bad she wasn't invited to these parties.

Out of the corner of her eye, she saw a familiar figure approaching and dropped into a crouch as Kirsten weaved her way behind the bar.

Jessica flinched as Michiru landed beside her and bent

down. "I see him. Looks like he's drinking a bottle of beer that's got a blue label. See if you can find one to drug and I'll make the switch."

"Can't you get the beer?" Jessica motioned at the bar. "Kirsten's back there."

Michiru gave her a warning look. "Figure it out. I want to keep an eye on him."

When Jessica didn't move, Michiru hauled her up. "She can't be that bad."

"She is and we can't afford the scene she'll make if she sees me here. The idea is to *not* tip off Bill about our presence, right?"

Michiru sighed. "Fine. I'll distract her. You just get the damn beer."

Michiru leapt back onto the counter. After confirming Bill hadn't moved, she turned and hollered hello to Kirsten.

As soon as Jessica heard Kirsten return the greeting, she scuttled behind the bar. She lifted the lids on a row of coolers and discovered that the third contained blue labeled beer.

She pulled out a dripping bottle and attempted to remove the cap. The crimped metal bit into her skin. Swearing under her breath, she tugged up the bottom of her tunic, wrapped it around the sharp edges, and tried again. The cap didn't budge.

Twist-off, my ass. She glared at the bottle.

Listening to ensure Kirsten and Michiru were still chatting, she reached up and blindly felt along the countertop for the bottle opener she had seen Kirsten using. The counter was disgusting. The parts that weren't sticky were wet. She had just grasped the opener's cool metal handle when Kirsten turned to leave and tripped over her foot.

She stumbled, spilling part of her drink down Jessica's back.

Cold soaked into her tunic and the sickly sweet, sharp smell of cola mixed with something alcoholic drifted to her nose. She kept her head down and her body still, hoping Kirsten was drunk enough not to notice.

Kirsten glared at her blearily and aimed a sharp kick. "Stupid bitch. Go pass out somewhere else."

Jessica grunted at the impact but didn't move until Kirsten left. She stood slowly, still clutching the beer in one hand and the bottle opener in the other.

"Wow." Michiru looked contrite. "My bitch-o-meter must be seriously off. You all right?"

Dropping the bottle opener onto the counter, Jessica rubbed her side. "Yeah. Par for the course with her. I'm just glad she didn't know it was me."

Jessica pried the beer cap off and tipped the powdered sedatives into the bottle. The beer frothed and she watched in dismay as white foam spilled down the sides. She slapped her palm over the top, hoping she'd managed to trap most of the medication inside. Finding the right dosage had been a delicate procedure, involving calculations of weight and the rate of sedative and alcohol metabolization. It wasn't something that could be screwed up without serious consequences.

Once the bubbles settled, Jessica held the beer up to the light and was relieved to see a layer of sediment on the bottom.

A hand suddenly snaked out of the crowd and snatched it from her grasp.

"Thanks," chirped a honeyed voice.

Jessica made a desperate grab for the bottle and captured the edge of a lacy sleeve. She reeled in the would-be thief and belatedly realized who the sleeve was attached to.

Kirsten stood on the other side of the bar looking murderous. She yanked her arm back, trying to shake Jessica's grip.

Jessica held on, wide eyes darting between the drugged beer and her adversary's reddening face. "This is mine. I'll get you another one."

"What the fuck are—" Kirsten spat out as she yanked her arm again.

A stream of amber sloshed down Kirsten's designer blouse and she screeched, "You bitch!"

Jessica saw her aiming the bottle and ducked. The beer flew past her head, shattering a smoked-glass mirror which ran the length of the bar.

She turtled and closed her eyes until the glass stopped plinking around her. Shaking her head and clothes to dislodge the shards, Jessica carefully tiptoed out from behind the bar. The uneven debris slipped and cracked under her shoes. She felt a sharp prick under a strap on her left shoe and limped away, seeking refuge in the nearest unoccupied corner.

Chapter 39

Jessica found a suitably dark nook to secret herself away in and eased her shoe off. Michiru slid in beside her.

After flicking a sparkling sliver of glass off her foot, Jessica glanced back at the bar.

Kirsten was surrounded by her minions, all nodding sympathetically as they guided her to a couch. They reminded Jessica of a circling flock of magpies. A finely chiseled guy sat down beside her, listening obediently as Kirsten held her ruined shirt away from her chest and sobbed on his shoulder.

It was the least of her worries, especially at the moment, but cold dread washed over her as she watched them.

Kirsten had it in for me before, but now she'll be out for blood.

She jammed her shoe back on and looked at Michiru. "What the hell are we going to do now? The beer's gone."

"We'll get another. No biggie." She grimaced. "Though the oddest things have a habit of becoming problems when you're around. Let me guess. We've got a problem?"

Jessica held up the empty baggie. "I only brought enough for one dose. I hadn't anticipated someone chucking the drink at my head. Silly me."

After a moment, Michiru clucked her tongue. "What about the candy man? I bet he's got something that'll do the trick."

"Candy man?" Then Jessica remembered the guy with lime green hair selling "candy" that they'd run into during their earlier rounds of the party. "You want to buy drugs?"

Pilfered prescription sedatives were bad enough. But this? They weren't just stepping over a line; they were performing a flamenco in full, crimson-feathered regalia all over it. Wasn't there something about the ends not justifying the means...or was it the other way around? She could never remember.

Jessica tried to form rational thoughts. "Okay. Keeping in mind that it's illegal and all, we also don't know the dealer. He could sell you anything from vitamins to rat poison."

Michiru shook her head. "Not me, you. If someone snaps a picture of me with a dealer, I can kiss any chance of a professional sports career goodbye."

"But, but..." Jessica stammered. "He could give me something dangerous. I don't know how to tell. Do you?"

"All drugs are dangerous Jess, illegal or not. We knew that coming in. I'm guessing most dealers rely on repeat customers, so just explain what you need it to do and ask how much to use."

Jessica's mouth hung open and Michiru gently pushed it closed with a finger.

Michiru searched through the jammed contents of her purse. A Swiss army knife and piece of chalk leapt for freedom before she gave in and upended the contents on the floor. She eventually stuffed the bizarre collection back in and held out a wad of crumpled bills.

"A roofie or something similar should work." Michiru pointed at the candy man, leaning against a wall near the makeshift dance floor. He appeared to be the only other steady person in the house.

Robotically taking the proffered money, Jessica searched her own pockets and pulled out a twenty. She stared at the bills.

Michiru put her hands on either side of Jessica's waist, turned her toward the dealer, and nudged her into forward motion.

She stumbled toward him and then froze like a deer in headlights. She had no idea how to start the transaction. Her only exposure to this sort of thing was from TV shows and movies. Somehow, she didn't think whipping out a gun and yelling, "Drop the stash, bitch!" was the best approach.

The dealer noticed her staring and sauntered over. "Hey, Red. What's your pleasure?"

Jessica blinked.

His grin widened the longer she stayed silent. "Well, shit. It's happened again. Don't tell me...you were blinded by my shockingly good looks from across the room and felt compelled to get a closer look?" He turned his head in profile and crossed his arms in an exaggerated supermodel pose.

Jessica managed a strangled, "Uh...no."

He put on a mockingly woebegone face for a few seconds, then turned back to her with a more serious, questioning, look.

Jessica's nervousness intensified under the scrutiny and she shuffled her feet, wincing as she put weight on her cut foot. "I mean...of course you're good looking...your hair is... bright...I like green...but that's not what...or why..." She mentally slapped herself and blurted out, "Do you sell roofies?"

His eyes narrowed into defensive slits. "Listen. If one of your friends had a bad time, it's not my problem. I'm not responsible for what people do with the product. I just sell it."

Jessica's anger flared. "Well, that's conveniently morally ambiguous. Must make sleeping at night easier. Weapons dealers use the same argument—they're not the ones actually pulling the trigger." Midway through her point she stumbled on the counter-argument. "Though, I guess if they're providing weapons to a group trying to free themselves from tyranny, it might be morally defensible. Can the outcome sometimes make an act ethical?"

The dealer quirked an eyebrow. "Depends on who wins. If the old regime wins, the dealers are criminals and hanged. If the dissidents win, the dealers are heroes who helped free their country. I run a business. Strictly supply and demand. Some customers are assholes and others are decent people who need this shit to get through the day. I'm not about to judge who should be able to buy what."

He pointed to a girl pressing her forehead against a window, her glassy eyes staring blankly into the darkness. "Maybe she needs some smack to forget she has to go home and be raped by her dad again." He motioned at a guy passed out on the coffee table, "Maybe he's got Crohn's and the only way he can eat without puking from the pain is to smoke a joint. Who am I to say no?"

"I get what you're saying, but there's some ugly consequences." Jessica shook her head, remembering her visit to the clinic. She caught sight of Michiru, who pointedly held up a beer bottle and waggled it at her. "Anyway, I didn't come over here for a debate, however interesting it is. You missed the point of my question." She leaned closer and whispered, "I want to *buy* a roofie."

"Say what?" He eyed her. "Shorty, if you want a guy, all you gotta do is ask. You've got the whole cutie next door thing going on. You don't need to resort to extreme measures."

Blushing, Jessica shoved the money at him. "Didn't you just finish saying what people do after they buy isn't your problem?"

"Well, yeah." The money disappeared. "You just don't seem the type. Do you even know what you're asking for?"

"I think so. I need something that'll knock a big guy out…preferably for an hour or two."

He chuckled. "You're planning some kind of prank. That's it, isn't it?" He shook his head. "It's always the innocent-looking ones."

"Yeah. A prank. Good think…uh, guessing."

Still chuckling, he searched his jacket and pulled out a baggie containing small, white pills. He handed one to Jessica, along with a twenty-dollar bill.

"Half price, 'cause you're the only one who hasn't treated me like hired help tonight. Just slip it into a drink. If he's big, I'd count on it wearing off quicker…maybe a half hour to an hour."

Jessica cringed. "A half hour isn't long enough. Can I give him two?"

The dealer shook his head. "Not a good idea. If he's got any kind of health problem, like heart trouble, asthma, he might not wake up."

Jessica palmed the pill and thanked him, but he grabbed her arm before she could leave.

"Wait a sec."

She turned back with an acute sense of panic, envisioning handcuffs and a badge, but was relieved to see that he was only holding a pen. His hand slid down her arm. She felt a gentle tickle on the back of her hand and stared in surprise at what he had written.

Apparently, his name was Ben.

"Give me a call sometime. I'd like to know how things went." He gave her a lopsided smile and sauntered off.

Jessica gazed at her hand.

Did he just hit on me? Nah. Probably just hoping for repeat business.

She looked up and saw that he was now mingling with the backyard partiers. His hair, tight jeans, studded belt, and black Sons of Anarchy shirt didn't exactly fit with this crowd, but he seemed perfectly at ease.

He couldn't like someone like me…could he?

* * *

Michiru watched Jessica bumble through the crowd back to where they had parted, no doubt lost in her own head. She would have kept wandering if Michiru hadn't snagged her.

"Did you get it?"

Jessica opened her hand to show the pill.

"I knew you'd pull it off." Michiru grinned and dropped the white disc into the new beer bottle. It foamed briefly as it hit the liquid and then drifted to the bottom. After swirling and checking to make sure it was dissolved, Michiru warned Jessica to stay put and made her way to Bill.

She wasn't sure what kind of reception she'd get, so she approached cautiously.

Bill was sitting in a recliner with a girl on his lap and a beer in hand. His other hand was down the girl's top.

Michiru was calculating how to switch her beer with his when Dean thumped an arm across her shoulders. He clumsily leaned his weight onto her as he swayed and drew her into the group before she had a chance to twist out of his grasp.

"Hey everybody. Look who I found!"

"Hi," Michiru said heartily, putting on her best smile. She

received a drunken chorus of greetings in return. Bill nuzzled the girl's neck and didn't respond.

Michiru watched him. It was evident the girl wasn't enjoying his enthusiastic fondling, but most of his attention was focused elsewhere. His eyes were intently tracking something across the room.

A chill ran down Michiru's spine, knowing she could guess Jessica's position by backtracking his gaze. She resisted the urge to look and continued to nod, smile, and laugh at the conversation around her.

Dean kept an arm draped over her and, if the hand wandering up and down her side was any indication, he was thinking about following Bill's example. She was just working on an exit strategy when Bill pushed the girl he was toying with too far.

He dropped his hand to her leg and slid it up to her crotch, bunching her skirt up so that his hand was the only thing preventing her exposure to the room at large.

The girl flushed bright red and struggled to get up. He chuckled nastily and said something in her ear that turned her struggles from outrage to fright. She lashed out with fists and elbows, catching him in the groin and head as she propelled herself off his lap. In the process, she knocked his beer flying.

Michiru extricated herself from Dean, ready to offer assistance, but all she needed to do was stand aside as the girl stormed off. Bill was up and out of the chair a second later, an ugly snarl on his face.

She hesitated to confront him directly, but stayed near, ready to take him down if needed. Michiru was fairly certain she could deliver an unconscious Bill the old-fashioned way without messing around with drugs. Leave it to Jessica to create the most complicated plan possible.

Dean and another guy grabbed Bill and jollied him back into the chair. When Dean offered to replace his beer, Michiru wordlessly presented hers. He passed it to Bill with a look of thanks.

Bill glared after the girl, but didn't try to follow. He took a hearty swig of his replenished drink and settled into the chair.

Michiru let out a breath she hadn't realized she was holding and watched Bill's eyes, searching for any sign of the shadow Jessica had described. They appeared to be an average pair of light-blue eyes. Despite the convincing weirdness of Halloween, a twinge of doubt niggled at her.

She shook it off. Even if all they did was give this ass a seriously uncomfortable night, she wouldn't regret it. One benefit of the roofie: He'd likely only have a vague recollection of what happened and, more importantly, who was involved.

Michiru chatted with the group, waiting for Bill to finish his beer. He'd turned sullen and brooding after his rage. She caught a glimpse of Jessica's copper hair from across the room. She was trying to hide behind a high-backed chair. Luckily, there were few people sober enough to wonder about her odd behavior.

There was a blur of movement in Michiru's peripheral vision and she instinctively dodged.

A bottle clipped the side of her head and shattered against a coffee table. She stumbled sideways as Bill lunged from his chair. His drugged condition slowed him enough that she evaded his clutching hands with a quick twist of her body.

"Bitch." He yelled. "I'm gonna snap your neck this time."

She shrugged off her shock and instinctively dropped into a bridging stance, waiting for his next move.

He took an unsteady step toward her before the roofie caught up with him and his knees buckled.

Bill crashed heavily into Dean, who'd been angling to intercept him again. They went down together in a heap of flailing arms and legs.

Everyone laughed until one of the girls abruptly crossed her legs. She hopped away, a dark stain spreading down her jeans. Several of the group trailed after the unfortunate girl, pulling out their phones.

Michiru listened as Dean and his friend debated where to dump the now unconscious Bill. The other guy wanted to stick him back in the chair, but Dean wanted him out of the house.

She poked Dean in the side. "Hey, my friend's got a car. If you guys bring him outside, we'll take him home."

He gave her an odd look. "Are you sure? I mean, he probably didn't mean to hit you with that, but…"

"People get stupid when they're drunk." She shrugged. "No hard feelings."

Dean and his friend looked at each other across Bill's slumped head. Dean shifted his grip and winced. "You're a better person than I am. But please, bring the car to us. I'm not hefting Gigantor around any longer than I have to."

Michiru grabbed Jessica on the way to the door and relayed the plan. Without a word, Jessica limped off to retrieve the car. Michiru followed Dean and his friend as they dragged Bill to the end of the driveway. As soon as the car pulled up, the boys brusquely shoved Bill into the backseat.

Michiru managed to insert the car door between herself and Dean before he could get his arms around her. He mumbled something vaguely coherent about catching up with her at school, and then staggered back to the house.

She studied Bill warily. His prone body twitched every now and then, but his eyes remained closed. There was something about him that set her nerves on edge, an indefinable sense of danger. Michiru had only experienced it once before, when she had narrowly avoided a six foot black mamba on her way to school in Nairobi. She'd listened to her gut then and survived. She decided to do the same now.

Prying a set of handcuffs out of her purse, she carefully slipped them onto Bill's wrists.

Michiru frowned when she saw the empty passenger seat. "Uh, where's Drew?"

"The trunk," Jessica replied, as if it was the most normal thing in the world. "I'll stop in a bit and let him out."

Michiru choked back a laugh. "This just keeps getting better. One guy in the trunk, another handcuffed in the back. I never thought we'd top Halloween, but this might just do it."

Jessica squeezed her eyes shut. "I certainly hope not." She motioned for Michiru to get in. "We'd better go. That pill might only last a half hour."

Michiru opened the passenger door, then hesitated. "Should I sit in the back to keep an eye on him?"

Jessica vigorously shook her head. "No. Ride up front. I want to limit our physical contact. I don't know what might provoke the entity to transfer."

Michiru had a disturbing thought, "So, how do we know the entity didn't jump into one of the guys who carried him out here, or someone else at the party?"

"Because my arm hurts like a sonofabitch whenever I'm near it." Jessica rubbed her right arm and turned to look at Bill, slumbering peacefully. "Plus, I don't think this thing can transfer without causing major pain. Not something you'd miss, trust me."

"Okay." Michiru slid in, confident that if champion worrywart Jessica wasn't panicked, it wasn't worth considering. She reached up to touch her pendant and remembered it wasn't there. "Right. Can I have my necklace back?"

"Shit," Jessica turned to face her. "Did you lose it? We'll have to go back and find it."

She looked so painfully grave that Michiru immediately dropped her joking tone. "I slipped it in your pocket when I sent you over to the dealer." She shrugged. "Bill kept watching us, even when we were at the bar. I figured since you said it glowed, it might not be such a good thing to wear while sneaking up on him."

Jessica's cheeks paled and then flushed a deep crimson.

"It's in your tunic."

Jessica patted her pockets and pulled it out. She shoved the necklace at Michiru. "I can't believe you did that," she snapped. "Not only was it dangerous to get close to Bill unprotected, but what if I'd lost it?"

"You didn't." Michiru re-tied the leather cord around her neck and had another thought. "Wait. Where's Drew going to sit?"

"Dunno. Maybe you'll have to sit on his lap," she said vindictively.

"Terrific." Michiru examined the foot well. "Bet I can squeeze in there if he pulls his feet up on the seat." Nodding with satisfaction, she dramatically pointed ahead. "To the bat cave, Robin."

Jessica grumbled as she took hold of the wheel and pulled away. "I'm pretty sure Batman did most of the driving."

Chapter 40

Tactical Advantage: Shadow host incapacitated. Primary Objective: Terminate Shadow. Method: Eliminate Shadow host. Probability of success: 42-95%. Channel damage likely. Extending area of influence to allow direct intervention. Probability of success increased to 79-98%.

* * *

The garage door scraped closed behind them. Drew and Michiru tumbled out of the car in a clumsy rush.

Despite a valiant effort, Michiru had not been able to fit in the foot well without risking spinal dislocation or chopping Drew off at the knees. Jessica had flatly refused to let him continue the journey in the trunk for fear of exhaust fumes, so Michiru had spent the trip on his lap. They had staunchly avoided eye contact with each other by glaring at Jessica.

After untangling herself from Drew, Michiru launched directly into a discussion about how to move Bill to the basement. The easiest and safest course they could think of was to wrap him in a sheet like a party cracker. This strategy satisfied both Jessica's requirement of limited contact and Michiru's need to ensure he was immobilized.

Leaving Drew and Michiru in uncomfortable silence, Jessica dashed off to acquire one of her parents' king-sized sheets. As soon as she opened the door to the house, Hamish ran up, wagging his tail. He dropped a soggy chunk of fabric at her feet. She recognized the pattern from their couch.

Grabbing the escapee, she ran upstairs and found her bedroom door wide open. In the tension of getting ready for the party, they must have forgotten to close it.

With an irritated huff, she shoved Hamish back into her room and surveyed the disaster zone. His reign of terror had evidently started here and ended downstairs in the living room. Her bedside table was lying on its side. Her lamp was on the floor with the shade bent as if he had used it like a hammock. All her blankets and sheets were bunched up in the middle of the bed.

Jessica felt around under her pillow and was relieved to find her pet sock still safely tucked away. She grabbed it and stroked the soft material. If ever she needed calm, the time was now. She stuffed the faintly glowing sock into her pocket and continued with her original quest, closing the bedroom door firmly but gently as Hamish attempted to shove his nose through the narrowing crack.

When Jessica returned to the garage, she spread the sheet out beside the car and warned Michiru in a flat voice, "Hamish got out."

"How?" Her eyes widened. "Your parents didn't come home did they?"

"I must have left my door open." She said flatly. "And trust me, you'd know if they were home. Looks like there was a shark feeding frenzy in the living room."

Michiru narrowed her eyes. "You're uncharacteristically calm."

Jessica yanked the car door open and stared at Bill. "I'm

too worried about the exorcism to give a shit about anything else. But I'm sure there'll be plenty of freaking out later. If I'm still around."

Michiru and Drew pulled Bill by his shirt out of the car onto the sheet and rolled him up. With one of them on either end, they half dragged, half carried him through the house and down the basement steps. By the time they reached the rec room, Drew was panting.

Michiru cautiously unwrapped Bill's face. "I think we hit his head a few times on the way down. He'll have some bruises, but he looks okay. He might be breathing a bit fast. Hard to tell."

Jessica rummaged through the pile of supplies she had collected for the ritual. "I'll work as fast as I can, but he's definitely going to wake up before I finish."

Nodding, Michiru watched their mummified captive pant and twitch. His movements were already more pronounced and frequent. Dumping the contents of her purse on the floor, she retrieved a small role of duct tape and placed a strip over Bill's mouth.

"What else can I do?" Michiru asked as Jessica dropped a handful of something green into a conch shell.

"Get Pinchy and figure out how to tether him so he can't crawl out of the circle."

She frowned. "Pinchy?"

"The lobster."

Michiru paused for a second and then headed for the stairs, muttering to herself, "She named it? Why would…" As she reached the top step, she hollered down to Jessica that the house phone was ringing.

"If it's important they'll leave a message." Jessica batted Drew away as he curiously examined her supplies. "Time for you to vamoose."

"What? Just when things get interesting. No way." He crossed his arms. "Why can't Mac leave?"

Jessica snorted, sure that if she had asked him to stay, he'd insist on leaving. "Because we only have two protections, Mac's necklace and the relic, which means only two of us can be down here. If you can convince her to give up the necklace, you're welcome to stay; otherwise I need you to wait upstairs, preferably in the garage or maybe the yard."

She shooed him out. In the midst of the tension, her fingers unconsciously sought out the calming oasis of her pet sock. She grabbed Drew halfway up the stairs and pressed the sock into his hand.

"I'm not saying this will help, but it might. It glows like the relic and necklace, only fainter."

"Does this mean I can stay?" Drew asked excitedly until he saw the limp green offering. "A sock?" He waggled it at Jessica. "It's not even a pair. What am I supposed to do with one sock? Threaten to shove it in Bill's ear if he comes up?"

"Listen. I don't really get it either, but the glow must mean something, so humor me and hold on to it, all right?" She held his gaze, trying to infuse her look with attitude.

Drew laughed and shoved the sock into his pocket. "Okay, okay. See? This is me, officially holding on to your sock." He frowned at his pocket and then looked at her pleadingly. "It's clean, right? Tell me you didn't just hand me a dirty sock for protection. Do you even like me?"

Jessica bit her lip. "It would lose its softness if it was washed." His face contorted and she added, "It's not like I wear it. I just pet it. It lives under my pillow. I'm sure it's clean."

"You keep a magic sock under your pillow?" He nodded

to himself. "You have some seriously unplumbed depths."

"I think the magic part is new." Jessica shuffled her feet. "I'd better get back to work. There's still things to set up."

Not many people knew about her pet sock and she wanted to keep it that way. Beth had found out during a sleepover when they were kids and teased her endlessly. *She's probably already blabbed about it to her new friends, along with everything else I didn't want anyone to know.* She should have been more careful about what she shared with Beth. Who knew how long she'd pay for that mistake.

She sighed and caught Drew's arm as he turned to leave. "You know, the ear thing might work. Just try not to touch him while you're sticking it in there."

Drew patted his pocket and wished her luck.

Jessica grabbed her notes for a last-minute review, trying to ignore the dull ache in her arm. After the epic fail of her last attempt, tonight's plan was more of a comprehensive, multi-phase approach, blending what she knew of traditional Catholic exorcisms with various wiccan rituals and Drew's skinwalker legend. She'd nicknamed the plan "Operation Shotgun" and had printed out meticulous step-by-step instructions. She turned the thick stack of papers on its side and twirled a strand of her hair. This was going to be a long haul.

A sudden chill washed over her and all the hairs on her body stood on end. She shivered and half-turned to check whether a window was open, but she knew what it had to be.

Bill's eyes were open and fixed on her. She stood rooted to the spot as the familiar shadow coiled and rippled across their surface.

Michiru bounded down the stairs, holding the lethargic lobster at arm's length. She halted mid-step when she saw Jessica's ashen face. Malice clogged the air and she redirected her attention to Bill.

He was lying perfectly still, but he had inched closer to Jessica. Her notes now drooped limply in her hand, forgotten.

"He's awake," breathed Jessica, her gaze locked with his.

"So I see." Michiru positioned herself between Jessica and Bill and waved the lobster at her. "I'll deal with him. You get on with whatever you need to do. Drew's going to stay in the garage. Said he'd try to do something about the car." She shrugged. "I told him to call the police and Father Nick if things go pear-shaped. Seriously, you named the lobster?"

Jessica glanced guiltily at the crustacean. "Pinchy's easier to say than lobster." At Michiru's dubious look she added, "Yes...I know we'll probably have to kill him."

"Really?" Michiru pointed to an old fish tank Jessica had pulled out of storage. It was full of water and the pump was running.

Jessica shuffled her feet. "Well...we might not have to. It's the last resort. People do keep them as pets, you know. I looked it up. All I need to do is..."

Michiru cleared her throat. "Focus, Jess."

Jessica went back to her notes as Michiru looped twine around the lobster's midsection. After tethering the other end to Bill's foot, she stationed herself beside him, marking his every move.

His gaze never faltered from Jessica. His body was as taught as a bowstring under the sheet.

After taking stock of the supplies for a third time, Jessica caught herself channeling Bakshi as she rearranged her herb containers by height. She was stalling. She couldn't help it. Even though everything on her equipment list was accounted for, she could not shake the feeling she had forgotten something.

Squaring her shoulders, she took a deep breath, collected her direction markers, and placed them around the room in preparation for the circle ritual. Turning to Michiru as she set the water bowl down, she warned, "Once I cast the circle, we have to stay inside until the exorcism is done or the entity might escape."

Michiru planted her feet and nodded. "I'm ready."

Chapter 41

Jessica felt Michiru's whole being center itself, as if a bar of light flared through her core, anchoring her firmly to *here* and *now*. She breathed in Michiru's calm, hoping to capture some of it for herself, as she collected her box of sea salt and notes. She tucked the glowing relic into the waistband of her leggings, where it would be in contact with her skin and handy if she needed to use it more actively.

"Keep your necklace on." Jessica's voice cracked as she noticed Bill watching her. The shadow stirred, moving beneath the flesh on his face, blackening his eyes as it passed. "If you lose it and the entity jumps into you…" her voice trailed off.

Michiru touched the luminous green charm and smiled. "It's solid and old, and the cord is strong. My neck would break long before it would."

Jessica's stomach lurched. She banished the image in her mind of Michiru lying on the floor, broken and still. There was no plan B if Operation Shotgun failed. The police wouldn't be able to do anything and Father Wojcikowski was so frail.

What if all I've succeeded in doing tonight is changing the location of my nightmare? And instead of some unknown person, it will be me or

Mac lying in a pool of blood and guts as the cops arrive.

She wilted inside. Their safety, Bill's life, everything relied on her. And who was she?

Jessica tried to take a step and couldn't.

Her mind screamed—*This isn't going to work. You'll make things worse. You'll make a mistake and screw everything up. You always do.*

Hot tears burned behind her eyelids. The words looped over and over, relentless in their denouncement. When she could no longer stand it, she wacked herself in the forehead with her mountain of notes. A sharp pain on her cheek finally succeeded in changing the channel. Never before had she been thankful for a paper cut.

She ordered the bitch in her head to shut the fuck up and let her get on with things. She had to try. She owed it to Chris.

Jessica straightened her spine, set her shoulders, lifted her foot…and took a step. She stared down in surprise and took another, silently congratulating herself for regaining the mobility of a two-year-old.

The circle ritual went quickly and Jessica sagged with relief when she felt a ripple of energy as the ends of her salt trail joined. She wasn't sure if the dizzy spell this time had more to do with the magic or the abrupt release of tension in her body.

Michiru had been dividing her attention between the room's occupants, but now her gaze was pinned to Bill. He was growling under his gag and spastically twisting his body. Pinchy tucked his bound claws under his torso and appeared to take a nap despite the occasional jerk on his tether.

Jessica retrieved her conch shell, laid a bundle of sweet grass over the herbs in the iridescent casing, and lit it. A pungent, organic smoke drifted up and filled the area with a tranquil haze. She fanned the smoldering grass, watching the eddies dance. The smoke stopped and curled back when it reached the outermost edge of the circle.

She flipped to the right page in her notes and recited the first of many verses in the Catholic exorcism. Her speech began stilted and unsure, but settled into a rhythm as her tongue grew accustomed to the Latin phrasing.

Even as the Latin became easier, Jessica found herself more and more at odds with the meaning behind the words. The tiresome naysayer in her head started in again: *If you don't believe in what you're saying, how can it work? You're screwing it up.*

She crouched near Bill, stifled her thoughts, and made the sign of the cross over both of them.

"Animadverto crux crucis of Senior; genitus, vos obnoxius vox!"

A rough, grating noise came from Bill. It took Jessica a second to recognize it as a laugh.

Spittle seeped from under the edge of his duct tape gag as he wriggled on the floor like a bloated maggot. Jessica gagged, wishing she hadn't chosen a pale yellow sheet. It only enhanced the sickening resemblance.

Steadying her voice, she continued reading the ritual. *"EGO iacio vos sicco, immunda phasmatis in nomen nostri Senior Jesus Sarcalogos. Genitus quod subsisto recedentia ex is creatura of Deus."*

She made a cross in the air over Bill again. His grim laugh echoed through the room, further shredding her tenuous veneer of confidence.

When she reached the final page, his laugh changed to a snarl and he thrashed around, swinging the startled lobster tied to his foot like a tetherball.

Dodging the airborne crustacean, Jessica yelled out the last paragraph and paused.

Michiru ducked as Pinchy flew by. "Is that it?"

Jessica nodded and grimly turned back to the start of the

exorcism. "Maybe it's my Latin. I dunno. The priest said some-times it had to be done several times. I'll try again."

Michiru, tired of playing dodgeball with an armored pro-jectile, stamped her foot down on the twine attaching Pinchy to Bill. "Take as long as you need. I'll make sure he doesn't go anywhere."

Leaning to the side with her foot on the string, Michiru grabbed a large sledgehammer from Jessica's pile and jabbed Bill's leg. He turned to snarl at her and she smiled meaningfully, patting the heavy implement.

Bill's movements quieted.

Jessica hoped the lobster was still alive. Her worry was assuaged as Michiru yelped and hopped to the side. She rubbed a red mark on her ankle where Pinchy had done his name proud. Jessica stifled a tension-laden giggle. One of the rubber bands around his claws must have come loose in his recent travels.

Another thought nudged its way into her conciousness: *Bill responded to Mac's threat, which means we can scare it with something less than shattering reality. Good for us, bad for Bill. Mac doesn't even have to try to be scary. It comes natural.*

With renewed vigor, she read the exorcism rite again and again. She focused her energy, willing the words to work, and each time she completed the ritual, her strength waned a little more. On the fourth recitation, the letters on the page began to swim together.

Her voice ground to a halt and she sank onto the floor, exhausted. A sheen of sweat covered her body and Jessica irri-tably peeled her tunic away from her skin.

Bill's head swiveled to find her and his hateful laugh started again. Jessica clamped her hands over her ears.

She didn't want it to end like this.

Pinchy waved his claws in the air and tried to scrabble away, only to be drawn up short by his leash. It was as if he knew what was coming.

The rational part of her mind chastised her: *It's just a dumb water bug with an instinct-driven, brainless nervous system.*

Her heart responded: *He's a living creature and deserves better than this.*

She saw her old fish tank, waiting patiently in the corner, and closed her eyes. This wasn't a choice she wanted to make, but it was like deciding to get off a rollercoaster as it crested the first drop. It was too late.

Another part of her, somewhere deep down, simply stated: *Life is unfair. Why should death be any different?*

She brusquely flipped to the last page of her notes. "It's not working, Mac."

Jessica's voice had never had such a ragged edge and Michiru tore her gaze from Bill to look at her friend.

The tight line of staples at the top of Jessica's notes caused several pages to flip back over the one she was reading. She tore the stapled stack apart in frustration and threw it to the ground. Swallowing loudly, she took a shaky breath and continued, "We're going to have to…" She couldn't finish the sentence, and instead pointed at Pinchy.

Michiru nodded. "What do you need me to do?"

Jessica pulled the relic from her waistband. Her hand shook as she clutched the shriveled glove. "This next part is going to be…unpleasant."

She pulled Michiru as far away from Bill as the circle border allowed. "I'll hold the relic against his skin. If it reacts like your pendant did, it should make things uncomfortable for the entity. I imagine he's going to struggle, so I need you to hold him down. In theory…"

Jessica took a deep breath. "In theory, as long as I keep myself and Bill in contact with the relic, and you have the necklace on, the only unaffected creature to jump into will be Pinchy." She winced as she said his name. "You still can't see the shadow?"

Michiru's shrewd gaze flicked over Bill's face and then back to Jessica. She shook her head.

"Right. So I'll warn you when it jumps into Pinchy. Then, I'll keep the relic against Bill while you take care of the lobster."

"Finally." Michiru cracked her knuckles. "Something I can do."

Bill twisted from side to side, trying to loosen the sheet and free his hands from the handcuffs. Thanks to the girls' wrapping skills, his movements largely served to further tighten the tangled material. His eyes widened in surprise as Michiru straddled his chest and roughly dropped her weight onto him. Air whooshed out of his lungs and his struggling momentarily ceased.

Jessica circled, searching for exposed skin. His face offered the only viable opportunity and she gingerly crouched at his head, pressing the glove against his forehead.

Bill's mouth gaped and a scream tore from him, as if every cell in his body simultaneously cried out for release. The tortured howl hit them like a physical blow. He twisted and lashed his head around, gnashing his teeth, trying to shake the relic.

Jessica fought to keep it in place, trying not to look into the void within his eye sockets.

Bill's strength increased with his panic and pain, until Michiru was barely able to hold on.

Realizing she was in trouble, Jessica threw herself across his chest, hoping her added weight would slow him down. The threesome writhed in a tangled knot of clashing wills.

All movement ceased as Jessica's phone rang, the cheery Britpop utterly incongruous with the background of growls, grunts, and snapping teeth from a second before.

Bill recovered first, taking advantage of the break in concentration to viciously knee Michiru in the back. The blow sent her flying into Jessica.

Michiru knocked the wind out of both of them when she landed. The ringtone stopped as Jessica's hipbone ground into Bill's sternum.

Fleetingly wondering who was calling in the middle of the night, Jessica levered herself up and jabbed a knee into Bill's side. She hoped it wasn't important.

She leaned her full weight on Bill, pressing the relic hard against him. He went still for a moment and then heaved up. While Jessica and Michiru fought to maintain their balance, the glove slipped sideways on his forehead, revealing an angry red blister under the now brightly glowing artifact.

"It's burning his face." Jessica yelled, panting from exertion and fear. "Pull the sheet down and I'll move it to his chest."

"I can barely stay on top of this fucker and now you want me to strip him?"

Bill twisted and Michiru fell to the side, bumping into Jessica again. Michiru struggled to force his body back to the floor without disturbing the relic.

"Please." Jessica gave her a beseeching look. "The entity's responsible, not Bill. Let's at least try to limit the damage."

Michiru hissed when she caught sight of his burnt skin. "Fine."

She retrieved a knife from her ankle sheath, yanked the sheet and Bill's shirt away from his chest, and sliced through the layers of fabric to expose a section of skin. The expertly honed knife left a thin line of blood drops down his chest, marking each time he bucked.

Jessica lifted the relic off his forehead and his scream changed to a harsh sucking noise. His chest swelled to grotesque proportions as he took in a huge breath. A violent convulsion racked his body, sending both girls skidding across the floor in opposite directions.

Nightmare pain blazed through Jessica's outstretched hand. She instinctively pulled away from the first vile feeler, but it was too late. The searching tentacle fused to her. She grasped frantically for the relic laying inches beyond her fingertips, but her spasming muscles pulled her farther away from it.

She searched for Michiru but the room was lost in a jumble of blinding lights, swirling and dancing around her, until she couldn't remember whether they were moving or she was. She opened her mouth to call for help, but her lungs were achingly empty.

Caustic tendrils wriggled up her arm like worms frantically crossing flooded pavement. It felt like her flesh was being stripped from her bones. The entity reached her chest and ate its way up to her brain. The sheer agony of it shattered her last conscious thought and dropped her into darkness.

Chapter 42

ALERT: Shadow intrusion. Channel compromised. Probability of Channel destruction exceeds tolerance. Emergency protocols activated. Direct manipulation of Channel permitted.

* * *

Michiru sat up, trying to convince the packing peanuts filling her head to morph back into brain cells. She guessed the pain in her head and proximity of the sledgehammer were connected, but that was unimportant. Agonizingly slowly, or so it seemed to her adrenaline laced body, she took stock of the room, located Bill, gathered herself, and lurched toward him.

* * *

Jessica drifted in an infinite abyss. She felt nothing, saw nothing, heard nothing. In that void, she began to lose herself. Her memories, her worries, her desires, her pain, everything flowed away, until there was nothing. And that nothing was bliss compared to what had come before.

And then...a voice, as soothing as a cool rush of mountain water over travel weary feet. The blanket of sound originated from somewhere both without and within. There were no words, just perfect, harmonious tones. The melody rippled through her, joining with her, promising all and demanding all. Teasing with secret potential. Drawing her down.

Curiosity; the last remnant of her being. Jessica's Achilles heel. It edged around her and tickled what was left of her consciousness.

Where am I? What's happening?

* * *

Michiru jammed an elbow against Bill's throat and realized he wasn't moving. His breathing was slow and his face was slack. She ripped the duct tape off his mouth, worried he couldn't breathe, and he let out a languid snore.

She was just starting to relax when a thumping noise started to one side. Fear clenched her gut as she turned to see Jessica's body locked in a violent seizure, the relic sitting inches from her hand.

There was a distortion in the air above her thrashing body. Smoke sealed in the protective dome with them was gathering in an odd cloud, resembling two intersecting circles.

* * *

The velvet voice ebbed through Jessica. Numbing peace spread, stripping away her thoughts and muzzling her mounting questions. A dark chamber in the back of her mind, that last intrinsic vestige of her being, questioned why.

She was supposed to be doing something. Jessica tried to remember. She fought the detached lethargy creeping through her until she forgot why she was struggling. Her mind reached into the shadows, grasping for reason, but the darkness offered nothing. Only the indistinct melody remained constant.

Jessica focused her dwindling essence on the voice and,

slowly, the sounds resolved. She strained to listen, to care. Words formed, each one almost completely drowned out by a cacophony of other voices suddenly tugging at the edges of understanding.

The voices organized, joining to convey one word: DAN-GER. She felt an echo of the screaming pain of moments? hours? before.

The liquid music that had drawn her to this place flowed around her. Armor for her spirit.

JOIN.

It was the ebullient lightness of dawn on the first day of summer. Release from the burden of cares and responsibility.

REST.

An image impinged itself on her cocoon of pure sound. Fuzzy outlines sharpened and resolved into two intersecting circles with an eye in the center.

Comprehension rushed through her, momentarily thawing her languid thoughts.

Of course. The symbol. The gatekeeper. Together. Just like Halloween. This depthless place, the sweet liquid music. She hadn't summoned it, but it was here anyway.

"What are you?" She sent out the voiceless query, hoping it would understand.

YOU CALL ME GATEKEEPER.

Her frustration rose. The gentle music surged around her, through her.

"Why are you here?"

FUNCTION: CONTROL ACTIVATED GATE.

"What gate? To where?" The only gate she'd toyed with lately was between the world of the living and the dead. *Is this what dead feels like? Not what I expected.*

GATE 20916 CONTAINS 7 DISTINCT SPACETIME FRACTURES.

Jessica was suddenly surrounded by a fine mist. At first it

looked gray, but upon closer inspection she saw a rainbow of color shimmering around each tiny droplet. The mist rotated. Lines developed, hair-thin intersections where the colors did not blend quite so perfectly into each other. At the instant each fracture crossed her view, she was blasted with sound and color.

She caught a brief glimpse of a ruined city. Massive stone buildings torn and crumbled. Three humanoid creatures at least twice her size covered in fantastically ornate plate armor huddled against one of the remaining walls. Dull thuds of explosions and the sound of shrieking metal.

The next fissure held a trackless desert. Sparse tufts of alien vegetation clung to crevices in rocks as the moaning wind endlessly shuffled sand across the landscape.

Then everything went gray. Perhaps a thick fog? It was gone too quickly to be sure.

Another turn and she was underwater, surrounded by waving strands of violet seaweed and thousands of darting, luminescent minnows.

There was a quick burst of discordant color, too quick to get any details, something that looked very much like a bank vault flashed past, and then she was staring down through overlapping jungle foliage.

Well, at least I'm not dressed like supper this time.

Then she was back in the formless, sightless darkness.

She felt an insistent pressure mounting against her from the gatekeeper...not against her body, since that didn't exist here, but against her mind, her soul. It wanted in. She tried to turn away, to retreat, only to realize she didn't know how. Could one move without a physical presence?

"What do you want from me?"

CHANNEL FACILITATES ORGANIZATION OF LOCAL POPULA-TION TO MAINTAIN GATE INTEGRITY. CURRENT TASK: ELIMINATE

SHADOW TO AVERT INFESTATION.

An image appeared—herself, naked, wrapped in black, tarry tentacles.

"What is it?"

CLASS 3 H-K SHADOW DRONE. PRE-INTERREGNUM LOCAL ORIGIN PSI HAZARD RELEASED FROM GATE 20916 ON ACTIVATION. PRIORITY 1 REMOVAL.

"That doesn't help. What's a Shadow Drone? I can't fight it if I don't understand it."

SELF-REPLICATING PSI WEAPON. PURPOSE: INFILTRATE HIERARCHY AND BREAK DOWN SOCIAL / ECONOMIC ORDER.

"Wait. It can replicate?"

CLASS 3: SELF-REPLICATING.

"How? Has it done it already?"

ONCE SUFFICIENT SUSTENANCE AQUIRED, DRONE DIVIDES EXPONENTIALLY. 97% PROBABILITY FIRST DIVISION ACHIEVED WITH CONSUMPTION OF CHANNEL.

She fought down her fear. "Okay, so does it just eat me whole or what? I mean, what exactly is it feeding on?"

WHAT YOUR SPECIES PRODUCES.

Her frustration built. "We make a lot of things. Be more specific."

FEAR. ANGER. PAIN.

Jessica searched the darkness, wishing the gatekeeper had a face, a body she could focus on and read. But there was nothing. Only those words. Was that how the gatekeeper viewed her?

Why would it even want to help if that's what it thinks of us?

SHADOW INFESTATION DESTABILIZES LOCAL POPULATION AND COMPROMISES GATE INTEGRITY.

DANGER. INSTRUCT CHANNEL TO JOIN.

The cool blue of the gatekeeper struggled to envelop her, but jagged red-tinged lightning held it at bay. The flashes pulsed in time with her thoughts.

Another echo of pain blazed across her consciousness.

White twinkles perforated the darkness around her, bringing light and the sensation of falling. She looked up and saw the bridge and a hand groping for her ankle. Blackness humped up from her foot, stretching to the fingers, releasing her from rage and pain as she fell. The bridge's cement support pillar was too close. Fear. Her body flailed. Above, Bill's agonized cries intensified. Her body twisted impotently, trying to avoid the cement abutment. Dark water lapped against concrete. Failure.

Suddenly, she was sitting under fluorescent light, studying fusion reactions in a physics book. One of her perfectly manicured nails traced the lines of a diagram. She reached out to poke her replica of deuterium dangling beside its companion, tritium, on the display stand Bakshi had lent her. She was amazed that such incredibly powerful forces could be wrapped into such a small space. The model atoms hung at an angle, artificially separated by powerful magnets. Visualizing masses of atoms swirling in a tight, hot mass, she lifted both hands and slowly pressed the atoms together. Voicing a subdued *kssshh*, she overcame their wobbling resistance and tapped them together. She flinched at the sudden burst of heat and light. The sharp scent of ozone mixed with the smell of burnt flesh. She stared at what was left of her hands. Searing pain eclipsed rational thought. Failure.

Jessica's basement popped into existence and she walked toward Michiru. Her friend's fear was palpable. Bill held her from behind, arms wrapped around her chest, squeezing until she went limp. Something scraped beside her. She looked down to see that she was dragging the head of the sledgehammer along the floor. Michiru's body tensed and she lashed out with a foot, catching Bill in the knee. There was a sickening crack and his leg buckled. They went down. Michiru struggled free.

Black whips extended from Jessica's body, striking Michiru. She let out a cry of pain so delicious Jessica felt drool slide down her chin. The room disappeared in shadow. Her vision cleared as Michiru stood, gathering herself to run. A shadow moved in Bill's eyes as he caught Michiru's pant leg. She fell. The sledge-hammer rose. Blackness. Michiru's tortured scream was never-ending. Failure.

JOIN. The gatekeeper's voice washed over her, absolving her sins, smoothing out her jagged emotions.

Jessica's will softened. What had her bumbling accomplished? She had failed Chris and Lindsey. She was about to fail Michiru, and Drew, and everyone else. She realized now, in this little disconnected pocket of time, that something like this had been inevitable since she stepped into the circle with Bill. Her only choice was whether to be consumed by the shadow or the gatekeeper.

She had always wondered what brought people to the point where they would sacrifice themselves in an effort to save others. How many of them had just been too caught up in solving a problem to notice?

However she had managed to get here, she was simply delaying the inevitable. She tried to will the flashes arcing from her body to cease, but that increased them. The only thing that helped was not thinking about them. She pretended she was watching a movie, that none of this was real. The more she detached herself, the fewer flashes there were.

REST.

Jessica tried, but the very act of thinking about relaxing and letting the gatekeeper take over seemed to prevent it.

I can't even give up right, she thought bitterly.

Despair washed over her. What was the point of thinking, planning? She screwed everything up. The world would be better off if she just stopped.

And she did.

* * *

Michiru watched the entwined smoke circles descend and sink into Jessica's body.

A sharp gasp broke through Jessica's purpling lips. Her eyes flew open and she spun until she was on all fours. She gagged. Her pupils dilated, swallowing her bright green irises. Convulsions wracked her body until the spine-cracking tension melted away, leaving her slumped and panting on the floor.

Bill shuddered. His body twisted and flipped unexpectedly, throwing Michiru sideways. Mindless mewls of agony spilled from his taut lips.

Jessica grabbed the relic and stood in one fluid motion, as if nothing had happened.

Michiru drew back. She didn't recognize the cold, detached eyes that locked with hers. There was an alien presence there that sent electric prickles cascading along her spine. This was no longer the Jessica she knew.

* * *

Calm certainty suffused Jessica, even as her head throbbed and her muscles strained against exhaustion.

The hatred emanating from the shadow felt like hot sun on a burn, but the gatekeeper's cool blue music had followed her out of the void. It surrounded her, promising strength and purpose. She relaxed into it, wrapping the energy around her body like a fluffy robe.

She crouched and grasped the sledgehammer near the heavy, metal head. Wrapping her other hand around the handle, she raised it high and calmly stepped to within perfect striking distance.

The host's body stilled as the shadow drone re-asserted control. In her altered state, Jessica saw it pulsing in the core of the host's skull.

It's so simple. Why didn't I think of this sooner? If I destroy the host's brain, the shadow won't have anywhere to hide.

* * *

Michiru gathered herself to leap as Jessica raised the hammer. She knew it was a futile effort. It had taken her too long to grasp Jessica's intention. She winced at the crack of metal on concrete, but there was no bright gush of blood. Something in Jessica had balked during the smooth downward arc, causing the hammer to swerve off course and smash into the floor beside Bill's head.

Chapter 43

Override control rejected by Channel. Channel non-receptive. Probability of success 48-64%. Generating new decision trees.

* * *

A blazing spear of denial shattered the gatekeeper's hold and cast Jessica into the light.

She had no purpose, no plan, no reasoned argument to present as to the wisdom of her choice. There were simply things she would not do. Murder topped the list.

The mortal weight of all her aches and strains returned in a rush, as if she'd just been dragged from a pool. She staggered back, eyes locked with Bill's predatory gaze. The horror of what she had almost done burrowed through her, freezing her from the inside out.

* * *

Relief flooded Michiru and she let out a long breath. Whatever alien presence had animated Jessica's features disappeared as she stumbled to the edge of the circle.

There was a movement to Michiru's right and she saw

Bill in a crouch, free from the sheet that lay tangled at his feet. His eyes were fixed on Jessica. The muscles in his arms bulged and the veins in his neck popped out as he strained against the handcuffs binding his hands behind his back.

Michiru closed the distance between them and landed a precisely timed roundhouse kick to his solar plexus. He wheezed and toppled to the ground.

"Welcome back," Michiru called out to Jessica, almost conversationally. "Care to explain what the hell happened?"

"Just as soon as someone explains it to me." The sledge-hammer fell from Jessica's hand with a clatter that sounded un-naturally loud. She glanced at the relic clutched in her other hand and shook her head. "No time to talk. We need to finish this."

Bill jerked forward and Michiru pulled her leg away. His teeth missed her by inches. A quick snap kick landed her heel on the side of his head and he went down again.

Taking advantage of his stunned state, Michiru jumped on him and dug her arm into his neck. He wrenched his body to the side and she jabbed his Adam's apple with her elbow, sending him into a coughing fit.

* * *

Jessica urged her straining muscles forward. As she approached, Bill redoubled his efforts despite the pressure on his neck and Michiru had to back off slightly or risk crushing his windpipe.

"Stupid bitch. You think you can stop me? Banish me?" He spat the words out with the venom of a rattler. "I am from you. In your every fiber. I am—"

His last words were choked off as Michiru viciously jammed her arm against his throat.

Jessica summoned her courage and threw herself back into the fight, helping Michiru hold him down. She thrust the relic against his exposed chest.

He let out a terrible scream as it seared his skin. He twisted and bucked, crashing the girls into each other as they struggled to stay on top.

Unable to protect her head while holding the glove in place, Jessica's eye socket met Michiru's elbow. The world grayed. Bright streaks of pain trailed across her vision.

Somewhere in the fog, a thick black tentacle floundered, and then another. The entity peeled away from Bill's body. Jessica felt part of it graze her arm and recoiled from the grating touch almost as fast as it did.

It's the same as the one on Halloween, only larger, and...darker.

Jessica's overextended muscles shook with exertion. Her energy was flagging and she wondered how near Michiru was to the end of her strength. She risked a quick glance and the pinched look on her friend's face said it all.

We haven't got long.

Her vision narrowed until all she saw was the brilliant relic against the gray relief of Bill's heaving chest. She summoned her strength and pressed it into him, reciting the one line she remembered from the exorcism ritual.

"*Male nocere, ab hoc corpore!*"

She poured all her remaining energy and hope into those words. Her sluggish mind no longer recalled their meaning. She didn't care. Her intention was clear: *Get out.* She knew now that was all that mattered.

Bill's violent thrashing intensified until both girls were reduced to stubbornly clinging to him, unwilling to let go and admit defeat. When Jessica was sure her arms would give out, he suddenly went still. So still, that she stared at his chest for a few dreadful moments until the next rise and fall.

Pressing the relic to his chest, she looked over and saw the shadow's urchin-like mass coalesce around Pinchy. The doomed lobster skittered back and forth in the center, claws gnashing at empty air, feelers spastically twitching in a grotesque parody of the entity's tentacle movements. The shadow huddled in on itself, perhaps adjusting to its new, decidedly low-rent accommodations.

Jessica weakly touched Michiru's arm, interrupting her examination of Bill's tranquil face. "It's in Pinchy." The words scraped along her throat. "More or less."

Michiru nodded sharply and stood to retrieve the sledgehammer.

"I'll guard Bill," Jessica panted. "Be careful. The shadow's still active and it feeds on emotions."

Michiru retrieved the sledgehammer and cautiously moved toward Pinchy. Jessica braced herself as the hammer rose.

Dozens of whip-like tentacles burst from the entity, extending in all directions, curving around the inside of the salt barrier, filling the space.

A closely packed group lashed out at Michiru. She dropped the sledgehammer and leapt back, away from Pinchy, but the wire-thin feelers were behind her too. A maze of livid red welts arose on her exposed skin.

Her pendant flared and the tentacles touching her sublimed under its glare, giving her a second to recover.

Jessica flattened herself on top of Bill, hoping the relic wedged between their bodies would be enough to protect them. She concentrated on the idea of the relic, imagining its green energy enveloping her and Bill.

Whether it had anything to do with her efforts, or not, it appeared to work. She felt the shadow's myriad fingers travel the length of her body, hovering millimeters above her flesh. A trail of goose bumps rose in their wake.

Bill squirmed under her, unconsciously edging away from the hostile promise in the tentacles. Jessica winced as his movements occasionally brought her into contact with them.

Michiru was not so lucky. Her pendant kept the entity from directly attacking her, but her blind ducking and weaving continually ran her into the burning extensions which swarmed around her.

Jessica yelled, "Mac. Stop moving." She tried to control her fear for Michiru, but the shadow must have sensed it. Its feelers redoubled their efforts, breaking through her shield with greater frequency.

Michiru whipped her head around and more angry ridges swelled on her cheek. "I can't see it, Jess. It feels like it's everywhere."

"It is. Stand still. Panicking is making it worse." Jessica lowered her voice, trying to sound more sure. "Trust me. Your pendant will hold it off."

Michiru eyed her uncertainly and then stilled.

"That's it. Your pendant's glowing like crazy and the shadow's backing off."

Michiru started to nod and stopped herself. "Okay. Keep telling me what's happening."

Jessica watched the entity. It was stretched out, testing the circle's boundary. Black threads squirmed through the air and jerked back when they reached the salt outline. They thrust up to the ceiling and down into the ground, searching for a break.

"It's trying to get out of the circle." Jessica stared at the line of salt. It suddenly seemed a very thin barrier. As much for her benefit as Michiru's, she said, "I dealt with the same kind of creature on Halloween and it couldn't get out. We're probably fine."

Michiru grimaced. "Probably?"

"Probably," Jessica said in a flat voice. "But we need to deal with Pinchy ASAP. The shadow's partially in him, but I don't think it fits. If you move very slowly, your necklace should drive it back as you go."

"Got it." Michiru closed her eyes and a serenity settled over her features. Her eyelids flickered open, she took a deep breath, and inched toward the center of the circle, and Pinchy. The dark filaments parted before her.

"It's working, Mac! Just keep on like that."

Michiru slowly crouched, picked up the sledgehammer, and moved toward the twitching lobster.

The closer she got, the thicker the tentacles were. Some pushed through to her skin, regardless of how carefully she moved. Their touch was quickly dispersed by her pendant's aura, but not before raising new red welts on her already inflamed skin. None of this registered on Michiru's determined face.

Against her will, Jessica's eyes followed the metal head as it swung down. Michiru's aim was true and her strike crushed Pinchy's head, splitting him into pieces. A writhing knot of darkness gathered in the gory carcass and then paled to a dull gray.

Michiru set her jaw against the pain of the whipping tentacles and raised the hammer again and again, until there was nothing left but a splatter of extinguished life.

* * *

With Pinchy's death, the entity's central mass and writhing tentacles steadily thinned, turning transparent. Its movement became disordered and its reach diminished, until the appendages melded back into the increasingly faint darkness pooled in Pinchy's remains.

Jessica's breath caught in her throat as Bill twitched under her and groaned. She slowly turned to look. One of his eyes was swollen shut, but the other fluttered open.

Groggy confusion glimmered in the clear blue orb as he tried to focus on her face. "Who..." He cleared his throat and croaked, "Who're you?"

Summoning as much authority as she could in her exhausted state, Jessica ordered him not to move.

Still feeling the effects of the roofie, his cracked lips spread in a contented grin and he slurred, "Yesh, ma'am."

Jessica's relief that he was conscious and free of the shadow was quickly supplanted by annoyance when he wiggled suggestively under her. She shifted position, hoping to remove any hint of romance, but everywhere she moved seemed worse. He continued rubbing his hips against her.

Losing her temper, Jessica swatted his shoulder. "Stop that."

He pouted, but after a moment apparently forgot what he was upset about and his silly grin returned.

Jessica stared at the spot where Pinchy had died for a long time, waiting for something to happen. She couldn't believe it was done, that this insane night, day, whatever, was over at last.

Her dazed mind registered someone talking. She looked at Michiru. She was standing with the hammer raised, ready for another hit.

"Did you say something?"

"I asked if you were okay." Michiru's eyes did not stray from her target.

"No, but I'm alive. You?"

Michiru nodded. "Same."

Jessica looked back to where the shadow had disappeared. Still nothing.

"I think it's gone. Really gone." Jessica wiped a drop from her eye, unsure whether it was sweat or tears.

Chapter 44

H-K Shadow Drone eliminated. Primary objective achieved.
Channel remains non-receptive.

* * *

Jessica gratefully slid off Bill and struggled into a sitting position.

Michiru eased down beside her and leaned into her shoulder, not entirely steady herself. She pulled her knees up, wrapped her arms around them, and stared at the floor. After a moment, she said, "Sorry I freaked out."

Jessica shook her head. "It's me who should be sorry. You couldn't see what was happening. I should have been your eyes."

"No. You were amazing." Michiru sighed. "I should have tried standing still, but I wasn't thinking. I let panic win."

A hysterical giggle escaped from Jessica before she could slap a hand over her mouth.

Michiru's head drooped lower.

"I'm not laughing at you." Jessica went to put a hand on Michiru's arm, but stopped herself when she saw the maze of welts. "I was just thinking about my panic attack earlier. I couldn't even move."

"Yeah, sure."

"No, really. At least you didn't have to whack yourself in the head to snap out of it." She raised a hand to her cheek, gently felt along several of her own welts, and winced when she came to a thin laceration. "I even managed to give myself a paper cut. How's that for stupid?"

"I wondered what the head banging was about." A reluctant smile tugged at the corners of Michiru's mouth.

They sat in silence, until Michiru cleared her throat. "So." She looked between Bill and Jessica. "What actually happened? You went a bit weirder than normal for a while there."

"I can't. Not yet." Jessica rubbed her throbbing temples. She didn't have the mental faculty to tie a shoelace at the moment. "I need to sort through it myself first."

Michiru nodded. "I understand. *Ame futte chi katamaru.* It takes a while to recover."

Jessica stared at her blankly, afraid one of them had suffered a stroke.

"Something my mum says. It means, 'After the rain, earth hardens.' I guess what I meant was, I understand if it's a while before you want to talk…if that makes sense." She shook her head. "I think I've caught your nervous babble. I must be tired."

Smiling weakly at the idea that Michiru counted those few sentences as babbling, Jessica forced herself to look back at Pinchy's remains. There was no sign of the shadow. She peered around the room and saw nothing but an occasional sparkle as dust motes floated through patches of light.

Jessica took the relic off Bill's chest and watched his face. His expression remained locked in blissfully drugged delirium. She felt a stab of envy—a feeling quickly squashed by the realization that she would never be content to remain unaware. She'd always choose knowledge, even if it was the more painful option.

She pried his good eye open. A slow, triumphant smile spread across her face. "It's gone, Mac. It's really gone. It worked." She heard the disbelief in her voice.

Michiru hugged her. "I knew you could do it." She let her go and then stiffly shifted into a crouch, levering Bill up into a sitting position. "Now we just need to sober him up and get that relic back to the church. How are we doing for time?"

All feelings of accomplishment abandoned Jessica. In the immediacy of the fight, she had blocked out everything but the next few seconds. Now, with her future once more extended, she forced herself to think ahead; the relic had to be returned, Bill had to be taken home, the house had to be cleaned, the garage door needed fixing, her mother's car—Jessica stopped when she felt the familiar light-headedness that accompanied a panic attack.

She checked her watch and frowned at the blank display. Shaking her wrist a few times, she muttered under her breath, "What a surprise. Something else I've broken."

Jessica struggled to her feet and headed for the stairs, but came to an abrupt stop at the salt outline. Cursing, she collected her scattered notes and riffled through the crumpled pages until she found the relevant section. Her bed was beginning to feel like the mythical pot of gold at the end of a rainbow.

She shuffled clockwise around the room three times as quickly as her shaky legs could manage, reciting the circle-opening ritual.

"I thank the energies for their assistance and bid them farewell. The circle is open but unbroken." She forced the words out in a feeble mumble as fatigue dragged at her limbs.

The barrier popped out of existence and the incense smoke dissipated. She felt marginally better with the circle down, her limbs less leaden.

She called back to Michiru, promising to put on a pot of coffee, and climbed the stairs. A serious infusion of energy was required before she could face the rest of the night.

The more she thought about it, the more sure she was that her exhaustion after Halloween, and now, had something to do with the rituals. It was more than physical exhaustion, it felt like someone had sucked the marrow from her soul.

Hope it's temporary. With my luck, I'll find out this magic crap is using up years of my life.

It was a sobering thought, and one that spurred her already pressing need to find out why the laws of physics appeared to have taken a holiday lately.

Chapter 45

A mantle of aromatic euphoria drifted around Jessica as she poured coffee beans into the grinder. They tinkled to the bottom of the machine, sounding like rain on a tin roof. She breathed in their earthy scent and hit the button, turning them into a beautiful, rich brown whirlwind. The promise of caffeinated goodness lulled her into quiet wellbeing.

There was a movement near the kitchen door. Jessica yelped and spun to see Drew brandishing a shovel as nonchalantly as possible, which wasn't very.

"Hey there." It sounded like a good-natured greeting, but his strained eyes suggested otherwise. "Shovel beats grinder."

Jessica frowned.

Drew nodded to her hands and she looked down to see she was wielding the grinder as if it were a weapon. Swallowing the lump in her throat, she shoved it back onto the counter.

"Holy crap." She managed a weak smile. "I forgot you were here."

"Ooooh, burn…you are *so* not good for a guy's ego." He propped the shovel against the wall and came into the kitchen, still keeping his distance, watching her closely.

"I was going to ask how things are going, but damn, your face says it all." He grimaced. "You've got some nasty-looking scratches."

"Welts." She ran a finger down her cheek and winced. "And a paper cut. You should see Mac. She got it a lot worse."

"Does she need help?"

Jessica shook her head. "They're healing pretty fast. The welts, not the paper cut. That still hurts like a mofo." She scrunched her sleeve up to check her arm and was pleased to find the inflamed skin was now no worse than a bad sunburn. "And you can stop looking at me like that. I'm not possessed."

Drew chuckled and visibly relaxed. "You must be fine. Bill never sounded that petulant." He dug in his pocket and tossed something at her. "Here, before I forget…"

Jessica was too slow to catch it, but she rolled her eyes as her pet sock landed on the counter beside her. He was testing. She picked up the green scrap and held it, giving him a look.

"The shadow's gone. For good, I think. And Bill's starting to come out of it. I'm making coffee in hopes of getting him on his feet quicker." She swayed and leaned against the counter as a wave of fatigue hit. "And keeping me on mine."

Drew guided her to a chair. "I'll make the coffee. You look less lively than the walking dead."

"Now who's bad for the ego?" Jessica snorted and shoved her pet sock into her pocket. "But that's pretty much how I feel…only without the need to chow down on brains. Though I wouldn't pass up a transplant. Mine's feeling a bit…minced. Now that would be an awesome medical breakthrough. 'Hmm, brain needs a rest today. Think I'll swap in my spare.' " She saw Drew's eyebrow rise and clamped her lips together. "Sorry. Have I mentioned I'm a bit overtired?"

"Believe it or not, I got that all on my own." He opened

and closed a few cupboards, and then asked, "Okay. I give up. Where are the filters?"

Jessica directed him and then slumped forward onto the kitchen table, laying her head on her arms. Just as she got comfortable, she belatedly remembered her phone going off in the middle of everything, and had a sudden terrible thought that something might have happened to her parents in Switzerland.

She fished out her wayward phone and stared at the blank screen. After trying the power button several times, she slapped the inert device onto the table.

"Fuck."

Drew turned to look at her. "What's up?"

"Doesn't matter. I just wish I could stop breaking things." She thumped her head onto the table, groaning as she hit a sore spot.

"That reminds me. Your landline rang a couple times. I didn't answer." Drew placed a glass of water at her elbow and headed for the basement with two more glasses. "I'll be right back."

Resolving to check her voicemail as soon as she had the time and a speck of energy, she hefted herself up. "Wait. I'm coming too. Don't fancy being on my own right now." She lurched into the pantry and emerged with a bag of candy.

They found Michiru half dragging a disgruntled Bill in circuits around the rec room. Jessica was relieved to see that Michiru's skin was recovering at the same rate as hers. The mass of red lines crisscrossing her face, stomach, and arms were fading to light pink, and she was moving with more ease.

As soon as Michiru saw the water, she dropped Bill onto the old sofa they'd shoved against the wall and gratefully downed both glasses.

"Remind me not to enter any drinking competitions with

you." Drew looked impressed as he retrieved the empty glasses. "More?"

Michiru nodded and flopped down on the couch.

Jessica called after Drew as he climbed the stairs, "Can you check on the coffee too?" She didn't bother disguising her desperation. Popping a handful of chocolate-covered peanuts in her mouth, she summoned the energy to chew and sank down beside Michiru.

"I know I told you not to let me, but I think I need to re-sort to coffee again. I've almost had it." Michiru's hand snaked over and the candy bag rustled.

Jessica grunted in response, hoping the sugar would kick in quickly.

Bill's hand landed heavily in Jessica's lap, spilling some of the M&M's. She slid the bag to her other side, out of his reach.

He pouted. "Awwww. Meanie. Mean mean meanie…" He trailed off into indistinct mumbles.

"This is going to take a while, isn't it?" Jessica huffed.

Michiru sighed and retrieved another handful of candy. "At least we've got chocolate."

Drew arrived with four steaming mugs of coffee. His long fingers were elegantly wrapped around the handles and Jessica thought she'd never seen anything so beautiful.

She fought back grateful tears as she warmed her hands on a mug and breathed in deeply. She imagined the heavenly vapors traveling down her throat and into her lungs, energizing every cell they met along the way.

Bill sagged sideways and knocked Michiru's arm, spilling a wave of coffee onto her leg. She raised an elbow to lever him off and Drew hopped forward to grab him before anyone sus-tained further injury. He shuffled Bill over and sat between him and Michiru.

Drew held a mug to Bill's mouth and was eventually able to convince him to drink by fooling him into believing it was a nice, frothy glass of beer. Bill screwed up his face in disgust at the first sip, but gradually warmed to the idea and began drinking on his own.

Somewhere through the lazy fog that had settled over her, Jessica noticed Drew's gentle attention to Bill and resolved to thank him, later, when speaking didn't feel like such a chore.

The room fell into silence for a time, broken only by sporadic slurping of coffee.

When Bill was done, Drew plucked the empty cup out of his hand, slipped an arm around his back, and hefted him upright. He waved Michiru back with his free arm. "Sit. I've got him."

Bill contemplated Drew, his one good eye squinting at the proximity. "Who are you?"

"Dude. Don't breathe your rancid beer fumes in my face. You could kill a skunk at ten paces." Drew turned his head away and started walking. The two of them staggered sideways, righted themselves, then swayed and stumbled in the other direction.

Jessica's head nodded forward and she jerked it back up, struggling to stay awake. It fell again, and this time, she didn't have the energy to raise it. The room faded into gray and then black.

* * *

Some time later, Michiru shook Jessica awake. She blearily looked around and saw that Bill was stumbling in a mostly straight line on his own, with Drew providing an occasional shove to keep him on course.

Michiru waved a steaming cup under Jessica's nose and

she groggily sat up. Wiping a bead of drool off her lip, she cradled the proffered coffee.

Drew steered Bill back to the couch and Michiru shoved another cup into his hands, asking, "What do you remember?"

He took a sip and then pulled the mug away from his swollen lips, dropping his gaze to the floor. After a while, he said, "Everything's blurry. Like a dream. But, I get flashes…" His face paled, bringing the purple bruises and pink lattice of welts on his skin into sharp relief. "Did I attack Coach? And Chris…oh God…he jumped…"

The mug fell to the floor, forgotten, as he locked his hands behind his head. He rocked back and forth, keening to himself, and then half stood, and sat again, staring at Jessica. "…and you…I wanted to kill you. Why? What the fuck is going on?"

"Settle down." Michiru gave him a warning look. "You remember anything else?"

He eyed her suspiciously. "Like what? You obviously have something in mind."

Jessica, Michiru, and Drew remained silent. Bill looked from one to the other, but even Jessica managed to keep her face blank.

Bill frowned. "I don't remember much. Mostly just anger and pain." He touched his bruised face and glared at Michiru. "And a vague feeling that most of this is your fault."

"Since you were trying to kill us at the time, consider yourself lucky." Michiru leaned back and stretched her arms out, cracking her knuckles. Bill flinched. "You've been causing trouble for weeks."

"Weeks?" He stood unsteadily and backed away from them. "Listen, I don't know what's going on. Maybe I wanted to hurt some people…and my dog…oh God…did I drown my dog?" He raised a fist to his mouth and bit his knuckle. "This is crazy. I wouldn't kill anyone."

Unable to bear his confusion and pain any longer, Jessica blurted out, "You were possessed by...something horrible. It was in Chris, and when he died, it went into you."

"Chris." Bill held his hands up, turning them slowly. "I tried to stop him. He wouldn't listen. He was talking crazy. I grabbed for him—" He curled his fingers into fists and then his body folded in half as he sank to his knees.

Jessica knelt beside him, reliving the horror with him. She now knew the truth of it. Chris hadn't wanted to die. He'd desperately fought to survive, right up to the end. But that pillar had been too close... She wasn't sure if her newfound insights into self-sacrifice made her feel better or worse.

She extended and retracted a hand several times, trying to work up the courage to touch Bill. Eventually, she patted his arm.

He leaned in and wrapped his arms around her as he let out a quaking sob.

Michiru sprang off the couch, but Jessica waved her back. Although restricting, Bill's hug wasn't threatening. His touch, his voice, practically everything about him was different now. The hatred had vanished. He was simply scared and broken, grieving the loss of a friend.

Jessica spoke to Michiru and Drew as she awkwardly patted his back. "We need to get him home."

Michiru frowned. "Drew will have to take him. We've got to get the relic back ASAP. If we're lucky, Father Nick didn't bother to pull it out yesterday, but I bet he'll want it for Sunday service."

"Great." Drew scowled at Bill. "Come on, numbnuts. Time to go." He helped Bill to his feet, a more involved task than expected as Bill refused to let go of Jessica. It was like prying a security blanket away from a distressed toddler.

Jessica wasn't sure why he had latched onto her, but it was better than the alternative. Kidnapping and drug charges would be so very inconvenient.

She followed them upstairs, selfishly hoping Bill's memories remained fuzzy.

Chapter 46

Jessica stared at her sneakers and then clumsily shoved her feet into them. By the time her second foot finally slid into place, she wasn't sure if she had the energy to get back up again. She dropped her head onto her knee and winced as a welt on her forehead contacted a bruise on her leg.

Her breath escaped in a single, ragged exhalation. When she looked up again, she found Bill watching her, a concerned groove crinkling his blistered forehead. There was a great deal of fear, grief, and despair in his eyes, but at least now he had a chance to heal.

She became lost in the vivid sapphire and white flecks radiating from his pupils like miniature lightning strikes. Life was a delicate thing. A collection of random atoms balanced on the knife-edge of being and not. Surely saving a life should cancel her debt?

A wave of guilt and sorrow broke over her. Tears welled and she sucked in a pained breath as her chest constricted. Nothing she'd done tonight erased her failure with Chris, and that failure sat in her gut like a ball of barbed wire. The thought that she might have saved him if she'd heeded the gatekeeper's first warning would haunt her to her last breath.

More guilt poured into the swelling reservoir as a new realization wiggled its treacherous way into her mind. She'd trade
Bill's watery blue eyes for Chris's kind gray ones in a heartbeat.

What kind of a person does that make me?

Jessica broke eye contact and tried to wrestle her emotions back into their shell as she pretended to search for her
keys. Bill backed off and stood sheepishly to the side. She
wiped a renegade tear on her shoulder and had almost regained
her composure when Drew's bike roared to life.

She jumped. The aggressive growl jangled every raw
nerve in her body. She scanned her neighbors' windows to see
if any lights flicked on and caught the flash of car headlights
turning down her street.

Adrenalin surged through her fatigued body. She ducked
behind the porch railing, dragging Bill down beside her. Her
heart thumped in her chest as the vehicle slowed and turned
into her driveway. She peered between the wooden slats and
saw Drew still poised on his bike, watching the car intently as it
stopped.

The driver's side door opened and Eric emerged, giving
Drew a wary look. He jogged to the porch, calling out Jessica's
name.

She rose from her crouch, not entirely sure why she'd
bothered hiding. Her recent lifestyle was generating some bad
habits.

Eric bounded up the steps, drew her in for a quick hug,
and then held her at arm's length. The way he looked her over,
at first worriedly, and then in confusion, reminded her that she
was still dressed for a party, and probably more than a bit of a
mess.

"Jess? Are you okay?" He saw Bill and backed away, pulling her with him. "Who are these guys? What's going on?"

"W...what are you doing here?" she asked, trying to wrap her mind around the sudden collision of her two, very different worlds.

He frowned and Jessica wondered if she would ever learn to not say the first thing that came into her mind.

The motorbike engine died and Drew sauntered back to the porch, offering Eric a polite nod. Although Drew was taller than Eric by a few inches, he was outclassed as far as muscle mass was concerned. He positioned himself behind Bill, a hulk anyone would think twice before tackling, and listened in with apparent interest.

Eric's frown deepened as he examined Jessica, moving her into the light by the open front door. "You smell like stale beer and pop. And what's up with your face? It's all red and blotchy. Are you having an allergic reaction?"

"No. It's..." Jessica shuffled her feet, attempting to think of an explanation that wouldn't alarm him further.

As she struggled to answer, Eric turned back to the guys. "Who the hell are you and what are you doing here at..." He checked his watch, "...almost six a.m.?"

"Holy shit! Is that the time?" Jessica whipped around to the graying eastern horizon and her heart rate increased.

The sound of scampering claws approached and Hamish shot out of the house. An excited blur of fur and wet tongue raced around everyone's legs. When the puppy reached Bill, he sniffed enthusiastically and yipped until he was picked up.

"Mish!" Bill gazed affectionately at the dog and then Jessica. "You saved him. I remember." Hamish licked his cheek, wiggling with excitement.

Eric watched in silence, his face flushing as he glanced between Bill and Jessica. "Looks like you two ran into the same thing." He waved at Bill's welts and inquired in a hard voice, "Poison ivy?"

The ensuing puzzled hush broke when Michiru appeared in the doorway, flashing a white sports bra as she casually pulled on one of Jessica's old sweatshirts. Surprise briefly registered on her face when she saw Eric, but she recovered quickly and smiled, extending a hand. "Hi. From the photos upstairs, I'm guessing you're Eric?"

Jessica ground her teeth, cursing Michiru's relaxed attitude. *Of all the times! This already looks bad enough without someone prancing around half dressed.*

Eric blinked at Michiru and then tilted his head to gaze past her at the disheveled entryway. One of the throw pillows from the living room sofa was lying in the hall, its feather innards strewn across the floor. A muscle in his cheek twitched as he clenched his jaw.

Michiru let her hand drop to her side when he made no move to take it. Casting a questioning look at Jessica, she slid past Eric and stationed herself next to the boys, giving Hamish a friendly pat he snuffled her shoulder.

Not sure what else to do, Jessica introduced Eric to everyone.

After an uncomfortable pause, Eric led her a few feet away and whispered, "Jess. Talk to me. Tell me that what I think is happening here, isn't. I've been trying to get a hold of you all night. I must have left a dozen messages. I've been worried sick."

"I'm fine...really...just tired, so I'm a bit muddled...and my cell's dead." Jessica self-consciously adjusted her tunic, wishing it wasn't quite as tight and low-cut. "What's so urgent that you needed to talk to me anyway? Are you okay?"

Eric's lips thinned. "You don't have a clue, do you?"

Jessica shook her head.

"Our date," he said flatly. "Los Abucheos. Eight-thirty. Ring any bells?"

Jessica closed her eyes. "That's what's been nagging at me!" It was a bitter relief. She'd screwed up, again, but at least the horrible feeling she'd missed something was gone. And, sad to say, it was by far the least worrying detail she could have forgotten.

"Jess." Eric took hold of her arms. "What is going on? I waited for an hour at the restaurant and then came here. When you weren't home, I tracked Kathy down, but she had no idea where you were, and Beth was AWOL as usual. I eventually had to go home, but I kept calling until about an hour ago. I got through and heard a bunch of…I don't know…yelling and growling? I figured you were in some kind of trouble."

He cast a suspicious glance at the rest of the group. "So I swipe my parent's car, drive back, and find…this, whatever this is." He pulled a dried sage leaf out of her hair. "Please tell me you didn't blow off our date and scare the living crap out of me to go on a double date with these guys."

"It's not like that. Bill was…" She rejected her initial impulse to tell the truth and searched for something more believable. "…drunk and couldn't go home, so we brought him here to sober up." Pleased that she'd both avoided lying and answering the core question, she continued, "We were just about to take him home."

"Really? All of you? On that?" He jabbed a finger at the motorbike. "Interesting. Think I'll stick around to watch this."

Jessica stared at the bike. Her mind felt like a fossilized snail coiled in her skull. "Uh," she drew the word out, trying to force her brain into action. She couldn't get past the image of everyone piled on the bike like a totem, with Hamish on top, ears flapping in the wind as they cruised down the street. "No. Of course not. That would be ridiculous and very unsafe." Her voice cracked and she swallowed. "Drew was going home, on his own. Mac and I were going to walk Bill back to his house."

"I see. And I suppose you found him drunk on your way to Los Abucheos?" Eric pulled her hand up to examine the name and number written on it.

"So, if that's Drew, and that's Bill," he said, pointing at them respectively, "Who's Ben? Tomorrow night's entertainment?"

A white-hot flash of anger shot through Jessica and she jerked her hand back. She glared off into the distance, wrestling with her temper, and saw a thin strip of pink creep over the shoulder of Coldwater Hill. She pressed the heels of her hands against her throbbing forehead.

"Listen. I screwed up and I'm sorry. I'll explain everything, but I have to do something right now. It's time sensitive. As soon as I'm done, I'll call you."

"What the fuck, Jess? We've always been straight with each other. Something is going on and you're trying to buy time to think up an excuse. So, no thanks. We'll talk now. Your friends can take Bill home."

Michiru touched Jessica's elbow, turning her slightly so she could retrieve the relic from her jacket without Eric seeing. "I can do this on my own. I don't mind."

"See? She doesn't mind." Eric sat down on the porch steps, resting his forearms on his thighs.

"Well, I do." Jessica snatched the relic back and glared at him. This was her mess and she wasn't going to just drop it on her friend. Plus, his assumption of control pissed her off. "Why is it suddenly so hard to trust me? You know I would never—"

"I thought I knew you." Eric interrupted. "But now…"

He let the statement hang and dropped his head forward, twining his hands between his knees until his knuckles turned white.

A light flicked on in a house across the street and Michiru hissed, "You two need to end this or take it inside. We're starting to attract attention."

Jessica and Eric simultaneously glared at her.

* * *

Drew sidled away, shoving Bill down the walkway in front of him. Although curious to see how Jessica dug herself out of this hole, he knew a good exit cue when one was presented. Being caught between Michiru and the solidly built Eric was an unpleasant enough prospect, without throwing in Jessica Wildcard Clarke. At the rate she was going, she'd probably turn them all into toads.

When he reached the driveway, he called back in a stage whisper, "I'll drop Bill off. No problem." He went to hand Bill the spare helmet, scowled at the beagle squirming in his arms, and then at his bike as if it had betrayed him.

"Well, that's not going to work." He moodily slung the helmets back onto the handlebars. "Guess we're hoofing it."

* * *

Jessica watched the guys set off down the street in a mostly straight line, thanks to Drew's guiding nudges.

Lowering her voice, she addressed Eric. "What's going on already doesn't make much sense, so me trying to explain things quickly while I'm half-conscious won't work. I should have found a way to tell to you sooner, but everything just snowballed. I know this isn't fair to you, but right now, I need you to go home. When I'm done, I'll call and we can talk…if that's what you still want."

She waved at Michiru to follow and started down the driveway, hoping Eric would back off.

He didn't. He kept pace with her. "Enough with all this cryptic shit, Jess. I'm not going anywhere. After what I've been through tonight, you owe me an explanation."

* * *

Michiru's muscles tensed in reaction to the fury rolling off Jessica like an incoming tide. Her own body and mind felt as resilient as overcooked noodles and she was impressed Jessica was keeping it together as well as she was.

"After what *you've* been through?" Jessica ground the words out between clenched teeth.

Eric ducked in front of them, forcing them to stop or alter their course.

Jessica planted her feet and glared up at him.

Michiru's protective instincts bristled and she resisted the urge to bodily throw Eric back into his car. She sighed. The hands-on approach was expedient, but rarely well received. She discreetly circled behind him, unsure how he would react to the blasting he was about to receive.

"I owe you?" Jessica said, her tone low with barely suppressed rage. "I'm done. Do you understand? Done! I don't owe anyone anything anymore. There's only so much I can do in a day and I blew way past that hours ago. Get out of my way." She pushed past him.

Eric kicked a stray rock. It thwacked into the wooden fence bordering the sidewalk, sending vibrations down its length. Jessica spluttered and batted at the air as she walked through a cloud of startled moths abandoning their disturbed shelter.

"Fine. Go." Eric yelled after her, ducking as a moth

flapped at his face. "I don't know when it happened, but you changed, Jess. You used to be a nice person."

Jessica's steps faltered and she spun back. "You know what? You're right. A month ago, I would have stood here explaining everything until you liked me again. But now I know that nice is a luxury. Go home, Eric." She walked off into the dawn mist, until she was no more than a blur in the shifting gray haze.

Eric threw his hands in the air and stared up at the fading stars.

Michiru wondered if she should say something. When nothing came to mind, she shrugged at him and jogged after Jessica.

He let out a frustrated growl and she glanced over her shoulder to see him stalking back toward the house.

* * *

Jessica swiped a sleeve across her eyes. "What you said earlier about hardening...when does that happen?" Her anger had deserted her, leaving an aching pit in her stomach.

"It's different for everyone." Michiru gave her a sympathetic smile. "Maybe things won't look so bad once everyone's cooled off."

Jessica peered at the empty street behind them. "Yeah. Maybe."

Lately, her maybes seemed to be herding together and piling up. Maybe she had done the right thing tonight. Maybe she was going to do the right thing now. Then again, maybe not.

Chapter 47

Michiru jogged down the sidewalk with Jessica wheezing loudly behind her, trying to keep up. They needed to gain back the time they'd lost dealing with Eric, but the going was slow. She stopped when Jessica doubled over in a coughing fit.

"We're almost there." She tried to sound encouraging as Jessica gasped for breath.

The pink streak on the horizon was widening and birds fluttered around, chirping excitedly with their mates. Michiru scowled at a particularly vocal tree.

This was usually her favorite time of day: Animals frolicking without fear of human intrusion, flowers shyly opening under the sun's touch. Mornings were all possibility. But not this one. This morning was a ticking time bomb, its dial relentlessly winding down to zero.

"We'd better keep moving. If we stop for too long, our muscles will seize up." She looped an arm through Jessica's and started forward again, this time at a walking pace.

Jessica's breathing normalized with the reduced speed, though it remained shallower and faster than Michiru was comfortable with.

"Why did you keep Eric out of the loop?" Michiru pressed her lips together. The question had been rolling around in her mind. She hadn't meant to ask, but now that she had, she figured she might as well get it all out. "I mean, I know you were worried he'd call the cops, but there's something else, isn't there? Anything I should worry about? He seems a bit...intense."

"No. He's not normally like that. Actually, I've never seen him like that." Jessica was silent for a moment and then sighed. "Two of my best friends buggered off just as this craziness started. I guess I was scared that I'd lose him too. So, I pretended everything was fine. And now, he's probably gone because of *that* boneheaded decision. Ironic, in a shitty way."

Michiru stared straight ahead, thinking she should have kept her mouth shut. This emotional stuff was beyond her expertise.

"What's wrong with me, Mac? I know I fucked up with Eric, and I wouldn't blame him if he never talks to me again, but I don't understand Beth and Kathy. Did they just wake up one day and decide I wasn't worth being around?"

"Sometimes things just don't work out." There was a lengthy silence. Michiru wondered if Jessica was waiting for more. "Uh, well, as far as I'm concerned, a friend who deserts you when you need them is a shitty friend and you're better off without them. If Eric really cares, he'll give you a chance to explain."

Jessica shrugged, not looking hopeful, and then jabbed a hand against her ribs. "Fuckin' hell. This stitch is killing me." She doggedly staggered on in silence.

Soon, the church gate loomed out of the fog. Jessica stopped in front of it, staring up at the wrought-iron points and twists. A weak smile played at the corners of her mouth. "You know, this doesn't seem so scary anymore. Painful, but not scary."

Michiru patted her on the shoulder, relieved the gate wouldn't prove as time-consuming a hurdle as it had the last time. "You want a leg up?"

Jessica shook her head and started climbing.

Michiru grinned and followed, easily outpacing her friend, who had to pause to find each new hand and foothold.

Jessica's journey over the metal barrier was not smooth, but she made it with only a few more bruises and abrasions than she started with. She landed with a gravel-scattering thud, brushed herself off, and set her shoulders. "Onwards and upwards," she croaked and set off to the chapel.

As Michiru watched Jessica limp away, her respect grew. Given the option, Jessica might choose to be a wimp, but she'd proven more than once tonight that she came through when it mattered. And, given how knackered she was, Jessica had to be feeling it worse.

Michiru caught up and pulled her off the gravel road onto the grass verge. Without the cover of rain to hide the crunching this time, the grass was the quieter path.

If they were going to keep this up, she'd have to do some training with Jessica. Get her into some kind of physical exercise regime. Maybe Drew too, if he stuck around. And they needed to work on self-defense. That was priority number one. She couldn't even fathom walking down a street or entering a room without taking stock of threats and working through scenarios in her mind. From several conversations she'd had with Jessica, it had become painfully obvious this was not part of her routine.

The girls crept through the churchyard as shadows desperately groped for each other in the gathering light. They rounded a bush and Michiru registered a movement…a musky smell…something…

She dropped into a crouch. Jessica stumbled into her and Michiru pulled her down.

There was a scrape of gravel and a glint of lupine eyes as a low, gray blur loped past.

The wolf stopped and turned to inspect them. The amber spheres paused on Jessica. There was a spark of recognition and, for a moment, it was more than animal. Then it blinked and the connection was gone. Its muzzle rose to catch a scent, whiskers and ears alert and twitching.

A twig snapped under Jessica's foot and the wolf growled, lowering its body, readying to fight or flee. The three stared at each other, unmoving, until a vigilant, pointed ear flicked to the side, picking up a distant sound. The wolf raised its nose to recover the trail and darted into the spruce trees.

Michiru waited, not trusting that it was gone. Something about the way it had looked at them was odd. Then again, she wasn't used to the wild animals here or convinced her mind was entirely functional at the moment.

She leaned close to Jessica's ear and whispered, "What the hell was that?"

"My next project." Jessica said, watching the trees intently. "I think I forgot to tell you about Sarah." An embarrassed flush darkened her cheeks. "I'll explain later. One thing at a time, right?"

Michiru raised an eyebrow as a howl drifted on the wind. She had mostly lived in cities, so she had a fair amount of experience dealing with human wildlife, but this rural living was fraught with a whole new set of complications—a wolf encounter was probably the most normal she could expect, based on recent experience. Not being able to anticipate what might happen next was both exhilarating and intensely frustrating.

They carried on toward the chapel, even more watchful of their surroundings. Michiru grimaced at the telltale rasping behind her and resisted the urge to snap at Jessica to pick up her feet. She'd make as much noise trying to explain as Jessica did shuffling through the grass. No wonder she tripped over everything.

Pausing to stare at a large, paw-shaped depression in a patch of wet dirt, Michiru wondered if she would eventually yearn for the dull monotony she had been so afraid she'd find here. The long, deep claw marks suggested she would.

They arrived at the church without any further encounters and stood huddled against the entry arch. Having already unlocked the door once, it proved little challenge for her, and they quickly made their way to the relic cabinet. She popped open its lock and then backed off to let Jessica deal with the glove.

Michiru sat on one of the hard wooden pews, wishing there were cushions. She rubbed her thighs, stretching out her stiffening muscles.

There was a flash of copper low and to her left. A muscle in her neck spasmed painfully as she whipped her head around.

She grinned at her jumpiness when she saw what it was. Michiru bent down to retrieve the penny and then paused, warily drawing her hand back. Disquiet prickled at the base of her skull. The coin was sitting at the tip of a spear of orange light that shouldn't be there. Her light-hearted mood dissolved.

She followed the beam to its source and saw the church door standing ajar. Cursing herself for not double-checking the latch, she stood and heard a faint footfall outside. She slid under the bench and threw the penny at Jessica, hoping she recognized the warning.

* * *

The coin bounced off Jessica's head and she dropped the relic case. It hit the cabinet with a resounding thud and she fretfully checked the glass for cracks. Finding the case intact, she ran her fingers over the wood cabinet top and felt a dent.

Jessica rubbed the back of her head and turned to glare at Michiru, wondering why she was throwing things.

She was nowhere to be seen.

A shadow slipped through the church door.

"Freeze," hollered a masculine voice. "Put your hands on your head."

Jessica froze, but the second part was problematic. One hand was already in position, spastically clutching a wad of hair, but her other hand was resting on the cabinet.

"I can't do both," she wheezed in shock.

Stark electric light flooded the church and an RCMP officer approached, pointing at the floor. His other hand hovered over the gun in his belt. "On the ground and put your hands behind your head…and then you can freeze, smartass."

Jessica managed to follow his order only because her legs chose that moment to give out. Her whole body went numb. She flopped her deadened hands onto her head and lay with her nose to the floor, listening to the rushing cannon beat of her heart.

The officer tugged her arms behind her back and cold steel encircled her wrists as handcuffs clicked into place. "You alone?"

She squeaked out a weak "Yes" and risked a sideways glance. There was still no sign of Michiru. If she was there, she must have found a cloak of invisibility in her bag of many things.

The officer warned her to stay put as he searched the chapel.

Maybe if I play dumb I can talk my way out of this? No. Bad idea. I'll babble and then who knows what will come out.

Jessica watched him methodically check between the pews and prayed that Michiru was long gone. She doubted the secret compartment in her bag would withstand a full police search, and being caught with knives, lock-picks, and whatever other interesting paraphernalia she had would make the situation considerably worse.

This is a fine thank-you for trying to do the right thing. She sneezed as dust went up her nose.

Jessica mentally gave the universe the middle finger. All the stories she'd read on the web about people being arrested for minor crimes and ending up mysteriously dead or forgotten in a cell flooded her mind. She felt doubly bad now for making fun of Drew for not wanting to tangle with the police.

The cop finished his search and came back. Jessica stared at her distorted reflection in his polished black boots. She was all nose. It would have been funny, except that it wasn't. She closed her eyes, silently rejoicing that Michiru had escaped detection.

Jessica was suddenly lifted to her feet. She teetered on wobbly legs, shivering from exhaustion and fright.

A loud, electronic squawk made her flinch and the officer grabbed her arm. She suspected it was to encourage her not to run, but she was glad for the added support.

He pushed the transmission button on his shoulder mic. "Control. 271 here. One adolescent female in custody. No sign of anyone else."

Jessica stopped breathing. She knew that call sign. She knew that voice.

The officer patted her down and pulled the relic out of her jacket pocket. He examined the shriveled hunk of leather, puzzled.

The radio crackled. "Copy that, Regina 271. Do you require backup?"

He dropped the relic into an evidence bag, along with her house keys, the folding knife Michiru had given her, a strip of paper she'd acquired from a fortune cookie a few weeks ago, and her pet sock. He gave her a funny look when he reached the last item.

"Negative on the backup. I think I can handle this one. See you in ten."

He escorted Jessica to the patrol car, helped her into the backseat, and went to meet an approaching figure, who turned out to be the pajama-clad priest.

The old man came closer, leaning on the cop's arm, and peered myopically in the window. He blinked in surprise when he recognized Jessica.

She slunk lower in her seat, wishing she had the ability to do something really useful like disappear in a puff of blue smoke.

But no, all I do is have disturbing dreams…and apparently depossess people. After a moment of wallowing, she reluctantly admitted both of those had been useful, but put in an urgent request for smoky escapes the next time strange abilities were being doled out. *And thick, flowy hair. All the best heroines have great hair.*

The patrol car rocked as the officer slid in and started the engine. Jessica watched the familiar landscape pass her window as they drove along the winding lane to the street. They were the same houses and trees and mailboxes and parked cars she saw every day. This was what she had wanted, what she had yearned for in the past weeks, months—for things to be the same—but now, a part of her rebelled.

Why were they the same? Shouldn't there be some kind of acknowledgement, some reaction in the world to what had happened? Something…anything?

Ghostly coils of steam rose from the road as the asphalt warmed under the rising sun's confident glow. It was going to be a beautiful day.

She looked up into the brightening sky and it struck her that maybe sameness *was* the response. Her gaze moved to the RCMP officer. Everyone had another day.

Dropping her aching head back onto the seat, Jessica tried not to think about what was coming. She stared at the spot on her door where a handle should have been and spent the remainder of the trip fending off a bout of claustrophobia.

Chapter 48

Jessica gratefully climbed out of her rolling cell when they arrived at the RCMP detachment. She preceded her escort through the doors with no resistance. He grunted a quick hello to the officer at the front counter and pulled out a chair for her at a desk in the bullpen.

Relaying her personal details felt reassuringly normal, until she reached the legal guardian part. Jessica's mind seized as she imagined the upcoming conversation with her parents.

She coughed, trying to talk around a lump which felt permanently lodged in her throat. The officer gave her an unimpressed look and slapped a glass of water down in front of her. She stared at it for a second and then leaned forward to slurp up a mouthful. The handcuffs jangled as she moved and he grudgingly held the glass for her.

After a few sips, Jessica cleared her throat and explained that her parents were in Switzerland. Her audience was skeptical. Just as their muddled conversation edged into outright argument, Father Wojcikowski arrived and bustled over to them.

"What is the meaning of all this?" Anxious, cataract-clouded eyes blinked at Jessica and she dropped her gaze to her running shoes.

The officer at reception abandoned his crossword puzzle and ushered the priest back to a row of seats by the front door, explaining politely that Constable Robyns would take his statement after he had processed Jessica. The priest stiffly sat, worrying at a button on his fraying overcoat.

Jessica gave Robyns her parents' cell phone numbers, which he promptly delivered to the front desk for confirmation.

She sank lower in her chair, feeling doom closing in on her like a hungry lioness. She hoped she'd gotten the numbers right. With her phone dead, it felt like half her brain was missing.

He returned shortly and perched on the edge of the desk, thoughtfully clicking his tongue. "I don't suppose you'd care to explain why you broke in? Maybe if I understand what happened, I can make things a little easier for you."

There it is, thought Jessica. *The question with no good answer. Well, not quite. There is an answer. And it's better than good, great even, possibly the best. Too bad I can't use it.*

Jessica didn't think she had enough energy left to be mad, but she surprised herself.

She let her head fall back and counted the stained squares in the drop ceiling as she considered what to say. Half-truths and misdirection seemed the order of the day. The hardest lies to catch were the ones that held some truth.

"I didn't break in. The door was open."

At least it was by the time I used it, she reasoned.

"You're saying the church wasn't locked?" His tone turned the question into an accusation.

Jessica nodded, hoping he was fishing.

Out of the corner of her eye, she saw Father Wojcikowski shakily accept a cup of tea. She swallowed loudly. Implying he had been negligent didn't sit well, but her options were limited.

"Even if that is the case, it doesn't explain *why* you were there. Most people don't skulk around churches in the middle of the night."

And there she was again, right back at that damn question. She wriggled uneasily in her chair, ignoring the urge to point out that it was actually stupid o'clock in the morning, not night. The cuffs pinched her skin and she adjusted her wrists, trying to find a more comfortable position.

Robyns dumped the bag of items he had taken from her onto the desk. He lined everything up and then studied the odd collection. Shoving the keys and knife to one side, he left the sock, fortune, and relic in the center, and stared some more.

In retrospect, Jessica mused, *the fortune was uncannily accurate.* "You will meet interesting people." She rolled her eyes. *Guess it forgot to mention they'd be possessed.*

"I've got it! It was a scavenger hunt, wasn't it?" He picked up the relic and examined the desiccated folds.

There was a whimper of protest from the reception area.

Constable Robyns leaned to the side to address the priest. "You recognize this?"

"Of course. It is the relic of Saint Aloysius." He spluttered and then paused to collect himself.

Robyns raised an eyebrow and transferred his gaze to Jessica. "I'm right, aren't I? It *was* a scavenger hunt." When she shrugged, he slapped his knee. "Thought so. Every year, somebody pulls this crap. I don't suppose you'll tell me who else is involved?"

She shook her head and stared at the floor.

He dropped his voice and leaned in closer. "Not even to spare that poor old guy another heart attack when he finds the next kid sneaking around his church?"

"Nobody else is going to bother him."

"I expect you're right. Your arrest should be a good enough deterrent," he said with an air of finality.

Robyns left to have a hushed conversation with the priest. Afterwards, they came back to the desk and the cop pulled his chair out for the old man.

The priest missed the offer, his attention wholly consumed by the relic. He picked it up, turning it in his hand as he examined its crevices and peaks until satisfied it was both genuine and undamaged.

He closed his eyes, made the sign of the cross, and then looked directly at Jessica. "The constable has explained his scavenger hunt theory, but I would like to hear what happened from you."

Jessica cleared her throat several times, unsuccessfully tried to meet his eyes, and aimed an earnest gaze at his left earlobe. "I didn't mean to cause so much trouble. I'm really sorry about everything. And I didn't want to scare anyone, especially you."

"Hmmmm. Yes. I see."

Jessica looked away, guessing from his tone that he hadn't missed her sidestepping the question.

The priest motioned to Robyns, who was hovering like a fly over an open jam pot. He pointed at Jessica's handcuffs. "Can you not take those off? They are hardly necessary."

Robyns looked like he was about to say something, but in the end just sighed, unclipped a key from his belt, and unlocked the handcuffs.

Jessica eased her stiff arms around to her lap, pleasantly surprised to note that the pattern of welts on her hands were now barely visible.

At least that's one less thing to explain, she thought, massaging her wrists.

"Jessica." The priest waited for her to look up before continuing. "You are an intelligent young woman. Whatever possessed you to do this?"

She searched his face, trying to determine whether the allusion was accidental or intentional. His brow was furrowed, but she read no covert motives in his expression, only well-intentioned and frank concern.

The front desk officer sauntered up and handed Robyns a computer printout. "Here's her paperwork. No priors. I got a hold of her parents. She wasn't lying. They're in Zurich, but her father's catching the next plane back. Problem is, it's a fifteen-hour flight and it'll take him a few hours to book a ticket and get to the airport." Before resuming his post, he solemnly shook his head at Jessica. "He's none too happy. You, my dear, are in a world of trouble."

"A world of trouble." Jessica repeated softly. "You have no idea." Her eyes glazed over and she fell back into silence.

Robyns turned to the priest. "If you'll take a seat at reception, I'll be right over to discuss what charges you'd like to pursue."

The old man studied Jessica. "I will not be pressing charges. There was no damage at the church and the relic is…" He sent a heartfelt look of gratitude toward the ceiling. "…mercifully safe. She has apologized and I do not think she will make such a poor decision again. Am I right?"

Jessica forced herself to meet his eyes. "I won't. Not if I have a choice in the matter."

Father Wojcikowski blinked at the odd wording, but nodded and laid a hand on her shoulder. "Growing up is difficult, especially when you are left to do so on your own. If you wish to talk, my door is open." An impish smile curved his lips. "Sometimes, it is even open when it is locked."

Constable Robyns threw the papers he was holding onto the desk, muttering incoherently.

A guilty flush crept up Jessica's neck as the priest continued, "Every one of us makes bad choices now and then. Even I have been known to make a few...what do you youngsters say...whoppers. The trick is to not repeat them." He patted her shoulder, retrieved the relic, and cradled it against his chest as he shuffled to the door.

After seeing him out, Robyns returned and slumped into his chair. He sat staring at Jessica until he cocked his head to the side and hollered at the front desk. "Hey Danny. How long 'til her dad gets here?"

"Maybe twenty hours. Probably more, knowing airlines and customs."

"Right. And I suppose the usual Saturday-night gang is in the back?"

Danny glanced at the metal door separating the bullpen from the holding cells. "Full house. The two you picked up on the DUI are still cooling their heels. Parents figured a night with us might straighten them out. Old Bob's in cell two. He's not going anywhere anytime soon." He paused and smiled. "That reminds me, he missed the bucket again. I cleaned up the last round, so it's your turn."

Robyns groaned and pinched the bridge of his nose.

"Set her up at Riley's desk with some magazines. If she causes trouble, we'll make her scrub Bob's cell." Danny made a face. "Trust me, kid. Be good, 'cause that's an ugly experience you won't forget."

Jessica bristled. *All they see is an irresponsible kid. They have no idea what I've been through, what almost happened.*

Robyns snorted. "Nice, but she can't sit out here for twenty bloody hours." He turned back to Jessica, sounding desperate. "There must be someone who can take you for a day. Any family member will do."

"I have a grandma in Saskatchewan." Jessica shrugged. "But it's like a seven-hour drive, and she's on a retreat."

Danny squinted at her from across the room. "Don't you hang out with McNeal's kid? What's her name, Elizabeth?"

A horrible feeling settled over Jessica. "Uh...no. Not anymore. Look, I promise I won't be any trouble. I'll just sit in a corner. I don't even need a chair. The floor is fine. You won't know I'm here."

Robyns ignored her. "Good thinking. McNeal's off today too. Call her dad back and see if he'll let us release her to him."

Danny nodded and picked up the phone.

Robyns leaned back in his chair. "Believe me, this is better. You don't want to be stuck here if you don't have to be."

Better? Jessica felt like the stuffing had been punched out of her. Beth witnessing any part of this was so monumentally NOT better. There would be some seriously juicy gossip making the rounds at school on Monday. And Beth would be in the center of the storm, in heaven.

Jessica rubbed her throbbing temples. *I might as well enlist and hope the army sends me somewhere far away. I wonder if they'd release me into the army's custody?* She considered the idea. *Nah. Based on the chaos I've stumbled into as a civilian, I'd hate to see what would happen with high-explosives added to the mix.*

Danny waved at Robyns. "Her dad said it was okay. I'll tell McNeal to get down here ASAP."

Robyns let out a pleased whistle. "See? It all worked out. You're lucky. You got off lightly this time. Make sure there isn't a next time."

She sighed, knowing in her bones there would be.

Why couldn't I have had a vision about the cops showing up at the church? She challenged the gatekeeper. *That would have been useful. But no, I dream about everyone else, so I can fix their shit, and then I'm left standing when the music stops.*

Jessica wilted as she thought about explaining things to her dad. She'd have to stick with Robyns's ridiculous scavenger hunt theory, and she wasn't convinced her parents would buy it.

The constable dropped a stack of papers into a shredder and handed her confiscated items back. She gratefully stroked her sock, trying to convince herself she wasn't a complete failure.

So things took a sour turn. I still accomplished the important bits. And nobody died. Overall, it's a win.

As the glowing green material slid through her fingers, she couldn't help but think that even it, her most longstanding and steadfast ally, looked unmoved as it drooped in silence.

Shortly, Beth's dad arrived with a very disgruntled daughter in tow. The rumpled hair and pajamas sticking out from under her coat suggested Beth hadn't been given time to get ready. She scowled when she saw Jessica.

Robyns pulled McNeal aside and talked out of earshot. Beth made no move toward Jessica. She waited by the door, impatiently scraping her shoe against an uneven tile.

Jessica laid her head on the desk and closed her eyes.

* * *

Something touched her shoulder and she woke with a snort. Jessica whipped around to see Beth's dad, which gave her another start as she tried to remember where she was.

Everything came crashing back and her shoulders slumped under the weight.

"We're ready to go if you are." McNeal smiled encouragingly from under his bushy moustache and helped her as she teetered upright.

It was like trying to stand in a canoe. After steadying herself against the desk, she made her way to the door, avoiding looking at Beth.

McNeal held the door open, frowning as Beth shoved past Jessica and stood mutely by the car. The girls piled into the back from either side and he wordlessly slid into the driver's seat, concern drawing his features tight.

As they pulled out of the parking lot, Beth snapped at Jessica, "You could at least slouch down. The whole town doesn't need to see this."

Her father gave her a sharp warning look through the rear-view mirror. "Elizabeth! There's no call to be rude. Apologize."

After a mumbled apology, Beth descended into a silent sulk and the girls stared out their respective windows with their backs turned to one another.

McNeal cleared his throat. "You look beat, Jessica. I'll set the cot up in Beth's room when we get home."

Jessica managed a wan smile, leaned her forehead against the cool window, and muttered, "Thanks."

She was so tired, she would have slept in a fiery pit of coals at the very mouth of hell. And sadly, that only sounded marginally worse than a cot in Beth's room.

"For a moment, after I woke you up, you looked scared, Jessica. I mean, *really* scared. Not something I expect to see in a sixteen-year-old." McNeal smoothed down the corners of his moustache.

Jessica watched the mirror as his gaze darted to his daughter and then back to her.

"What Robyns said happened doesn't sound like you at all. Did you get in over your head with something? Is there someone you're worried about? Scared of?"

Crap. What do I do now?

She knew from experience that McNeal was sharp. They had never been able to get away with anything at Beth's house. It was as if he had an anti-lie sphere around him. There was no way she could sell the scavenger hunt to him. Certainly not when her brain felt like melted Swiss cheese.

Jessica closed her eyes and pretended to be asleep. She didn't pretend for long. The stress and exertion of the last few days caught up with her all at once, and she fell into an uneasy slumber.

Chapter 49

The next time Jessica opened her eyes, she was wrapped in a warm blanket with a longhaired Persian cat doing a convincing impression of a hat. Rolling over, she pulled the gray fluff ball to her chest and petted him until his purrs rumbled through her sore muscles like a gentle massage.

She stayed in that languid state between sleep and waking for a while, soothed by the fuzzy energy thief as she watched a golden sunbeam work its way up the wall.

She was at Beth's. She smiled and sneezed.

Ah yes. The morning toxic cloud.

Fumes from her friend's extensive perfume collection always got up her nose. Mostly because Beth sprayed ten times more than she needed into the air and then walked through the noxious mist—to get even coverage, she claimed. Jessica snorted and sneezed again.

Rubbing her nose, she wondered what they would do today.

She sighed. They'd end up at the mall. They always did. There was probably homework she should be doing.

Jessica eased onto an elbow to check the bed beside her

and saw that Beth wasn't there. Frowning, she checked her watch and stared at the blank face. The last few hours, days, and weeks rolled over her foggy mind in a succession of slow, bruising realizations.

Her prevailing sense of calm and normalcy shattered. A gray haze crept in at the edges of her vision, obscuring the cozy room. The cheerful sunbeam mocked her as the world receded.

Struggling upright, she propped herself against Beth's bed. Her throat tightened and cold sweat slicked her body. The cat glared as his heat source moved, and when she started wheezing, he skittered off.

Jessica clawed at her twisted tunic and undid several buttons. It felt like there was a snake coiled around her, slowly squeezing the air out of her lungs.

Desperately needing to focus her racing mind, Jessica concentrated on the comforter she had kicked off. Through the encroaching haze, she followed the maze of wrinkles and tried to slow her breathing, repeating in her head, *I can move. I'm free.* She wiggled her fingers, twirled her wrists, and flexed her legs as she fought off her chronic nightmare of being pinned in a capsized kayak, drowning. Despite her efforts, darkness closed in.

The door banged open and Beth dropped a plate on the floor beside the cot without looking at her.

"Boy, when you want attention, you sure know how to get it. Couldn't you have picked something that wouldn't drag me into your little drama? Or was that the point? Tell me you didn't do this to get back at me."

She eventually noticed Jessica's spastic breathing and sighed long-sufferingly. "Great. Now you're having one of your attacks. You know...I have better things to do than play nursemaid. I was supposed to go to a matinee with Matt, but

Dad made me cancel. Don't you ever think about anyone else?"

Jessica ground her teeth and focused on the labyrinthine valleys and peaks in the blanket. She drew in a gulp of polluted air. With Beth's return, the scent of perfume was overpowering.

Jessica waved at the window. "Open," she gasped between shallow breaths.

Beth scowled as she shoved the window open. "Wouldn't kill you to say please. Nice. Now it's freezing in here."

She grabbed a pink cashmere sweater from her dresser and pulled it on. "Are you going to do this for much longer?" Her tone was clipped, but a touch of worry had crept in.

When Jessica didn't answer, she asked hesitantly, "Should I get Dad, or call 911?"

A cool breeze flowed over Jessica, replacing the cloying chemical fumes with the rich, musky scent of autumn. She breathed deeply and was seized with the sudden desire to see beyond the room's confining walls. Crawling onto Beth's bed, she leaned against the window frame and felt her throat and chest loosen slightly.

"Give me a sec." Jessica took another deep breath. "I think it's okay."

A gnarled old birch stood a few feet from the window, its bare branches swaying gracefully in the wind. Her gaze traveled down the rough silver trunk to the leaf-scattered ground. Buried roots locked it in place from birth to death. Every year it sprouted new leaves, nurtured them, and then lost them to stand naked and alone through the bitter winter. And yet there remained something joyously defiant and free in the way its limbs danced and waved, playing with the breeze.

The wind whispered through the branches and Jessica strained to hear, feeling strangely certain that it held a deep truth.

A brown leaf blew onto the windowsill and Jessica picked it up. She caressed the dried veins and wrinkled skin before letting it go, as Michiru had done after their first visit to the church.

That seems so long ago now, she thought, watching it twirl away.

Looking back at the tree, she smiled. "You don't lose them, do you? You let them go, so you that can grow."

"What?" Beth asked querulously.

All the fear and anger Jessica had been holding in melted away. The pain of betrayal and rejection was still there—she suspected it would be for a while—but it lost some sharpness in the realization that it wasn't Beth's fault. Jessica had betrayed herself. And that was something she could fix.

She turned back to contemplate her old friend. For a time their lives had intersected and they had grown together. But seasons change. Their paths diverged. Jessica cringed, recalling how desperately she had clung to their friendship, too scared of the unknown to let go.

Well, the unknown came and kicked my ass anyway, but I'm still standing.

She picked at a chip of paint on the sill. The unknown was scary, scarier than she could ever have imagined, but she saw now what she couldn't back then—that she couldn't force people to be what she wanted any more than she'd let anyone, or anything, dictate who she was.

"Listen. I know you'll spread this around school tomorrow—" Beth started to protest and Jessica held up a hand. "It's what you do." She locked her gaze with Beth's. "I want you to know that I don't care. I did something good, something important. That's all that matters. And you were right. It's time we moved on. I'll always be thankful for the good times we had, but I need people in my life I can count on, and that just isn't you. It never was."

A small, sad smile played at the corners of Jessica's mouth. "You'll always be my first best friend." She slid off the bed and hugged Beth, who stiffened, looking at her as if she'd sprouted a giant pineapple on her head.

Beth backed away as soon as Jessica released her. "You've totally lost it."

"No. Not lost, just let go."

"You're not making sense."

"On the contrary, my dear Watson, I think I've finally gleaned some sense from the senseless." She grinned, knowing Beth wouldn't get it, and picked up the plate. "Oooooh, sandwiches. I'm starving. Thanks."

Jessica perched on the edge of the bed and ravenously tucked into the most delicious egg salad sandwich she had ever tasted. She started to ask Beth to thank her dad and then realized she was gone.

The bed jiggled as she looked around. A magazine fell off the side table exposing an alarm clock. 5:33 p.m. T minus ten hours and her father would be here. It took several swallows to dislodge the bread and egg wedged in her throat.

Dealing with her parents and classmates would be a nightmare, but there had been a lot of those lately, and she was starting to get used to them. She stared at the remaining corner of sandwich, remembering the fury of the entity and the icy depths of the gatekeeper.

A tree branch tapped against the house and she reminded herself that even the worst storms passed, eventually.

Right? she silently asked the tree.

Tap, scratch, tap.

Jessica decided that was birch-code for yes.

Besides, there was nothing her parents or classmates could throw at her to compare with last night. And she had survived that. Her body and mind might be battered, but they were not broken. She was not broken.

Jessica popped the last bite into her mouth and scraped up the crumbs on the plate, wondering if it would be rude to ask for more.

Chapter 50

Channel interface unstable. Revert to first contact pro-
tocol. 95% probability interregnum exceeded 1000 years.
Primary objective: Maintain gate integrity. Secondary
objective: Guide local population's adaptation to gate.

* * *

Beth was true to form. By the time Jessica dragged herself to
school Monday morning, everyone knew about her weekend
brush with the law. The usual suspects pointed and whispered
as she walked down the hall, but she tuned them out.

She must have started texting people as soon as I left. Guess I
called that one.

As the day ground on, Jessica was increasingly amazed at
the havoc word of mouth played with facts. The rumors ranged
from the fairly mundane ("She was high on something and
tried to break into a church") to the ridiculous ("She was a
vampire caught performing a blood rite in the graveyard").

She didn't think anyone seriously believed the latter until
a girl with bottle-black hair wearing a T-shirt with a picture of a
wolf on it timidly stopped her in the hall. She asked if she could
join Jessica's clan, intimating she was willing to let them drink

her blood.

Jessica's first reaction was to lump her in with all the idiots spreading insane rumors and blow her off, but the warring hope and fear of rejection in the girl's eyes forced her to rethink. She experienced a moment of mental vertigo, recalling herself from a month ago.

If there were entities that possessed people, a Sarah-wolf roaming the streets, and spirits that talked to her from mirrors, why couldn't there be vampires? What if this girl actually ran into one? What if she was turning into one and needed someone to talk to?

Feeling guilty, Jessica gently told the girl that she wasn't a vampire, but that she'd let her know if she came across any. She walked away, hoping that problem wouldn't fall into her lap any time soon.

The last bell of the day finally rang and Jessica wandered down the less-traveled halls to science club. She felt numb. The kind of numbness that sets in after the tenth time you've smacked your hand into the corner of a table. Even her blush had worn out, and that had never happened before.

The handcuffs clipped to the side of her backpack jangled against a locker as she brushed past. She had found the furry purple offering attached to her locker after lunch and taken a shine to them. At least they were imaginative and potentially useful, unlike the muffin impaled with an old nail file someone chucked at her in the cafeteria.

She flicked a speck of coconut icing off her sweater and contemplated the growing list of people she'd like to restrain and rage at for a while. If only the handcuff donor knew...

If her tormentors expected her to burst into tears and hide, they were out of luck today. Her mental-freak-out bar had been raised a few notches.

She came across a group idling beside a set of lockers. One of them called out, "Psssst. Jailbird…don't drop the soap, unless you like it that way." A chorus of snickers erupted.

"You'll never find out." She gave them a bored look and kept walking.

Another one for the list, she thought, reminding herself it was only a month and a half until Christmas holidays. *I can hold out. I just need to focus on what's important and not get caught up in this stupidity.* She sighed. *Probably easier said than done.*

If all her days were like this one, they were going to pass achingly slowly, but she suspected the rest of her time would vanish all too quickly. There was lycanthropy research to be done. She'd seen Sarah around school occasionally, but had yet to figure out how to approach her. And then there was the gatekeeper and the gate it had shown her. She had no idea where to even start with that, but at least she knew where her visions were coming from now, and possibly her newfound ability to see glowing auras around people and objects. She needed to find out exactly what being a Channel entailed. Blindly trusting the gatekeeper again was out, but they would have to find a way to work together.

Jessica rounded a corner and smiled when she saw Drew outside the science lab. A friendly face was a rare and cherished commodity lately. She wasn't looking forward to facing Boxer and his crew, and since Kathy hadn't made any effort to talk to her, she was sure there wouldn't be support from that quarter.

Drew gestured in quick, irritated motions as he argued with Sam and Bobby. "For the last time, find your own ride home. I've got my own shit to take care of."

Jessica leaned against a nearby locker, wondering exactly when her life had become so fucked up that this routine argument was now the most comforting part of her day.

Sam narrowed his eyes at Drew. "What's up with you? You're turning into an ass-kissing nerd. What's so great about this stupid club, anyways?"

"Well, this might come as a shock, but I kinda thought I'd learn something. Jess and I have this wicked project…"

Sam rolled his eyes. "Ugh. Not that geeky dwarf again. You guys will make a great couple. Introducing Mr. and Ms. Dweeb. I fear for your kids. The two of you will bore them to death."

"No way." Bobby elbowed Sam. "She might be weird, but that's the chick who got pinched for screwing in the church. She's hardcore."

Drew's scowl deepened. "She wasn't having sex…" Sam and Bobby leaned forward, obviously hoping for details. "Never mind. You guys don't listen worth shit anyway. If you don't get a move on, you'll miss the bus."

"So it's like that, is it?" Bobby peered down his nose at Drew. "What, she put out quick or something?"

Drew stared at him for a few seconds and then shook his head. "Seriously. Drop it." He crossed his arms. "If you two super-studs think my plans are so lame, I'd like to hear what you have in mind."

Sam and Bobby looked at each other.

"Dunno." Sam shuffled his feet. "Probably meet up with Tate at the old water tower. He's got a new rifle with some kind of laser scope."

Drew looked unimpressed. "Think I'll stick with my plans. I can't miss science club today anyway. I need to talk to Jess."

The guys whistled suggestively.

"Oh, shut up," growled Drew. "She wasn't around at lunch. Have either of you seen her? She's supposed to meet me..."

Bobby grinned and pointed to where Jessica was loitering. She raised a hand. "Hey."

Drew joined her, blushing.

Sam and Bobby trailed behind him and Drew pointedly called over his shoulder, "I'll call if I get out early. See ya."

They made no move to leave, and he turned to face them. "Piss off already, unless you want to help us evaluate similarity metrics for preference ranking?"

Drew, Bobby, and Sam silently stared each other down until Sam shrugged. "Whatever. Like we want to hang with you anyways."

He spun on his heels and waved a hand at Bobby. "Come on. Let's get the fuck out of here." Sam directed a glare at Jessica. His dark eyes ranged over her body and returned to her face. "Let him play with his white trash. There isn't enough of her to hold his attention for long."

Bobby glanced between Drew and Jessica, his eyes widening slightly when he noticed the handcuffs on her bag. Jessica grinned and reached back to pet the fur. His cheeks darkened and her smile widened.

Bobby mumbled a quick bye to Drew and trotted after Sam.

Jessica raised an eyebrow. "Hmmmm. I'm guessing Sam's the jealous type."

Drew massaged his temples. "Those two give me a headache on a good day, but Sam's been extra annoying lately. He's worried about Neave. Doesn't make it okay for him to be an ass though. Actually, everyone's pretty worried about her. We figured she'd call to let someone know she was okay, but nothing. She must've really booked it."

He watched his departing friends. "Between work and

weirdness, I haven't had much time to spend with Sam." He let out a long breath. "Truth is, I don't know what to say to him."

"So don't say anything." Jessica shrugged. "Sometimes it's just nice to have people around. Especially someone you don't have to explain yourself to."

"Speaking of explaining." Drew leaned close to her. "Where have you been? You never called Sunday, though if there's any truth in the stories I've heard, I understand why. And you pulled a Houdini at lunch."

"Yeah. Sorry about that. I meant to call, but Dad took my laptop away and your number was on my cell, which is totally fried. Even the SIM got scrambled. Oh…and lunch… thanks to Dad, I get to spend it in the counselor's office. He totally freaked…"

Mr. Bakshi poked his head out of the lab. "You two planning on joining, or should I mark you absent and let your parents sort it out, Miss Clarke?"

She groaned. "No. I'm coming."

"I've been instructed to make you sign in." Bakshi held out a clipboard and pen.

Drew slipped by them and headed for the back row as Jessica scribbled on the paper.

"Check it out. Better heat up the baby bottle." Boxer made a suckling noise at Jessica and laughed.

Drew swept an arm out as he passed Boxer's lab bench. The joker's binder hit the floor and burst, scattering papers across the room.

"Hey!" Boxer jumped up and took a step toward Drew, fists balled.

"Whoops." Drew innocently held up his hands and backed away, taking no pains to hide his smug grin.

Mr. Bakshi cleared his throat as he retrieved a comb from

his lab coat and smoothed a wayward curl. "That's quite enough. Andrew, help James retrieve his papers and then both of you can sit down. We have work to do and I've had it with these silly interruptions." He tossed his clipboard onto his desk, grimaced as it landed askew, and then carefully lined it up with the corner.

Jessica picked up some stray papers and handed them to Drew, whispering, "Thanks."

"Anytime." Drew dumped the messy pile on Boxer's desk with a feral grin and followed her to the back.

Settling onto his customary stool, he pretended to pay attention to Bakshi, and whispered, "Never a dull moment. You want a ride home after?"

Jessica nodded. "If you have time. I'm still pooped and there's a lot…" She snapped her mouth closed as Bakshi stopped talking and shot her a look. Opening her workbook, she flipped to a blank page and wrote "later" on the top corner. She slid it over to Drew and he nodded, flourishing his pen over the paper.

The next time Jessica looked down, she barely managed to stifle a laugh. Staring back at her from the page was a caricature of Bakshi wearing military epaulettes on his lab coat, sternly leveling his pointer at a row of beakers wearing combat helmets.

Drew grinned, keeping his head faced forward so the teacher wouldn't suspect distraction.

Jessica wiped moisture from the corner of her eye. He knew how putrid this day had been. He saw through her walls as if they were glass. And although he would never admit it, under all his joking and blustering, he cared. And that meant the world.

Chapter 51

Bakshi dismissed the group after an hour. They had barely cleared the lab door before Drew's patience expired. He started probing Jessica for details and she pulled him off to the side.

She ran through a hurried account of what had happened at the church, anxiously grabbing his hand to check his watch.

Her description was as muddled as her mind, which was swimming with pieces of information that should fit together, but didn't. On the surface, the sequence of events seemed simple, but there were dark shadows within shadows, and everything defied reason.

Drew stopped her when she described running into the wolf. "You think it was Sarah?"

"Pretty sure."

"Sounds like you interrupted a hunt. She's getting braver. We'll have to talk to her soon. She could get hurt if she keeps running around town, or hurt someone else."

"Right." Jessica squared her shoulders and shored up her mind as she entered work mode. "We need to dig up more information on lycanthropy ASAP. I want something tangible to give her, other than a sympathetic ear. Can you email me what your uncle knows?" She absently twirled a strand of hair, thinking furiously. "I can imagine how well this talk will go. There just isn't a good way to interject lycanthropy into normal conversation."

"Better bring a big, juicy bone. Give her something to chew on, other than you." He chuckled as Jessica rolled her eyes. "I'll talk to Uncle this week and get you what I can. Let's hope he's feeling more lucid." Drew leaned against a locker and gestured for her to continue.

She felt a pang of sympathy for his uncle. Was he, like her, struggling to fit logic into an illogical world? Jessica shrugged to herself and was about to relate how the police showed up, when she saw Michiru jogging down the hall toward them.

Jessica waved to get her attention. "Hey, stranger."

Michiru stopped beside them. "I'm so glad I caught you. Practice ran late and I thought you'd be gone." She looked Jessica directly in the eye and then dropped her gaze. "Jess, I am *so* sorry. I tried to warn you at the church…"

Jessica rubbed the back of her head and grinned. "I know. Still have the lump to prove it."

Michiru grimaced. "Sorry. I…I should have noticed sooner. It's all my fault. I let myself get distracted and you paid the price. And I shouldn't have split. I'm a shitty friend."

"You're not." Jessica laid a hand on her arm. "And trust me, leaving was the best thing you could have done, though you'll have to explain how the hell you did it. That was freaking amazing. Anyways, Father Wojcikowski didn't press charges and the cops convinced themselves I was on some stupid scavenger hunt. If you had stayed and the cops had found your lock picks and whatever else you had…it would have been a different story."

"Scavenger hunt?" Michiru shook her head. "Weird. But you're okay? I phoned last night and your dad said you weren't allowed to talk. I couldn't find you at lunch, and then with that killer test in physics...I totally failed that, by the way." She trailed off and sighed. "Everything seems to go wrong at once."

"Welcome to my life." The corner of Jessica's mouth quirked. "Breathing and relatively pain free, with a side of seriously confused, about covers how I am at the moment. Talking about stuff is going to be hard because Dad's monitoring and scheduling my every move. Nobody's allowed over unless it's school related and he disabled wi-fi on the router, so I have to use the desktop in Mom's office to get on the internet." Jessica snorted. "Or so he thinks. I'll pick up a pre-paid data stick so I can have a bit of freedom, though I'll need to be miserly with bandwidth." She looked at Michiru. "That reminds me. Can I borrow your cell? I snuck in an email to Eric yesterday and I'd like to see if he's replied."

Michiru held out her phone. "Keep it for the night and call him. Please don't explain what's been going on in an email. It's too easily archived. And steer clear of keywords that might attract big brother's attention."

Drew and Jessica blinked at her, shocked.

"What?' Michiru shrugged. "I'm not a total luddite."

Jessica read the time on the screen before she shoved the phone in her pocket. "Shit. I've got to be home soon." She started down the hall, flanked by her friends. "Drew's giving me a lift, but if you'll tag along, Mac, I can at least get through what happened with the police and...oh my gods...what happened when Dad got back. He totally flipped out."

The trio stopped at Michiru's locker and then headed to the parking lot.

When they reached Drew's truck, Jessica stared at the

hole where the passenger door used to be. Twisted remains of door hinges jutted from the frame. She decided not to mention it and clambered onto the seat, shuffling over to make room for Michiru.

Drew slid behind the wheel and Jessica asked in a quiet voice, "Can we make a quick pit stop?"

He jiggled the key in the ignition, trying to find the right angle. "Sure. Where to?"

"The bridge." Jessica watched jealously as Michiru easily vaulted onto the seat beside her.

"No problemo. Don't suppose there'll be any impromptu skinny-dipping?"

Jessica and Michiru leveled identical "not on your life" looks at him.

He shrugged, unperturbed. "Can't blame a guy for hoping."

"What's with the lack of door?" Michiru asked as she tugged on her seatbelt and stared at the vacant space beside her.

Drew's face tightened. "My brother decided to solve the sticky-door problem with the help of a lamppost." He jerked a thumb at the truck bed as the engine coughed. "At least he picked it up. It's a bitch to find and fit a new door." He grinned at Michiru. "Don't worry. I'll make sure to turn the corners extra fast so you don't get bored."

"Bring it on." She wrapped a hand around the "oh shit" handle.

"Please don't," Jessica pleaded, huddling down to avoid the chill gusts of November wind. She was glad she was in the middle. Michiru seemed unfazed by the weather and situation, as usual.

They drove through town to the highway and headed west toward the dam. Drew mostly behaved himself as Jessica caught them up on major events.

"…I nearly keeled over when Dad walked by the basement door and asked why he smelled fish. But I totally lucked out. Somewhere between the flight, Mom's car, and the trashed couch, his brain must have fried itself, because after that he just went to bed. I managed to clean the basement before he saw it and he never mentioned anything about the garage door."

She cuddled closer to Michiru's heat. "And, FYI, lobster guts turn into seriously nasty glue when they dry. Not good." She twined her fingers together. "I still feel bad about Pinchy."

Jessica closed her eyes against the incessant flapping of her hair and dug in her pockets. She pulled out a pencil, gathered her hair on top of her head, jammed the pencil through the messy clump, and enjoyed a brief moment of victory. Then the truck bounced over a pothole and her makeshift bun uncoiled, dropping the pencil behind the seat. Jessica sighed.

Michiru handed her a spare hair elastic. "Forgot to mention…I didn't see Bill today, so I talked to some of his friends. Turns out his parents sent him to a health retreat. They think he had a mental breakdown."

"Thanks," Jessica said, relieved to cross one worry off her list. "I kept stressing that he'd had a bad reaction to the roofie, or that he'd gotten a concussion and hadn't woken up, or that he'd done something to hurt himself and we should have stayed with him longer." She stopped when Michiru put an arm around her.

"I wouldn't have just left him, you know." Drew cast an exaggeratedly hurt look at Jessica. "He'd come out of shock by the time we got to his house. That was slow going, let me tell you. He forgot where he lived. Anyway, I made sure his parents were up because he was still pretty upset. Kept talking about Chris. I'm lucky I didn't end up at the police station with you.

Should have seen the look his mom gave me. If I keep this up, the parents in town are going to start demanding the police charge me with DBI."

"What the hell are you on about now?" Michiru asked, eyeing him warily.

"DBI: Delivered By Indian." He shook his head and glanced over at Jessica, who was chewing her bottom lip. "We did everything we could for him, Jess, and then some. He has to work through the rest."

Jessica rubbed her temples. "It's hard to know when to stop. But even when I know, it's hard to actually do the stopping."

"We'll just have to remind each other, then." Michiru's smile wavered. "You really aren't mad at me for taking off at the church?"

"No. Honestly, if I had your ninja agility, I'd have vamoosed too."

"No you wouldn't." Michiru held her gaze. "You'd have stuck around until the bitter end and you wouldn't have taken off on anyone, let alone a good friend."

Jessica looked away, moved by the confidence in her voice. She wished she shared it. "Well, I've never been accused of having much sense."

Michiru let out a snort of laughter and covered her mouth, looking startled. "I've picked up your laugh."

Drew snorted and sent both girls into peals of laughter.

"Must be catching." He grinned as he turned off the highway and drove down to the boat launch below the bridge. "You know, a month ago all I wanted was to get out of here— off the Rez, away from Coldwater, out of the fucking province if I could. Every day with the same people, listening to the same bitching and lame insults, going through the same boring-ass bullshit just to get by. And now, you couldn't make me leave. Who'd have thought?"

The way Michiru glanced over at him made Jessica wonder if they had more in common than they cared to admit.

"Right...why suffer the indignity of repetitious insults when you can hang out with me and be subject to a whole fleet of new and exciting ones." Jessica sighed. "I liked knowing what tomorrow looked like. I miss that."

Michiru hopped out of the truck when they stopped and Jessica followed, staring up at the bridge's gray underbelly. She tried to resist, but her eyes sought out the spot where Chris had fallen. Her gaze traversed the distance between the metal guardrail and the base of the abutment.

If it weren't for the gatekeeper, I would have been lost in the shadow's world of rage and hatred. I can't imagine the strength it must have taken to shake loose its hold. But Chris did. He did it to save his friend. His last act was completely selfless and, unfortunately, completely wasted.

She trekked up the hill to the bridge, stopping when she reached the section of railing cluttered with dead flowers, teddy bears, and freezer-bagged sympathy cards. Drew and Michiru followed silently.

Jessica crouched to read the messages. They were numerous and heart wrenching. So many people cared about him. Their loss and regret poured into hers.

She stood abruptly, overwhelmed, and looked past the railing at the lake's calm, slate blue surface. "I haven't been here since before Chris died." Her voice cracked and she swallowed loudly. "I didn't have the guts. Still don't, but I figured..." She frowned. "I don't know what I figured."

Michiru caught hold of a weathered stuffed bear dangling precariously on a string. Pulling a small roll of duct tape from an inside jacket pocket, she refastened the bear to the railing and patted it on the head.

Jessica fought back tears as she stared at the sad little creature. Left out in the wind and rain. No shelter. No hope. Gawked at by passersby. Just another conscript holding the line in a battle that's already lost.

She shook her head. "After everything that happened, everything we did, I thought…I hoped coming here, facing this place, would bring me some peace. An ending. But there's nothing. Just this." She gestured at the memorial. "Dead flowers and spent memories."

"Not all dead." Michiru hopped down into a sheltered ditch and came back with a late-blooming weed. She tucked it between the bear and the railing, smiling as the small yellow flowers swayed cheerfully in the breeze.

"I should have brought something." Jessica stared at her empty hands.

Drew hesitated and then put a hand on her shoulder. "You brought yourself. That's enough."

"I wish I believed that." Jessica closed her eyes. "Chris was a good person, one of the best, and some fucking evil thing used him and then just threw him away. Like he was disposable. Well, he wasn't. How do you make sense of a world where that can happen?"

"Most tragedies are senseless," Michiru said. "Whoever's left standing has to make it mean something. Make it count."

"Nothing changes what happened." Jessica turned her back on the memorial and headed down the hill to the truck. "Chris is still gone."

"But Bill isn't." Michiru kept pace beside her. "You'll never save everyone, Jess. Chris died trying to protect a friend and you chose to pick up where he left off. There's your sense."

Drew nodded. "She's right. That's the most any of us can hope for: That someone will carry forward what's important to us when we're gone. I want a Jessica around when my time is up. Someone has to keep Mac in line." He tried to dodge the swat Michiru aimed at him and failed. "See? I already need your help."

Jessica smiled. He was trying to cheer her up, but she could tell by the haunted look he cast at the lake that he felt the weight of this place and what had happened here.

The world wasn't right. Maybe it never would be. But there were others who saw and cared enough to try to make a difference. There were two of them walking beside her. And that was something. Maybe it was everything.

THANK YOU TO OUR READERS

Writing this novel was a lot of fun. We hope you enjoyed getting to know the characters and their world as much as we did. Please consider leaving a review to share your impressions or send an email to feedback@braevitae.com.

Visit **www.braevitae.com** for links to our other stories.

ABOUT THE MIST WARDEN SERIES

The series continues with Book Two: Curse Bound. Check in at **www.mistwarden.braevitae.com** for the latest publication schedule and extra behind-the-scenes information.

ABOUT THE AUTHORS

REBECCA BRAE is a freelance writer, artist, and fog enthusiast, with a background in sociology and weird pets. ADRIAAN BRAE is a software developer and tech-geek, with a passion for languages and martial-arts. Their divergent interests can be challenging at times but their love of new ideas, storytelling, and Lego always brings them together.

Made in the USA
San Bernardino, CA
06 January 2015